PENGUIN CLASSICS

THE KREUTZER SONATA

AND OTHER STORIES

Count Leo Nikolayevich Tolstoy was born in 1828 at Yasnaya Polyana in the Tula province, and educated privately. He studied Oriental languages and law at the University of Kazan, then led a life of pleasure until 1851 when he joined an artillery regiment in the Caucasus. He took part in the Crimean war and after the defence at Sebastopol he wrote *The Sebastopol Stories*, which established his reputation. After a period in St Petersburg and abroad, where he studied educational methods for use in his school for peasant children in Yasnaya, he married Sofya Andreyevna Behrs in 1862. The next fifteen years was a period of great happiness; they had thirteen children and Tolstoy managed his vast estates in the Volga Steppes, continued his educational projects, cared for his peasants and wrote *War and Peace* (1865–8) and *Anna Karenin* (1874–6). *A Confession* (1879–82) marked an outward change in his life and works: he became an extreme nationalist and moralist, and in a series of pamphlets after 1880 he expressed such theories as rejection of the State and Church, indictment of the demands of the flesh, and denunciation of private property. His teaching earned him numerous followers in Russia and abroad, but also much opposition and in 1901 he was excommunicated by the Russian holy synod. He died in 1910 in the course of a dramatic flight from home, at the small railway station in Astapovo.

David McDuff was born in 1945. He was educated at the University of Edinburgh, where he took his PhD in 1971 with a thesis on the poetry of the Russian modernist Innokenty Annensky, having spent several periods of study in the Soviet Union. After some years of foreign travel and freelance writing, he worked as a co-editor of the literary quarterly *Stand*, and also with Anvil Press Poetry in London. His publications comprise a large number of translations of foreign verse and prose, including poems by Joseph Brodsky and Tomas Venclova, as well as contemporary Scandinavian work; a *Selected Poems* of Osip Mandelstam (1975 and 1983); a *Complete Poems* of Edith Södergran (1984) and *No I'm Not Afraid*, the selected poems of Irina Ratushinskaya (1986). His first book of verse, *Words in Nature*, appeared from Ramsay Head Press, Edinburgh, in 1972. At present he is engaged in translating nineteenth-century Russian prose works for the Penguin Classics. These include translations of Dostoyevsky's *The House of the Dead* (1985), *Poor Folk and Other Stories* and *Uncle's Dream and Other Stories* (1988), Tolstoy's *The Sebastopol Sketches* (1986), and Nikolai Leskov's *Lady Macbeth of Misensk* (1987)

Leo Tolstoy

THE KREUTZER
SONATA

and

Other Stories

Translated with an introduction by

David McDuff

PENGUIN BOOKS

PENGUIN BOOKS

Published by the Penguin Group
Penguin Books Ltd, 27 Wrights Lane, London W8 5TZ, England
Penguin Books USA Inc., 375 Hudson Street, New York, New York 10014, USA
Penguin Books Australia Ltd, Ringwood, Victoria, Australia
Penguin Books Canada Ltd, 10 Alcorn Avenue, Toronto, Ontario, Canada M4V 3B2
Penguin Books (NZ) Ltd, 182–190 Wairau Road, Auckland 10, New Zealand

Penguin Books Ltd, Registered Offices: Harmondsworth, Middlesex, England

This translation first published 1983
7 9 10 8 6

Copyright © David McDuff, 1985
All rights reserved

Printed in England by Clays Ltd, St Ives plc
Typeset in VIP Palatino

CONTENTS

TRANSLATOR'S INTRODUCTION

Tolstoy's work on *The Kreutzer Sonata* was prolonged and characterized by a high degree of complexity: with certain interruptions, it lasted not less than two years, during which he also wrote the comedy *The Fruits of Enlightenment*, the tale *The Devil*, some works on art and a number of other articles and essays.

The embryo of the tale is to be found in an unfinished fragment dating from the end of the 1860s and bearing the title *The Wife-murderer*. This fragment does little more than illustrate that the central problem it deals with – the moral situation of a husband who murders his wife – was one that preyed on Tolstoy's mind at least from the time of his marriage to Sofya Andreyevna Behrs in 1862. The development of the ideological and thematic framework of *The Kreutzer Sonata* was long and tortuous, and was intimately connected with the moral, religious and existential crisis that led to Tolstoy's temporary abandonment of 'artistic' literary forms, and to his writing of *Confession* and *What I Believe*, and his retranslation and reordering of the New Testament.

In a letter to his children's tutor, V. I. Alekseyev, dated 10 February 1890, Tolstoy explained his own attitude to the tale which had become such a centre of public controversy and discussion: 'The substance of what I was writing was just as new to me then as it is now to those who are reading it. In this regard there was opened to me an ideal so distant from everything I was occupied with at the time that at first I was stricken with horror and did not want to accept it; subsequently, however, I grew convinced of its truth, saw the error of my ways and rejoiced at the joyful transformation that awaited me and others.'

It is impossible to determine exactly when Tolstoy began work on the tale. A letter to G. A. Rusanov of 14 March 1889 does, however, give us an approximate dating: 'The rumour concerning the tale is grounded in fact. Two years ago I wrote the rough draft of a tale on the theme of sexual love, but so carelessly and unsatisfactorily that I haven't even bothered to revise it – if I were to take up this idea again, I should rewrite the whole thing.' Thus it would appear that the first draft dates from 1887. It was apparently written as a dramatic monologue for the actor V. N. Andreyev-Burlak,* who came to visit Tolstoy at Yasnaya Polyana on 20 June 1887. According to Sofya Andreyevna, the monologue was based on a story told by Andreyev-Burlak to Tolstoy: '[He] recalled how he had once met a man in a train who had told him of the unhappiness he had experienced as a result of his wife's infidelity, and it was this plot Levochka made use of.'

The earliest draft of the tale bears only a moderate resemblance to its later, finished version. It is considerably shorter, as befitting a piece intended for stage delivery or recital at a soirée, and it contains none of the extended general discussions that are such an important feature of *The Kreutzer Sonata*. The action is compressed. Pozdnyshev's wife's lover is not a musician, but a painter; indeed, there is no mention of music anywhere in this draft. The first and last meetings of Pozdnyshev's wife and her lover, and also the murder itself, take place at a country dacha, not in the Pozdnyshev household. Pozdnyshev is said to be a chemist – not a musician – by training: throughout the narrative he is referred to as a scientist, a chemist, and even a professor of chemistry.

Not satisfied with this first attempt, Tolstoy continued to work away at successive versions of the tale throughout 1888. Several factors played a part in the development and elaboration of the original material. Among the most important of these was his increasing preoccupation with questions of married life, in particular those relating to sexuality and chastity. This was a concern to which he gave expression in his correspondence with his disciple, V. G. Chertkov. Only a

---

* Andreyev-Burlak was noted for his performances of 'literary' monologues, in particular Gogol's *Diary of a Madman* and Marmeladov's confession from Dostoyevsky's *Crime and Punishment*. The influence of both these writers is quite strongly in evidence in all the drafts of *The Kreutzer Sonata*.

few years previously, Tolstoy had been urging Chertkov to marry for the sake of his health and moral welfare; the direction in which Tolstoy's thoughts on this matter were now moving may be seen in the following letter to Chertkov, written from Yasnaya Polyana and dated 9 October 1888:

> The question of sexual relations between husband and wife, and to what extent they are justified, is one of the most important questions of practical Christianity, and is of the same order as the question of property; it preoccupies me constantly. As always, this question is resolved in the Gospels and, as always, so far removed are our lives from this resolution that not only have we been unable, do we remain unable, to put it into practice – we are not even able to understand it. 'But he said unto them, All men cannot receive this saying, save they to whom it is given. For there are some eunuchs, which were so born from their mother's womb: and there are some eunuchs, which were made eunuchs of men: and there be eunuchs, which have made themselves eunuchs for the kingdom of heaven's sake. He that is able to receive it, let him receive it' (Matthew xix, 11–12). What does this so frequently and inaccurately quoted passage mean but that Jesus's reply to people's questions about what they should do concerning their sexual feelings, what they should strive for, what the ideal of mankind should be, expressed in language that is comprehensible to us, is: 'Make yourselves eunuchs for the kingdom of heaven's sake. Whoever achieves that makes the highest achievement possible, and even those who are unable to achieve it will be all right as long as they strive towards it. He that is able to receive it, let him receive it.'
>
> I think that for the good of mankind both men and women ought to strive for absolute chastity – then, and only then, will mankind become what it is supposed to be. It must set its sights beyond the goal in order to arrive at the goal. If, on the other hand, as is the case in our own society, people consciously go out of their way in order to have sexual intercourse, they inevitably end up in unlawfulness and debauchery. If people consciously go out of their way to live not for the belly, but for the spirit, their attitude towards food will be the one it ought to be; but if, on the other hand, people take great pains to prepare sumptuous feasts for themselves, they inevitably end up in unlawfulness and debauchery.

This was only the first of a whole series of letters to Chertkov, whose request for 'a reply to my question about family life'

brought about a veritable deluge of advice from Tolstoy on an
area of human life that had always been to him most crucial
and problematic. In a letter of 6 November 1888, the personal
is quickly disposed of, to make room for more general matters:
'The first thing I must say in this connection is that in speaking
of the manner in which a husband and wife should live
together, I do not mean to imply that I have lived, or am living
as I ought to; not only that, I am firm in the knowledge,
derived from my own experience, of how one ought to live
only because I have *not* lived in the way one ought to . . .'
Tolstoy then proceeds to a discussion of the origins and
practicalities of marriage:

> First there is the feeling of amorousness, a feeling that has the
> greatest power over human beings. It is initiated between persons
> of different sex who have not known one another previously, and
> it leads to marriage, the instantaneous result of which is the
> conception of a child. A pregnancy ensues, as a result of which the
> husband and wife experience a cooling of their carnal relations with
> one another – a cooling which would be most marked and would
> have the effect of severing carnal intercourse altogether, as is the
> case with animals, were it not for the fact that people consider such
> carnal intercourse as a legitimate source of enjoyment. This cooling
> between the partners, which is replaced by a concern for the growth
> and nursing of the child, continues until the infant is weaned, and
> in a good marriage (and here one may perceive the difference
> between human beings and cattle) the weaning of the infant
> coincides with a resurgence of the feeling of amorousness *between
> the same partners.* However far we may be from this, it is nevertheless
> beyond question that this is how it ought to be. And for these
> reasons
>   1. Sexual intercourse when the woman is not ready to conceive
> (i.e. when she has no menstrual periods) is without rational
> justification, and is merely a form of carnal pleasure – and a very
> ignominious and shameful pleasure, as every man of conscience
> will admit, being similar to the most infamous, unnatural sexual
> perversions.
>   2. Everyone knows and agrees that sexual intercourse weakens
> and exhausts human beings and that its weakening effect is felt in
> the most essential sphere of human activity, the spiritual one.
> Moderation, say the defenders of the present order, but there can

be no question of moderation where the violation of the laws of reason is concerned. But the harm caused by excess (and intercourse when the woman is not ready to conceive is excess) may still not be too great for the man if restraint is observed (the very use of the word 'restraint' in such a context is repellent), if he only has carnal relations with one woman – yet what is moderation for the husband will be a terrible excess for the wife who is pregnant or nursing.

I believe that the backwardness and hysterical tendencies of women are largely caused by this. This is what the emancipation of woman should consist in: that she become one flesh with her husband, cease to be the servant of the Devil as she is at present, and become the servant of God. A remote but great ideal. And why should we not strive towards it? In my view, marriage should be like this: the couple become intimate as a result of the overmastering pressure of being in love, a child is conceived, and the husband and wife, avoiding everything that may interfere with the growth and nursing of the child, avoiding all fleshly temptation – not, as at present, arousing it – live together as brother and sister. Otherwise the husband, who before his marriage has led a life of debauchery, will transfer his debauched habits to his wife, will infect her with the same sensuality and will place upon her the intolerable burden of being at one and the same time a mistress, an exhausted mother and a sick, irritable and hysterical human being. And her husband will love her as a mistress, ignore her as a mother and hate her for her irritability and hysteria, which he himself has produced and continues to produce. This, in my view, is the key to all the sufferings that are concealed in the vast majority of families.

The way I envisage it is that the husband and wife will live together as brother and sister; the wife will carry her child, bear it, and nurse it in peace and quiet and without interruption, growing morally in stature all the while, and only when she is ready to conceive again will they once more abandon themselves to their amorousness for one another, which will last for a week and then be followed by another period of calm. In my view, this amorousness is like the pressure of steam that would cause a boiler to burst if the safety valve were not released. The valve is only opened when the pressure has reached a very high level; at other times it is kept assiduously closed, and our goal must be to close it as tightly as possible and to place a weight on it in order to keep it from opening. This is how I interpret the words: 'He that is able to receive it, let him receive it' – i.e. let each man try to abstain from marrying for as long as possible, and when he does marry let him live with his wife as a brother lives with his sister. And the steam will gather and open the valves – but it is not for us to open them, as we do at present, regarding sexual intercourse as a legitimate source of pleasure. It is only legitimate when we are unable to abstain from it and when it breaks through against our will . . .

In the world of men it is considered a very good thing to take enjoyment in sexual love, just as it might be thought a good thing to open the safety valves and let the steam out of them; in God's world, however, the only good is to live the true life, to work for God with one's talent: i.e. to love other people, their souls, and of them first and foremost one's own wife, and help her in the comprehension of the truth, not interfere with her ability to perceive it by making her the instrument of one's pleasure – in other words, to work in the way that the steam does, and to take all measures to see that it does not go into the safety valves.

'But then the human race will die out.' For one thing, no matter how hard people may try to refrain from sexual intercourse, the fact remains that the safety valves exist because they are necessary, and that children will be born. And anyway, why should we tell ourselves lies? In defending our indulgence in sexual intercourse, are we really concerned with the extinction of the species? What we are really concerned with is our own pleasure. This is something that needs to be said. The human race die out? What will die out is man the animal. What a terrible misfortune that would be! Just as the animals of prehistoric times died out, so, probably, will the human animal (considered in terms of its appearance in space and time). Let it die out. I am no more sorry for this two-legged animal than I am for the ichthyosaurs etc. What I care about is that the true life should not die out, the love of creatures that are able to love. And not only will this not die out if the human race comes to an end because people renounce the pleasures of lust for the sake of love, but it will grow an immeasurable number of times greater, and this love will grow correspondingly greater, and the creatures that experience it will become such that the continuation of the human species will not be necessary for them. Carnal love is only necessary in order that such creatures may be made from human beings.

This, broadly, is the ideological framework within which *The Kreutzer Sonata* developed into its final versions, and it also represents the raw material for the Postface which Tolstoy wrote for the tale. It is a familiar framework, representing a logical development of arguments from earlier phases of his thinking on these matters. The concept of 'man the animal', in particular, is one he had treated before, nowhere so straightforwardly, perhaps, as in the tale *Strider: The Story of a Horse* (1886), where human beings, considered as animals, are seen as being inferior to the rest of animal creation. Man is a misfit in the animal kingdom: his task is to transcend his animal nature, which is in contradiction with his spirit and reason and is merely an encumbrance and a hindrance to his further growth, but it is a task he either shirks or ignores.

Three events which took place during 1888 and 1889 were instrumental in shaping the structure and content of the final versions of *The Kreutzer Sonata*. The first of these related to the plot of the tale; the other two were a support and reinforcement of the 'ideal', the conclusion 'so distant from everything I was occupied with at the time', at which Tolstoy had initially been 'stricken with horror' – the notion that the ultimate aim and aspiration of mankind must be the attainment of total chastity – and which found its expression in Pozdnyshev's elaborate, extended monologue.

In the spring of 1888, a performance of Beethoven's 'Kreutzer Sonata' took place in the Tolstoy family's Moscow home. The musicians were the young violinist Yuli Lyasota and Tolstoy's son Sergey. Also present were Andreyev-Burlak and the distinguished painter Repin. Tolstoy was well acquainted with the sonata, but this performance of it made an especially strong impression on him. Once more he returned to the idea of writing a dramatic monologue on the theme of a husband who murders his wife; this time, however, the plot would be fused with the inspiration provided by the music. Tolstoy proposed to Repin that he should paint a canvas on the same theme, likewise entitled *The Kreutzer Sonata*. The picture would be exhibited at an evening gathering, and Andreyev-Burlak would recite the tale written by Tolstoy. Nothing came of this project, and of the three artists, Tolstoy was the only one to fulfil his part of the plan. What the incident appears to confirm, however, is that this hearing of

Beethoven's work was in some way deeply significant for Tolstoy, himself an accomplished pianist and a keen lover of music.*

On 17 November 1888, Tolstoy wrote to Chertkov that he had recently received from America a copy of a book 'by a certain woman doctor' which was absorbing his entire attention. This was *Tokology – A Book for Every Woman*, a recently published gynaecological manual dealing with practical aspects of pregnancy, childbirth and child care, by an American general practitioner named Alice Bunker Stockham. Chapter 11 of this work is entitled 'Chastity in the Marriage Relation', and advocates 'the observance of the law of continence' which

> will do much to palliate the many nervous symptoms of pregnancy. I have known women so sensitive during gestation that even a touch or a kiss from the husband caused nausea and other distressing symptoms ... The sexual relation at this time exhausts the mother and impairs the vitality of the child, inducing in its constitution precocious sexual development. The mind should be free from the subject, and every substance that has a tendency to promote desire should be studiously avoided. For this reason separate beds and even sleeping rooms for husband and wife are to be recommended.

Many features of this chapter, including a number of rhetorical flourishes and turns of phrase, found their way into the final drafts of *The Kreutzer Sonata*, where at times Pozdnyshev almost appears to be speaking with Stockham's voice. Stockham visited Tolstoy at Yasnaya Polyana in the autumn of 1889.

In April 1889, while deep in his work on the tale, Tolstoy was startled and impressed, as by some act of providence, by the arrival of another package from the United States, this one containing tracts and brochures by members of the American Shaker community. These also preached absolute chastity. Tolstoy wrote to Chertkov on 10 April:

---

* Tolstoy's son Sergey recorded that 'music would sometimes affect him against his will, and even torment him, and he would say: *"Que me veut cette musique?"* '

Are you familiar with their teaching? Especially that part of it that is against marriage, i.e. not against marriage *per se*, but in favour of an ideal of purity that is superior to marriage. This is a question that preoccupies me constantly, and as just that − a question. I am not in agreement with the solution proposed by the Shakers [voluntary castration], but I cannot help admitting that their solution is much more sensible than our universally accepted institution of marriage. The real reason why I can't find an answer to the question is because I am an old man, and a repulsive, debauched old man at that . . .

On 3 July 1889, Tolstoy made the following entry in his notebook: 'The mother's selfishness. In the sense that work is a fine thing, but its value depends on what use it serves. And since the children were an expression of her selfishness, they brought nothing but torment.' On 4 July he noted in his diary:

This morning and yesterday evening thought long and clearly about *The Kreutzer Sonata*. Sonya is copying it out, it is disturbing her, and last night she spoke of the young woman's disillusionment, of the sensuality of men, so alien at first, and of their lack of sympathy with children. She is unjust, because she wants to justify herself, while in order to understand and to tell the truth, one must repent. The whole drama of the tale, which has never once gone out of my mind during all this time, is now clear in my mind. He has cultivated her sensuality. The doctors have forbidden her to have any more children. She is fed to satiety, dressed in chic clothes, and there are all the temptations of art. How could she fail to fall? He must feel that he himself has led her to this, that he really murdered her when he conceived this hatred for her, that he sought out a pretext for murdering her and was glad of it. Yes, yesterday the muzhiks confirmed that the *klikushi* [hysterical peasant women] are always married women, never unmarried girls. So it must be that the phenomenon is caused by sexual excess.

The nine drafts of the tale indicate that during this period its writing was something of an obsession for Tolstoy. This is confirmed by further diary and notebook entries, all of which point to the fact that the task of construction was arduous and frustrating. Something of Tolstoy's ambivalence to what he eventually produced may be seen in the letter he wrote to the critic N. N. Strakhov on 6 November 1889: 'Thank you, Nikolay

Nikolayevich, for your letter. I greatly valued your criticism, which was much more lenient than I had expected. I know that from an artistic point of view this work is beneath all criticism . . . None the less, I have left it as it is, not out of laziness, but because I am unable to put it right. But I don't mind this, because I am secure in the knowledge that what I have written is by no means without use; on the contrary, it may be of great use to other people, and be to some extent new to them.'

That the tale's 'use' and 'novelty' were indeed among its most immediately appealing features was given vivid confirmation by the way in which, not yet completed, it was wrested from its creator's hands and transformed into a piece of public property. Before Tolstoy had even had time to prepare his ninth and final draft, the text of the eighth draft began to circulate in handwritten, lithographed and hectographed copies. On 28 October 1889, a copy in the handwriting of Tolstoy's son Mikhail was brought from Yasnaya Polyana to St Petersburg by M. A. Kuzminskaya, whereupon it was immediately read aloud at a gathering held at the Kuzminskys' flat, where further copies were made. On the following day the tale was read aloud in the office of *Posrednik* (*The Intermediary*), the religious–philosophical journal edited by Chertkov. Since Kuzminskaya had to return to Yasnaya Polyana immediately, as soon as the reading was over the manuscript was divided up into sections, and by the following morning a complete new copy was ready. 'In this manner,' wrote Yu. O. Yakubovsky, 'within three days, against the wishes of the author, the manuscript of *The Kreutzer Sonata*, in its first version, received distribution in St Petersburg. But this proved to be merely a drop in the ocean; in many houses copies were made on domestic hectographs, and these received instant distribution in the new and second-hand bookshops, where they sold at a price of 10–15 rubles apiece.'

Tolstoy's daughter Aleksandra records in her memoirs:

It is hard to convey now what took place when, for example, *The Kreutzer Sonata* and *The Power of Darkness* first appeared. Before they had even been passed for the press hundreds, even thousands of copies of them were made, which went from hand to hand, were translated into every language and were read everywhere with incredible passion; it sometimes seemed that the public had forgotten all its personal concerns and was living exclusively for the sake of the works of Count Tolstoy . . . The most important political events were seldom the object of such overwhelming and universal attention.

Strakhov informed Tolstoy that people no longer said 'How do you do?' when they met, but 'Have you read *The Kreutzer Sonata*?' Copies of the tale's eighth draft soon reached Moscow, and from there found their way far and wide throughout the provinces of Russia. Tolstoy's archive in Moscow contains a very large number of letters from all over Russia and from abroad containing readers' reactions to the tale in its unfinished version. This 'edition' also provoked a number of responses from other writers, both Russian and foreign, and was even responsible for inspiring several literary works, of which the most significant is the short story *Apropos of the Kreutzer Sonata* by N. S. Leskov. The story bears an epigraph which is a paraphrase of a quotation from the eighth draft of Tolstoy's tale: 'Every young girl is morally superior to any man, because she is incomparably more pure than he is. A girl who marries is always superior to her husband. She is superior to him both when she is still a girl and when she becomes a woman in our conditions of society.' It is significant that this passage was excised by Tolstoy when he came to write the ninth draft, indicating his disapproval of Leskov's 'tolerant' view of marital infidelity as expressed in the story.

It was partly in reply to this and other 'misunderstandings' of the tale, and partly as a result of pressure from his prospective publisher, Chertkov, that Tolstoy wrote the Postface to *The Kreutzer Sonata*. There was also the problem of the controversy and outrage that had accompanied the distribution of the eighth draft – in some quarters Tolstoy had been accused of preaching immorality and of attempting to deprave the young (the Archbishop of Kherson pronounced anathema on him as 'a sheep in wolf's clothing'); in others, he was thought to have gone mad. Some response on the part of the author was clearly called for. It was work that cost him much effort and labour. After a number of drafts, he finally arrived at the version published as Appendix 1 to the present volume, in which the ultimate ideal of humanity is envisaged as perfect chastity, and the concept of 'Christian marriage' exposed as an absurd contradiction in terms.

There seemed at first little likelihood that the censor would ever permit the tale to be published in printed form. When it was submitted for consideration in its final version, a copy was passed to Tsar Aleksander III, who made the tale the subject of an imperial banning order. This was, however, not the first time that one of Tolstoy's writings had fallen into the 'forbidden' category, and Sofya Andreyevna, who was preparing a new volume of her husband's collected works, saw a possibility that permission might be forthcoming for her to include *The Kreutzer Sonata* in it. Thus it was that the warnings of Pobedonostsev and other advisers to the Tsar went unheeded. Although it was not until 1891 that Sofya Andreyevna was able to procure an interview with Aleksander, when she asked him to remove the banning order he replied: 'Yes, we might allow you to print it in the complete works, because not everyone could afford to buy the full set, and it would not be too widely disseminated.'

Sofya Andreyevna agreed to edit the text of the tale, toning down its language and removing some of its sexual explicitness. In all, she made some two hundred alterations, and it was in this bowdlerized form that *The Kreutzer Sonata* was eventually published, along with some other related material, as Volume XIII of the *Collected Works*. Not until the appearance in 1933 of Volume 27 of the Jubilee Edition was *The Kreutzer Sonata* published in Tolstoy's original ninth redaction: this is the text that has been used for the present translation.

In giving permission for the publication of *The Kreutzer Sonata*, the Tsar had stipulated that it should *only* be obtainable as Volume XIII of the entire series; he had not realized that it could be published separately.

I have decided to write your majesty about unpleasant matters [began a letter from Pobedonostsev, the head of the Holy Synod]. If I had known in advance that the wife of Leo Tolstoy had requested an audience of your majesty, I would have begged you not to receive her. What has happened is what one might have feared. Countess Tolstoy returned from you with the thought that her husband has in you a defence and justification for all those things in him over which the healthy-minded and religious people of Russia are indignant. You permitted her to print *The Kreutzer Sonata* in the complete collection of the works of Tolstoy. It might have been possible to foresee how they would make use of this permission. This complete collection consists of thirteen volumes, which can be placed on sale separately. The thirteenth volume is a small book, in which have been published, together with *The Kreutzer Sonata*, certain slight articles in the same spirit. They have placed this book on sale separately, and already three separate editions of it have appeared. Now this book is in the hands of Gymnasium students and young girls. On the road from Sevastopol, I saw it on sale in the station and being read in the trains. The book market is full of the thirteenth volume of Tolstoy . . . (Quoted in E. J. Simmons, *Leo Tolstoy*, John Lehmann, 1949, pp. 498–9).

Although Sofya Andreyevna had acted in good faith, the Tsar was greatly displeased with this 'misdemeanour', as he saw it, and Pobedonostsev's letter, which also contained a vitriolic attack on the whole of Tolstoy's thinking and teaching, became the signal for a campaign of reprisals taken against him by the Church. It set the seal on a deep antagonism between Tolstoy and the Church–State complex of Imperial Russia that was to last until the writer's death in 1910, and even beyond it (it is significant that even though the Soviet cultural authorities were quick to exploit Tolstoy's anti-Church writings to the full, a text such as *What I Believe*, filled as it is with attacks on State power, has even today not received any wide publication in the Soviet Union.

What, nearly a hundred years on, has *The Kreutzer Sonata* to say to us? As a work of prose fiction it undoubtedly suffers from numerous defects – improbability, long-windedness, structural weakness and much else besides. Its 'sexual' theme, once the focus of a profound social and political scandal, can hardly shock us today. On the other hand, its treatment of female sexuality and the problems attendant upon it may have a certain relevance to our own times. Should we approach the tale as an autobiographical confession, a text in the same lineage as the *Confession* of 1879 or the tract *What I Believe* of 1883? There is much to be said for such a view of the work. Certainly, the device of Pozdnyshev, the half-mad, 'Dostoyevskian' central character, is only partly successful. We constantly have the feeling that Tolstoy is hiding behind it. Every so often the disguise seems to break down, revealing the writer's anguished features. Sofya Andreyevna had no illusions whatsoever on this matter. For her, the tale was a nightmarish act of callous indiscretion aimed at her and her children by a man she was beginning to fear and hate, a monstrous outpouring in public of the most intimate secrets of her marriage to him. Until the end of 1888, Tolstoy had continued to cling to the idea that marriage as an institution was a good in itself. Then, suddenly, as we have seen, he reached the conclusion that absolute chastity was the ultimate ideal towards which mankind must strive. The year 1889, with its intensive bouts of work on *The Kreutzer Sonata* and its Postface, saw him decide that marriage was not one of the forms of service to God. Without further ado, he consigned his own marriage to a private scrap-heap – from now on he would devote his energies to the realization of the Kingdom of God upon earth. Living almost as a guest in his own home, he now regarded family life as an empty frivolity and sexual relations with his wife as an evil to be fought and resisted. As she copied her husband's diary, Sofya Andreyevna could not help but see a marked similarity between these latest jottings concerning his struggle to preserve his chastity ('The Devil fell upon me,' he wrote. 'It was so shameful, as after a crime,' or 'What if a child should be born? How shameful, especially where the children are concerned. They will work out when it took place, and they will read what I am writing [*The Kreutzer Sonata*]') and the diary entries from the 1850s she had been

given to read at her betrothal on the subject of his struggle with
the 'devil' of sex. She saw her twenty-seven years of married life
– with their constant childbearing, her devotion to her husband
and all the hard and persevering work she had put into support-
ing his literary career – fall into ruins before her very eyes. The
whole episode of her petition to Aleksander must be seen as a
desperate attempt on her part to project the work as a piece of
literature, to deny its confessional nature and to protect her own
reputation and that of her family.

Despite all this, however, there is a sense in which *The
Kreutzer Sonata* transcends the level of autobiographic self-
laceration, and in which it moves beyond the social and
historical ramifications of its subject-matter. The profound
personal and spiritual crisis that brought Tolstoy to the verge
of suicide at the age of fifty, the influence of which may clearly
be observed in the final part of *Anna Karenina* and the effects
of which are described in *Confession*, was to a large extent
connected with a sense of being imprisoned in the world, of
being excessively enmeshed in the details of personal life and
of a literary career. The vision of cosmic terror and salvation
that concludes *Confession* is an act of freeing, a breaking of the
bonds of place and time that had hitherto held the author's
spirit captive. The tale *The Death of Ivan Ilyich* (1886) conveys
Tolstoy's personally experienced sense of life's meaninglessness in the face of physical death. Yet Ivan Ilyich's death itself
is an intensely meaningful process, an act of liberation: ' "It is
finished!" someone said above him. He heard these words and
repeated them within his own soul. "Death is finished," he
said to himself. "It doesn't exist any more." '

Similarly, in Pozdnyshev's murder of his wife, we may see
an act of rebellion against life's meaninglessness in the face of
domination by the reproductive urge, institutionalized in
marriage. Much has been made of Tolstoy's supposed 'mis-
ogyny', of his typification of woman as a 'devil' – yet it is not
woman herself Tolstoy condemns, rather the social institutions
that compel her to play a role he considers degrading, and the
instinct of sex itself, which he sees as having no relevance to
the essential human condition, being an attempt by the Devil

to divert the attention of human beings from their struggle to realize the Kingdom of God upon earth. While it is impossible to eradicate the sexual instinct from human relations altogether, Tolstoy considers that it should be tolerated only as a necessary evil: the human race will continue, even though its days, like those of the dinosaurs once, may be numbered. The aim, the purpose of humanity is, however, not to reproduce itself, but to be more loving, more Christ-like, more nearly a part of the Kingdom of God, and this aim can only be achieved by the practice of chastity. Pozdnyshev's wife dies as the victim of a cruel and inhuman world which sees the reproduction and reinforcement of its physicality as more important than the realization of spiritual goals. Starting from the despairing cry of 'Life is evil!', Tolstoy moved towards the premiss that 'God is life', and finally to the conclusion that 'Life without faith is impossible.' In *The Kreutzer Sonata* and its Postface he gives us a record of that journey, mapped out in terms of his own intimate, personal tragedy.

During the latter part of 1889 and early 1890 Tolstoy began to work on a second tale devoted to this theme. It developed rather differently, however. *The Devil* is the result of a fusion of two stories taken from real life: that of 'Fridrikhs', a judicial investigator from Tula whose involvement with and murder of a peasant girl named Stepanida bear many resemblances to Tolstoy's final narrative; and the story of Tolstoy's own involvement with Aksinya Bazytskaya, a peasant girl on his estate at Yasnaya Polyana, which lasted from 1858 until 1860. This affair evidently made a deep and lasting impression on Tolstoy: even as late as 1908 we find references to it in his diary, passages which were a source of great distress to Sofya Andreyevna when she finally read them after her husband's death – as was her reading of *The Devil* itself in 1909, when Tolstoy still had more than a year to live. The tale was not published until 1911, in the edition of *Posthumous Works* edited by Chertkov.

While *The Devil* does not possess the demonic intensity of *The Kreutzer Sonata*, as a tale it is considerably better constructed. It is also cast in a lighter key, and although the outcome of the action is tragic (the alternative variants of the ending present either murder or suicide as a solution to Irtenev's plight), one has the sense that on one level, at least, this story of a much younger man's obsession represented a kind of idyll for the ageing Tolstoy. Although the bulk of the writing dates from around the same time as *The Kreutzer Sonata*, the emotional detachment and lightness of touch seem more typical of the 'twentieth-century' Tolstoy: gone are the ideological passages, the laborious God-seeking of the works of the 1880s. The narration is swift, injected with touches of humour, and the action is clear and concise.

The way in which Tolstoy gradually recovered his artistic poise after the decade-long crisis of the 1880s may be seen, not in the ill-conceived and overblown *Resurrection*, but in the shorter prose works which followed the composition of the two tales on 'sexual love': *Master and Man* (1895), and the posthumously published *The Forged Coupon, After the Ball, Father Sergius* and *Hadji-Murat*. In *The Forged Coupon*, Tolstoy gives artistic treatment, most successfully, of his doctrine of non-resistance to evil, first outlined in *What I Believe*. The first part of the tale, in which the evil of the schoolboys' forgery is gradually compounded until it climaxes in Pelageyushkin's murder of Maria Semyonovna is skilfully offset by the second part, which describes a gradual progress away from darkness towards the light shed by the Gospels. The compression and tautness of the narrative are unparalleled in Tolstoy's literary output, with the possible exception of *Hadji-Murat*. *After the Ball* depicts the evil that Tolstoy saw as the motive power behind 'secular' society, a power from which there can be no escape except through a renunciation of that society and its values.

The Kreutzer Sonata was the product of a central crisis in Tolstoy's life as an artist, thinker and religious believer. In itself problematic from an artistic point of view, it none the less made possible the final period of Tolstoy's creative development. Although the tension between art and ideology is not resolved in it, any more than it is in the last part of *Anna Karenina*, the struggle for resolution did ultimately lead to a form of reconciliation between the pedagogic and creative impulses in Tolstoy's psyche, and made possible the writing of works in which the two at last successfully joined hands.

THE
KREUTZER SONATA

But I say unto you, That whosoever
looketh on a woman to lust after her
hath committed adultery with her
already in his heart.
(Matthew v, 28)

His disciples say unto him, If the case of the man be so
with his wife, it is not good to marry.

But he said unto them, All men cannot receive this
saying, save they to whom it is given.

For there are some eunuchs, which were so born from
their mother's womb: and there are some eunuchs, which
were made eunuchs of men: and there be eunuchs, which
have made themselves eunuchs for the kingdom
of heaven's sake. He that is able to receive it,
let him receive it.
(Matthew xix, 10–12)

I

This took place in early spring. It was the second uninterrupted day of our journey. Every so often passengers who were only going short distances would enter the railway carriage and leave it again, but there were three people who, like myself, had boarded the train at its point of origin and were still travelling: a plain, elderly lady with an exhausted-looking face, who was smoking cigarettes and was dressed in a hat and coat that might almost have been those of a man; her companion, a talkative man of about forty, with trim, new luggage; and another man who was rather small of stature and whose movements were nervous and jerky – he was not yet old, but his curly hair had obviously turned grey prematurely, and his eyes had a peculiar light in them as they flickered from one object to another. He was dressed in an old coat that looked as though it might have been made by an expensive tailor; it had a lambskin collar, and he wore a tall cap of the same material. Whenever he unfastened his coat, a long-waisted jacket and a Russian embroidered shirt came into view. Another peculiar thing about this man was that every now and again he uttered strange sounds, as if he were clearing his throat or beginning to laugh, but breaking off in silence.

Throughout the entire duration of the journey this man studiously avoided talking to any of the other passengers or becoming acquainted with them. If anyone spoke to him he would reply curtly and abruptly; he spent the time reading, looking out of the window, smoking or taking from his old travelling-bag the provisions he had brought with him and then sipping tea or munching a snack.

I had the feeling that his solitude was weighing him down, and I tried several times to engage him in conversation. Each time our eyes met, however, which was frequently, as we were sitting obliquely opposite one another, he would turn away and start reading his book or gazing out of the window.

Shortly before evening on that second day, the train stopped at a large station, and the nervous man stepped outside, fetched some boiling water and made tea for himself. The man with the smart luggage, a lawyer, as I later discovered, went to have a glass of tea in the station buffet with his travelling companion, the cigarette-smoking lady in the man's coat.

During their absence several new passengers entered the carriage. They included a tall, clean-shaven old man whose face was creased all over in wrinkles; he was evidently a merchant, and he wore a polecat fur coat and a cloth cap that had an enormous peak. He sat down opposite the places temporarily vacated by the lawyer and the lady, and immediately launched into a conversation with a young man who looked like an estate manager and who had also entered the carriage at this station.

My seat was diagonally opposite theirs, and since the train was not in motion I could, when no one was passing down the carriage, overhear snatches of what they were saying. The merchant started off by telling the other man that he was on his way to visit his estate, which lay just one stop down the line; then, as such men always do, they began to discuss trade and prices, the current state of the Moscow market, and eventually, as always, they arrived at the subject of the Nizhny Novgorod summer fair.[1] The estate manager embarked on a description of the drinking and antics of a certain rich merchant they both knew, but the old man would not hear him out; instead, he began to talk about the jamborees he himself had taken part in at Kunavino[2] in days gone by. Of his role in these he was evidently proud, and it was with open delight that he related how once, when he and this same mutual acquaintance had been drunk together in Kunavino, they had got up to some mischief of a kind that he could only describe in whispers. The estate manager's guffaw filled the entire carriage, and the old man laughed along with him, exposing a couple of yellow teeth to view.

Not expecting to hear anything of interest, I rose and left my seat with the aim of taking a stroll along the platform until it was time for the train to depart. In the doorway I bumped into the lawyer and the lady, who were chattering animatedly to one another as they found their way back to their seats.

'You won't have time,' the talkative lawyer said to me. 'The second bell's going to go any minute now.'

And so it was: before I had even reached the end of the line of carriages the bell rang. When I got back to my seat I found the lawyer and the lady deep in energetic conversation. The old merchant sat opposite them in silence, looking severely in front of him and chewing his teeth from time to time in disapproval.

'So then she just told her husband straight out,' the lawyer was saying with a smile as I made my way past him. 'She said she couldn't and wouldn't live with him any more, because . . .'

And he began to say something else, something I could not make out. More passengers came trooping in behind me; then the guard walked down the carriage, followed by a porter in a tremendous hurry, and for quite a long time there ensued such an uproar that no conversation could possibly be heard. When things had quietened down again and I could once more hear the lawyer's voice, the conversation had evidently passed from the particular to the general.

The lawyer was saying that the question of divorce was very much the object of public discussion in Europe just now, and that cases of this type were cropping up in our own country with an ever-increasing degree of frequency. Noticing that his voice had become the only one in the carriage, the lawyer cut short his homily and turned to the old man.

'There was none of that sort of thing in the old days, was there?' he said, smiling affably.

The old man was about to reply, but at that moment the train began to move and, taking off his cap, he began crossing himself and reciting a prayer in a whisper. The lawyer waited politely, averting his gaze. When he had finished his prayer and his thrice-repeated crossing of himself, the old man put his cap fairly and squarely back on his head, rearranged himself in his seat, and began to speak.

'Oh there was, sir. It's just that there wasn't so much of it, that's all,' he said. 'You can't expect anything else nowadays. They've all gotten that well educated.'

As the train began to gather speed it kept rattling over points, and it was not easy to hear what he was saying. I was interested, however, and I shifted my seat so as to be closer to him. The interest of my neighbour, the nervous man with the light in his eyes, had also plainly been aroused, and he continued to listen while staying where he was.

'But what's wrong with education?' said the lady, with a scarcely perceptible smile. 'Was it really better to get married in the old way, with the bride and bridegroom never even setting eyes on one another beforehand?' she continued, replying, as many women do, not to what the person she was addressing had actually said, but to what she thought he was going to say. 'You didn't know whether you were even going to like the man, let alone whether you'd be able to love him; you got married to the first man who came along and spent all the rest of your life in misery. Do you think that was better?' she said, making it clear that her words were addressed primarily to the lawyer and myself, and only in the last instance to the old man with whom she was talking.

'They've all gotten that well educated,' repeated the old merchant, surveying the lady contemptuously and letting her question go unanswered.

'I'd like to hear you explain the connection you see between education and marital discord,' the lawyer said, with a faint smile.

The merchant was about to say something, but the lady cut in before him.

'No, those days have gone,' she said. But the lawyer would not allow her to continue.

'Just a moment, let him say what's on his mind.'

'Education leads to nothing but a lot of silliness,' said the old man, firmly.

'People who don't love one another are forced to get married, and then everyone wonders why they can't live in harmony together,' said the lady hurriedly, turning an appraising eye on the lawyer, myself and even on the estate manager, who had risen out of his seat and was leaning his elbows on its back, listening to the conversation with a smile. 'After all, it's only animals that can be mated at their masters' will; human beings have inclinations and attachments of their own,' she went on, apparently from a desire to say something wounding to the merchant.

'You're wrong there, missus,' said the old man. 'The true difference is that an animal's just an animal, but human beings have been given a law to live by.'

'Very well, but how are you supposed to live with someone you don't love?' asked the lady, still in a hurry to express her opinions, which doubtless seemed brand-new to her .

'People didn't make such a fuss about all that in the old days,' said the merchant in a serious voice. 'That's all just come in lately. First thing you hear her say nowadays is "I'm leaving you." It's a fashion that's caught on even among the muzhiks. "Here you are," she says; "here's your shirts and trousers, I'm off with Vanka, his hair's curlier than yours." And it's no good arguing with her. Whereas what ought to come first for a woman is fear.'

The estate manager looked first at the lawyer, then at the lady, and finally at me; he was only just keeping back a smile, and was preparing to treat what the merchant had said with either ridicule or approval, according to how it went down.

'What sort of fear?' asked the lady.

'Fear of her *hu-u-u*sband, of course. That kind of fear.'

'Well, my dear man, those days have gone, I'm afraid,' said the lady, with an edge of malice in her voice.

'No, missus, those days can never be gone. Eve, the woman, was created from the rib of man, and so she will remain until the end of time,' said the old man, with such a stern and triumphant shake of his head that the estate manager at once decided that victory was on the side of the merchant, and he burst into loud laughter.

'That's only the way you menfolk see it,' said the lady, not ceding defeat, and giving us all an appraising look. 'You've granted yourselves freedom, but you want to keep women locked up in a tower. Meanwhile you've decided you're going to allow yourselves anything you want.'

'No one's decided anything of the kind. It's just that a home profits nothing from a man's endeavours, and a woman is a fragile vessel,' the merchant continued earnestly.

The merchant's solemn, earnest tone of voice was evidently having a persuasive effect on his audience. Even the lady appeared to have had some of the wind taken out of her sails, though she showed no sign of giving up the struggle.

'Yes, well, but I think you would agree that a woman is a human being, and that she has feelings just as a man has, wouldn't you? So what's she supposed to do if she doesn't love her husband?'

'If she doesn't love him?' echoed the merchant darkly,

making a grimace with his lips and eyebrows. 'She'd better love him.'

The estate manager seemed to find this line of argument particularly attractive, and he made a noise of approval.

'Oh, no she hadn't,' said the lady. 'If there's no love there in the first place, you can't force it.'

'And what if the wife's unfaithful to the husband?' asked the lawyer.

'That mustn't happen,' said the old man. 'You have to be on the look-out for that kind of thing.'

'But what if it does happen? It does, after all.'

'There's some as it happens to, but not the likes of us,' said the old man.

No one ventured anything for a while. The estate manager shifted a little closer. Apparently not wishing to be left out of things, he gave a smile and said: 'Oh, but it does, you know. There was a scandal with one of the lads on the estate where I work. It wasn't easy to tell whose fault it was, either. Married a loose woman, he did. She started her flirting around, but he was the homely type, and he had a bit of education. First jump she had was with one of the clerks in the office. The lad tried to make her see reason, but there was no stopping her. All kinds of filthy tricks she got up to. Started stealing his money. So he beat her. Didn't do any good, she just went from bad to worse. She started playing around – if you'll pardon the expression – with a heathen, a Jew he was. What was the lad supposed to do? He threw her out. Now he lives as a bachelor, and she walks the streets.'

'So he was an idiot,' said the old man. 'If he'd never given her any leeway in the first place but had kept her properly reined in, she'd no doubt still be living with him to this day. You mustn't allow them any freedom from the word go. Never trust a horse in the paddock or a wife in the home.'

At this moment the guard arrived to take the tickets for the next station. The old man gave up his ticket.

'Yes, you have to rein them in early on, those womenfolk, otherwise it all goes to pot.'

'But what about that story you were telling us just then about those married men going on the spree in Kunavino?' I could not resist asking.

'That's something altogether different,' said the merchant, and lapsed into silence.

When the whistle blew he got up, fetched his travelling-bag from under his seat, drew his overcoat tightly around him and, raising his cap to us, went out on to the brake platform.

II

As soon as the old man had gone, several voices took up the conversation again.

'That fellow was straight out of the Old Testament,' said the estate manager.

'A veritable walking *Domostroy*,'³ said the lady. 'What a barbarous conception of woman and marriage!'

'Yes, we're a long way behind the European idea of marriage,' said the lawyer.

'What these people don't seem to understand,' said the lady, 'is that marriage without love isn't marriage at all; love is the only thing that can sanctify a marriage, and the only true marriages are those that are sanctified by love.'

The estate manager listened, smiling. He was trying to memorize as much of this clever talk as he could, for use on future occasions.

The lady's homily was interrupted half-way through by a sound that seemed to come from behind me and might have been a broken laugh or a sob. When we turned round, we saw my neighbour, the solitary, grey-haired man with the light in his eyes; he had evidently become interested in our conversation and had come closer to us without our noticing. He was standing up, his hands leaning on the back of his seat, and he was plainly in a state of great agitation. His face was red, and a muscle in one of his cheeks was twitching.

'What's this love . . . love . . . love . . . that sanctifies marriage?' he stammered.

Observing the state of agitation he was in, the lady tried to make her reply as gentle and thorough as possible.

'True love . . . if true love exists between a man and a woman, then marriage, too, is possible,' said the lady.

'Yes, but what's true love?' said the man with the light in his eyes, smiling timidly and awkwardly.

'Everybody knows what love is,' said the lady, visibly anxious to bring this conversation to an end.

'I don't,' said the man. 'You'd have to define what you mean . . .'

'What? It's very simple,' said the lady, though she had to think for a moment. 'Love? Love is the exclusive preference for one man or one woman above all others,' she said.

'A preference lasting how long? A month? Two days, half an hour?' said the grey-haired man, and he gave a laugh.

'No, not that kind of preference, you're talking about something else.'

'What she means,' said the lawyer, intervening and designating the lady, 'is firstly that marriage ought to be based primarily on affection – love, if you like – and that only if this is present does marriage offer something that is, as it were, sacred. Secondly, that no marriage which is not based on natural affection – love, if you like – carries with it any moral obligation. Have I understood you correctly?' he asked, turning to the lady.

By a movement of her head, the lady indicated her approval of this exposition of her views.

'It follows, therefore . . .' the lawyer began, pursuing his discourse. But by this time the nervous man, whose eyes were now on fire, was clearly restraining himself only with difficulty.

Without waiting for the lawyer to conclude, he said: 'Yes, that's exactly what I'm talking about, the preference for one man or one woman above all others, but what I'm asking is: a preference for how long?'

'How long? A long time, sometimes for as long as one lives,' said the lady, shrugging her shoulders.

'But that only happens in novels, not in real life. In real life

Leo Tolstoy

a preference like that lasts maybe a year, but that's very rare; more often it's a few months, or weeks, or days, or hours,' he said, evidently aware that this opinion would shock everyone, and pleased at the result.

'What are you saying? No, no! Sorry, but no!' we all three of us burst out together. Even the estate manager made a noise of disapproval.

'I know, I know,' said the grey-haired man in a raised voice, louder than any of us. 'You're talking about the way things are supposed to be, but I'm talking about the way things actually are. Every man experiences what you call love each time he meets a pretty woman.'

'Oh, but what you're saying is dreadful! Surely there's an emotion that exists between people called love, a feeling that lasts not just months or years, but for the whole of their lives?'

'Definitely not. Even if one admits that a man may prefer a certain woman all his life, it's more than probable that the woman will prefer someone else. That's the way it's always been and that's the way it still is,' he said, taking a cigarette from his cigarette case and lighting it.

'But there can be mutual affection, surely,' said the lawyer.

'No, there can't,' the grey-haired man retorted, 'any more than two marked peas can turn up next to one another in a pea-cart. And besides, it's not just a question of probability, but of having too much of a good thing. Loving the same man or woman all your life – why, that's like supposing the same candle could last you all your life,' he said, inhaling greedily.

'But you're just talking about physical love. Wouldn't you admit that there can be a love that's founded on shared ideals, on spiritual affinity?'

'Spiritual affinity? Shared ideals?' he repeated, making his sound again. 'There's not much point in going to bed together if that's what you're after (excuse the plain language). Do people go to bed with one another because of shared ideals?' he said, laughing nervously.

'I'm sorry,' said the lawyer. 'The facts contradict what you're saying. Our own eyes tell us that marriages exist, that the whole of humanity or at least the greater part of it lives in a married state and that a lot of people manage to stay decently married for rather a long time.'

The grey-haired man began to laugh again. 'First you tell me that marriage is founded on love, and then when I express my doubts as to the existence of any love apart from the physical kind you try to prove its existence by the fact that marriages exist. But marriage nowadays is just a deception!'

'No, sir, with respect,' said the lawyer. 'All I said was that marriages have existed and that they continue to exist.'

'All right, so they exist. But why? They've existed and they continue to exist for the sort of people who see in marriage something that's sacred, a sacrament that binds them in the eyes of God. Marriages exist for those people, but not for the likes of you and me. Our sort enter into a marriage without seeing in it anything except copulation, and it usually ends either in infidelity or violence. Infidelity is easier to put up with. The husband and wife simply pretend to everyone that they're living in monogamy, when in actual fact they're living in polygamy and polyandry. It's not very pretty, but it's feasible. But when, as is most often the case, the husband and wife accept the external obligation to live together all their lives and have, by the second month, come to loathe the sight of each other, want to get divorced and yet go on living together, it usually ends in that terrible hell that drives them to drink, makes them shoot themselves, kill and poison each other,' he said, speaking faster and faster, not letting anyone else get a word in, and growing hotter and hotter under the collar. No one said anything. We all felt too embarrassed.

'Yes, there's no doubt that married life has its critical episodes,' said the lawyer, endeavouring to bring to an end a conversation that had grown more heated than was seemly.

'I can see you've recognized me,' said the grey-haired man quietly, trying to appear unruffled.

'No, I don't think I have the pleasure . . .'

'It's not much of a pleasure. Pozdnyshev's the name. I'm the fellow who had one of those critical episodes you were talking about. So critical was it, in fact, that I ended up murdering my wife,' he said, making his noise again. 'Oh, I say, I'm sorry. Er . . . I didn't mean to embarrass you.'

'Not at all, for heaven's sake . . .' said the lawyer, not quite sure himself what he meant by this 'for heaven's sake'.

But Pozdnyshev, who was not paying any attention to him, turned round sharply and went back to his seat. The lawyer and the lady whispered to one another. I was sitting beside Pozdnyshev and I kept quiet, not knowing what to say. It was too dark to read, so I closed my eyes and pretended I wanted to go to sleep. We continued in this silent fashion until the train reached the next station.

While the train was at a standstill, the lawyer and the lady moved along to another carriage as they had arranged to do earlier on with the guard. The estate manager made himself comfortable on the empty seat and went to sleep. As for Pozdnyshev, he continued to smoke cigarettes and sip the tea he had made for himself at the previous station.

When I opened my eyes and looked at him, he suddenly turned to me with an air of resolve and exasperation: 'I think perhaps you're finding it unpleasant to sit next to me, since you know who I am? If that's so, I'll move.'

'Oh, no, please don't.'

'Well, would you like some tea, then? It's strong, mind.' He poured me a glass of tea. 'What they were saying . . . It's all wrong, you know . . .'

'What are you talking about?' I asked.

'Oh, the same thing – that love they keep going on about, and what it really is. You're sure you'd not rather be getting some sleep?'

'Quite sure.'

'Well then, if you like, I'll tell you how that love of theirs drove me to the point where I did what I did.'

'By all means, if it's not too painful for you.'

'No, it's keeping quiet about it that's the painful part. Have some more. Or is it too strong for you?'

The tea was the colour of tar, but I swilled down a glass of it all the same. Just then the guard passed down the carriage.

Pozdnyshev followed him angrily with his gaze and did not start speaking again until he was gone.

III

'Very well, then, I'll tell you ... You're absolutely sure you want me to?'

I repeated that I did, very much. He said nothing for a moment. Then, rubbing his face in his hands, he began: 'If I'm going to tell you, I'll have to start at the beginning, and tell you how and why I got married, and what I was like before my marriage.

'Before my marriage I lived the sort of life all men do, in our social circle, that is. I'm a landowner, I've got a university degree, and I used to be a marshal of nobility. As I say, I lived the sort of life all men do – a life of debauchery. And, like all the men of our class, I thought that this debauched existence was perfectly proper. I considered myself a charming young man, a thoroughly moral sort of fellow. I wasn't a seducer, had no unnatural tastes, and didn't make debauchery into my main aim in life, as many young men of my age did, but indulged in it with decency and moderation, for the sake of my health. I avoided women who might have succeeded in tying me down by having babies or forming attachments to me. Actually, there probably were both babies and attachments, but I behaved as if there weren't. Not only did I regard this as moral behaviour – I was proud of it.'

He paused and made his sound, as he apparently did whenever some new idea occurred to him.

'And that's the really loathsome thing about it,' he exclaimed. 'Debauchery isn't something physical. Not even the most outrageous physicality can be equated with debauchery. Debauchery – real debauchery – takes place when you free yourself from any moral regard for the woman you enter into physical relations with. But you see, I made the acquisition of that freedom into a matter of personal honour. I remember the agony of mind I once went through when I was in too much of a hurry to remember to pay a woman who had probably fallen in love with me and had let me go to bed with her. I just couldn't rest easy until I'd sent her the money, thereby demonstrating that I didn't consider myself morally obliged towards her in any way. Don't sit there nodding your head as if you agreed with me!' he suddenly shouted at me. 'I know what you're thinking! You're all the same, you too, unless you're a rare exception, you see things the way I did then. Oh I say, forget that, I'm sorry,' he continued. 'But the fact is that it's horrible, horrible, horrible!'

'What is?' I inquired.

'The abyss of error we live in regarding women and our relations with them. It's no good, I just can't talk calmly about it. It's not merely because of that episode, as the other gentleman called it, but because ever since I went through it my eyes have been opened and I've seen everything in a completely new light. Everything's been turned inside out, it's all inside out! . . .'

He lit a cigarette and, leaning forward with his elbows on his knees, began to tell me his story.

It was so dark that I could not see his face, only hear his forceful, pleasant voice raised above the rattling and swaying of the carriage.

IV

'Yes, it was only after the suffering I endured, only thanks to it that I came to understand what the root of the trouble was, saw the way things ought to be, and thus obtained an insight into the horror of things the way they were.

'If you want to know, this is how and when it all began, the sequence of events that led up to that episode of mine. It started shortly before my sixteenth birthday. I was still at grammar school then. My older brother was a first-year student at university. As yet I had no experience of women, but like all the wretched boys of our social class I was no longer innocent. For more than a year I'd been exposed to the corrupting influence of the other boys. Woman – not any woman in particular but woman as a sweet, ineffable presence – woman, any woman, the nakedness of woman already tormented me. The hours I spent alone were not pure ones. I suffered in the way ninety-nine per cent of our youngsters suffer. I was horrified – I suffered, prayed, and succumbed. I was already corrupted, both in my imagination and in reality, but I had still not taken the final step. In my lonely way I was going from bad to worse, but so far I had not laid my hands on any other human being. But then one of my brother's friends, a student, a *bon vivant*, one of those so-called "jolly good chaps" (an out-and-out villain, in other words), who had taught us to play cards and drink vodka, persuaded us to go with him to a certain place after a drinking-bout one evening. My brother was still a virgin, like myself, and he fell that very same night. And I, a fifteen-year-old boy, defiled myself and contributed to the defilement of a woman without the slightest understanding of what I was doing. After all, never once had I heard any of my elders say that what I was doing was wrong. And it's not something you hear said nowadays, either. It's true that it's in the Ten Commandments, but you know as well as I do that they're only useful for giving the school chaplain the right answers on examination day, and even then they're not a great deal of help – much less so, for example, than knowing when to use *ut* in conditional clauses.

'That's the way it was: none of the older people whose opinions I respected ever told me that what I was doing was wrong. On the contrary, the people I looked up to told me it was the right thing to do. I was told that, after I had done it, my struggles and sufferings would ease. I was told this, and I read it. My elders assured me that it would be good for my health. As for my companions, they said it entailed a kind of merit, a certain bravado. Accordingly, I could see nothing but good in it. The danger of infection? But that, too, is taken care of. Our solicitous government takes pains to see to it. It supervises the orderly running of the licensed brothels and ensures the depravation of grammar-school boys. Even our doctors keep an eye on this problem, for a fee of course. That is only proper. They assert that debauchery is good for the health, for it's they who have instituted this form of tidy, legalized debauchery. I even know mothers who take an active concern for this aspect of their son's health. And science directs them to the brothels.'

'Why science?' I asked.

'What are doctors, if not the high priests of science? Who are the people responsible for depraving young lads, claiming it's essential for their health? They are. And having made such a claim, they proceed to apply their cures for syphilis with an air of the utmost gravity.'

'But why shouldn't they cure syphilis?'

'Because if even one per cent of the effort that is put into curing syphilis were to be employed in the eradication of debauchery, syphilis would long ago have disappeared from memory. But our efforts are employed not in eradicating debauchery, but in encouraging it, making it safe. Anyway that isn't the point. The point is that I, like nine out of ten, if not more, young men, not only in our own class but in all the others as well, even the peasantry, have had the horrible experience of falling without succumbing to the natural temptation of the charms of any one woman in particular. No, it wasn't a case of my being seduced by a woman. I fell because the society I lived in regarded what was a fall either as a bodily function that was both legitimate and necessary for the sake of health, or as a diversion that was thoroughly natural for a young man and was not only pardonable, but even innocent. I myself didn't know it was a fall; I simply began to indulge in something that was half pleasure and half physical necessity – both, I was assured, perfectly proper for young men of a certain age. I began to indulge in this debauchery in the same way as I began to drink and smoke. Yet there was something strangely moving about that first fall. I remember that immediately after it was over, right there in the room, I felt terribly, terribly sad; I wanted to weep, weep for my lost innocence, for my relation to women which had been forever spoiled, corrupted. Yes, the simple, natural relation I had had to women had been ruined for ever. From that day on I ceased to have a pure relation to women, nor was I any longer capable of one. I had become what is known as a fornicator. Being a fornicator is a physical condition similar to that of a morphine addict, an alcoholic or a smoker of opium. Just as a morphine addict, an alcoholic or a smoker of opium is no longer a normal individual, so a man who has had several women for the sake of his pleasure is no longer a normal person but one who has been spoiled for all time – a fornicator. And just as an alcoholic or a morphine addict can immediately be recognized by his features and physical mannerisms, so can a fornicator. A fornicator may restrain himself, struggle for self-control, but never again will his relation to women be simple, clear, pure, that of a brother to a sister. A fornicator can be instantly recognized by the intent look with which he examines a woman. I, too, became a fornicator and remained one, and that was my undoing.'

V

'Yes, that's how it happened. After that it got worse and worse; I became involved in all kinds of moral deviations. My God! I recoil in horror from the memory of all my filthy acts! I, whom all my friends used to laugh at because of what they called my innocence! And when one looks at our golden youth, at our officers, at those Parisians! And when all those gentlemen and myself, debauchees in our thirties with hundreds of the most varied and abominable crimes against women on our consciences, go into a drawing-room or a ballroom, well scrubbed, clean-shaven, perfumed, wearing immaculate linen, in evening dress or uniform, the very emblems of purity – aren't we a charming sight?

'Just give some thought for a moment to the way things ought to be and the way things actually are. This is the way things ought to be: when one of these gentlemen enters into relations with my sister or my daughter, I go up to him, take him aside and say to him quietly: "My dear fellow, I know the sort of life you lead, how you spend your nights and who you spend them with. This is no place for you. The girls in this house are pure and innocent. Be off with you!'' That's how it ought to be. Now how things actually are is that when one of these gentlemen appears and starts dancing with my sister or my daughter, putting his arms round her, we rejoice, as long as he's rich and has connections. Always supposing, of course, that after Rigolboche⁴ he considers my daughter good enough for him. Even if there are consequences, an illness ... it doesn't matter. They can cure anything nowadays. Good heavens, yes, I can think of several girls from the highest social circles whose parents enthusiastically married them off to syphilitics. Ugh, how vile! But the time will come when all that filth and deception will be shown for what it is!'

He made his strange sound several times and began to sip his tea. The tea was horribly strong, and there was no water with which to dilute it. I felt it was the two glasses of the stuff I had already drunk that were making me so agitated. The tea must also have been having an effect on him, for he was growing more and more excited. His voice was increasingly acquiring a singing, expressive quality. He shifted position constantly, now removing his hat, now putting it on again, and his face kept altering strangely in the semi-darkness where we sat.

'Well, and so that's the way I lived until I was thirty, without ever for one moment abandoning my intention of getting married and building for myself the most elevated and purest of family lives, and with that end in view I was keeping an eye out for a girl who might fill the bill,' he continued. 'I was wallowing in the slime of debauchery, and at the same time looking for girls who might be pure enough to be worthy of me! I rejected a lot of them because of that – because they weren't pure enough; but at last I found one whom I considered worthy of me. She was one of the two daughters of a Penza landowner who had once been very rich but had lost all his money.

'One evening after we'd been out boating and were going home together in the moonlight, I sat beside her and admired her curls and her shapely figure, hugged by the tight silk of the stockinet dress she was wearing. I suddenly decided that she was the one. That evening it seemed to me that she understood everything, all I was thinking and feeling, and that all my thoughts and feelings were of the most exalted kind. All it really was was that silk stockinet happened to suit her particularly well, as did curls, and that after a day spent close to her I wanted to get even closer.

'It's really quite remarkable how complete the illusion is that beauty is the same as goodness. A pretty woman may say the most stupid things, yet you listen, and you don't notice the stupidities, it all sounds so intelligent. She says and does things that are infamous, yet to you they seem delightful. And when at last she says something that is neither stupid nor infamous, as long as she's pretty, you're immediately convinced that she's quite wonderfully intelligent and of the very highest morality.

'I returned home positively beside myself with enthusiasm and decided that she was the acme of moral perfection and consequently worthy of being my wife. I proposed to her the very next day.

'What a tangled mess it all is! Out of a thousand men who get married, not only in our own class but also, regrettably, among the common people as well, there's scarcely one who hasn't already been married ten times, if not a hundred or even a thousand times, like Don Juan, before his marriage. (Nowadays there are, it's true, as I've heard and observed, pure young men who know and sense that this is no laughing-matter, but a great and serious undertaking. May God give them strength! In my day there wasn't one chap in ten thousand like that.) And everyone knows this, yet pretends not to. In novels the hero's emotions are described in detail, just like the ponds and bushes he walks beside; but while they describe his *grand amour* for some young girl or other, they say nothing about what has taken place in the life of this interesting hero previously: there's not a word about his visits to brothels, about the chamber-maids, the kitchen-maids, the wives of other men. Even if indecent novels of this type do exist, they're certainly not put into the hands of those who

most need to know all this – young girls. At first we pretend
to them that this debauchery, which fills up the lives of half
the inhabitants of our towns and villages, doesn't exist at all.
Subsequently we grow so accustomed to this pretence that we
end up like the English, secure in the honest conviction that
we are all of the very highest morality and that we live in a
world that is morally perfect. The poor girls take it all very
seriously. I know my own wretched wife did. I remember that
after we'd got engaged I let her read my diary,[5] so she could
get some idea of the sort of life I'd been leading previously
and in particular some knowledge of my last affair, which she
might have found out about from other people and which I
therefore considered it necessary to tell her about. I remember
her horror, despair and perplexity when she learned about it
and the whole thing dawned on her. I could see she was
thinking of leaving me. If only she had!'

He made his sound, fell silent, and took another mouthful
of tea.

VI

'No, all the same, it's better the way it turned out, better the
way it turned out!' he cried suddenly. 'It served me right! But
that's all in the past now. What I was trying to say was that it's
only the poor girls who are deceived. Their mothers know,
especially the ones who've been "educated" by their husbands,
they know perfectly well what goes on. And although they
pretend to believe that men are pure, their actual behaviour is
altogether different. They know the right bait to use in order
to catch men, both for themselves and for their daughters.

'It's only we men who don't know, and we don't know
because we don't want to know. Women know perfectly well
that the most elevated love – the most "poetic", as we call it –
depends not on moral qualities but on physical proximity and
also on things like hair-style, or the colour and the cut of a
dress. Ask any experienced coquette who has set herself the
task of ensnaring the attentions of a man which she would

rather risk: to be accused of lying, cruelty and even of whorish behaviour in the presence of the man she is trying to attract, or to appear before his gaze in an ugly, badly made dress – and she will always choose the former. She knows that our man's lying when he goes on about lofty emotions – all he wants is her body, and so he will willingly forgive her the most outrageous behaviour. What he won't forgive, however, is an outfit that is ugly, tasteless or lacking in style. A coquette's knowledge of this is a conscious one; but every innocent young girl knows it unconsciously, as animals do.

'That's the reason for those insufferable stockinets, those fake posteriors, those bare shoulders, arms – breasts, almost. Women, especially women who've undergone the "education" provided by men, know very well that all talk about higher things is just talk, that all a man really wants is her body, and all the things that show it off in the most enticing fashion possible. And that's what they give him. You know, if only one is able to kick the habit of all this squalor that's become second nature to us and takes a look at the life of our upper classes as it really is in all its shamelessness, one can see that what we live in is a sort of licensed brothel. Don't you agree? I can prove it to you if you like,' he said, not letting me get a word in. 'You may say that women of our class act out of interests that are different from those of the women in the whorehouses, but I say that the contrary is true, and I can prove it. If people differ as regards the purpose, the inner content of their lives, that difference will inevitably be reflected in outward things, and those will differ, too. But look at those poor despised wretches, and then cast a glance at our society ladies: the same exposure of arms, shoulders, breasts, the same flaunted, tightly clad posteriors, the same passion for precious stones and shiny, expensive objects, the same diversions – music, dancing, singing. Just as the former seek to entice men by all the means at their disposal, so do the latter. There's no difference. At a rule, we may say that while short-term prostitutes are generally looked down upon, long-term prostitutes are treated with respect.'

VII

'Yes, and so I fell into the trap of all those stockinets, those curls and fake bottoms. I was an easy catch, because I'd been brought up under those special conditions created for amorous young people, who are cultivated in them like cucumbers in a greenhouse. Yes, the stimulating, superabundant food we eat, together with our complete physical idleness, amounts to nothing but a systematic arousal of lust. I don't know whether you find that astonishing or not, but it's a fact. I myself had no idea of all this until quite recently. But now I can see it. And that is what I find so infuriating, that no one has any idea of what's really going on, and everyone says such stupid things, like that woman just now.

'Yes, this spring there were some peasants working on the railway embankment close to where I live. The normal food of a young peasant is bread, kvas and onions; it keeps him lively, cheerful and healthy; he works at light tasks out in the fields. He goes to work for the railway, and is fed on kasha and a pound of meat a day. But that day involves sixteen hours of labour, during which he has to trundle a wheelbarrow weighing some thirty pounds, and he soon uses up the meat. It's just right for him. But look at us: every day each of us eats perhaps two pounds of meat, game and all kinds of stimulating food and drink. Where does it all go? On sensual excesses. If we really do use it up in that way, the safety valve is opened and everything is all right. If, on the other hand, we close the safety valve, as I did mine from time to time, there immediately results a state of physical arousal which, channelled through the prism of our artificial way of life, expresses itself as the purest form of love, sometimes even as a platonic infatuation. I, too, fell in love that way, like everyone else. And it was all there: all the ecstasy, the tender emotion, the poetry. In actual fact, this love of mine was the product of, on the one hand, the efforts of the girl's mother and dress-makers, and on the other, of the excessive quantities of food I had consumed during a life of idleness. If, on the one hand, there had been none of those boat trips, those dress-makers with their waistlines, and so on, and say my wife had gone around in an ill-fitting housecoat and spent her time at home, and if, on the other hand, I had been living the normal life of a man who consumes just as much food as is necessary for him to be able to do his work, and the safety valve had been open – it happened to be closed at the time – I would never have fallen in love and none of all this would ever have happened.'

VIII

'Well, this time it all clicked together: my state of mind, her dress and the boat trip. And it worked. Twenty times before it hadn't worked, but now it did – the way a trap does. I'm quite serious. Marriages nowadays are set like traps. Only stands to reason, doesn't it? The girl's grown up now, she'll have to be married to someone. It all seems so simple, as long as the girl's not a freak and there are men around who want to get married. That's the way it was done in the old days. When a girl came of age, her parents arranged a marriage for her. That's how it was done, and that's how it's done all over the world to this very day: among the Chinese, the Hindus, the Muslims, among our own common people. That's how it's done among at least ninety-nine per cent of the human race. It's only we one per cent or less of debauchees who've decided that's not good enough and have thought up something new. And what is that something new? It's girls sitting in line while men come and go in front of them as if they were at a market, making their choice. As they sit there waiting, the girls think, not daring to say it out loud: "Choose me, dearest! No, me. Not her, me: look what nice shoulders and all the rest of it I have." We men walk up and down, take a look, and are very pleased with what we see. "I know what they're up to," we say to ourselves, "but I won't fall into their trap." We walk up and down, we take a look, we're thoroughly gratified that all this has been arranged for our benefit. We look, are taken off our guard for a moment – and slam! There's another one caught!'

'But how do you think it ought to be?' I asked. 'Should the woman be the one to propose?'

'I honestly don't know: but if we're going to have equality, then let's have real equality. It may well be that matchmaking is a degrading business, but this is a thousand times more so. At least under the old system the rights possessed by both parties and their chances of making a decent match were equal, but nowadays a women is like a slave in a market or a piece of bait for a trap. Just you try to tell a mother or even the girl herself that all her activities are directed towards catching a husband. Dear Lord, what an insult! And yet that's all they do, and they've nothing else with which to fill their time. What's so awful is seeing even poor innocent young girls engaged in this activity. If only it were done out in the open, but no, it's all trickery, deceit. "Ah, the origin of species, how interesting! Oh, Liza's so interested in painting! And you'll be going to the exhibition? How educational! And the troika rides, and the theatre, and the symphony concert? How wonderful! My Liza's simply mad about music. Oh, do tell me why you don't share these convictions! And boating, too . . ." And all the while there's just one thought in her head: "Take me, take me, take my Liza! No, me! Go on, just for a trial!" Oh, horror! Lies!' he concluded, and, drinking up what was left of the tea, set about clearing away the glasses and the rest of the tea things.

IX

'You know,' he resumed, as he put the tea and sugar away in his travelling-bag, 'it's this domination by women we're suffering from, it all stems from that.'

'What domination?' I asked. 'All the rights and privileges are on the side of men.'

'Yes, yes, that's just the point,' he said, interrupting me. 'That's exactly what I'm trying to tell you, that's what explains this curious phenomenon: from one point of view, it's perfectly correct to say that woman has been brought to the lowest degree of subjection, but from another point of view it's equally true to say that she's the dominant one. Women are exactly like the Jews, who by their financial power compensate for the oppression to which they're subjected. "Aha, you just want us to be merchants, do you? All right, then, it's as merchants that we'll lord it over you," say the Jews. "Aha, you just want us to be the objects of your sensuality, do you? All right, then, it's as the objects of your sensuality that we'll enslave you," say women. Women's lack of rights has nothing to do with them not being allowed to vote or be judges – those matters don't constitute any sort of right. No, it has to do with the fact that in sexual relations she's not the man's equal. She doesn't have the right to avail herself of the man or abstain from him, according to her desire, to select the man she wants rather than be the one who's selected. You may say that would be monstrous. Very well. Then the man shouldn't have these rights, either. The way things are at present, the woman is deprived of the rights possessed by the man. And, in order to compensate for this, she acts on the man's sensuality, forces him into subjection by means of sensuality, so that he's only formally the one who chooses – in actual fact it's she who does the choosing. And once she has mastered this technique, she abuses it and acquires a terrible power over men.'

'But where's the evidence of this special power?' I asked.

'Where? All around us, in everything. Just go into the shops of any large town. There's millions of rubles worth of stuff there; you could never put a value on the amount of labour that's gone into producing it. Yet look: in nine out of ten of those shops is there even one article that's intended to be used by men? All life's luxury articles are made in order to meet the demands of women, and be consumed by them. Just look at all those factories. By far the majority of them produce useless ornaments, carriages, furniture, playthings for women. Millions of human beings, generations of slaves perish in factories doing this convict labour merely in order to satisfy the caprice of women. Women are like empresses, keeping nine tenths of the human race in servitude, doing hard labour. And all because they feel they've been humiliated, because they're been denied the same rights men have. And so they take their revenge by acting on our sensuality and ensnaring us in their nets. Yes, that's where the trouble lies. Women have turned themselves into such effective instruments for acting on our senses that we can't even speak to them with equanimity. No sooner does a man go near a woman than he falls under her spell and loses his head. Even in my previous life I always used to get an uneasy sensation whenever I set eyes on a woman dressed in a ball-gown, but now that sight inspires me with genuine terror: I really do see in her something that's dangerous to men, something that's against all law, and I feel like calling for the police and appealing to them for protection against this danger, demanding that the hazardous object be confiscated and taken away.

'Yes, you may laugh!' he shouted at me. 'But it's no laughing matter. I'm convinced that the day will come, and perhaps before very long, when people will realize this and be amazed that there could have existed a society which tolerated actions so disturbing to public order as the ornamentation of the body, something that's so openly provocative of sensuality, yet is permitted to women in our society. It's just as if we were to set traps along all the thoroughfares men use in their daily business . . . it's even worse that that! Why is it that gambling's against the law, while women displaying themselves in prostitutes' garb that excites sensuality aren't? They're a thousand times more dangerous!'

X

'Well, anyway, that's how I too was caught. I was what's called "in love". It wasn't just that I thought she was the acme of perfection – during the time I was engaged to her I thought I was the acme of perfection, too. After all, there's no good-for-nothing who, after looking round for a bit, can't find other good-for-nothings worse than himself in certain respects, and thus find a reason for pride and self-congratulation. That's the way it was with me: I wasn't marrying for money – material interests weren't involved as they were for the majority of my friends, who were getting married for the sake of either money or connections – I was rich, she was poor. The other thing I was proud of was that while my friends were all getting married with the intention of continuing to live in polygamy as they had done before, I had the firm intention of remaining monogamous after my wedding – and my pride in this knew no bounds. Yes, I was a dirty pig, and I thought I was an angel.

'My engagement was a brief one. I can't recall that time now without a sense of shame. What an abomination! We usually assume, don't we, that love is something spiritual, not sensual? Well, if love is spiritual, a spiritual relation, its spirituality ought to be expressed in words, in our conversations, our chats with each other. Of that there was none. Whenever we were left alone together we had a dickens of a job finding anything to say to one another. It involved a kind of sisyphean labour. As soon as you thought of anything to say, you said it – then you had to be silent again, and try to think of something else to say. There was nothing to talk about. Everything we could think of to say about the life that lay ahead of us, about our plans and our living arrangements, we had already said, and what was there left? If we'd been animals, we'd have known that talking was not what we were supposed to be doing. In this situation, however, we were supposed to talk – yet there was nothing to talk about, since what occupied our thoughts was not something that could be dealt with by means of conversation. Add to this the outrageous custom of offering each other sweetmeats, our brutish gorging on candies and desserts, and all those revolting wedding preparations: the talk about the apartment, the bedroom, the beds, the dressing-gowns, the night clothes, the linen, the toilettes. You'd agree, I think, that if people get married according to the *Domostroy*, in the manner that old man was describing, all those things like feather quilts, trousseaus and beds are just details that accompany the sacrament. But in our day, when out of ten men who get married there's hardly one who believes in the sacrament or even that what he's doing carries any particular obligation with it, when out of a hundred men there's hardly one who hasn't been married before, and out of fifty hardly one who hasn't married with the intention of being unfaithful to his wife at the first opportunity, when most men view the trip to church merely as a peculiar condition set down for their being able to possess a certain woman – think what a dreadful significance all those details acquire. In the end they turn out to be what the whole thing boils down to. It's a kind of sale: an innocent girl is sold to some debauched individual, and the sale is accompanied by certain formalities.'

XI

'I got married the way everyone gets married, and the much-vaunted honeymoon began. What vulgarity there is in the very name!' he spat contemptuously. 'When I was in Paris once, I went on a tour of all the city sights; lured by a billboard, I went in to have a look at a bearded lady and a so-called "aquatic dog". The first turned out to be nothing but a man in a woman's low-cut dress, and the second a dog that had been forced into a seal-skin, swimming around in a bath-tub. It was all of very little interest; but as I was on my way out, the man in charge of the show politely followed me to the door and, when we got outside, pointed to me, saying to the people who were standing there: "Ask this gentleman if it's worth seeing! Roll up, roll up, one franc a time!" It would have pricked my conscience to say that the show wasn't worth a visit, and the man was no doubt banking on that. That's probably how it is for people who've experienced the entire beastliness of a honeymoon and who refrain from disillusioning others. I didn't disillusion anyone, either, but now I can see no reason why I shouldn't tell the truth. I even think it's necessary for the truth about this matter to be told. A honeymoon is an embarrassing, shameful, loathsome, pathetic business, and most of all it is tedious, unbearably tedious! It's something similar to what I experienced when I was learning how to smoke: I felt like vomiting, my saliva flowed, but I swallowed it and pretended I was enjoying myself. It's like the pleasure one gets from smoking: if there's to be any, it comes later on. A husband and wife have to educate themselves in this vice if they're to get any pleasure out of it.'

'Why vice?' I asked. 'I mean to say, you're talking about one of the most natural human activities there is!'

'Natural?' he said. 'Natural? No, I tell you, quite the contrary's true, I've come to the conclusion that it isn't . . . natural. No, not . . . natural, at all. Ask children about it, ask any uncorrupted young girl. When my sister was still very young she married a man twice her age, a thoroughly debauched character. I remember how startled we were when, on the night of her wedding, pale and in tears, she came running out of the bedroom and, trembling all over, declared that not for anything, not for anything in the world would she do what he wanted her to do – she couldn't even bring herself to say what it was.

'You claim it's natural. Eating is natural. Eating is something joyful, easy and pleasant which by its very essence involves no shame. But this is something loathsome, ignominious, painful. No, it's unnatural! And an uncorrupted young girl – of this I'm convinced – never fails to hate it.'

'But,' I said, 'how else can the human race continue?'

'Oh yes! As long as the human race doesn't perish!' he said with malevolent irony, as if he had been expecting this response as a familiar one, made in bad faith. 'To preach that one must abstain from procreation so that the English lords may continue to gorge themselves at their ease . . . that's all right. To preach that one must abstain from procreation in order to make the world a more agreeable place to live in . . . that's all right, too. But just try to insinuate that one ought to abstain from procreation in the name of morality . . . God in heaven, what an uproar will ensue! Is the human race going to disappear from the face of the earth just because a couple of dozen men don't want to go on living like pigs? But I'm sorry, excuse me. The light's getting in my eyes – do you mind if we pull the shade over it?' he said, pointing to the lamp.

I said I had no objection, and then with the haste that
marked all his actions he got up on his seat and pulled the
woollen shade over the lamp.

'All the same,' I said, 'if everyone thought like that, the
human race would disappear.'

He did not reply at once.

'You ask how the human race would continue?' he said,
settling himself down again opposite me; he had spread his
legs wide apart and was leaning his elbows on his knees. 'Why
should it continue, the human race?' he said.

'Why? We wouldn't exist, otherwise.'

'And why should we exist?'

'Why? So we can live.'

'But why should we live? If life has no purpose, if it's been
given us for its own sake, we have no reason for living. If that
really is the case, then the Schopenhauers and the Hartmanns,[6]
as well as all the Buddhists, are perfectly right. And even if
there is a purpose in life, it seems obvious that when that
purpose is fulfilled life must come to an end. That's the
conclusion one reaches,' he said, visibly moved, and obviously
treasuring this idea. 'That's the conclusion one reaches.
Observe that if the purpose of life is happiness, goodness,
love or whatever, and if the goal of mankind is what it is
stated to be by the prophets, that all men are to be united by
love, that swords are to be beaten into ploughshares and all
the rest of it, what prevents it from being attained? The
passions do. Of all the passions, it is sexual, carnal love that is
the strongest, the most malignant and the most unyielding. It
follows that if the passions are eliminated, and together with
them this ultimate, strongest passion, carnal love, the goal of
mankind will be attained and there will be no reason for it to
live any longer. On the other hand, for as long as mankind
endures, it will follow some ideal – not, needless to say, the
ideal of pigs and rabbits, which is to reproduce themselves as
abundantly as possible, nor that of monkeys and Parisians,
which is to enjoy sexual pleasure with the greatest degree of
refinement possible, but the ideal of goodness, goodness that

is attained by means of abstinence and purity. Men have always striven for this ideal, and they continue to do so. But just look at the result.

'The result is that carnal love has become a safety valve. If the present generation of men hasn't yet attained its goal, that's merely because it has passions, the strongest of which is the sexual one. And since that passion exists, a new generation also exists, and thus a possibility of the goal being attained in the next generation. If this generation doesn't manage to do it, there will always be another one to follow it, and so it will continue until the goal has been attained and men have been united with one another. What would things be like if this were not the case? Imagine if God had created human beings in order to achieve a certain goal and had created them either mortal, but without the sex instinct, or immortal. If they'd been made mortal, but without the sex instinct, what would the result have been? They would have lived for a while, and failed to attain their goal; in order to achieve his aim, God would have had to create a new human race. If, on the other hand, they'd been created immortal, let us suppose (though it would be more difficult for beings of this sort to correct the error of their ways and approach perfection than it would for new generations to do so) that after many thousands of years they attained their goal... what good would they be then? What could be done with them? Things are still best the way they are at present... But perhaps you don't care for that sort of an argument, perhaps you're an evolutionist? The outcome's still the same. In order to defend its interests in its struggle with the other animals, the highest form of animal life – the human race – has to gather itself into a unity, like a swarm of bees, and not reproduce infinitely: like the bees, it must raise sexless individuals, that's to say it must strive for continence, not the excitement of lust, towards which the entire social organization of our lives is directed.' He fell silent for a moment. 'The human race disappear? Is there anyone, no matter how he views the world, who can doubt this? I mean, it's just as little in dispute as death is. All the churches teach the end of the world, and all the sciences do the same. So what's so strange about morality pointing to the same conclusion?'

He said nothing for a long time after this. He drank some more tea, put his cigarette out, and transferred some fresh ones from his bag to his old, stained cigarette case.

'I follow your meaning,' I said. 'It's a bit like what the Shakers[7] preach.'

'Yes, and they're right,' he said. 'The sex instinct, no matter how it's dressed up, is an evil, a horrible evil that must be fought, not encouraged as it is among us. The words of the New Testament, that whosoever looks on a woman to lust after her has already committed adultery with her in his heart, don't just apply to the wives of other men, but expressly and above all to our own.'

XII

'In our world it's exactly the other way round: even if a man's thoughts run on sexual abstinence while he's still single, as soon as he gets married he ceases to think it of any importance. Those trips away after the wedding, that seclusion into which the young couple retires with the sanction of their parents – all that's nothing more nor less than a licence for debauchery. But the moral law has a way of paying us back if we ignore it. No matter how hard I tried to make our honeymoon a success, nothing came of it. The whole episode was repellent, embarrassing and tedious. And it was not long before it became unbearably irksome. It started to get that way very early on. On the third day, or maybe it was the fourth, I noticed that my wife seemed to be in a listless frame of mind; I asked her what the matter was and tried to put my arms around her, thinking that was what she wanted. But she pushed me away and burst into tears. Why? She was unable to tell me. She felt depressed and ill at ease. Probably her worn-out nerves had given her an insight into the truth about the vileness of our relationship: but she couldn't express it. I continued to question her and she told me she was missing her mother. Somehow I suspected this wasn't really true. I began to reason with her, but without pursuing the subject of her mother. I didn't realize she was just depressed, and that this talk about her mother was simply an excuse. But she immediately flew into a temper because I'd passed her mother over in silence, as if I hadn't believed what she'd been telling me. She said she could see I didn't love her. I scolded her for being capricious, and suddenly her face completely altered: now, instead of depression, it expressed irritation, and she began to accuse me in the most biting terms of cruelty and egotism. I looked at her. Her entire countenance expressed the most consummate hostility and coldness — hatred, almost. I remember how horrified I was when I saw this. "How can this be?" I thought. "Love is supposed to be the union of souls, and now this! It isn't possible, this isn't the woman I married!" I tried to calm her down, but I ran up against an intransigent wall of such cold and embittered hostility that before I'd had time to gather my wits I was seized with irritation, and we began to say a whole lot of nasty things to each other. That first quarrel had a terrible effect on me. I call it a quarrel, but it wasn't really a quarrel; it was just the revelation of the abyss that actually separated us. Our amorous feelings for each other had been drained by the gratification of our senses, and we were now left facing each other in our true relation, as two egotists who had nothing whatever in common except our desire to use each other in order to obtain the maximum amount of pleasure. I said it was a quarrel, what took place between us. It wasn't a quarrel, it was just the bringing out into the open of our true relationship, which followed upon the appeasement of our sensual desire. I didn't realize that this cold and hostile attitude was actually the one that was normal to us, and that was because at the beginning of our life together it was very soon obscured from us by a new sublimation of our sensuality, a new infatuation with each other.

'I thought what had happened was that we had quarrelled and then made it up, and that nothing of this kind would happen again. During this same first month of our honeymoon, however, we soon reached a second stage of satiety: once again we stopped being necessary to each other, and we had another quarrel. This second quarrel had an even worse effect on me than the first one had had. "So the first one wasn't an accident," I thought. "It was bound to happen, and it'll happen again." Our second quarrel struck me all the more forcibly because it arose from the most improbable of pretexts. It had something to do with money. I've never been stingy with money, and I certainly would never have been grudging with it where my wife was concerned. All I remember is that she managed to interpret something I had said to imply that I was attempting to use my money in order to dominate her, that I'd made my money into the basis of an exclusive right over her – some absurd, stupid, evil nonsense that was unworthy of either of us. I lost my temper, and began to shout at her for her lack of tact, she accused me of the same thing, and thus it started all over again. Both in what she was saying and in the expression of her face and eyes I once again saw that cold, cruel hostility that had so shaken me previously. I remembered quarrels I had had with my brother, my friends, my father. But never had there been between us the personal, envenomed hatred that made its appearance here. After some time had passed, however, this mutual hatred was once again obscured by our 'love' – our sensuality, in other words – and once again I consoled myself with the thought that these two quarrels had been mistakes that could be made up for. But then there came a third, and a fourth, and I realized that they were no accidents, that this was how it was bound to be, that this was how it was going to be in future, and I was appalled at the prospect. I was tortured, moreover, by the dreadful thought that I was alone in having such a wretched relationship with my wife, and that everything was quite different in other people's marriages. At that stage I was still unaware that this is the common experience, that everyone believes, as I did, that theirs is an exceptional misfortune, and that everyone hides their shameful and exceptional misfortune not only from the eyes of others but also from themselves, and that they refuse to admit its existence.

'It set in right at the start of our married life together, and it continued without a break, increasing in intensity and bitterness. Even in the very first weeks I knew in the bottom of my heart that I'd been *trapped*, that this wasn't what I'd been expecting, that not only was marriage not happiness, it was something exceedingly painful and distressing. But, like everyone else, I refused to admit this to myself (I'd still not have admitted it to myself even now if the whole thing hadn't come to an end) and I hid it not only from others, but also from myself. It amazes me now that I didn't realize the situation I was in. I ought to have understood it then, for our quarrels used to start from the kind of pretexts that made it impossible, later on, when it was all over, to remember what they'd been about. Our intelligences had no time in which to lay a foundation of satisfactory pretexts beneath the increasing hostility we felt for one another. But even more remarkable were the flimsy reasons we would find for patching up our differences. Sometimes there were talks, explanations, even tears, but sometimes . . . ugh, how vile it is to remember it even now – sometimes, after we had both said the cruellest things to one another, suddenly, without a word, there would be looks, smiles, embraces . . . Ugh! What loathsomeness! How could I have failed to see the vile mediocrity of it all even then . . . ?'

XIII

Two passengers got on and found seats for themselves further up the carriage. He remained silent until they had seated themselves, but as soon as they were settled he continued, evidently never losing the thread of his thought for a second.

'The vilest thing of all about it,' he began, 'is that in theory love's supposed to be something ideal and noble, whereas in practice it's just a sordid matter that degrades us to the level of pigs, something it's vile and embarrassing to remember and talk about. After all, nature didn't make it vile and embarrassing for no reason. If it's vile and embarrassing, it ought to be seen as such. And yet it's quite the contrary: people behave as though what was vile and embarrassing were something beautiful and noble. What were the first signs of my love? They were that I abandoned myself to animal excesses, not only quite unashamedly, but even taking pride in the fact that it was possible for me to indulge in them, without ever once taking thought for her spiritual or even her physical well-being. I wondered in astonishment where this relentless animosity we felt towards each other could possibly be coming from, yet the reason for it was staring me in the face: this animosity was nothing other than the protest of our human nature against the animality that was suffocating it.

'I was astounded at the hatred we felt for one another. Yet it couldn't have been any otherwise. This hatred was nothing but the mutual aversion experienced by accomplices to a crime – both for inciting to it and for perpetrating it. What other word can there be for it but crime, when she, poor creature, became pregnant in the very first month, and yet our piglike relationship continued? Perhaps you think I'm losing the thread of my thought? Not a bit of it! I'm still telling you the story of how I murdered my wife. They asked me in court how I killed her, what I used to do it with. Imbeciles! They thought I killed her that day, the fifth of October, with a knife. It wasn't that day I killed her, it was much earlier. Exactly in the same way as they're killing their wives now, all of them . . .'

'But how did you kill her?' I asked.

'Look, this is what's really astounding: no one is willing to admit what's so clear and self-evident, the thing doctors know and ought to tell people about, instead of keeping quiet on the subject. It's so simple. Men and women are made like animals, so that carnal love is followed by pregnancy, and then by the nursing of young, both states in which carnal love is harmful for the women and her child. There's an equal number of men and women. What follows from that? The answer would seem to be quite clear. It surely doesn't require a great deal of intelligence to come to the conclusion the animals arrive at – abstinence, in other words. But oh, no. Science has managed to discover things called leucocytes that float about in our bloodstream, and has come up with all sorts of other stupid bits of useless information, yet it's unable to grasp this. At any rate, one's never heard it say anything on the subject.

'And so for the woman there are really only two ways out: one is to turn herself into a freak of nature, to destroy or attempt to destroy in herself her faculty of being a woman – a mother, in other words – so that the man can continue to take his pleasure without interruption; the other isn't really a way out at all, just a simple, gross and direct violation of the laws of nature, one that's practised in all so-called "decent" families. In other words, the woman has to go against her nature and be expectant mother, wet-nurse and mistress all at the same time; she has to be what no animal would ever lower itself to be. And she doesn't have the strength for it, either. That's where all the hysteria and "nerves" come from, and it's also the origin of the *klikushi*, the "possessed women" that are found among the common people. You don't need great powers of observation to see that these *klikushi* are never pure young girls, but always grown women, women who have husbands. It's the same in our class of society. It's equally the case in Europe. All those nerve clinics are full of women who've broken the laws of nature. But after all, the *klikushi*, like the patients of Charcot, are out-and-out cripples; the world's full of women who are only semi-crippled. To think of the great work that's accomplished in a woman when she bears forth the fruit of her womb, or when she gives suck to the child she's brought into the world. What's in the process of growing there is what will give us perpetuity, what will replace us. And this sacred work is violated – by what? It's too dreadful even to contemplate! And we carry on with our talk of freedom and women's rights. It's just as if a tribe of cannibals were to fatten up its captives before eating them, all the while assuring them of its concern for their rights and freedom.'

This was all rather original, and it made an impression on me.

'Yes, but what then?' I said. 'If that's really how it is, a man would only be able to make love to his wife once every two years, but men . . .'

'Men can't survive without it,' he chipped in. 'Once again our dear priests of science have managed to convince everyone that this is true. I'd like to see those witch-doctors compelled to perform the duties they say women must carry out as being so necessary to men, what would they have to say for themselves then, I wonder? Tell a man he needs vodka, tobacco and opium, and all those things will become necessities for him. The way they see it is that God had no idea of what human beings needed, and that he made a mess of things because he didn't consult them, the witch-doctors. You only have to take a look round to see there's something wrong. The witch-doctors have decided that men must satisfy their lust – it's a need, a necessity, and yet here are things like child-bearing and breast-feeding getting in the way. What's to be done about it? Send for the witch-doctors, they'll sort it out. And so they have. Oh, when will those witch-doctors and all their tricks be shown up for what they really are? It's high time. Now it's even got to the point where people go insane and shoot themselves, and all because of this. How can it be otherwise? The animals seem to know that their offspring assure the continuation of their species, and they stick to certain laws in this regard. It's only man who doesn't know these laws, and doesn't want to know them. He's only concerned with obtaining the greatest possible amount of pleasure. And who is this? The king of nature – man. You'll notice that the animals copulate with one another only when it's possible for them to produce offspring; but the filthy king of nature will do it any time, just so long as it gives him pleasure. More than that: he elevates this monkey pastime into the pearl of creation, into love. And what is it that he devastates in the name of this love, this filthy abomination, rather? Half of the human race, that's all. For the sake of his pleasure he makes women, who ought to be his helpmates in the progress of humanity towards truth and goodness, into his enemies. Just look around you: who is it that's constantly putting a brake on humanity's forward development? Women. And why is this so? Solely because of what I've been talking about. Yes, yes,' he repeated several times, and began to rummage about in search of his cigarettes. At last he found them and lit one, in an obvious attempt to calm himself down.

XIV

'So that's the sort of pig's existence I led,' he resumed, in the same tone of voice. 'And the worst of it was that, living in this filthy way, I imagined that because I didn't allow myself to be tempted by other women, I was leading a decent, married life, that I was a man of upright morality with not a stain of guilt on my conscience, and that if we had quarrels, it was her fault, the fault of her character.

'Needless to say, it wasn't her fault. She was just like all women, or the majority of them, anyway. She'd been brought up in the way the situation of women in our society demands, the way in which all upper-class women without exception are and have to be brought up. You hear a lot of talk these days about a new type of education for women. That's all hot air: women's education is exactly the way it ought to be, given the prevailing attitude towards women in our society – the real attitude, that is, not the pretended one.

'The type of education women receive will always correspond to the way men see them. After all, we know what men think of women, don't we? *Wein, Weiber und Gesang* – even the poets write things like that in their verses. Examine the whole of poetry, painting and sculpture, starting with love-poetry and all those naked Venuses and Phrynes, and you'll see that in them woman's an instrument of pleasure, just as she is on Trubnaya Street, on the Grachevka,[8] or at the court balls. And observe the devil's cunning: if pleasure and enjoyment are what's being offered, we might as well know that there's enjoyment to be had, that woman's a sweet morsel. But that's not the way of it: from the very earliest times the knights of chivalry professed to deify woman (they deified her, but they still viewed her as an instrument of pleasure). Nowadays men claim to have respect for woman. Some will give up their seats to her, pick up her handkerchief, recognize her right to occupy any post whatsoever, participate in government and so forth. They say this, but their view of her remains the same. She's an instrument of pleasure. Her body's a means of giving pleasure. And she knows it. It's like slavery. Slavery's just the exploitation by the few of the forced labour of the many. And so, if there's to be no more slavery, men must stop exploiting the forced labour of others, they must come to view it as a sin or at least as something to be ashamed of. But instead of this, all they do is abolish the outer forms of slavery – they arrange things so that it's no longer possible to buy and sell slaves, and then imagine, and are indeed convinced, that slavery doesn't exist any more; they don't see, they don't want to see, that it continues to exist because men go on taking satisfaction in exploiting the labour of others and persist in believing that it's perfectly legitimate for them to do so. And for as long as they believe this, there will always be those who are able to do it with more strength and cunning than others. It's the same where the emancipation of woman is concerned. The reason for the condition of slavery in which woman is kept hasn't really got much to do with anything except men's desire to exploit her as an instrument of pleasure, and their belief that this is a very good thing. Well, and so they go emancipating woman, giving her all sorts of rights, just the same as men have, but they still continue to regard her as an instrument of pleasure; that's how she's brought up as a child and how later on she's moulded by public consensus. And there she is, still the same humiliated and debauched slave, while men continue to be the same debauched slave-masters.

'They've emancipated woman in the universities and the legislative assemblies, but they still regard her as an object of pleasure. Teach her, as is done in our society, to consider herself in the same light, and she will for ever remain an inferior being. Either, with the help of those sharks of doctors, she'll prevent herself conceiving offspring, and so will be a complete whore, will descend to the level, not of an animal, but of a material object; or else she'll be what she is in the majority of cases: mentally ill, hysterical and unhappy, as are all those who are denied the opportunity of spiritual development.

'Schools and universities can do nothing to change this. It can only be changed by a radical shift in the opinion that man has of woman, and that woman has of herself. That shift will only occur when woman comes to consider virginity the most exalted condition a human being can aspire to, and doesn't, as she does at present, regard it as a shame and a disgrace. As long as this is lacking, the ideal of every girl, no matter how well educated, will be to attract as many men, as many males, as she can, so she can make her choice from among them.

'The fact that this one is rather good at mathematics, and that one can play the harp – that alters nothing. A woman's happy and gets everything she wants when she succeeds in bewitching a man. That's her main task in life. That's the way it's always been, and that's the way it'll go on being. A young girl in our society lives that way, and she continues to live that way after she gets married. She needs to live like this when she's a young girl so she can make her choice, and she needs to do it when she's a married woman so she can dominate her husband.

'The only thing that can put a stop to it or at least suppress it for a time is children, and then only if the woman isn't a monster, that's to say, if she breast-feeds them herself. But here again the doctors interfere.

'My wife, who wanted to breast-feed and did breast-feed our five subsequent children, had a few problems with her health after the birth of our first child. Those doctors who cynically made her undress and probed every part of her body, actions for which I had to thank them and pay them money, those pleasant doctors decided that she shouldn't do any breast-feeding, and thus throughout that early phase of our life together she was deprived of the only thing that might have prevented her from indulging in coquetry. Our child was fed by a wet-nurse – in other words, we exploited the wretchedness, poverty and ignorance of a peasant woman, and enticed her away from her own child in order to look after ours, to which purpose we dolled her up in a fancy bonnet trimmed with silver lace. But that wasn't the problem. The problem was that no sooner had she escaped from pregnancy and breast-feeding than the female coquetry that had lain dormant within her made a quite flagrant reappearance. And, every bit as flagrantly, the torments of jealousy reawoke in me: they continued to plague me throughout the whole of my married life, as they can't fail to plague men who live with their wives the way I lived with mine – immorally, in other words.'

XV

'Never once, throughout all my married life, did I cease to experience the tortures of jealousy. And there were periods when I suffered particularly badly in this way. One of those periods occurred when, after the trouble with her first child, the doctors told her not to do any breast-feeding. At this time I was particularly jealous, in the first instance, because my wife was undergoing that restlessness that is characteristic of a mother and is inevitably brought on by such an arbitrary interruption of her life's natural rhythm; and, in the second instance, because when I saw with what ease she threw aside the moral obligations of a mother, I correctly, though unconsciously, drew the conclusion that she would find it just as easy to throw aside her obligations as a wife, especially since she was in perfect health and, in spite of what the dear doctors told her, subsequently breast-fed all our other children herself, and did it excellently.'

'I can see you don't like doctors,' I said. I had observed that at the very mention of them his voice acquired a peculiarly malevolent intonation.

'It isn't a question of liking them or not liking them. They've ruined my life, just as they've ruined and continue to ruin the lives of thousands, hundreds of thousands of people, and I can't help putting two and two together. I can see they're just trying to earn money, like lawyers and the rest, and I'd gladly give them half my income – anyone who understands what it

is they do would gladly give them half of what they own –
provided only that they shouldn't interfere with our marriages
or ever come anywhere near us. I mean, I haven't got any
statistics, but I know of dozens of cases – there's a vast number
of them – where they've murdered the child while it was still
in its mother's womb, claiming she was unable to give birth
to it, and where the mother has subsequently given birth to
other children without difficulty; or else it's the mothers
they've murdered, on the pretext of carrying out some operation or other on them. No one even bothers to count these
murders, just as no one ever counted the murders of the
Inquisition, because they were supposed to be for the good of
mankind. It's impossible to put figures on the number of
crimes they've committed. But all those crimes are as nothing
compared to the moral rot of materialism they've brought into
the world, especially through woman. And all that's quite
apart from the fact that if they were to follow the doctors'
instructicns regarding the infection they say is rife everywhere
and in everything, people would have to seek not union but
disunion; according to the doctors' version of things, everyone
ought to keep apart from one another and never take the
spray-syringe of phenol acid (which they've found doesn't
have any effect, anyway) out of their mouths. But even that's
not important. No, the real poison is the general corruption of
human beings, of women in particular.

'Nowadays it's simply not done to say: "You're living badly,
you ought to try to live better." It's not done to say that either
to yourself or to someone else. If you're living badly, it's
because your nerves aren't functioning properly, or something
of that sort. So you have to go to the doctors. They'll prescribe
you thirty-five copecks' worth of medicine, and you'll take it.
You'll just make yourself worse, and then you'll have to take
more medicines and consult more doctors. As a trick, it fairly
takes your breath away!

'But again, that's not important. What I was trying to say
was that she breast-fed her children herself, perfectly well, and
that it was only her pregnancies and breast-feeding that saved
me from the tortures of jealousy. If it hadn't been for that,

everything would have happened sooner than it did. Our children protected both of us. In the space of eight years she had five of them. And she breast-fed them all herself.'

'Where are they now, your children?' I asked.

'My children?' he echoed, in a frightened tone of voice.

'I'm sorry, perhaps you don't want to be reminded of them.'

'No, it's all right. The children were taken into custody by my sister-in-law and her brother. They wouldn't let me have them back. I'm supposed to be a kind of madman, you know. I'm on my way home from visiting them now. I saw them, but they won't let me have them back. They think I might bring them up so they're not like their parents. And they have to be the same. Well, what can I do? Naturally they won't let me have them back, and they don't trust me. I don't even know myself whether I'd have the strength to bring them up. I think probably I wouldn't. I'm a wreck, a cripple. I've only got one thing. It's what I know. Yes, I know something it'll take other people quite a while to find out about.

'At any rate, my children are alive, and they're growing up to be the same savages as everyone else around them. I've seen them, three times I've seen them now. There's nothing I can do for them. Nothing. I'm going down south now, home. I've got a little house and garden down south.

'No, people aren't going to find out what I know for quite a while to come. If it's a question of whether there's a lot of iron or other metals in the sun or the stars, they soon get to the bottom of it; but if it's something that exposes our pigsty behaviour – they find that hard, terribly hard!

'At least you're listening to me, and I'm grateful for that.'

XVI

'You mentioned children just now. Again, what awful lies we spread about children. Children are God's blessing on us, children are a delight. It's all lies, you know. All that may have been true once upon a time, but it isn't nowadays. Children are a torment, nothing more. Most mothers know this, and will sometimes be quite frank about it. Most mothers in our well-off section of society will tell you they're so scared their children are going to fall ill and die, they don't want to have any, and even if they do have children, they don't want to breast-feed them in case they grow too attached to them and suffer as a result. The pleasure their baby gives them with the grace and charm of its being, of its little arms and legs, of the whole of its young body, the enjoyment they receive from their baby is not as great as the suffering they endure – not even because it falls ill or dies, but because of their fear that it may do so. Once they've weighed the advantages against the disadvantages, it seems to them that having children is disadvantageous, and therefore undesirable. They say this boldly and frankly, imagining that these feelings stem from their love of children, from a good and praiseworthy sentiment they're proud of. They don't notice that by talking like this they do nothing but negate love and affirm their own selfishness. They find less enjoyment than suffering in the grace and charm of their baby because of the fear they have for its safety, and so they don't really want this child which they are going to love. They don't sacrifice themselves for a being they love, what they do is sacrifice to themselves a being that's intended to be loved.

'It's obvious that this isn't love but selfishness. But not one hand will be raised to condemn them, these mothers from well-off families, for their selfishness, when it's remembered what agonies of suffering they go through on account of the health of their children, thanks once again to those doctors and the role they play in the lives of our better-off citizens. Even now I have only to recall the manner of my wife's existence, the condition she was in, during that early phase of our life together when she had three, then four children and was entirely absorbed in them, in order to be seized with horror. That was no life we led. It was a kind of perpetual state of danger, escape from it, then fresh danger, again followed by desperate efforts at escape, and then – another escape; constantly the sort of situation there is on board a ship that's in the process of sinking. It sometimes used to seem to me that it was all an act she was putting on, that she was just pretending to be worried about the children in order to score points over me. This way of behaving settled every problem so simply and flatteringly in her favour. It sometimes seemed to me that everything she said and did on these occasions had some kind of ulterior motive. Yet she herself suffered terribly, and constantly punished herself with guilt about the state of her children's health, about their illnesses. It was an ordeal for her, and for me as well. And she couldn't have done anything else but suffer. After all, her attachment to her children, her animal instinct to feed, caress and protect them, were just as strong in her as they are in the majority of women; she did not, however, have what the animals have – an absence of reason and imagination. The hen isn't afraid of what may happen to her chick, knows nothing of all the diseases that may attack it, or of all those remedies human beings imagine will save them from sickness and death. And the hen's chicks are not a source of torment to her. She does for them what it's natural and agreeable for her to do: her children are a delight to her. And when one of her chicks starts to show signs of being ill, the range of her concerns is very limited: she feeds the chick and keeps it warm, secure in the knowledge that what she's doing is all that is necessary. If the chick dies, she doesn't ask herself why it has died, or where it's gone, she merely clucks for a while, then stops, and goes on living as before. But that's not how it is for our unfortunate women, and that's not how it was for my wife. Quite apart from all the talk about illnesses and their treatment, about the best methods of rearing children and educating them, she was surrounded on all sides by a great mass of divergent and constantly changing rules and regulations, both printed and spoken. Children should be fed like this, with this; no, not like that, not with that, but like this; how they should be dressed, what they should be given to drink, how they should be bathed, put to bed, taken out for walks, how to see they get enough fresh air – every week we (or rather she) discovered new rules affecting all this. As if it were only yesterday that children had started being brought into the world. And if the feeding method was wrong, if the bathing was done in the wrong way or at the wrong time, and the child fell ill, then it was all her fault, as she hadn't done what she was supposed to do.

'That was if the child was healthy. And even that was torture. But just wait till it fell ill – then the fat was really in the fire. All hell would be let loose. There's a common notion that illness can be treated, and that there's a science devoted to this purpose, with people – doctors – who know all about it. Not all of them do, but the very best ones do. Right, so your child's been taken ill, and your task is to find one of those very best doctors, one who's able to save lives, and then your child will be all right; but if you can't find one of those doctors, or you don't live in an area where there is one – your child's had it. And this wasn't a faith in any way exclusive to her, it was the faith adhered to by all the women in her set, and all she ever heard from every side was: "Yekaterina Semyonovna's lost two of hers, because they didn't call in Ivan Zakharych; Ivan Zakharych saved Marya Ivanovna's eldest girl, you know. And then look at the Petrovs: they took the doctor's advice in time, he told them to get the children out of the home and they were split up and moved into various hotels and they survived – if they hadn't been separated they'd have died. And then there was that woman who had the delicate child; the doctor advised her to move down south, they did, and the child was all right." How could she have not been plagued by misery and anxiety all her life when the lives of her children, to whom she was devoted as an animal is devoted, were dependent on her being able to find out in time what Ivan Zakharych had to say? And what Ivan Zakharych would say, nobody knew, least of all Ivan Zakharych himself, since he was very well aware that he didn't really know anything at all and was quite unable to offer any kind of help, but just kept improvising blindly so that people wouldn't stop believing he did know something. After all, if she'd really been an animal, she wouldn't have suffered like that; if she'd really been a human being, she'd have believed in God, and she'd have said and thought what the peasant women say: "The Lord gave, and the Lord hath taken away; we're all in the hands of God." She'd have considered that the lives and deaths of all God's creatures, her own children included, fell outside the jurisdiction of human beings and were dependent upon God alone, and then she wouldn't have been tormented by the thought that it was in her power to prevent the deaths and illnesses of her children – but this she didn't do. The way she saw the situation was like this: she'd been given some extremely weak and fragile creatures to look after, creatures that were susceptible to an infinite number of disasters. For these creatures she felt a passionate, animal devotion. What was more, although these creatures had been delivered into her care, the means by which they could be preserved from danger had been concealed from us, but revealed instead to complete strangers, whose services and advice could only be obtained for large sums of money, and even then not always.

'The whole of the existence my wife led with her children was for her, and consequently for me as well, not a joy but a torment. How could she not have suffered? She suffered continually. We might just have calmed down after some scene of jealousy or outright quarrel and be thinking that now we'd be able to get on with our lives for a while, do a bit of reading or thinking; yet no sooner had one settled down to some task or other than the news would arrive that Vasya was being sick, or there was blood in Masha's stool, or Andryusha had a rash, and then it would all be over, life would once more cease to be possible. Where would one have to go galloping off to now, which doctors would have to be sought out, where would the child have to be taken? And then the enemas would start, the temperatures, the mixtures and the doctors' visits. No sooner would this be at an end than something else would crop up. We had no stable, regular family life. All we had was, as I've told you, a constant running battle against dangers both real and imaginary. That's the way it is for the majority of families nowadays, you know. In my own family it took a particularly nasty form. My wife was the maternal type, and she was easily gulled.

'So it wasn't just that our having children made our lives no better – it actually poisoned them. More than that: the children constantly gave us new pretexts for quarrelling. The older they grew, the more frequently they themselves were the reason for our falling out with one another; not only that – they were the weapons in a battle. It was as if we were fighting one another through our children. We each had a favourite child – a favourite weapon. My weapon was usually our son Vasya, the eldest child, while hers was usually our daughter Liza. And that wasn't all: when the children started getting a bit older and their personalities started to mature, they turned into allies whom we each tried to win over to our own side. They suffered terribly because of that, the poor children, but we were far too preoccupied with our never-ending war to pay any attention to them. The girl was on my side, while the eldest, our son, who looked like his mother and was her favourite, was often really nasty to me.'

XVII

'Well, that's the way we lived. We grew more and more hostile to each other. And it finally got to the point where it was no longer our disagreements that were responsible for our hostility to one another – it was our hostility that created our disagreements. Whatever she might say to me, I would disagree with it before she had even opened her mouth, and exactly the same was true of her.

'By the fourth year of our marriage we both seemed to have accepted, almost as if it had been decided for us, that we were never going to be able to understand each other or agree about anything. We'd already given up trying to settle our arguments. We each obstinately stuck to our own point of view about even the most simple things, but particularly about the children. Thinking back on it now, I can see that the opinions I used to defend were by no means so dear to me that I couldn't have got along without them; no, the point was that the opinions she held were the opposite of mine, and yielding to them meant yielding to . . . her. This I was not prepared to do. Neither was she. I think it's probable she always considered

herself entirely in the right where I was concerned, and as for
me, I saw myself as a saint in comparison with her. When we
were left alone together we either had to remain silent or else
carry on the sort of conversations I'm convinced animals have
with one another: "What's the time? Bedtime. What's for
dinner today? Where are we going to go? Is there anything in
the newspaper? Send for the doctor. Masha's got a sore
throat." We had only to stray out of this impossibly narrow
focus of conversation by as much as a hair's breadth, and our
mutual irritation would flare up again. Quarrels would erupt
over things like the coffee, a table-cloth, a cab, or a lead at
whist – none of them things that were of the slightest
importance to either of us. I used to boil inwardly with the
most dreadful hatred for her! Sometimes I'd watch the way
she poured her tea, the way she swung her leg or brought her
spoon to her mouth; I'd listen to the little slurping noises she
made as she sucked the liquid in, and I used to hate her for
that as for the most heinous act. I didn't notice it then, but I
was regularly affected by bouts of animosity that used to
correspond to the bouts of what we called "love". A bout of
"love" would be followed by one of animosity; a vigorous bout
of "love" would be followed by a long bout of animosity, while
a less intense bout of "love" would be followed by a correspondingly shorter bout of animosity. We didn't realize it
then, but this "love" and animosity were just two sides of the
same coin, the same animal feeling. To live like that would
have been insufferable if we'd understood the situation we
were in, but we didn't understand it – we weren't even aware
of it. It's the salvation as well as the punishment of human
beings that when they're living irregular lives, they're able to
wrap themselves in a blanket of fog so that they can't see the
wretchedness of their situation. That's what we did. She tried
to forget herself in a frantic round of concerns, always hastily
attended to: the furniture, her clothes and those of her
children, the children's health and their education. As for
myself, I had my own anaesthetic, the anaesthetic of work,
hunting and cards. We were both constantly busy. We both
sensed that the busier we were, the more opportunity we

would have for being nasty to one another. "It's all very well for you to make faces," I used to think, "but you've plagued me all night with your scenes and I've got a meeting today." "It's all very well for you," she used not only to think, but say out loud, "but I haven't been able to get a wink of sleep all night because of the baby."

'And so we continued to live, in a perpetual fog, without ever becoming aware of the situation we were in. If what finally happened hadn't happened, and I'd gone on living like that until my old age, I think that even when I was dying I'd have thought I'd had a good life, not an unusually good one, perhaps, but not a bad one either, the sort of life everyone has; I would never have come to perceive the abyss of unhappiness, the loathsome falsehood in which I was wallowing.

'We were like two prisoners in the stocks, hating each other, yet fettered to each other by the same chain, poisoning each other's lives and trying not to be aware of it. I didn't know then that ninety-nine per cent of all married couples live in the same hell I lived in, and that this can't be otherwise. I didn't know that then, either with regard to other people or with regard to myself.

'It's amazing what coincidences can take place in a life that's regularly led, or even in one that's not! Just at the point where the parents have made life intolerable for each other, an urban environment becomes necessary for the sake of the children's education. And thus the need for a move to town becomes apparent.'

For a while he said nothing, but made his peculiar noises a couple of times. Now they really did sound like stifled sobs. The train was approaching a station.

'What time is it?' he asked me.

I looked at my watch. It was two a.m.

'You're not tired?' he asked.

'No, but you are.'

'Oh, I'm just short of breath. Look, excuse me, I'm just going out for a moment to get myself a drink of water.'

And he went stumbling off up the carriage. As I sat there on my own I ran over in my mind all the things he had been telling me, and so absorbed in my thoughts did I become that I failed to notice him returning through the door at the opposite end.

XVIII

'Yes, I keep getting led off the point,' he said when he had sat down again. 'I've changed a lot of the ideas I used to have, there are a lot of things I see differently now, and I have this need to talk about it all. Well, anyway, we went to live in town. Life's more bearable for unhappy people there. In town a man can live for a hundred years and never notice that he's long been dead and buried. There's never any time to study your conscience; you're busy all the time. There's business, social life, looking after your health, keeping up with the arts, attending to the health of your children, arranging their education. One moment you may have to receive this person, go and visit that person; the next, you may have to go and see this or that exhibition, attend this or that concert. You know how it is: at any given moment there are one, two or even three celebrities in town whom you simply mustn't miss. One moment you're taking some treatment or other, or arranging treatment for somebody else; the next, it's teachers, tutors, governesses, and yet life is as empty as it can possibly be. Well, that's how we lived, and that way we didn't feel so acutely the pain caused by the fact of our living together. More than that: in those early days we were kept busy in the most marvellous fashion, setting ourselves up in a new town, in a new apartment, with the added diversion of trips from the town to the country and back again.

'We spent one whole winter like that. During the second winter of our marriage there took place an event no one noticed at the time, one which seemed quite trivial but which lay at the root of all that was to happen subsequently. She was ill, and those reptiles had forbidden her to have any more children and had taught her a method of contraception. I found this revolting. I struggled against it, but she held firm with a frivolous obstinacy, and I yielded to her. The last excuse for our pigsty existence – children – had been removed, and our life together became even more repulsive. Even though it may be hard for him to feed them, a muzhik or a working man's children are necessary to him, and for this reason his marriage relationship has a justification. But for our sort of people children aren't necessary – they're a superfluous worry, an extra expense, co-inheritors, a burden. And the pigsty existence we lead has no justification whatsoever. We either get rid of our children by artificial methods, or we view them as a misfortune, a consequence of imprudent behaviour, which is even more loathsome. There's no justification for it. But morally we've sunk so low that we don't even see the need for a justification. Nowadays the greater part of the educated classes indulges in this debauchery without the slightest shadow of remorse.

'There's no remorse left because in our section of society there's no moral conscience except the conscience – if you can call it that – represented by public consensus and criminal law. Yet neither of these are violated. There's no reason for anyone to feel guilty in the face of public opinion, since *everyone*, from Marya Pavlovna to Ivan Zakharych, does it. Why should one add to the number of paupers there already are, or deprive oneself of the possibility of leading a social life? No more is there any reason to feel guilty in the face of the criminal law or to be afraid of it. It's only whores and soldiers' wives who drown their children in ponds or throw them down wells; they, of course, should be locked up in prison, but we do it all in our own good time and without any mess.

'We lived like that for another two years. The method the reptiles had prescribed was obviously beginning to be effective; she had rounded out physically and had grown as pretty as the last ray of summer. She was aware of it, and she started to take an interest in her appearance. A kind of provocative beauty radiated from her, and people found it disturbing. She was thirty years old, in the full flower of her womanhood; she was no longer bearing children; she was well fed and emo-

tionally unstable. Her appearance made people uneasy. Whenever she walked past men she attracted their gaze. She was
like an impatient, well-fed horse that has had its bridle taken
off, the same as ninety-nine per cent of our women. I could
sense this, and it scared me.'

XIX

Suddenly he got up, moved over to the window and sat down
there.

'Excuse me,' he said and, fixing his gaze on the window, sat
there in silence for something like three minutes. Then he
gave a deep sigh and came back to sit opposite me once more.
His face had now altered completely; his eyes wore a beseech-
ing expression, and something that might almost have been a
smile creased his lips strangely. 'I'm getting a bit tired, but I'll
tell you the rest of it. There's a lot of time yet; it's still dark out
there. Yes,' he began once more, as he lit a cigarette. 'She'd
rounded out a bit since she'd stopped having children, and
that illness of hers – her constant suffering on account of the
children – had begun to clear up; well, it didn't really clear up,
but it was as though she'd come to after a bout of drunkenness,
as though she'd recovered her senses and realized that God's
world was still there with all its delights, the world she'd
forgotten about and had no idea of how to live in, God's world,
of which she knew absolutely nothing. "I mustn't let it slip!
Time flies, and one doesn't get it back again!" I reckon that's
the way she thought, or rather felt, and it was impossible she
could have thought or felt any differently. She'd been brought
up to believe that there was only one thing in the world worth
bothering about – love. She'd got married, she'd managed to
get a bit of that love she'd been told about, but it was far from
being what she'd been promised, what she'd expected, and it
had brought her a lot of disillusionment and suffering; what
was more, it had involved this quite unforeseen torment –
children! This torment had worn her out. And then, thanks to
those obliging doctors, she'd discovered it was possible to

avoid having children. She'd been overjoyed, had tried the method for herself and had started to live again for the one thing she knew anything about – love. But love with a husband who was bemired in jealousy and rancour wouldn't do. She began to imagine another love that was fresh and pure – that's the way I figure it, at any rate. And then she started looking around her as though she were expecting something to come her way. I could see this, and I couldn't help feeling uneasy. Quite often it would happen that as she carried on a conversation with me through the intermediary of others – that's to say, she'd be talking to other people while really addressing herself to me – she'd come out boldly and half seriously, completely oblivious to the fact that an hour ago she'd said the exact opposite, with the statement that a mother's cares are simply an illusion, a worthless one at that, and that it's not worth sacrificing oneself for the sake of one's children when one's young and able to enjoy life. She had started to devote less attention to the children, and no longer had such a desperate attitude towards them; she was spending more and more time on herself and on her appearance (though she tried to conceal the fact), on her amusements and also her accomplishments. She took up the piano again with enthusiasm – previously she had let it go completely. That was how it all started.'

Again he gave the window a weary look. Almost immediately, however, he made a visible effort to pull himself together, and continued: 'Yes, and then this man appeared.' He faltered and made his peculiar nasal sounds a couple of times.

I could see it was torture for him to mention this man, to remember him and talk about him. But he made the effort and, as if he had tugged clear some obstacle that was in his way, he continued in a resolute tone of voice: 'He was a rubbishy fellow, as far as I could see or judge, and not because he'd acquired this importance in my life, but because he really was what I say he was. Anyway, the fact that he was so mediocre only went to prove how irresponsible she was being. If it hadn't been him, it would have been someone else, it had to happen.' Once again he fell silent. 'Yes, he was a musician, a violinist; not a professional musician, but part professional, part man of the world.

'His father was a landowner, one of my own father's neighbours. He – the father – had suffered financial ruin, and his children – he had three boys – had all found settled positions; only this one, the youngest, had been delivered into the care of his godmother in Paris. There he'd been sent to the Conservatoire, as he was musically gifted, and he'd emerged from it as a violinist who played at concerts. As a man, he was . . .' Obviously experiencing an impulse to say something bad about him, he restrained himself and said quickly: 'Well, I don't really know what sort of a life he led, all I know is that during that year he turned up in Russia, and turned up, what's more, in my own home.

'He had moist eyes, like almonds, smiling red lips, and a little moustache that was smeared with fixative; his hair was styled in the latest fashion; his face was handsome in a vulgar sort of way, and he was what women call "not bad-looking". He was slight of physique, but not in any way malformed, and he had a particularly well-developed posterior, as women have, or as Hottentots are said to have. I believe they're also said to be musical. He tried to force a kind of brash familiarity on to everyone as far as he could manage, but he was sensitive and always ready to drop this mode of address at the slightest resistance, and he never lost his outward dignity. He dressed with that special Parisian nuance: buttoned boots, brightly coloured cravats and the like – all the sort of garb foreigners adopt when they're in Paris, the sort of thing that makes an impression on women because of its distinctiveness and novelty. His manner had a superficial, affected gaiety. You know that way of talking all the time in allusions and desultory snatches, as if to say, "You know all that, you remember, you can fill in the rest for yourselves."

'He and his music were the real cause of it all. At my trial the whole thing was made to look as though it had been caused by jealousy. Nothing could have been further from the truth. I'm not saying jealousy didn't play any part at all, mind

– it did, but it wasn't the most important thing. At my trial they decided I was a wronged husband who'd killed his wife in order to defend his outraged honour (that's the way they put it in their language). So I was acquitted. During the court hearings I tried to explain what was really at the bottom of it all, but they just thought I was trying to rehabilitate my wife's honour.

'Whatever her relationship with that musician was, it wasn't important to me, any more than it was to her. What was important was what I've been telling you about – my pigsty existence. It all happened because of that terrible abyss there was between us, the one I've been talking about, the terrible stress of our mutual hatred for each other that made the first pretext that came along sufficient to cause a crisis. In the last days our quarrels became terrifying; they were particularly shattering because they alternated with bouts of animal sensuality.

'If it hadn't been him, it would have been some other man. If jealousy hadn't been the pretext, some other one would have been found. I insist on the fact that all husbands who live as I lived must either live in debauchery, get divorced, or kill themselves or their wives, as I did. If there's any man alive to whom this doesn't apply, he's an extremely rare exception. You know, before I brought it all to an end in the way I did, I was several times on the verge of suicide, and she'd also tried to poison herself on several occasions.'

XX

'Yes, that's the way it was, even quite a short time before it happened.

'It was as though we were living in a kind of truce and couldn't find any reason for breaking it. One day as we were talking, the subject of a dog came up. I said it had won a medal at a dog show. She said it hadn't been a medal, just a special mention. An argument began. We started to jump from one subject to another, and the accusations began to fly:

"Yes, yes, I've known that for ages, it's always the same: you said . . ." "No, I didn't." "I suppose you think I'm lying!" I suddenly got a feeling that at any moment now that terrible quarrel was going to start, the one that would make me either want to kill myself or kill her. I knew it was about to begin, and I was afraid of it in the way one's afraid of a fire starting. I tried to keep myself under control, but the hatred had gained complete mastery over me. She was in the same sort of state, only worse, and she was purposely misinterpreting my every word, twisting its meaning. Everything she said was steeped in venom; she was trying to hurt me where she knew I was most sensitive. The longer it went on, the worse it got. I shouted: "Shut up!" or something like that. She went skittering out of the room and into the nursery. I tried to detain her in order to finish what I was saying and prove my point, and I seized her by the arm. She pretended I was hurting her, and she screamed: "Children, your father's beating me!" "Don't tell lies!" I shouted. "This isn't the first time he's done it!" she screamed, or something of the kind. The children went running to her, and she calmed them down. "Stop play-acting!" I said. "Everything's play-acting to you," she replied. "You'd kill someone and then say they were play-acting. Now I can see what you're really like. You actually want things to be like this!" "Oh, I wish you were dead!" I shouted. I remember the horror those terrible words filled me with. I had never thought I'd be capable of uttering such terrible, primitive words and I was amazed at the way they leapt out of me. I shouted those terrible words and then fled to my study, where I lay down and smoked one cigarette after another. Eventually I heard her going out into the hall and getting ready to go off somewhere. I asked her where she was going. She didn't answer. "Well, she can go to hell for all I care," I said to myself. I went back to my study, lay down again and continued to smoke. A thousand different plans of how I might take my revenge on her and get rid of her, making it look as though nothing had happened, came into my head. I thought about all this, and as I did so I smoked, smoked, smoked. I thought of running away from her, of hiding, of going to America. I got to the point where I dreamed that I had in fact got rid of her and of how marvellous it was going to be now: I'd meet another, beautiful woman, entirely different from my wife. I'd get rid of my wife because she'd die, or I'd get a divorce, and I thought of how I'd do it. I was aware I was getting muddled, that I wasn't thinking about the right things – but I went on smoking to stop myself being aware of it.

'But the life of the household went on as before. The governess arrived, and asked "Where's madame? When's she coming back?" The butler appeared, to ask if he should serve the tea. I went into the dining-room; the children, especially Liza, the eldest girl, who already knew what was going on, looked at me questioningly and disapprovingly. We sipped our tea in silence. She still hadn't returned. The whole evening passed, she still didn't come back, and two emotions kept alternating inside me: animosity towards her making my life and the lives of all the children a misery by her absence when I knew she intended to come back again; and fear that she might not come back, that she might do away with herself. I wanted to go and look for her. But where would I look? At her sister's? It would have been stupid to go there asking for her. Oh, let her go: if she wanted to make our lives a misery, let her make her own life miserable too. That was probably what she wanted, anyway. And next time it would be even worse. But what if she wasn't at her sister's, what if she was trying to do away with herself, or had even done so already? Eleven o'clock, twelve, one a.m. I didn't go into our bedroom, it would have been stupid to lie there alone, waiting, and I didn't want to sleep in my study. I wanted to be busy with something, write letters, read; I couldn't do anything. I sat alone in my study, suffering, angry, listening. Three a.m., four a.m. – still no sign of her. Towards morning I fell asleep. When I woke up, she still wasn't back.

'Everything in the house continued as before, but everyone was perplexed and looked at me questioningly and reproachfully, assuming it was all my fault. And still the same struggle was going on inside me: animosity because she was making my life a misery, and worry lest anything should have happened to her.

'At about eleven o'clock that morning her sister arrived, acting as her emissary. And the usual things were said: "She's in a terrible state. What on earth have you been doing?" "Oh, it was nothing." I said something about how impossible she was, and that I hadn't done anything.

' "Well, it can't go on like this, you know," said her sister.

' "It's all up to her, not to me," I said. "I'm not going to take the first step. If she wants a divorce, we'll get a divorce."

'My sister-in-law went away empty-handed. I'd spoken boldly, on the spur of the moment, when I'd told her I wouldn't take the first step, but as soon as she'd left and I'd gone out of the room and seen the children looking so scared and wretched, I suddenly felt ready to take that first step. I would even have been glad to take it, but I didn't know how to. Once again I started to wander about the house; I smoked cigarettes, drank vodka and wine with my lunch and attained the goal I unconsciously desired: not to see the stupidity, the vulgarity of the situation I was in.

'She arrived at about three o'clock that afternoon. She didn't say anything when we met. I thought perhaps she'd calmed down a bit, and I started to tell her that I'd been provoked by her accusations. With the same severe look of terrible suffering on her face she told me she hadn't come for explanations but in order to fetch the children; it was impossible for us to go on living together. I started to say it wasn't I who was the guilty one, that she'd driven me beyond the limits of my endurance. She gave me a solemn, severe look, and then said: "Don't say any more, you'll regret it."

'I said I couldn't bear melodramatics. Then she shrieked something I couldn't make out, and rushed to her room. I heard the sound of the key turning in her door: she'd locked herself in. I knocked, but there was no answer, and I went away in a fuming rage. Half an hour later, Liza came running to me in tears.

' "What is it? Has something happened?"

' "It's gone all quiet in Mummy's room!"

'We went to investigate. I pulled at the double door with all my might. She hadn't fastened the bolt properly, and both halves of the door opened. I went over to her bed. She was lying awkwardly atop her bed with her petticoat and her high boots still on, and she was unconscious. On the bedside table there was an empty phial of opium. We brought her round. There were more tears and, at last, a reconciliation. Yet it was not really a reconciliation: within each of us the same animosity continued to burn, mingled now with irritation at the pain this fresh quarrel had caused, pain for which each of us blamed the other. In the end, however, we had to bring it to some sort of conclusion, and life took its accustomed course. Quarrels of this kind, and occasionally even worse ones, were constantly breaking out, sometimes once a week, sometimes once a month, sometimes every day. On one occasion I even went to the lengths of getting myself a passport for foreign travel – the quarrel had been going on for two days – but then once more we had a semi-explanation, a semi-reconciliation – and I stayed put.'

XXI

'So that's the way things were between us when this man appeared. This man – Trukhachevsky's his name – arrived in Moscow and came to see me. It was in the morning. I asked him in. There'd once been a time when we'd been on familiar "thou" terms with one another. Now he tried, by means of phrases inserted between his use of "thou" and "you", to commit us to the "thou" form, but I put the emphasis fairly and squarely on "you", and he immediately complied. I didn't like the look of him from the very outset. But it was a strange thing: some peculiar, fatal energy led me not to repulse him, get rid of him, but, on the contrary, to bring him closer. After all, what could have been simpler than to speak to him coldly for a couple of minutes and then bid him farewell without introducing him to my wife? But no, of all things, and as if on purpose, I started to talk about his playing, saying that I'd heard he'd given up the violin. He said that, on the contrary, he was playing more than ever before nowadays. He recalled that I had been musical too, in the old days. I said that I'd let my playing go, but that my wife played the piano rather well.

'It was quite remarkable! From the very first day, the very first hour of our meeting, my attitude towards him was such as it ought really to have been only after what eventually took place. There was something fraught in my relations with him: I found a special significance in each word, each expression either of us uttered.

'I introduced him to my wife. The conversation immediately turned to music, and he offered to play duos with her. My wife was, as she always was during those last days, very elegant and alluring, disturbingly beautiful. It was obvious that she _did_ like the look of him from the very outset. What was more, she was delighted at the prospect of having someone to play the violin with her – so fond of playing duos was she that she used to hire the services of a violinist from the local theatre orchestra – and her joy was written all over her face. Having cast a glance at me, however, she immediately understood the way I felt and altered her expression accordingly, and a game of mutual deception got under way between us. I smiled pleasantly, trying to make it look as though nothing could be more agreeable to me than the thought of them playing duos together. He, surveying my wife in the way all debauched men look at pretty women, tried to make it appear as though all he was interested in was the subject of the conversation, which was of course what interested him least of all. She tried to appear indifferent, but the combination of my jealous-husband look, with which she was familiar, and his lustful ogling evidently excited her. I saw that right from that first meeting her eyes began to shine in a peculiar way and that, probably as a result of my jealousy, there was immediately established between them a kind of electric current which seemed to give their faces the same expression, the same gaze, the same smile. Whenever she blushed or smiled, so did he. They talked for a while about music, about Paris, about various trivial matters. He got up to go and, with a smile on his lips, his hat resting on his thigh which from time to time gave a sudden quiver, he stood looking now at her and now at me, as if he was waiting for what we would do next. I remember that moment so well, as it was then that I could have decided not to invite him back, and then nothing would have happened. But I looked at him, and at her. "Don't think I'm jealous," I said to her mentally. "Or that I'm afraid of you," to him. And I invited him to bring his violin with him one evening and play duos with my wife. She looked at me in surprise, blushed and began to make excuses, saying that her playing wasn't good enough. This excuse-making irritated me even further, and I became all the more insistent. I remember the strange feeling I had as I looked at the nape of his neck, at its white flesh with the black hairs standing out against it, parted in the middle, as he moved away from us with his peculiar, bobbing, almost birdlike gait. I'm not exaggerating when I tell you that man's presence used to drive me out of my mind. "It's up to me to arrange things so I need never set eyes on him again," I thought. Yet to act like that was tantamount to admitting I was afraid of him. No, I wasn't afraid of him! That would be too degrading, I told myself. And right there and then in the hallway, knowing that my wife could hear me, I insisted that he should bring his violin along that very same evening. He promised to do so, and left.

'That evening he arrived with his violin and they played duos. It took them quite a while to get their playing organized: they didn't have the music they wanted, and my wife couldn't sight-read. I was very fond of music, and I took an interest in their playing, fixed his music stand for him, and turned the pages. And they managed to play a few pieces: some songs without words, and a Mozart sonata. He played excellently, with what they call a good tone. More than that: he played with a refinement and nobility of taste that were quite out of keeping with the rest of his character.

'He was, of course, a far better player than my wife, and he helped her along, at the same time managing to say nice things about her playing. He was a model of good behaviour. My wife seemed only to be interested in the music, and she behaved in a simple, natural sort of way. I, on the other hand, although I pretended to be interested in the music, spent the entire evening being tortured by jealousy.

'From the first moment that his eyes met those of my wife, I saw that the beast which lurked in them both, regardless of all social conventions and niceties, asked "May I?", and replied "Oh yes, certainly." I saw that he hadn't at all expected to find in the person of my wife, a Moscow lady, such an attractive woman, and was clearly delighting in his discovery. For there was no doubt at all in his mind that she was willing. The only problem was how to stop her insufferable husband from getting in the way. If I'd been pure, I wouldn't have understood this, but, like the majority of men, I too had thought this way about women before I'd got married, and so I could read his mind as if it were a printed book. I was particularly tormented by the fact that I could see beyond any doubt that the only feeling she had in my regard was a constant irritation, broken only by our habitual bouts of sensuality, and that this man, because of his outward elegance, his novelty and undoubted musical talent, would, as a result of the intimacy arising out of their playing together, and of the effect produced on impressionable natures by music, especially violin music, inevitably not only appeal to her, but would unquestionably and without the slightest hesitation conquer her, crush her, twist her round his little finger, do with her anything he wanted. I couldn't fail to see this, and I suffered horribly as a result. Yet in spite of this or perhaps in consequence of it, some force compelled me against my will to be, not simply extra-polite, but even kindly disposed towards him. Whether it was for my wife's sake that I did this, or for his, in order to show him I wasn't afraid of him, or whether it was in order to pull the wool over my own eyes – I don't know. All I do know is that right from the start of our dealings with each other I found it impossible to be straightforward with him. I had to be nice to him, if I wasn't to end up killing him on the spot. I regaled him with expensive wine at dinner, expressed my admiration of his playing, smiled particularly amicably whenever I spoke to him and invited him to come to

our house again and play duos with my wife the following
Sunday. I told him I would invite some of my musical friends
to come and listen to him. And that's how it ended.'

Pozdnyshev, greatly agitated now, changed his position and
made his peculiar noise.

'It's strange, the effect that man's presence had on me,' he
began again, making a visible effort to remain calm. 'Coming
home from an exhibition the following day or the day after,
I entered the hallway and suddenly felt something heavy, like
a stone, fall on my heart. At first I couldn't work out what it
was. It had to do with the fact that as I'd walked through the
hallway I'd noticed something that had reminded me of him.
It was only when I got to my study that I was able to work
out what it had been, and I went back into the hallway to
make sure. No, I hadn't been seeing things: it was his
overcoat. You know, one of those fashionable men's overcoats.
(Though I wasn't aware of doing so at the time, I paid the
most minute attention to everything that was connected with
him.) I made inquiries: yes, I was right, he was here. I made
for the ballroom, entering it from the schoolroom, not the
drawing-room end. My daughter Liza was in the schoolroom,
reading a book, and the nurse was sitting at the table with
the youngest girl, helping her to spin a saucepan lid or
something of the kind. The door into the ballroom was closed:
I could hear regular arpeggios coming from inside, and the
sound of their voices, talking. I listened, but I couldn't make
out what they were saying. It was obvious that the piano-
playing was meant to drown out their voices, and perhaps
their kisses, too. My God! The feelings that rose up in me!
I'm seized with horror whenever I think of the wild beast
that lived in me during that time. My heart suddenly con-
tracted, stopped beating, and then started again like a ham-
mer. The principal feeling I had was the one there is in all
angry rage, that of self-pity. "In front of the children, in front
of the nurse!" I thought. I must have been a dreadful sight,
for Liza gave me a strange look. "What should I do?" I
wondered. "Go in? I can't. God knows what I might do." But
I couldn't go away, either. The nurse was looking at me as

though she understood my situation. "No, there's nothing for it, I'll have to go in," I said to myself, and swiftly opened the door. He was sitting at the grand piano, playing those arpeggios with large, white, arched fingers. She was standing in the crook of the piano, looking at some musical scores she had opened out. She was the first to see me or hear me, and she glanced up at me quickly. Whether she was frightened but pretending not to be frightened, or whether she really wasn't frightened at all, I don't know, but she didn't bat an eyelid, didn't even move, but just blushed, and then only after a moment or two.

' "How nice that you're back; we can't decide what to play on Sunday," she said, in a tone of voice she wouldn't have used if we'd been alone. This, together with the fact that she'd said "we", meaning the two of them, made me furious. I greeted him in silence.

'He shook my hand and, with a smile that to me seemed downright mocking, began to explain to me that he'd brought some music over so my wife could practise it before Sunday, and that they couldn't come to an agreement as to what they should play – whether it should be something more on the difficult, classical side, like a Beethoven sonata, or just short pieces. It was all so normal and straightforward that there was nothing I could find any fault with, yet at the same time I was convinced it was all a pack of lies, that they had agreed on a plan to deceive me.

'One of the most tormenting things for jealous husbands (and in our section of society all husbands are jealous) is that peculiar set of social conventions which permits the greatest and most dangerous degree of intimacy between the sexes. You'd make a laughing-stock of yourself if you were to try to prevent the kind of intimacy there is at balls, the intimacy there is between a doctor and his female patients, the intimacy that's associated with artistic pursuits – with painting, and especially music. People practise the noblest art of all, music, in pairs; the art necessitates a certain intimacy, yet there's nothing at all suspect about it – it's only a stupid, jealous husband who will see anything undesirable in it. Yet at the same time everyone knows that it's precisely these pursuits, music in particular, that cause most of the adulteries in our class of society. I'd evidently embarrassed them by the embarrassment I myself had shown. For a long time I could find nothing to say. I was like an upturned bottle from which the water won't flow because it's too full. What I wanted to do was shout at him and turn him out of the house, but once again I felt I had to be nice to him, affable to him. So I was. I made it appear as though I approved of it all, and again under the influence of that strange feeling that made me treat him all the more kindly the more unbearable I found his presence, I told him that I had the greatest confidence in his taste, and advised my wife to do the same. He stayed just long enough in order to dispel the unpleasant atmosphere that had been created by my walking into the room in silence, looking afraid – and left in the pretence that now they had decided what they would play the following evening. I, on the other hand, was fully convinced that in comparison with what was really on their minds, the question of what they were going to play was a matter of complete indifference to them.

'I accompanied him out through the hallway with especial politeness (how could one fail to accompany out a man who had arrived with the express purpose of shattering one's peace of mind and destroying the happiness of a whole family?). I shook his soft, white hand with a peculiar effusiveness.'

XXII

'All that day I didn't say a word to my wife – I couldn't. The mere sight of her aroused such hatred in me that I even frightened myself. At dinner she asked me in front of the children when it was I was leaving. The following week I was due to travel to the provinces to attend a meeting of the local zemstvo.[9] I told her the date of my departure. She asked me if I needed anything for the journey. I made no reply, but sat at the table for a while in silence, and then, just as silently, went off to my study. During those last days she never came into my room, particularly at that hour. I lay there in my study, fuming with anger. Suddenly I heard familiar footsteps. And into my head came the terrible outrageous thought that, like the wife of Uriah, she wanted to conceal the sin she had already committed, and that with this purpose in view she was coming to see me in my room at this unprecedented hour. "Can she really be coming to my room?" I wondered, as I listened to her approaching footsteps. "If she is, it means I was right." And an unutterable hatred of her arose within me. The footsteps came nearer, nearer. Perhaps she would go past, into the ballroom? No, the door creaked, and there in the doorway was her tall, beautiful silhouette. Her face and eyes had a timid, ingratiating look which she was trying to conceal but which was evident to me and the meaning of which I knew only too well. I had nearly choked, so long had I held my breath, and, continuing to look at her, I grabbed my cigarette case and lit a cigarette.

' "Well, what's this? A woman comes to sit with you for a while and all you do is light a cigarette," she said, and sat down on the sofa close to me, leaning against me.

'I moved away so as to avoid touching her.

' "I see you're unhappy about me wanting to play duos on Sunday," she said.

' "I'm not in the slightest unhappy about it," I replied.

' "Do you think I haven't noticed?"

' "Well, I congratulate you for noticing. I haven't noticed anything, except that you're behaving like a flirt."

' "Oh, if you're going to start swearing like a cabby, I'd better go."

' "Go then, but just remember that even if you don't think our family's good name's of any importance, I do, and it's not you I care about (you can go to hell for all I care) but our family's good name."

' "What? *What* did you say?"

' "Just go. For God's sake go!"

'I don't know whether she was just pretending, or whether she really didn't have any idea of what I was talking about, but she took offence and flew into a temper. She got up, but didn't go away; instead she remained standing in the middle of the room.

' "You've really become impossible," she began. "You'd wear out the patience of a saint." And trying, as always, to be as wounding as she possibly could, she reminded me of how I had behaved towards her sister (on one occasion I'd lost my temper with her sister and been rudely offensive to her; she knew that this had caused me a lot of pain, and it was here that she chose to insert her dart). "Nothing you say or do will surprise me after this," she said.

' "Yes, go on, insult me, humiliate me, drag my good name in the mire and then claim I'm the guilty one," I said to her inwardly, and suddenly I was seized by a feeling of animosity towards her more terrible than any I'd ever experienced before.

'For the first time I felt a desire to give my animosity physical expression. I leapt to my feet and went up to her; I remember that at the very moment I got up I became aware of my animosity and asked myself whether it was a good thing for me to abandon myself to this feeling, and then told myself that it was a good thing, that it would give her a fright; then immediately, instead of fighting off my animosity, I began to fan it up in myself even further, rejoicing in its steadily increasing blaze within me.

' "Go, or I'll kill you!" I shouted suddenly, going up to her and seizing her by the arm, consciously exaggerating the level of animosity in my voice. I must really have appeared terrifying, as she suddenly lost her nerve to the point where she didn't even have the strength to leave the room, but merely said: "Vasya, what is it, what's wrong with you?"

' "Go!" I roared, even more loudly. "Otherwise you'll drive me mad, and I won't be responsible for my actions any more!"

'Having given vent to the full frenzy of my rage like this, I revelled in it, and was filled with a desire to do something extraordinary, something that would illustrate the pitch of rabid fury I had reached. I had a horrible wish to beat her, to kill her, but knew I couldn't do it, and so in order to continue giving expression to my frenzied rage, I grabbed a paperweight from my writing-desk, and with another shout of "Go!", I hurled it to the floor, narrowly missing her. I judged the shot excellently. She ran for the door, but stopped on her way out. And then without further ado, while she could still see it (I did it for her to see), I began to take other things – the candle-holders, the ink-well – off my desk and threw them to the floor as well, shouting: "Go! Away with you! I won't be responsible for my actions!"

'She left – and I immediately stopped what I'd been doing.

'An hour later, the nurse came to me and told me my wife was having a fit of hysterics. I went to have a look; she was sobbing, laughing, unable to get a word out. Her whole body was trembling. She wasn't shamming – she really was ill.

'Towards dawn she calmed down, and we had a reconciliation under the influence of the feeling to which we gave the name "love".

'In the morning, when after our reconciliation I confessed to her that I'd been jealous of her and Trukhachevsky, she wasn't at all upset and burst into the most artless laughter, so strange, as she said, did it seem to her, this idea that she might be interested in a man like that.

' "Do you really think any woman with self-respect could feel anything for a man like that beyond the enjoyment of hearing him play? I tell you what, if you like, I'll never see him again. I won't even have him here on Sunday, even though all the guests have been invited now. You can write and tell him I'm not well, and that'll be that. The worst thing would be for anyone, especially him, to think that he's dangerous. And I'm far too proud to let anyone think that."

'And, you know, she wasn't lying, she really believed what she was saying. By saying this she was hoping to make herself feel contempt for him, and so protect herself from him, but she couldn't manage it. Everything was against her, particularly that damned music. So that's how it all ended up: on Sunday evening the guests arrived as invited, and the two of them played together again.'

XXIII

'I think I need hardly tell you that I was very vain. In the sort of life our set leads, if a man's not vain he doesn't have much to live for. Well, that Sunday I went out of my way to see to it that the dinner and the musical evening were organized with the maximum possible good taste. I personally supervised the buying of the food for the dinner, and I issued all the invitations myself.

'By six that evening the guests had all assembled, and he appeared wearing tails and a dicky with vulgar diamond studs on it. He was behaving in a free and easy manner, replying hastily to any question that was put to him, with an understanding, acquiescent smile – you know, the kind of expression that conveyed that everything others said or did was exactly what he'd been expecting. I noted all the things that were *mauvais ton* about him now with especial satisfaction, because they helped to put my mind at rest and demonstrate to me that he was so much my wife's inferior that she would never be able, as she put it, to stoop that low. By now I'd stopped allowing myself to feel jealous. For one thing, I'd had a basinful of that particular torture, and I needed a rest; for another, I wanted to believe my wife's assurances, and so I did believe them. But in spite of not being jealous, I couldn't behave naturally towards either of them, and this was true both during dinner and throughout all the earlier part of the evening, before the music started. I kept watching their movements, their looks.

'The dinner was as such dinners usually are – tedious and artificial. The music began fairly early. Oh, how well I remember all the details of that evening. I remember how he produced his violin, the way he opened the case, removed the cloth that had been specially sewn for him by some lady or other, took the instrument out and began tuning it. I remember the way my wife sat down at the piano, trying to appear indifferent, while in actual fact she was extremely nervous – her nervousness being mostly due to fears about her own ability – and then the customary As on the piano, the plucking and tuning of the violin, the setting up of the music. Then I remember how they looked at one another, glanced round at the audience and began to play. She took the first chord. His face assumed a stern, severe, sympathetic expression and, as he gave attention to the sounds he was making, he searched the strings with careful fingers and provided a response to the piano. And so it began . . .'

He paused and made his sounds again several times in succession. He seemed to be on the point of continuing, but sniffed and paused once again.

'They played Beethoven's "Kreutzer Sonata". Do you know its first movement, the presto? You know it?' he burst out. 'Ah! It's a fearful thing, that sonata. Especially that movement. And music in general's a fearful thing. What is it? I don't know. What is music? What does it do to us? And why does it do to us what it does? People say that music has an uplifting effect on the soul: what rot! It isn't true. It's true that it has an effect, it has a terrible effect on me, at any rate, but it has nothing to do with any uplifting of the soul. Its effect on the soul is neither uplifting nor degrading – it merely irritates me. How can I put it? Music makes me forget myself, my true condition, it carries me off into another state of being, one that isn't my own: under the influence of music I have the illusion of feeling things I don't really feel, of understanding things I don't understand, being able to do things I'm not able to do. I explain this by the circumstance that the effect produced by music is similar to that produced by yawning or laughter: I may not be sleepy, but I yawn if I see someone else yawning; I may have no reason for laughing, but I laugh if I see someone else laughing.

'Music carries me instantly and directly into the state of consciousness that was experienced by its composer. My soul merges with his, and together with him I'm transported from one state of consciousness into another; yet why this should be, I've no idea. I mean, take the man who wrote the "Kreutzer Sonata", Beethoven: he knew why he was in that state of mind. It was that state of mind which led him to perform certain actions, and so it acquired a special significance for him, but none whatever for me. And that's why that kind of music's just an irritant – because it doesn't lead anywhere. A military band plays a march, say: the soldiers march in step, and the music's done its work. An orchestra plays a dance tune, I dance, and the music's done its work. A Mass is sung, I take communion, and once again the music's done its work. But that other kind of music's just an irritation, an excitement, and the action the excitement's supposed to lead to simply isn't there! That's why it's such a fearful thing, why it sometimes has such a horrible effect. In China, music's an affair of state. And that's the way it ought to be. Can it really be allowable for anyone who feels like it to hypnotize another person, or many other persons, and then do what he likes with them? Particularly if the hypnotist is just the first unscrupulous individual who happens to come along?

'Yet this fearful medium is available to anyone who cares to make use of it. Take that "Kreutzer Sonata", for example, take its first movement, the presto: can one really allow it to be played in a drawing-room full of women in low-cut dresses? To be played, and then followed by a little light applause, and the eating of ice-cream, and talk about the latest society gossip? Such pieces should only be played on certain special, solemn, significant occasions when certain solemn actions have to be performed, actions that correspond to the nature of the music. It should be played, and as it's played those actions which it's inspired with its significance should be performed. Otherwise the generation of all that feeling and energy, which are quite inappropriate to either the place or the occasion, and which aren't allowed any outlet, can't have anything but a harmful effect. On me, at any rate, that piece had the most shattering effect; I had the illusion that I was discovering entirely new emotions, new possibilities I'd known nothing of before then. 'Yes, that's it, it's got absolutely nothing to do with the way I've been used to living and seeing the world, that's how it ought to be,'' I seemed to hear a voice saying inside me. What this new reality I'd discovered was, I really didn't know, but my awareness of this new state of consciousness filled me with joy. Everyone in the room, including Trukhachevsky and my wife, appeared to me in an entirely new light.

'After the presto they played the attractive but unoriginal andante with its rather trite variations, and then the finale, which is really weak. Then, at the request of members of the audience, they played things like Ernst's "Elégie", and various other brief encores. These were all quite pleasant, but none of them made one tenth of the impression on me that the presto had done. They all came filtering through the impression the presto had made on me. I felt cheerful and buoyant all evening. As for my wife, I'd never seen her looking as she did that evening. Her radiant eyes, her serenity, the gravity of her expression as she played, and that utterly melting quality, the weak, pathetic, yet blissful smile on her lips after they'd finished – I saw all this, but I didn't attach any particular significance to it, beyond supposing that she had experienced the same feelings as I had, and that she, like myself, had discovered, or perhaps rather remembered, emotions that were new and unfamiliar. The evening ended satisfactorily, and everyone went home.

'Knowing that I was due to travel away for the zemstvo meeting in two days' time, Trukhachevsky told me on his way out that he hoped to repeat the pleasure of that evening when he was next in town. I took this to mean that he didn't consider it permissible to visit my house when I wasn't there, and this pleased me. It turned out that, since he would have left town by the time I was back, we wouldn't see one another again.

'For the first time I shook his hand with real satisfaction, and thanked him for the pleasure he had given me. He also said a final goodbye to my wife. Their mutual farewells seemed to me the most natural and proper thing in the world. Everything was fine. My wife and I were both very pleased with the way the evening had gone.'

XXIV

'Two days later, having said goodbye to my wife in the best and most tranquil of moods, I went off to the provinces. In my particular district there was always an enormous amount of business to attend to, and the place had a life of its own; it was a little world apart. On each of my first two days in the district town I spent ten hours in the zemstvo headquarters. On the second day a letter from my wife was brought to me in the council chamber. I read it there and then. She wrote about the children, about our uncle, about the nurse, about things she had bought and then in passing, as if in reference to the most ordinary event, about a visit she'd had from Trukhachevsky: he'd apparently brought her the music he'd promised her and had suggested they play together again, but she had refused. I couldn't remember him having promised to bring any music: it had seemed to me at the time that he'd said a definitive goodbye, and what she described gave me a nasty jolt. However, I had so much to do that there wasn't any time to reflect about it, and it was only in the evening, when I got back to my lodgings, that I read her letter through again properly. It wasn't just the fact that Trukhachevsky had been to the house again in my absence. The whole tone of the letter seemed forced to me. The rabid beast of jealousy began to snarl in its kennel, trying to get out, but I was afraid of that beast, and I hastily locked it up inside me. "What a loathsome thing jealousy is!" I told myself. "Nothing could be more natural than what's in her letter."

'And I lay down on the bed and began to think about the matters I had to attend to the following day. I always had a lot of trouble getting to sleep when I was away at those zemstvo meetings – it also had to do with the unfamiliar surroundings – but on this occasion I managed to fall asleep almost at once. But then – you know the way it sometimes happens, that you're seized by a sort of electric shock, and you wake up? I woke up like that, with my head full of thoughts about her, about my carnal love for her, about Trukhachevsky and about the two of them making love together. I shrank inwardly with rage and horror. But I began to reason with myself. "What rubbish," I told myself. "You've got absolutely no grounds for thinking like that, nothing of the kind's happening, nor has it happened already. And how can you humiliate yourself and her by supposing such horrors? Some hired fiddler, known to be a worthless individual, suddenly taking up with an honourable woman, the respectable mother of a family, *my* wife? What an absurdity!" was what one part of me was thinking. "How could it possibly be otherwise?" was what the other part thought. "There couldn't be anything more simple or straightforward: it was for the sake of that simple, straightforward thing that I married her, for the sake of it that I've lived with her, it's the only thing about her which I actually want and which other men, including that musician, therefore also want. He's an unmarried man, in good health (I can still remember the way he used to crunch the gristle in his chop and greedily seize the rim of his wineglass in his red lips), sleek and well fed, and not merely quite without principles but obviously an adherent of certain special ideas of his own about how best to take full advantage of the pleasures that came his way. And between them they have the bond of music, the most refined form of sensual lust. What can possibly hold him back? Nothing. On the contrary, everything is drawing him in that direction. Would she be able to hold him back? I don't even know who she is. She's a mystery, just as she's always been, just as she'll always be. I don't know her. I only know her as an animal. And nothing can or should hold an animal back."

'It was only then that I began to remember the way they had looked that evening when, after they'd finished the "Kreutzer Sonata", they played some passionate little encore – I don't recall the composer – some piece that was so voluptuous it was obscene. "How could I have gone away like that?" I wondered, as I began to remember the look on their faces. "Surely it must have been obvious that everything took place between them that evening? And surely I must have seen then that there was no longer any barrier between them? Not only that, but that both of them, especially her, were experiencing a kind of shame after what had occurred between them?" I remembered how weakly, pathetically and blissfully she had smiled as I came up to the piano, how she had wiped the perspiration from her blushing face. Even then they had been avoiding each other's eyes, and it was only at supper, when he was passing her a glass of water, that they looked at each other and gave each other a little smile. With horror now I recalled those looks, those barely perceptible smiles. "Yes, it's all taken place between them," said a voice inside me, yet almost immediately another voice said something quite different. "What's come over you? That's impossible," said that other voice. I started to get a sinister feeling, lying there in the dark, and I struck a match: the little room with its yellow wallpaper suddenly filled me with a kind of terror. I lit a cigarette; you know how it is when your mind starts to spin round in the same circle of insoluble problems – you smoke. I smoked one cigarette after another, in an endeavour to cloud my intelligence and make the problems go away.

'I didn't get any sleep at all that night, and at five a.m. I decided I couldn't stand any more of this nervous tension and would go home immediately. I got up, woke the caretaker who acted as my servant and sent him off to fetch some horses. I sent a note to the zemstvo, saying I'd been called away to Moscow on urgent business and asking them to replace me with one of the other members. At eight a.m. I got into a carriage and began my journey.'

XXV

The guard came in and, noticing that our candle had burned down, he extinguished it without putting a new one in its place. Outside it was beginning to get light. Pozdnyshev kept silent, sighing heavily all the time the guard was in the carriage. He continued his story only when the guard had left; and all that could be heard in the semi-darkness was the rattling of the windows of the moving carriage, and the estate manager's regular snoring. In the half-light of the dawn I could no longer make out Pozdnyshev's features. All I could hear was his voice, which was growing more and more agitated, fuller and fuller of suffering.

'I had to go thirty-five versts[10] by horse and carriage, and then after that there was an eight-hour rail journey. The conditions were just right for a carriage ride. It was frosty autumn weather, with brilliant sunshine. You know, the time of the year when the calks in the horseshoes leave their imprints on a road surface that's even, without a single rut in it. The roads were smooth, the light was bright and the air was invigorating. I really enjoyed that carriage ride. Once it had got light and I'd started my journey, I'd felt a load lift from my shoulders. As I looked at the horses, the fields, the passers-by, I forgot where it was I was going. At times I had the illusion that I was just out for a drive, and that none of what had given rise to this journey had ever taken place. And I experienced a strange joy in those moments of self-oblivion. Whenever I remembered where I was going, I would say to myself: "It'll all be clear soon enough; don't worry your head about it." Moreover, halfway through the journey there occurred an event that delayed me and proved even more diverting: the carriage broke down and had to be repaired. This breakdown was very significant, as it meant that I got to Moscow not at five p.m., as I'd planned, but at midnight, and didn't reach home until one in the morning – I missed the fast mail train, and had to take the ordinary passenger service. All the business of being towed by a cart, getting the repair done, paying the bill, having tea at the inn, chatting with the innkeeper – all that took my mind off things even further. By twilight everything was ready, and I set off once more; it was even better driving by night than it had been by day. There was a new moon, the frost was light, the road still perfect, the horses galloped, the coachman was in a good mood; I rode along, enjoying myself, because I was completely unmindful of what awaited me; or perhaps it was because I knew only too well what awaited me, and was saying farewell to the joys of life. But this tranquillity of spirit I experienced, this ability to suppress my emotions, all that came to an end when the carriage journey was over. As soon as I got into the railway coach I lost all control over my imagination: it began to paint for me, in the most lurid fashion, a rapid sequence of pictures which inflamed my jealousy, and each of which was more cynical than the last. They were all of the same thing – of what was happening there, in my absence, of her being unfaithful to me. I was consumed with rage, indignation and a kind of strange, drunken enjoyment of my own hurt pride as I contemplated these pictures, and I couldn't tear myself away from them. I couldn't help looking at them, I couldn't erase them from my mind, and I couldn't stop myself dreaming them up. But that wasn't all: the more I contemplated these imaginary pictures, the more I believed they were real. The luridness with which they appeared before me seemed proof that what I was imagining was in fact reality. It was as though some devil was inventing the most abominable notions and suggesting them to me against my will. I suddenly remembered a conversation I'd once had long ago with Trukhachevsky's brother, and I used it in order to lacerate my feelings with a kind of triumphant ecstasy, making it relate to Trukhachevsky and my wife.

'It had been a very long time ago, but I still remembered it. Once, when I'd asked Trukhachevsky's brother if he ever went to brothels, he'd replied that a respectable man wouldn't go to some dirty, loathsome place where he might run the risk of catching an infection, when it was always possible to find a respectable woman. And now his brother had found my wife. "It's true that she's not all that young any more, she's lost one of her side teeth and she's a bit on the puffy side," I imagined him thinking, "but there you are, you have to make the best of what's available." "Yes, he thinks he's doing her a favour by taking her as his mistress," I reflected. "And what's more, she's safe. No, that's outrageous! What am I thinking of?" I said to myself in horror. "There's nothing of that kind, nothing. There aren't even any grounds for supposing anything of that kind. After all, didn't she tell me herself that she found the very idea of my being jealous of him degrading to her? Yes, but she was lying, she's always lying!" I cried out loud – and it started again . . . There were only two other passengers in the carriage, an old woman and her husband, both of whom were very untalkative, and when they got out at one of the stations I was left alone. I was like a wild animal in a cage: at one moment I'd leap up and go to the window, at another I'd pace stumblingly up and down, willing the train to go faster; but the carriage just went on shaking and vibrating all its seats and windows, exactly like ours is doing now . . .'

And Pozdnyshev leapt to his feet, took a few paces and then sat down again.

'Oh, I'm so afraid, so afraid of railway carriages; I get stricken with horror in them. Yes, it was horrible,' he continued. 'I told myself I was going to think about something else; I'd think about the keeper of the inn, say, where I'd had tea. And immediately I saw him in my mind's eye, the old, long-bearded innkeeper with his grandson, a boy the same age as my Vasya, standing beside him. My Vasya! Now he was seeing a musician embracing his mother. What must be taking place in his poor soul? But what did she care? She was in love . . . And it all began to seethe within me again. "No, no . . . Very well," I thought, "I'll fix my mind on the hospital I inspected yesterday. And that doctor who had a moustache like Trukhachevsky's. And the way he impudently . . . They were both deceiving me when they told me he was leaving town." And again it began. All my thoughts led back to him. I suffered horribly. I suffered mainly because of my ignorance, my doubts, my ambivalence, my not knowing whether I ought to love her or hate her. So intense was my suffering that I remember that the thought occurred to me – I found it greatly appealing – that I might get out on to the track and throw myself on the rails under the train, and thus make an end of it all. Then at least I wouldn't be able to doubt and hesitate any more. The only thing that prevented me from doing this was my own self-pity, which immediately gave way to a surge of hatred for my wife. For him I felt both a strange hatred and a consciousness of my humiliation and of his triumph, but for her I felt nothing but the most terrible hatred. "I'm not just going to commit suicide and let her off that way; she's at least got to suffer a bit, and realize how I've suffered," I said to myself. At every station I got out of the train in an attempt to take my mind off it all. I saw some men drinking in one of the station buffets, and I went in and ordered some vodka. There was a Jew standing beside me. He too was drinking. He started talking to me and, willing to do anything rather than sit alone in my carriage, I accompanied him along to his grimy, smoky, third-class compartment, the interior of which was spattered with the husks of sunflower seeds. There I sat down beside him, and he droned away, telling me various anecdotes. I listened to him, but I couldn't follow what he was telling me, as I was still thinking about my own problems. He noticed this, and began to demand that I pay more attention. At that point I got up and went back to my own carriage. "I must think about it carefully," I said to myself. "Is it really true, what I suspect, and is there really any reason for me to torture myself like this?" I sat down and tried to think it over calmly and quietly; but no sooner had I done so than it all started up again: instead of following a calm, reasoned argument, my head was filled with pictures and imaginings. "Think how often I've tortured myself like this," I said to myself, as I remembered the similar attacks of jealousy I'd had previously. "Yet every time it was a false alarm. That's probably the way it'll be this time, as well. I'll find her peacefully asleep; she'll wake up, be delighted to see me, and her words and eyes will tell me that nothing's happened and that all my suspicions are groundless. Oh how good that would be!" "Oh no, it's happened that way too often, this time it's going to be different," said a voice inside me, and it started again. Yes, that was the nature of my punishment! If I'd wanted to discourage a young man from running after women, I wouldn't have taken him to a syphilis clinic, I'd have taken him into my own soul and shown him the devils that were tearing it apart! What was really so horrible was that I felt I had a complete and inalienable right to her body, as if it were my own, yet at the same time I felt that I wasn't the master of this body, that it didn't belong to me, that she could do with it whatever she pleased, and that what she wanted to do with it wasn't what I wanted. And that there was nothing I could do to stop either him or her. He was like some Vanka-Klyuchnik[11] before the gallows, singing a song about how he'd kissed her sweet lips, and so forth. And he had the upper hand. With her there was even less I could do. Even if she hadn't been unfaithful to me yet, she wanted to, and I knew she wanted to, and that made it even worse. It would have been better if she'd actually done it and I'd known about it, so there wouldn't have been this uncertainty. I wouldn't have been capable of saying what it was I wanted. I wanted her not to want what she couldn't help wanting. It was complete and utter madness.'

XXVI

'At the station before the terminus, after the guard had been along to collect the tickets, I got my things together and went out on to the brake-platform. My awareness of what now lay close at hand – the resolution of the entire conflict – was making me even more nervous. I was cold and my jaws started to shake so that my teeth chattered. I shuffled mechanically out of the station with the rest of the crowd, hailed a cab, got into it and set off home. As we rode along I observed the few passers-by, the yard-keepers,[12] the shadows thrown by the street-lamps and by my cab, now in front, now behind, and thought very hard about nothing. After we'd gone about half a verst, my feet started to feel chilled, and it came back to me that I'd taken off my long woollen socks in the train and had put them in my travelling-bag. But where was my travelling-bag? Had I left it in the train? No, I hadn't, it was there. But where was my wicker trunk? It flashed into my mind that I'd forgotten all about my luggage. However, when I discovered that I still had the luggage ticket, I decided it wasn't worth going back just for the trunk, and we travelled on.

'Even though I try hard now, I can't remember the state of mind I was in at that moment. What were my thoughts? What did I want? I've absolutely no idea. All I can remember is that I knew some terrible and very important event was about to take place in my life. Whether that important event did in fact take place because I was thinking like this, or whether it took place because I had a foreboding that it would, I don't know. It may even be that after what happened, everything that went before has taken on a gloomy tinge in my memory. The cab drove up to the porch of our house. It was one o'clock in the morning. There were several cabs standing outside the house; their drivers were waiting for fares, as there were lights in the windows (the lights were on in the ballroom and drawing-room of our apartment). Not stopping to ask myself why there might be lights on so late in our apartment, I climbed the stairs in the same expectation of some terrible event, and rang the doorbell. The door was opened by Yegor, our good, hard-working, but not very intelligent manservant. The first thing that struck my eyes was Trukhachevsky's overcoat hanging with the other coats on the coat-stand in the hallway. I ought to have been surprised, but I wasn't – it was as if I'd been expecting this. "So it's true," I said to myself. When I'd asked Yegor who the visitor was, and he'd told me it was Trukha-chevsky, I asked him if there were any other visitors. ' "No others, sir," he said.

'I remember the tone of voice in which he replied to me, as if he were anxious to please me and to dispel any uneasiness I might have that there might be other visitors. "No others, sir." "I see, I see," I said, as if I were talking to myself. "And the children?"

' "All well, sir, praise be to God. They're all asleep long ago."

'I could hardly breathe, and I couldn't stop the shaking in my jaws. "That means it's not the way I thought it was," I said to myself. "I used to think, 'disaster' – and yet everything would turn out to be just the same as before. It isn't like that this time; this time it's all happened, everything I used to think about and imagine, only now it isn't imaginings but reality. It's here, all of it . . ."

'I almost burst out sobbing, but the Devil immediately whispered to me: "If you go and cry and be sentimental,

Leo Tolstoy

they'll just part quietly, there won't be any evidence, and you'll spend the rest of your life in doubt and agony." And immediately my self-pity evaporated, and was replaced by a strange feeling – you won't believe this – a feeling of joy, that now my suffering was at an end, that now I'd be able to punish her, get rid of her, give my hatred free rein. And indeed, I did give free rein to my hatred – I became a wild beast, a ferocious and cunning wild beast.

' "No, don't, don't," I said to Yegor, who was about to go into the drawing-room. "I tell you what you can do: take a cab down to the station and fetch my luggage. Look, here's the ticket. Off you go, now."

'He went along the passage to get his coat. Afraid that he might disturb them, I followed him to his little room and waited while he put his coat on. From the drawing-room, which lay through another room, voices and the sound of plates and knives were audible. They were eating, and hadn't heard the bell. "If only they don't come out now," I thought. Yegor put on his coat, which had an astrakhan collar, and went out. I opened the door for him and closed it behind him, and I felt an eerie sensation at being alone and knowing what I had to do next. How I was going to do it, I didn't yet know. All I knew was that now it had all taken place between them, that the fact of her guilt was now established beyond all question and that now I was going to punish her and bring my relations with her to an end.

'Previously I had always hesitated, and told myself: "But what if it's all untrue, what if I'm mistaken?" This time there was none of that. It had all been irrevocably settled. Without my knowledge, alone with him, at night! That showed a disregard that was total. Or perhaps it was even worse: the audacity and the insolence of her crime were intentional, and aimed at serving as a mark of her innocence. It was all quite transparently obvious. There could be no doubt whatsoever. I was only afraid that they might try to make a run for it, think up some new way of pulling the wool over my eyes, thus depriving me of my evidence and my chance of punishing her. And in order the more quickly to catch them, I crept on tiptoe to the ballroom where they were sitting, not through the drawing-room, but through the passage and the two nurseries.

'The boys were asleep in the first nursery. In the second, the nurse was stirring, on the point of waking up, and I pictured to myself what she would think when she discovered what had happened; at this notion I was seized by such self-pity that I couldn't keep my tears back, and so as not to wake the children I ran back into the passage on tiptoe and along to my study, where I threw myself on the sofa and wept out loud.

' "I'm an honest man, I'm the son of my parents, all my life I've dreamt of family happiness, never once have I been unfaithful to her . . . yet look! Five children, and she's kissing a musician because he's got red lips! No, she isn't human, she's a bitch, a repulsive bitch! Right next door to a room full of children she's pretended to love all her life. And to have written me the things she did! To throw herself into his arms so brazenly! For all I know, it may have been this way all along. Perhaps all these children that are considered mine were really sired by the manservants! And tomorrow I'd have arrived home and she'd have come out to greet me with hair done in that special way, with that twist of hers and those graceful, indolent movements" — I saw before me the whole of her loathsome, attractive presence — "and the wild beast of jealousy would have taken possession of my heart for ever and torn it to shreds. What will the nurse think, and Yegor? And poor little Liza? She already knows something. This brazenness! This lying! This animal sensuality which I know so well," I said to myself.

'I wanted to get up, but I couldn't. My heart was beating so violently that I couldn't stay standing upright. That was it, I was going to die of a stroke. She was going to kill me. That was exactly what she wanted. What did killing matter to her? Oh no, that would be doing her far too great a favour, I wasn't going to give her that satisfaction. Yes, here I was to sit, while in there they ate and laughed and . . . Even though she'd lost the first freshness of her girlhood, he wasn't going to turn his nose up at her; actually she wasn't at all bad-looking, and, most important of all, she didn't pose any danger to his precious health. "Why didn't I just strangle her there and then?" I asked myself, remembering the moment when, a week ago, I'd shoved her out of my study and then smashed things. I vividly remembered the state of mind I'd been in at the time: not only did I remember it, I now felt the same desire to smash and destroy that I'd felt then. I wanted to act. All considerations other than those related to action went abruptly out of my head. I entered that state a wild animal knows, or the state that's experienced by a man who is under the influence of physical excitement at a time of danger, and who acts precisely, unhurriedly, but without ever wasting a moment, and with only one end in view.'

XXVII

'The first thing I did was to take off my boots. Then, in my stockinged feet, I went over to the wall above the sofa where I kept my guns and daggers hanging, and took down a curved, damask-steel poniard that had never once been used and was horribly sharp. I removed it from its sheath. I remember that the sheath fell down behind the sofa, and that I said to myself: "I'd better see I find it afterwards, otherwise it'll get lost." Then I took off my overcoat, which I'd been wearing all this time and, treading softly in my stockinged feet, made for the drawing-room.

'I crept quietly up to the door, and then suddenly opened it. I remember the look on their faces. I remember it because it gave me an excruciating joy. It was a look of terror. That was exactly what I wanted. I'll never be able to forget the expression of desperate terror that came over both their faces in the first split-second they caught sight of me. As I remember it, he was sitting at the table, but when he saw me, or heard me, he leapt to his feet and froze with his back to the cupboard. His features wore a quite unmistakable look of terror. So did hers, but there was something else there, too. If all she had done was look terrified, it's quite possible that what took place might never have happened; but in that facial expression of hers – at least that's how it seemed to me in that first split-second – there was also a kind of annoyance, she looked as though she were put out at having her love-life interrupted, her happiness with him. It was as if all she cared about now was that no one should prevent her from being happy. These expressions stayed on their faces only for an instant. His terrified look quickly gave way to one that asked a question: was it going to be possible to lie or not? If it was, then they'd better start now. If it wasn't, then something else was going to begin happening. But what? He threw her a questioning look. When she looked back at him, it seemed to me that her expression of annoyance had turned into one of concern for him.

'For an instant I froze there in the doorway, clutching the poniard behind my back. At that same moment he smiled and started to say, in a tone of voice that was nonchalant to the point of being absurd: "Oh, we were just playing a little music together . . ."

' "Goodness, I wasn't expecting . . ." she began simultaneously, adopting the same tone of voice.

'But neither of them managed to get to the end of their sentences. That same rabid frenzy I had experienced a week previously once more took possession of me. Once again I felt that compulsion to destroy, to subjugate by force, to rejoice in the ecstasy of my furious rage, and I abandoned myself to it.

'Neither of them managed to finish what they were saying . . . That something else, the thing he was afraid of, the thing that blew all their words to kingdom come in one instant, began to happen. I rushed at her, still keeping the poniard hidden in case he tried to stop me plunging it into her side, under the breast. That was the spot I'd chosen right from the outset. In the very moment I attacked her, he saw what I was doing, and seized my arm – something I'd never expected he'd do – shouting: "Think what you're doing! Someone help!"

'I wrenched my arm free and went for him without a word. His eyes met mine, and suddenly he turned as white as a sheet, even his lips turned pale; his eyes started to glitter in a

peculiar way, and then suddenly – this was something else I
hadn't been expecting – he ducked under the piano and was
out of the room in a flash. I was about to rush after him, but
there was something weighing me down by my left arm. It
was her. I tried to pull myself away, but she hung on to me
even more heavily and wouldn't let go. This unexpected
impediment, her weight and the physical contact with her,
which I found revolting, inflamed me even further. I was in a
rabid frenzy, and I knew I must be a fearful sight, and was
glad of it. I swung my left arm round as hard as I could, and
my elbow struck her full in the face. She screamed and let go
of my arm. I wanted to run after him, but I reflected that it
would be ridiculous to run after one's wife's lover in one's
stockinged feet; I didn't want to look ridiculous, I wanted to
look terrifying. In spite of the terrible fury that gripped me, I
was constantly aware of the impression I was making on
others, and this consideration even guided my actions to a
certain extent. I turned and looked at her. She'd slumped on
to a *chaise-longue*; snatching with one hand at her eyes, which
I'd hurt, she was observing me. In her face there was fear and
hatred of me: I was the enemy. It was the kind of fear and
hatred that could only be inspired by her love for another man.
Yet I might still have held myself in check and not done what
I did, if only she hadn't said anything. But she suddenly began
to speak, as she attempted to seize the hand in which I was
holding the poniard.

' "Think what you're doing! What is this? What's wrong
with you? There's nothing, nothing, nothing . . . I swear it!"

'I might still have managed to put it off a little longer, but
what she had just said – from which I drew quite the opposite
conclusion, namely that everything *had* taken place between
them – demanded a reply. And the reply had to be in keeping
with the state of mind into which I'd worked myself, which
was rising in a non-stop crescendo, and which could not but
continue to rise. Even frenzied rage has its laws.

' "Don't lie, you repulsive bitch!" I began to yell, grabbing
her arm with my left hand. But she tore herself free. Then,
without letting go of the poniard, I gripped her throat in my

left hand, threw her back and started to strangle her. How hard her neck was . . . She seized my hands in hers, trying to tear them free of her throat, and as if this were the signal for which I'd been waiting, I struck her with the poniard as hard as I could in her left side, beneath the ribs.

'When people tell you they don't remember what they did when they are in a mad fit of rage, don't believe a word of it – it's all lies, nonsense. I remembered everything afterwards, and I've never ceased to remember it for one second. The more steam my rage got up, the more brilliantly the light of consciousness flared within me, making it impossible for me not to be aware of everything I was doing. I can't claim that I knew in advance what I was going to do, but I was aware of each action I took at the moment I performed it, and sometimes, I think, a little before. It was as if it had been arranged like this so I could repent, so I could tell myself I was capable of stopping if I wanted to. I knew that I was striking her with the poniard under the ribs, and that it was going to go in. At the moment I did it, I knew I was doing something horrific, something the like of which I had never done before, and that it was going to have terrible consequences. But that awareness came and went like a flash of lightning, and was instantly followed by the act itself. I was blindingly aware of that act, too. I felt – I can remember it now – the momentary resistance of her corset, and of something else as well, and then the way the poniard sank into something soft. She grabbed at the poniard with both hands, lacerating them on the blade, but she couldn't stop it from going in. For a long time afterwards, in prison, when a change of heart had taken place in me, I used to think about that moment, remembering what I could of it, and weighing it up in my mind. I would remember that for a split-second – only a split-second, mind you – before I did what I did, I had a terrible awareness that I was killing, that I'd killed a woman, a defenceless woman, my wife. I remember the horror of that awareness even now, and putting two and two together I think that once I'd stuck the poniard into her, I must have pulled it out again (I even have a dim memory of doing this), in an attempt to set right what I'd done and put a stop to it all. For a second I stood without moving, waiting to see what would happen, and whether everything was going to be all right again. She leapt to her feet and screamed: "Nurse, he's killed me!"

'The nurse had heard the noise, and was standing in the doorway. I continued to stand there, waiting, unable to believe what had happened. But then suddenly the blood came gushing out from under her corset. It was only then that I realized it couldn't be put right again, and I immediately made up my mind that there was no need for it to be put right, that this was just what I'd wanted, and what I'd been obliged to do. I waited a little, until she'd fallen down, and the nurse, with a scream of "Lord Almighty!", had run to her side, and only then did I throw down the poniard and stalk out of the room.

' "It's no good getting all worked up, I must be aware of what I'm doing," I told myself, looking neither at her nor at the nurse. The nurse was screaming, calling for the maid. I stalked along the passage, and, after I'd told the maid to go and help, went into my room. "What am I going to do now?" I wondered, and immediately knew the answer to my question. As I walked into my study, I made straight for the wall, took down a revolver, examined it – it was loaded – and placed it on the desk. Then, taking care to retrieve the sheath from behind it first, I sat down on the sofa.

'I sat there for a long time. I thought about nothing, remembering nothing. Along the passage I could hear people moving about. I heard someone come into the house, followed by someone else. Then there was a noise, and I saw Yegor come into my room carrying the wicker trunk he'd fetched from the station. As if anyone needed it now!

' "Haven't you heard what's happened?" I asked him. "Tell the yard-keeper to inform the police."

'He made no reply, and went away. I got up, locked the door, found my cigarettes and matches, and had a smoke. I'd hardly finished my cigarette when sleep overcame me and rendered me senseless. I remember I dreamed that she and I were on friendly terms again, that we'd had a quarrel but had made it up; we still had a few outstanding differences, but we were friends once more. I was woken by a knocking at the door. "That'll be the police!" I thought. "After all, I've just committed a murder, I think. Or maybe it's her, and nothing has happened." There was more knocking. I didn't go to see who it was, I was trying to make up my mind whether it had all really happened or not. Yes, it had. I had a memory of her corset's resistance, of the way the poniard had sunk into her, and a chill ran down my spine. "Yes, it happened, all right," I said to myself. "And now it's my turn." But even as I silently formed these words, I knew I wasn't going to kill myself. It was a strange thing: I remembered how many times before I'd been on the point of committing suicide; even that day in the train it had seemed easy to me, easy because I'd thought of how it would put the fear of God into her. Now, however, not only was I unable to kill myself – nothing could have been further from my thoughts. "Why should I?" I asked myself, and there was no reply. The knocking came again. "Right," I said to myself. "The first thing I must do is find out who that is. I'm not in any hurry." I put the revolver back on the desk and covered it with a newspaper. Then I went to the door and undid the latch. It was my wife's sister, that kind-hearted, brainless widow.

' "Vasya! What's happened?" she said, and the tears she always had ready started to flow.

' "What do you want?" I asked her, rudely. I knew there was absolutely no excuse for my being rude to her, nor would any purpose be served by it, but I couldn't think of any other tone of voice to adopt.

' "Vasya! She's dying! Ivan Fyodorovich said so." Ivan Fyodorovich was my wife's doctor and adviser.

' "Is he here?" I asked, and all my hatred for her seethed up again. "Well, what of it?"

' "Vasya, go in and see her. Oh, this is terrible," she said.

' "Go in and see her?" I said, phrasing the words in the form of a question to myself. And I immediately knew the answer, knew that I must go in and see her, that when a husband had murdered his wife, as I had done, the correct thing was for him to go in and see her. "If that's the correct thing to do, then I must go in," I told myself. "And if I have to, I'll still have time," I thought, apropos of my intention to commit suicide. I followed my sister-in-law out.

'   "Wait," I said to her. "I'll look ridiculous without my boots, let me at least put a pair of slippers on." '

XXVIII

'And it really was quite remarkable! Once again, as I emerged from my study and passed through the familiar rooms, once again there rose within me the hope that nothing at all had happened. But then the smell of that vile stuff doctors use – iodoform, phenol acid – or whatever it is – hit my nostrils. No, it had happened all right, all of it. As I passed the nursery I caught sight of Liza. She was looking at me with frightened eyes. For a moment it even seemed to me that all five children were in there, and that they were all looking at me. I went up to her bedroom. The maid came to the door, let me in and left. The first thing that leapt to my gaze was her light-grey dress draped over a chair; the dress was stained black all over with blood. She was lying on our double bed, on my side of it (it was easier of access), her knees raised. She was lying almost supine, on a pair of pillows, and she was wearing an unbuttoned bed-jacket. Some stuff or other had been applied to the place where the wound was. There was a heavy smell of iodoform in the room. What struck me most forcibly was her face: it was swollen, and along part of her nose and under one eye it was blue with bruises. This was the result of the blow I'd given her with my elbow when she'd been trying to hold me back. She had no beauty at all now, and I felt there was something repulsive about her. I stood still on the threshold.

'   "Go in, go in to her," said my sister-in-law.

'   "Yes, I expect she wants to confess," I thought. "Shall I forgive her? Yes, she's dying, and so can be forgiven," I said to myself, trying to be magnanimous. I went in and walked right up to her. She looked up at me with difficulty – she had a black eye – and she said, haltingly: "You've got what you wanted, you've killed me . . ." And through all her physical suffering, her nearness to death, even, I saw displayed on her face the same inveterate look of cold, animal hatred I knew so well. "Even so . . . I won't . . . let you have . . . the children . . . She" – her sister – "will look after them . . ."

'The thing I thought most important – the question of her guilt, her unfaithfulness – she didn't even seem to think worth mentioning.

' "Yes, admire what you've done," she said, looking towards the door, and she gave a sob. Her sister was standing in the doorway with the children. "Yes, there it is, there's what you've done."

'I looked at the children, at her battered face with its bruises, and for the first time I forgot about myself, about my marital rights and my injured pride; for the first time I saw her as a human being. And so insignificant did all that had hurt me and made me jealous appear, and so significant what I'd done, that I wanted to press my face to her hand and say: "Forgive me!" – but I didn't dare to.

'She fell silent, closing her eyes, and obviously without the strength to speak any more. Then her disfigured face began to quiver and was creased with a frown. Feebly, she pushed me away.

' "Why did all this happen? Why?"

' "Forgive me," I said.

' "Forgive? That's all nonsense! . . . If only I wasn't going to die! . . ." she screamed, heaving herself up and transfixing me with her feverishly glittering eyes. "Yes, you've got what you wanted! . . . I hate you! . . . Ah! Ah!" she cried, evidently in delirium now, and afraid of something. "Go on, kill me, kill me, I'm not afraid . . . Only kill all of us, all of us, him too. He's gone, he's gone!"

'After that, her fever became continuous. She couldn't recognize anyone any more. She died towards noon that same day. Before then, at eight a.m. to be precise, I'd been taken to the local police station and from there to prison. And there I remained for eleven months awaiting trial. During that time I thought a great deal about myself and my past life, and I grasped what it had all been about. I began to grasp it on my third day. It was on that third day that they took me there . . .'

He was about to say something else, but could not hold back his sobbing, and had to stop. Pulling himself together with an effort, he continued:

'I only began to grasp it when I saw her in her coffin . . .' He gave a sob, but continued hastily, at once: 'It was only when I saw her dead face that I realized what I'd done. I realized that I'd killed her, that it was all my doing that from a warm, moving, living creature she'd been transformed into a cold, immobile waxen one, and that there was no way of setting this to rights, not ever, not anywhere, not by any means. If you've never experienced that, you can't possibly understand . . . Oh! Oh! Oh!' he cried several times, and fell silent.

For a long time we sat there saying nothing. He sobbed and shook silently, and I looked at him.

'Well, *prostite*[13], forgive me . . .'

He turned away from me and lay down on the seat, covering himself up with his plaid. When we reached the station where I had to get off – this was at eight a.m. – I went over to him in order to say goodbye. Whether he was asleep or merely pretending, he didn't stir. I touched him with my hand. He threw off the plaid, and it was clear he had not been asleep.

'*Proshchayte*, goodbye,' I said, offering my hand.

He took it, and gave me the barest smile, though it was so pathetic that I felt like crying.

'Yes, *prostite*, forgive me . . .' he said, repeating the word with which he had brought his story to an end.

THE
DEVIL

But I say unto you, That whosoever
looketh on a woman to lust after her
hath committed adultery with her
already in his heart.
 And if thy right eye offend thee, pluck it out, and cast it
from thee: for it is profitable for thee that one of thy
members should perish, and not that thy whole body
should be cast into hell.
And if thy right hand offend thee, cut it off, and cast it
from thee: for it is profitable for thee that one of thy
members should perish, and not that thy whole body be
cast into hell.
(Matthew v, 28–30)

I

A brilliant career lay ahead of Yevgeny Irtenev. He had all that
it took: an excellent home education, a first-class degree from
the Faculty of Law at St Petersburg University, connections,
obtained through his recently deceased father, in the very
highest social circles, and even the beginnings of a position in
a government ministry under the patronage of the minister
himself. He also had a private income; it was quite a large
income, though not very secure. His father had lived abroad
for part of the year and had spent the rest of his time in St
Petersburg, making an annual allowance of six thousand
rubles to each of his two sons – Yevgeny and Andrey, who
was a bit older and served in the Horse Guards. He himself,

together with his wife, had managed to get through a fortune. The only time he had ever visited his estate had been for two months each summer, and he had never concerned himself with the running of it, leaving all that to an overfed manager who never concerned himself with the running of it either, but whom he had trusted completely.

When, after the death of their father, the brothers came to divide up the property, there proved to be so many debts outstanding that the family attorney advised them to renounce their inheritance and make do with the estate of their grand-mother, which was valued at a hundred thousand rubles. However, a neighbour of the estate, a landowner who had had dealings with old man Irtenev, had one of his promissory notes and had come to St Petersburg especially on that account, told the young men that in spite of all the debts there was a very good chance that they could clear up all the practical business and still manage to keep back a large capital sum. All they had to do was sell the wood and a few bits of vacant land, keeping the 'goldmine' – Semyonovskoye, with its four thousand desyatinas[14] of black earth, its sugar factory and its two thousand desyatinas of water-meadows – for themselves. It just required a bit of application. They would have to settle in the village on a permanent basis and run the place sensibly, with a due regard for economy.

So it was that, when he paid a visit to the estate that spring (his father had died during Lent) and made a tour of inspec-tion, Yevgeny decided to give up his government position, settle in the village with his mother, and devote himself to getting the most out of the property. With his brother, to whom he was not particularly closely attached, he came to the following arrangement: he undertook to pay him either an annual allowance of four thousand rubles, or a lump sum of eighty thousand, in return for which the elder brother would agree to give up his share of the inheritance.

This done, he went with his mother to live in the manor house at Semyonovskoye, and set about running the estate with zeal, but also with caution.

It is usually considered that old men are the natural

conservatives, while young men are natural innovators. This is not really so. Young men are the natural conservatives – young men who want to live but who don't think, or don't have time to think, about how they ought to live and who therefore take as their model the lifestyle of those who have lived before them.

Yevgeny was no exception. Ensconced now in Semyonovskoye, he had as his dream, his ideal, the resurrection of the type of life that had been lived there not in his father's day – his father had been hopeless at practical things – but in the day of his grandfather. In all that affected the house, the garden and the way things were run, he now began – making certain adjustments in keeping with the times, of course – to resurrect the general spirit that had reigned during his grandfather's lifetime: everything on a grand scale, concern for the welfare of all, good order, the organization of services and amenities – all of which involved a great deal of hard work. The demands of the creditors and the banks had to be met, and to this end land had to be sold and terms of credit arranged. Money also had to be found with which to continue (in some places by renting out land, in others by the use of hired labour) the farming of Semyonovskoye's enormous, four-thousand-desyatina tillage and the running of the sugar factory; the house and garden had to be taken in hand so they did not give an impression of dereliction and decay.

There was a lot of work to do, but Yevgeny had a good deal of strength, both physical and intellectual. He was twenty-six years old, of average height, powerfully built, with muscles that had been developed by physical exercises. He was a sanguine type, and his cheeks had a high, vivid colour; his teeth were brilliantly white, his lips bright red, and his hair was thin, soft and curly. His only physical defect was his near-sightedness, which he had brought upon himself by using spectacles; now he could not manage without a pince-nez, which had already set its imprints upon his aquiline nose. Such was his physical appearance. As for his personality, it could be said that the better you knew him, the better you liked him. His mother had always been fonder of him than of any of her other children, and now that her husband had died she not only lavished all her attention on her favourite son, she made him into the focus of her entire life. But she was not the only one who felt this way about him. The friends he had made at school and university had not only had a special place in their hearts for him, they had held him in respect. He had always had this kind of effect on other people, as well. It was impossible for anyone not to believe what he said, impossible to suspect any deceit or untruth when confronted with such an open, honest face, and especially such open, honest eyes.

Indeed, his personality was of great assistance to him in the business matters he now had to attend to. A creditor who might have turned down another man had confidence in him. A manager, an elder or a muzhik who might have played dirty and hoodwinked another man, forgot all about such trickery under the benign effect of dealing with someone who was so kind-hearted and straightforward, and who, most important of all, was as good as his word.

It was the end of May. After some wheeling and dealing, Yevgeny had finally managed to make arrangements in the town for the vacant land to be released from its mortgage so that it could be sold to a merchant. He had then borrowed money from this same merchant with which to renovate his stock of horses, bulls and carts, and, even more importantly, with which to start the construction of a badly needed farmhouse. The work got under way. Timber was being carted in, the carpenters had already got down to business, and eighty cartloads of manure were in the process of arriving, even though the entire project still hung by a thread.

II

Right in the middle of all these concerns, something happened which, although it was not important, caused Yevgeny rather a lot of trouble at the time. Up till now he had lived the way all young, healthy single men live: he had had relations with various kinds of women. He was not a libertine, but neither, as he liked to tell himself, was he a monk. And he had only indulged in this in so far as it was necessary for his physical well-being and his intellectual freedom, as he put it. It had started when he was sixteen. And so far it had all gone smoothly – smoothly in the sense that he hadn't given himself up to debauchery, had never once lost his head over any of the women he had had, and had never caught any diseases. Initially he had had relations with a seamstress in St Petersburg, but then she had become infected, and he had made other arrangements for himself. This side of his life had been so well organized that it had never given him any trouble.

But now here he was in his second month at Semyonovskoye, and he had not the faintest idea of how to make the necessary arrangements. The involuntary abstinence was beginning to have a bad effect on him. Would he have to go into town to get what he wanted? But whereabouts in town? And how was he going to arrange it? Such were the questions that troubled Yevgeny Ivanovich; and since he had made himself believe that this was what he had to do, and this was what he needed, it really did become a necessity for him. He felt he was no longer a free agent. Every time he caught sight of a young woman, he found himself following her with his eyes.

He did not think it would be right for him to have relations with a girl or a woman in Semyonovskoye. From what he had been told, he knew that both his father and his grandfather had differed completely from other landowners of their day in this respect, and had never had liaisons with their female serfs. He determined that he would not, either. As time went by, however, and he began to feel more and more constrained and pictured to himself with horror what might befall him in the god-forsaken town, he told himself that since serfs were a thing of the past nowadays, there was really nothing to stop him making arrangements in the village. The main thing was to do it in such a way that no one found out about it, and to do it not out of lust but for the sake of his health, as he said to himself. Having taken this decision, he became even more uneasy. Whenever he talked to the elder, the muzhiks or the carpenter he found himself bringing the conversation round to the subject of women, and if women were what they already happened to be talking about he would try to spin the conversation out as long as possible. As for women themselves, he found himself paying more and more attention to them.

III

To take a decision like this in private was one thing, however; to carry it out in practice was another. He couldn't just approach some woman all by himself. Which one would he choose? Where would they do it? It would have to be arranged through some third party, but who could he turn to?

One day when he was out in the woods he happened to call in at a gamekeeper's hut in order to get himself a drink of water. The gamekeeper had been one of his father's huntsmen. Yevgeny Ivanovich started to talk to him, and the gamekeeper began telling stories about the high old times they'd had on hunting expeditions in days gone by. It occurred to Yevgeny Ivanovich that it might not be such a bad idea to arrange what he had in mind out here in the hut, or in the woods. The trouble was that he didn't know how to go about it, or whether old Danila would arrange it for him. 'Perhaps if I suggest it to him he'll be horrified, and then I'll look really silly; but maybe he'll agree to it without any bother,' he thought, as he listened to Danila's stories. Danila went on to relate how they had once strayed rather far afield and had ended up staying the night with the deacon's wife, and how he had once fixed up a woman for the landowner Pryanichnikov.

'Yes, I can ask him,' thought Yevgeny.

'Your father, God rest his soul, never went in for that kind of nonsense.'

'No, I can't,' thought Yevgeny. However, in order to test the ground, he said: 'How did you ever come to get mixed up in an unpleasant business like that?'

'What's unpleasant about it? She was glad to do it and my Fyodor Zakharych was well satisfied. He gave me a ruble.

Anyway, how was he going to manage, otherwise? Needed his oats, he did, same as other men. Never said no to a drop of vodka, either.'

'Yes, I can ask him,' thought Yevgeny, and without further ado took the plunge.

'You know, Danila . . .' He could feel himself blushing scarlet. 'You know, I've been having an awful time.' Danila smiled. 'I'm not a monk, after all. I'm not used to it.'

He felt stupid saying this, but was relieved to see that Danila's attitude was one of approval.

'Why, sir, you should have told me ages ago, that's easily seen to,' he said. 'All you have to do is tell me which one you want.'

'Oh, it's really all the same to me. Well, of course, as long as she isn't ugly and hasn't any diseases.'

'I take your meaning!' said Danila, cutting him short. He thought for a bit. 'Ha, there's one really nice bit of stuff,' he began. Once again Yevgeny blushed. 'A lovely bit of stuff. She was married last autumn,' said Danila, starting to whisper now, 'but her husband can't do anything. Think what that's worth to a hunter, eh?'

Yevgeny was well and truly frowning with embarrassment by this time.

'No, no,' he managed to get out. 'That's not what I want at all. On the contrary (what could possibly be on the contrary?), all I want is one who's free of disease and won't cause any trouble. A soldier's wife, or something like that . . .'

'I've got the very one for you, sir. It's Stepanida you'll be wanting. Her husband works in the town, she's just like a soldier's wife. And she's that good-looking, and clean with it. You'll be well satisfied, sir. I was just saying to her the other day, you ought to go looking elsewhere, and she . . .'

'All right, so when can it be?'

'Tomorrow, if you want. I'll look in and fetch her on my way to buy tobacco. When it's dinner-time come here, or to the bath-house behind the kitchen garden. There won't be a soul about. Everybody sleeps after dinner.'

'Very well, then.'

As he made his way home, Yevgeny was gripped by a terrible sense of unease. 'What will it be like? What's a peasant woman like? What if she's horrible and ugly? No, they're pretty,' he said to himself, remembering the ones he had seen. 'But what will I say to her? How will I behave with her?'

He was not himself for the whole of the rest of that day. At twelve noon the following day he went back to the game-keeper's hut. Danila was standing in the doorway. He said nothing, but turned his head meaningfully in the direction of the wood. Yevgeny felt all the blood rush to his head, and he made for the kitchen garden. There was no one there. He approached the bath house. There was no one there, either. He took a quick look inside, came out again and suddenly heard the snap of a twig breaking. He looked round, and there she was, standing in a thicket on the other side of a small ravine. He rushed down into the ravine in order to get across to her. There were nettles in the ravine, he hadn't noticed them. He got badly stung, his pince-nez fell from his nose, and he scrambled up the opposite bank. Dressed in a white embroidered apron and a red-brown peasant skirt, her head covered by a bright red kerchief, barefoot, fresh, firm and pretty, she stood there, smiling shyly.

'There's a path, you should have gone round,' she said. 'I've been here for ages. Ever so long.'

He went up to her and, looking quickly around him first, touched her.

A quarter of an hour later they parted company. He found his pince-nez, and went off to the hut to see Danila. When Danila asked him 'Satisfied, master?', he gave the old man a ruble. Then he went home.

He was satisfied. It was only at the beginning that he had felt embarrassed. But his sense of shame had quickly passed. And it had been good. What was especially good was that now he felt calm, relaxed and cheerful. As for her, he hadn't really been able to see her properly. He remembered her as being clean, fresh, quite good-looking, and natural, with no airs and graces. 'Who's her husband?' he wondered. 'Pechnikov, did he say? Which Pechnikov would that be, now? There are two families of them, aren't there? She must be old Mikhaila's daughter-in-law. Yes, that's probably who she is. He's got a son who lives in Moscow. I must ask Danila about it some time.'

From that day on, the major drawback to life in the country – involuntary abstinence – was removed. Yevgeny's thoughts were no longer subject to distraction, and he was able to concentrate on the business of running the estate without interference.

The task Yevgeny had taken on was, however, very far from being an easy one: it sometimes seemed to him that he would not be able to last the course and that it would end with him having to sell the estate, and all his labours going for nothing. Worse still, that it might end with it being perfectly obvious that he hadn't been able to last the course, that he had failed to complete the task he had set himself. That was what worried him most. No sooner would he manage to plug up one gap than another, unexpected one would appear.

During all this time, more and more of his father's old debts, previously unknown, came to light. It became clear that during the latter days of his life his father had borrowed right, left and centre. When in May the property had been divided up, Yevgeny had believed that at last he knew everything. But suddenly, in the middle of the summer, he received a letter from which it transpired that a widow named Yesipova was still owed a sum of twelve thousand rubles. There was no promissory note, just a plain receipt which the family attorney said could be disputed. All Yevgeny wanted to know was whether the debt was a valid one or not.

'Mother, who's Kaleriya Vladimirovna Yesipova?' he asked, when he met his mother at dinner as usual.

'Yesipova? Oh, she was one of your grandfather's pupils. Why do you ask?'

Yevgeny told his mother about the letter.

'She ought to be ashamed of herself. After your father giving her all that money!'

'But do we owe her *this* money?'

'Well, I don't quite know how to put it. It isn't really a debt; your father, in his infinite goodness . . .'

'Yes, but did father consider it as a debt?'

'I really couldn't tell you. I don't know. All I know is that you've enough troubles already without that one.'

Yevgeny could see that Marya Pavlovna, his mother, didn't know what to say, and was testing him.

'From what you say it sounds as though it's a debt that will have to be paid,' he said. 'I'll go and have a word with her tomorrow. We'll see if the payment can't be deferred.'

'Oh, I'm so sorry for you. But you know, it's best this way. Yes, tell her she'll have to wait for a bit,' said Marya Pavlovna, evidently put at ease by this response, and proud of her son's determination.

Another thing that made Yevgeny's life particularly difficult was the fact that his mother, although she lived in the same house with him, had not the slightest understanding of the position he was in. All her life she had been accustomed to living on such a grand scale that she could not even imagine her son's predicament, which was that one of these days things might work out in such a way as to leave them destitute; Yevgeny might have to sell everything and support her by paid employment, which given his situation could earn him no more than two thousand rubles a year at the very most. She did not understand that they could only avoid such an outcome by cutting down their expenditure on all sides, and so was unable to comprehend why Yevgeny was so careful about little things like gardeners, coachmen, servants and even the meals they ate. What was more, like most widows she held the memory of her departed husband in a kind of reverential awe, quite unlike the attitude she had had towards him when he had been alive, and she would never have admitted that things he had done or arrangements he had made might have been bad ones, and need to be put right.

By dint of great exertions, Yevgeny was managing to run the garden with only two gardeners, and to keep up the stables with only two coachmen. In her innocence, his mother thought that by not complaining about the meals which the old manservant-cook prepared, or about the fact that the paths in the park were not all swept clean, or that instead of proper footmen they only had a boy, she was doing all that a mother could by way of sacrificing herself for her son. Similarly, in this matter of the new debt, which for Yevgeny was more or less the death-blow to all his attempts at good management, she saw merely one more instance of her son's noble character. Another reason why she was not particularly worried about his material situation was that she was sure he would make a brilliant marriage which would set everything to rights again. And indeed, it was in his power to make the most brilliant of marriages. She could think of a dozen families who would be happy to see their daughters married to him. And she wanted to arrange it as soon as possible.

IV

Yevgeny, too, dreamed of marrying, but not in the way his mother envisaged it. He found her view of marriage as a means of setting his financial affairs in order a repellent one. He wanted to marry honourably, for the sake of love. As it was, he eyed the girls he knew, and those who came his way, and tried to imagine what it would be like to be married to one of them, but so far nothing had come of it. Meanwhile, to his considerable surprise, he found that his relations with Stepanida showed no signs of abating; indeed, they were even acquiring a certain degree of steadiness. So far was Yevgeny from being a libertine, so ashamed had he been of performing that secret and, he sensed, ignoble act, that on no account could he bring himself to make arrangements to repeat it. After that first rendezvous he had rather hoped he would never see Stepanida again. It turned out, however, that after a while he was once more overtaken by the restlessness he ascribed to that cause. But this time the restlessness was not an anonymous one: into his consciousness this time floated those same black, brilliant eyes, that same low voice, saying 'ever so long', that same smell of something fresh and strong, and those same high breasts lifting up the apron, and all of this in that thicket of hazels and maples, awash with vivid light. In spite of the shame he felt, he went to see Danila again. And a second midday rendezvous in the woods was arranged. This time Yevgeny managed to get a better look at her, and everything about her seemed appealing to him. He tried to engage her in conversation a little, asked her about her husband. As he had thought, her husband was Mikhaila's son, and lived in Moscow where he was employed as a coachman.

'But look here, I mean, how is it you can . . .' Yevgeny was about to ask how she could be unfaithful to him like this.

'How is it I can what?' she asked. She was obviously intelligent and quick off the mark.

'Well, how is it you can make love with me like this?'

'Oh, that,' she said, full of high spirits. 'I'm pretty sure he gets his fun over there. Why shouldn't I have mine, too?'

She was obviously putting on this display of pertness and bravado especially for his benefit, and he found it charming. Even so, he could not bring himself to make another rendezvous with her. Not even when she suggested they might meet without involving Danila, towards whom she seemed somewhat coolly disposed, did he give his assent. He was hoping that this meeting would be their last. He found her appealing. He thought that such intercourse was a necessity for him, and that there was nothing wrong in it; deep within him, however, sat a sterner judge who did not approve and who hoped this was going to be the last time – or, if he did not hope that, at least did not wish to be party to the arrangement and did not want to make preparations to repeat it.

In this way the entire summer went by; during its course they met on perhaps a dozen occasions, each time through the mediation of Danila. There was one time when she was unable to show up because her husband had arrived back from town, and Danila suggested another woman. Yevgeny refused with disgust. Then her husband went back to town again, and their rendezvous continued. Initially it was all done through Danila, but later on Danila would merely fix a time, and Stepanida would make her way to the rendezvous in the company of a woman called Prokhorova, as married peasant women were not allowed to go around on their own. Once, at the very time for which one such rendezvous had been arranged, a family came to visit Yevgeny's mother, bringing with them the one girl she really wanted for her son, and there was no way that he could escape. When at last he managed to get away, he made as though for the barn, and then took the path round through the woods to the place where they were to meet. She was not there. However, in the place where they usually made love, all the shrubs and saplings – the bird-cherry, the hazel, even the young maple as thick as a fence-post – had been snapped and broken. She had waited, become worked up and angry, and had playfully left this for him as a reminder. He stood around for a while, then for a while longer, and finally went off to see Danila in order to ask him to tell her to come the following day. She did, and was just the same as ever.

Thus the summer went by. It was always in the woods that they arranged to meet. Only once, when autumn was approaching, did they meet in the barn that stood in Stepanida's back yard. It never entered Yevgeny's head that this relationship might be important to him in any way. Stepanida – he never thought about her. He gave her money, and that was that. What he didn't know and didn't suspect was that the entire village knew about the affair, that she was the object of envy, that her people at home were taking money from her and egging her on, and that all her ideas of right and wrong had been completely undermined by the influence of money and family. The way she saw it was that if people were envious of her then what she was doing must be all right.

'It's only for the sake of my health,' Yevgeny told himself. 'I know it isn't right, and even if no one's saying anything, they all, or at least some of them, know about it. The woman who comes with her knows. And since she knows, she's bound to have told others. But what can I do about it? I know I'm behaving badly,' he would say to himself, 'but what am I supposed to do? Anyway, it's not going to be for very long.'

Yevgeny's main worry was Stepanida's husband. For some reason he felt at first that her husband must be a sorry-looking fellow, and that this to a certain extent justified his behaviour. But then one day he saw the husband and was quite taken aback. The husband was a handsome, well-dressed man who looked no worse than he did, and probably even better. When he next met Stepanida he told her he had seen her husband and had been most impressed by his fine appearance.

'There isn't another man like him in all the village,' she said with pride.

This surprised Yevgeny. From then on, the thought of the husband started to worry him even more. Once, when he happened to be at Danila's hut, Danila said to him in the course of conversation: 'Mikhaila was asking me the other day: is it true the young master's living with my son's wife? I said I didn't know. Well, I said, better the master than some muzhik.'

'And what did he say?'

' "Oh, it's all right," he said. "Just wait, though, I'll find out what's going on, and then I'll give her what for." '

'Well, if her husband came back I'd give her up,' thought Yevgeny. But the husband went on living in town, and for the time being their relationship continued. 'When I have to, I'll break it off, and that'll be that,' he thought.

This seemed to him beyond all doubt. His certainty had much to do with the fact that during the summer he was intensely preoccupied with various matters: the layout of the new farmhouse, the harvest, the building work and, above all, the payment of the debts and the sale of the vacant land. These were things that absorbed him to the exclusion of all else; they occupied his thoughts all day, from the time he got up in the morning till the time he went to bed at night. They represented the life that was real. His relations – he did not even use the word 'affair' – with Stepanida were, on the other hand, something of very little account. It was true that when he was taken by the desire to see her, it was so overwhelming that he couldn't think of anything else. But this was of short duration: a rendezvous was arranged, and afterwards he would forget about her for weeks on end, sometimes even as long as a month.

That autumn Yevgeny had to make frequent trips to the town, and it was there that he made the acquaintance of the Annensky family. The Annenskys had a daughter who had just finished a course at a young ladies' institute. To the great chagrin of Marya Pavlovna, it came about that her son, as she put it, 'cheapened himself' by falling in love with Liza Annenskaya and asking for her hand in marriage.

After that his relations with Stepanida came to an end.

V

In the way that it is always impossible to say why a man chooses one woman rather than another, so it is impossible to say why Yevgeny chose Liza Annenskaya. There were all sorts of reasons, both positive and negative. One reason was that she was not the very rich girl his mother wanted him to marry; another was that towards her own mother she displayed an attitude of naive helplessness; yet another was that while she was no self-advertising beauty, she was not bad-looking either. The principal reason was, however, that Yevgeny had come to know her just at a time when he was ready to marry. He fell in love because he knew he was going to get married.

At first he had merely taken a fancy towards Liza Annenskaya; but once he had made up his mind that she was to be his wife, he conceived a much stronger emotion towards her: he felt he was in love with her.

Liza was tall, slender and long. Everything about her was long: her face, her nose, which pointed not outwards but downwards, her fingers and her feet. The colour of her face was very delicate, yellowy-white with a soft glow; her hair was long, soft, light brown and curly, and she had beautiful eyes that were clear, gentle and artless. These eyes made a particular impression on Yevgeny, and whenever he thought of Liza he saw them looking at him – clear, gentle and artless.

Such was her physical appearance. He knew nothing of what she was like as a person – all he could see was those eyes. They told him everything he needed to know. And what they told him was this.

Ever since, at the age of fifteen, she had started at her institute, Liza had consistently fallen in love with all the attractive men who had come her way, and had only been happy when she was in love. When she had left the institute she had continued to fall in love with all the young men she had met and, needless to say, had fallen in love with Yevgeny on her very first acquaintance with him. It was this susceptibility that gave her eyes the curious expression which so fascinated Yevgeny.

That particular winter she had already fallen in love with two young men at the same time, thrilling with excitement not only whenever they came into the room, but whenever their names were mentioned. When, however, her mother let it drop that Irtenev might have serious intentions towards her, so infatuated with him did she immediately become that she almost stopped thinking about the other two; and when Irtenev started to attend their balls and social gatherings, danced with her more than he did with the other girls, and only seemed to be interested in whether she loved him or not, her infatuation with him became positively morbid – she had dreams about him and fancied she saw him in her room at night, and all other men ceased to have any significance for her. But when he proposed to her, and their planned union received its blessing, when they kissed and were formally betrothed, she had no desire other than to be with him, to love him and be loved by him. She was proud of him, was touched and moved by him and by herself, and by her love for him. The better he got to know her, the more he returned her love. He had never expected to encounter such a love, and it made his own feelings all the more powerful.

VI

At the onset of spring he went to Semyonovskoye in order to take a look round and give instructions concerning the running of the estate, with particular regard to the house, which was being redecorated in preparation for the wedding.

Marya Pavlovna was unhappy about the choice her son had made, but only because the match was not as brilliant as it could have been, and because she disliked Varvara Alekseyevna, Yevgeny's future mother-in-law. She had no idea of whether Varvara Alekseyevna was a nice person or not, and she had not given the matter any reflection. She had, however, perceived at their very first meeting that Varvara Alekseyevna was not a woman of social distinction, not *comme il faut*, not a lady, as Marya Pavlovna expressed it to herself, and this vexed her bitterly. It vexed her because she set great store by social distinction; she knew that Yevgeny, too, was very sensitive in this regard, and foresaw no end of problems arising from it. On the other hand, she did like the girl. She liked her mainly because Yevgeny did. She had to like her. And Marya Pavlovna was quite prepared to do so and be completely sincere about it.

Yevgeny found his mother in a state of joyful happiness. She was putting the house in order and had intended to leave as soon as her son arrived with his young wife-to-be. Yevgeny urged her to stay. And the issue remained unresolved. In the evening, after tea, Marya Pavlovna played her usual game of patience. Yevgeny sat with her and took an interest in the game. This was the time of day when they had their most intimate chats with one another. As she was finishing one game of patience, and before beginning another, Marya Pavlovna gave Yevgeny a quick look and began, somewhat hesitantly, 'Oh, there was something I've been meaning to say to you, Zhenya. Of course I don't know anything about it, but as a general rule I'd advise you that before you marry it's absolutely essential that you wind up all your bachelor affairs, so that nothing can upset you or, pray God, your wife. Do you understand what I mean?'

And indeed, Yevgeny was not slow to gather that Marya Pavlovna was alluding to his relations with Stepanida, which had come to an end as long ago as the previous autumn, and that, as lonely women are prone to do, she ascribed a far greater importance to those relations than what they had actually possessed. Yevgeny went rather red in the face, not so much from embarrassment as out of annoyance that his dear, kind mother should go meddling – even if it was only out of love for him – in things that were none of her business, things she did not and could not possibly understand. He said he had nothing to hide, and had always taken care to behave in such a way that there could never be anything to interfere with his marriage.

'Well, my dear, that's wonderful news. Please, Zhenya, don't be angry with me,' said Marya Pavlovna in embarrassment.

But Yevgeny could see that she hadn't finished, and had not said what she really wanted to say. Such indeed proved to be the case. After a little while she began to tell him how, when he had been away, she had been asked to be a godmother by . . . the Pchelnikovs.

This time it was not annoyance nor even embarrassment that made Yevgeny go red in the face, but a strange presentiment of the importance of what he was about to be told, an involuntary recognition that ran quite counter to his normal way of thinking. It was as he expected. As if she were simply making pleasant conversation, Marya Pavlovna happened to mention that this year all the women in the village seemed to be having boys, and that this must mean there was going to be a war soon. The young Vasin woman and the young Pchelnikov woman had both had their first children recently, and both had been boys. Marya Pavlovna had meant to slip this in casually, but when she saw how red in the face her son had gone and observed the nervous way in which he removed his pince-nez, gave it a flick, put it back on his nose again and hurriedly lit a cigarette, she herself grew embarrassed. She fell silent. He too said nothing, unable to think of anything with which to break the silence. That was how they knew that each had understood the other.

'Yes, the main thing is that there should be fair dealing in the village, and no favourites, as there were in your grandfather's day.'

'Mother,' said Yevgeny all of a sudden, 'I know why you're saying this. You're worrying your head over nothing. My marriage is so sacred to me that there's nothing for which I'd ever put it in jeopardy. Anything that may have happened when I was a bachelor is all over and done with now. I never got involved in any serious affairs, and there's no woman who's entitled to anything from me.'

'Well, I'm glad to hear it,' said his mother. 'I know how fastidious you are in such matters.'

Yevgeny interpreted these words of his mother's as a tribute that was his due, and made no reply.

Next morning he set off for town, his head full of his bride-to-be, or anything at.all, in fact, except Stepanida. But almost as if it had been planned that way in order to remind him of her, as he drove up to the church he started meeting people who were going home from it on foot and in carriages. He met the old man Matvey with his son Semyon, some young lads and girls, and then two married women; one of these women was rather older than the other, who was smartly dressed and wearing a bright red kerchief, and who looked vaguely familiar. She was walking along lightly and cheerfully, carrying a baby in her arms. As he drew level with them, the older woman stopped short and bowed to him in the old-fashioned way, while the younger one with the baby merely inclined her head; from under the kerchief he caught the brilliance of smiling, merry eyes that were familiar to him.

'Yes, it's her, but that's all over now, and there's no point in giving her a second glance. And the child's probably mine,' flashed through his mind. 'No, that's all rot. She had a husband, she used to make love with him, too.' He did not even bother to start doing the necessary calculations, so firmly was it implanted in his head that it had been necessary for his health, that he had paid his money, and that had been that;

there was no bond of any kind between her and himself, there
never had been, nor could there or must there ever be. It was
not a matter of him suppressing the voice of his conscience;
no, it was simply that his conscience had nothing to tell him.
And after the talk he had had with his mother, and this
encounter, he dropped her completely from his mind. Nor did
he encounter her again.

The week after Easter, Yevgeny and Liza were married in
town. They left for Semyonovskoye immediately after the
wedding. The arrangements at the house were of the kind
usually made for a young couple. Marya Pavlovna wanted to
leave, but they both – Liza, especially – prevailed upon her to
stay. So instead of leaving, she merely moved into one of the
annexes.

And so for Yevgeny a new life began.

VII

The first year of Yevgeny's marriage was a difficult one. It was
difficult because after the wedding all the business to do with
the estate which he had somehow managed to put off dealing
with during his courtship now suddenly descended on him.

It was going to be impossible for them to free themselves
from all the debts. The dacha had been sold, and the major
debts paid; yet there still remained debts outstanding, and
there was no money with which to meet them. The estate
brought in a fair amount, but he had had to send some of that
money to his brother, and then on top of that there had been
all the expense of the wedding, which had left them with
hardly any ready cash at all; the sugar factory would be unable
to operate and would have to be closed down. The only way
out of this mess was for him to use his wife's money. When
she discovered the plight her husband was in, Liza herself
insisted he do this. Yevgeny gave his consent, but only on
condition that they took out a deed of purchase on half of the
estate in her name. He did this not for his wife's sake, needless
to say – she found it rather offensive – but in order to placate

his mother-in-law. These concerns, with their varying alter-
nations of success and failure, were one of the things that
poisoned Yevgeny's life during that first year. Another was
his wife's ill health. In the autumn of that same first year,
seven months after the wedding, Liza had an unpleasant
accident. She had taken the charabanc out to meet her husband,
who was returning from town. The horse, normally a very
docile creature, had suddenly started to frisk and prance; she
had taken fright and had jumped out. The jump had been a
relatively lucky one – a wheel might have caught her – but she
was pregnant, and that same night the pains started. She had
a miscarriage, and it took her a long time to recover from it.
The loss of the expected child, his wife's illness, the attendant
upset to his routine and, more than anything else, the presence
of his mother-in-law, who had arrived the moment Liza had
been taken ill – all this made the year even more trying for
Yevgeny.

Despite all these trying circumstances, however, towards
the end of the first year Yevgeny began to feel better. For one
thing, the aim he had set himself of reconstituting his family's
fortune and reviving in a new form the sort of life that had
been led on the estate in his grandfather's day was, albeit
slowly and with difficulty, in the process of being achieved.
Now there could be no more talk of their having to sell the
whole estate in order to meet their debts. The most important
part of the estate – even if it had been transferred to his
wife's name – had been saved, and as long as the beet harvest
was a good one and the prices favourable, in the new year
they could expect their situation of tension and economic
need to give way to one of complete prosperity. There was
that for a start.

The other thing was that, however much he had expected of
his wife, he had never expected to find in her what he had in
fact discovered. Not only was this not what he had expected
– it was far better. Tender scenes, ecstatic expressions of
affection – these there had not been, or only very mutedly,
even though he had tried to arrange them. What there had
been was something quite different: life had not only become

more cheerful, more pleasant – it had become easier. He had no idea why this should be, but it was so.

The reason was that immediately after the wedding Liza had made up her mind that Yevgeny Irtenev was the loftiest, cleverest, purest and most noble man in the whole world, and that it was therefore incumbent upon everyone to serve him and do whatever was pleasing to him. But since it was impossible to make everyone do this, she was going to have to do it herself, as far as she could. So she did, and all her emotional energy went into finding out and guessing what he wanted, and then doing it, no matter what it was or how difficult it might be.

She possessed, too, what constitutes the principal charm of association with a loving woman: the ability, derived from her love for her husband, to see into his innermost thoughts. She perceived – often, he used to think, better than he himself did – his slightest change of mood, his slightest inflection of feeling, and adapted her behaviour accordingly. So it was that she never gave him cause for offence, but invariably exerted a moderating influence on his depressions and a heightening one on his moods of elation. And it was not only his feelings she understood, but also his thoughts. She had an instant understanding of matters one might have thought would have been completely alien to her – agricultural problems, for instance, or questions to do with the factory and the assessment of personnel – and she was not only able to chat with him about all this, but often, as he himself said, to be a useful and irreplaceable adviser to him about it all. She viewed people, objects and everything else in the world exclusively through his eyes. She loved her mother, but when she saw that Yevgeny disliked her mother's interference in their lives, she immediately took her husband's part, and went about it with such determination that he had to chide her for it.

In addition to all this, she possessed an enormous amount of tact and good sense. Most important of all, she had about her an air of silent calm. Everything she did, she did so it was not noticed; all that could be observed were the results of her industry; cleanliness, order and elegance in all things. Liza had understood at once what the ideal of her husband's life consisted of, and she strove to attain, and by the orderly way in which she ran the house indeed did attain the very things he wanted. As yet they had no children, but of that, too, there were hopes. That winter they took a trip to St Petersburg, where they consulted an obstetrician who assured them that Liza was in perfect health and that there was absolutely nothing to prevent her having children.

This dream, too, was realized. Towards the end of the year she became pregnant again.

The one thing that . . . poisoned would be too strong a word, let us say threatened their happy life together was her jealousy. She kept it in check and did not display it, but she suffered from it frequently. It was not simply that Yevgeny could not love anyone else, because there was no woman on earth who was worthy of him (the question of whether she herself was worthy of him did not arise) – it was that, for this same reason, no woman might dare to love him.

VIII

This was the pattern of their daily lives: he would get up early, as he always did, and make himself busy about the estate, paying a visit to the factory where work would already be in progress, and sometimes going out into the fields. When it got round to ten o'clock he would come back to the house for coffee, which he had on the terrace in the company of Liza, Marya Pavlovna and an uncle who lived with them. After conversation – which was often quite heated – over coffee, they would go their separate ways until it was time for dinner. They dined at two. Afterwards they might take a walk or go out for a drive. In the evening, when he came back from the estate office, they would have a late glass of tea together, and sometimes he would read aloud while she worked, or, if guests were present, there would be chamber music or conversation. If he went away on a business trip somewhere he would write her a letter and receive one from her every day. Sometimes she would travel along with him, and then they would have a particularly happy time. On their name days they would have guests to the house, and he would derive pleasure from her talent for seeing that everyone had an enjoyable time. He would see and hear that everyone was full of admiration for her, this young, charming hostess, and he loved her for it all the more. Everything was going swimmingly. She bore her pregnancy with ease and they both began, if somewhat timidly, to make plans about the way they would rear their child. The method of upbringing, the principles to be applied in it – all this was in Yevgeny's hands. Her only desire was to carry out his wishes obediently. Yevgeny even started to dip into medical textbooks, and had every intention of rearing his child according to all the precepts of medical science. It went without saying that she was in complete agreement with everything he told her; she began to sew up 'warm' and 'cold' swaddling blankets, and got a cradle ready. Thus began the second year of their marriage, and the second year they had spent together.

IX

It was just before Whitsun. Liza was in the fifth month of her pregnancy and, although she was being careful, she was cheerful and active. Both their mothers were staying with them under the pretext of being there to keep an eye on her and look after her, and were, needless to say, only succeeding in making her thoroughly nervous by their constant bickering. Yevgeny had taken up farming with particular zeal, and was completely immersed in the details of a new large-scale processing technique for sugar-beet.

Just before Whitsun, Liza decided that the house would have to be given a thorough cleaning, which it had not had since Easter, and she called in two charwomen to help the servants wash the floors and the windows, beat the furniture and carpets, and spread loose covers over everything. The charwomen arrived early in the morning, put their iron cauldrons of water on to heat, and set to work. One of the women was Stepanida, who had recently weaned her little boy and had gone pestering the estate clerk, with whom she was now having an affair, to let her do cleaning work up at the house. She wanted to get a good look at the new mistress. Stepanida was living alone, as previously, without her husband, and she had had a series of affairs, first with Danila, who had caught her stealing firewood, then with Yevgeny, and now with this young lad, the clerk. Of Yevgeny she had no thoughts whatsoever. 'He's got a wife now,' she said to herself. 'But it'll be fun to see the mistress, and the way she's running the house; they say she's had it done up really nicely.'

Yevgeny had not seen her since that day he had met her with her child. Since she had had the baby to look after, she had not been doing any work, and he seldom passed through the village. That morning, the day before the Whit holiday, he got up early, at five a.m., and set off to visit a field which was lying fallow and was due to be spread with phosphorite. He left the house before the charwomen came in, while they were still busy out at the stove with their cauldrons.

Cheerful, satisfied and with a good appetite, Yevgeny came back to the house to have his breakfast. At the gate he dismounted from his horse and, having given it into the charge of a gardener who happened to be passing, he walked the remaining distance to the house, swiping at the tall grass with his whip and, in the way that people often do, repeating to himself something he had said not long ago. The words he kept repeating were 'Phosphorite will repay'; but what or whom they would repay, he neither knew nor greatly cared.

Someone was beating a carpet on the lawn. All the furniture had been carried out of the house. 'Good Lord! What a cleaning Liza's organized! Phosphorite will repay. There's a wife for you. Yes, a wife among wives,' he said to himself, quickly summoning up a mental picture of her in her white housecoat, her face radiant with happiness, as it nearly always seemed to be whenever he saw her. 'Yes, I'd better change my boots, or else that phosphorite will repay, or smell like manure, rather, and my wife's in that way of hers again. What way might that be? Ah yes, another little Irtenev's growing inside her,' he thought. 'Yes, phosphorite will repay.' And, smiling at his own thoughts, he made to push open the door of his study.

But no sooner had he started to apply pressure to the door than it seemed to open of its own accord, and he collided face to face with a woman who was coming towards him carrying a bucket; she had tucked up her skirt, she was barefoot, and her sleeves were rolled up as high as they would go. He moved to one side to let her past, but she also moved to one side, adjusting her kerchief, which had been knocked askew, with the back of a wet hand.

'Come along, I won't go in, if you . . .' Yevgeny began; then suddenly, recognizing her, he stopped.

She glanced at him with eyes that were merrily smiling. Then, untucking her skirt so that it covered her legs, she went out through the doorway.

'What nonsense is this? What on earth? . . . It can't be true!' said Yevgeny to himself, giving his head a toss as though to drive away a fly, annoyed with himself for having noticed her. In spite of his annoyance, however, he could not take his eyes off her body as it swayed to the rhythm of her supple and powerful walk, off her bare feet, her arms, her shoulders, the attractive folds of her chemise and her red peasant skirt, which was tucked up high above her white calves.

'And what am I looking at her for, anyway?' he wondered, and he lowered his eyes so as not to see her. 'Yes, I'll have to go in as if nothing had happened, and fetch another pair of boots.' He turned and faced his room again, but had hardly gone five paces into it when, not knowing why or on whose command, he looked round once more in order to catch another glimpse of her. At that moment she was turning the corner of the passage, and as she did so she also looked round to get a glimpse of him.

'Oh! What am I doing?' he exclaimed inwardly. 'She'll only get ideas into her head. In fact, she's probably got them already.'

He went into his wet study. Another woman, old and emaciated, was still in there, scrubbing. Yevgeny tiptoed his way across the dirty puddles towards the wall, where his other pair of boots was. He was just about to go out again when the woman herself left.

'Now she's gone, the other one, Stepanida, will come back – on her own,' someone inside him started to predict.

'Oh God! What am I thinking of, what am I doing?' He grabbed his boots and ran with them out into the hallway; there he put them on, brushed himself down and went on to the terrace where both mothers were already sitting having their coffee. Liza had obviously been waiting for him, and she came out on to the terrace at the same time as he did, but through a different door.

'Oh God, if only she knew, she who thinks I'm so honest, so pure, so innocent, if only she knew!' he thought.

Liza greeted him as always, with a radiant countenance. Today, however, he thought she looked somehow especially pale and yellow, long and weak.

X

Over coffee, as often happened, there was one of those conversations, peculiar to ladies, in which there is no logical connecting thread whatsoever, but which are evidently held together by something, as they go on interminably.

The two ladies were exchanging barbed remarks with one another, and Liza was artfully manoeuvring between them.

'I'm awfully sorry we didn't manage to finish cleaning your room for you before you got back,' she said to her husband. 'It's just all the clearing out there is to do.'

'Well, how are you? Did you manage to get some sleep after I left?'

'Yes, I slept. I feel fine.'

'How can a woman in her condition possibly feel fine in this unbearable heat when all the windows in her house face straight into the sun?' said Varvara Alekseyevna, Liza's mother. 'And not a screen or an awning anywhere. I always had awnings.'

'But the terrace is in the shade from ten o'clock onwards,' said Marya Pavlovna.

'That's the way to catch a chill, sitting in the damp,' said Varvara Alekseyevna, quite oblivious to the fact that this completely contradicted what she had just finished saying. 'My doctor always says that you can never diagnose an illness if you don't know the character of the patient. And he knows, believe me; he's a leading physician and we pay him a hundred rubles a visit. My late husband didn't hold much with doctors, but he never spared any expense for my sake.'

'How can a man spare expense on the woman he's married when her life and that of their child may depend . . . ?'

'Well, of course, if she's got money she doesn't have to depend on her husband so much. But a good wife defers to her husband in all matters,' said Varvara Alekseyevna. 'Liza's simply still rather weak after her illness, that's all.'

'Oh no, mother, I feel absolutely fine. Haven't they given you any boiled cream?'

'I don't want it. Fresh cream will do.'

'I did ask Varvara Alekseyevna if she wanted any. She said she didn't,' said Marya Pavlovna, as if in self-justification.

'That's right, I don't want any.' And, in order to bring this awkward conversation to a close, and as if she were making some magnanimous concession, Varvara Alekseyevna turned to Yevgeny and asked him: 'Well, and so have you finished spreading those phosphates?'

Liza went dashing off to fetch the boiled cream.

'But I don't want any, I don't want any.'

'Liza! Liza! Not so quickly, dear,' said Marya Pavlovna. 'Those quick movements are so bad for her.'

'There's nothing will do her any harm as long as her mind's at rest,' said Varvara Alekseyevna, as though hinting at something, even though she knew perfectly well that there was nothing to hint at.

Liza returned with the cream. Yevgeny sipped his coffee and listened gloomily. He was used to this kind of conversation, but today he found its absurdity particularly irritating.

He wanted to reflect on what had just happened to him, and this empty prattle was getting in the way. Having finished her coffee, Varvara Alekseyevna left the terrace in a worse frame of mind than she had been in before. Liza, Yevgeny and Marya Pavlovna stayed on, and their conversation was simple and pleasant. Even so, Liza, whom love had rendered more sensitive, noticed at once that something was troubling Yevgeny, and she asked him if he had something on his mind. He had not been prepared for this question, and he answered somewhat hesitantly, saying it was nothing. This reply made Liza ponder even more. There was something troubling him, and troubling him very deeply; that was as plain to her as the fact that a fly had landed in the milk. But he would not tell her what it was.

XI

After breakfast they all attended to their separate tasks. Yevgeny, according to a time-honoured habit, went off to his study. There, instead of getting on with the business of reading and writing letters, he sat down and began to smoke one cigarette after another as he turned things over in his mind. He had been shocked and upset by the reawakening within him of the unclean feeling from which, since the time of his marriage, he had believed himself to be immune. Since his wedding, he had never once experienced that feeling either for Stepanida or for any other woman apart from his wife. On many occasions now he had felt a profound relief at this sense of immunity, yet now this one seemingly trivial incident had revealed to him that he was not immune after all. What troubled and tormented him now was not that he had given into this feeling, that he desired her – he did not even want to think about that – but that the feeling was alive in him and that he would have to be on his guard against it. He had not the slightest doubt that he would succeed in conquering it.

He had one letter to answer, and a document to draw up. He

sat down at his writing-desk and began to work. By the time he had finished, he had forgotten all about what had been worrying him, and he went outside with the intention of visiting the stables. But again, as ill luck would have it – he did not know whether it was by accident or design – no sooner had he emerged on to the porch than a red peasant skirt and a red kerchief came round the corner, and she walked past him, swinging her arms and swaying her hips. Not only that – once she had gone by, she started to run almost playfully, and caught up her female companion.

Once again it all rose in his imagination: the brilliant noon, the nettles and, in the shade of the maples behind Danila's hut, her smiling face as she bit some leaves.

'No, I can't let it go on like this,' he told himself. He waited until the women were out of sight, and then went over to the office. It was right in the middle of the dinner-break, and he hoped he might catch the estate manager there. He did. The estate manager had just woken up from his nap. He was standing in the office, stretching, yawning and surveying the cattleman, who was saying something to him.

'Vasily Nikolayevich!'

'At your service, sir.'

'I want to have a word with you.'

'At your service, sir.'

'Finish your business with the cattleman first.'

'Can't you just carry it?' said Vasily Nikolayevich to the cattleman.

'It's too heavy, Vasily Nikolayevich.'

'What's he talking about?' asked Yevgeny.

'Oh, a cow's gone and had her calf out in the fields,' said Vasily Nikolayevich. 'Well, all right, then, I'll have a horse harnessed up right away. Tell Nikolay Lysukh to get an open cart ready.'

The cattleman went off.

'Well, you see, it's like this,' began Yevgeny, blushing and conscious of doing so. 'It's like this, Vasily Nikolayevich. When I was a bachelor here, I did a few things I shouldn't have . . . Maybe you've heard? . . .'

Vasily Nikolayevich smiled with his eyes and, obviously feeling sorry for his master, said: 'Is it about Stepashka, sir?'

'Well yes, it is. Look, this is what I wanted to say to you. Please, please don't hire her to do cleaning work up at the house. You must understand that it puts me in a very difficult situation . . .'

'Yes, I think you've got Vanka the clerk to thank for that, sir.'

'So please . . . Well, and are they going to spread the rest of the phosphorite today?' asked Yevgeny, in order to cover up his embarrassment.

'Yes, I'm just off to see to it now, sir.'

And there the matter rested. Yevgeny regained his calm, in the hope that since he had gone for a whole year without seeing her, things would continue like that. 'Besides, Vasily will tell Ivan the clerk, Ivan will tell her, and she'll realize I don't want her in the house,' he told himself, and was glad he had summoned up the courage to have a word with Vasily, however hard it had been for him to do so. 'Anything, anything's better than that uncertainty, that shame.' He shuddered at the mere recollection of the crime he had committed in his thoughts.

XII

It had cost Yevgeny a certain moral effort to overcome his sense of shame and tell Vasily Nikolayevich about what was troubling him. The effort had brought him calm. Now he felt that everything was all right again. Liza noticed at once that he seemed quite to have regained his composure and that ne even appeared to be in a better mood than usual. 'It was probably our mothers getting at one another that upset him,' she thought. 'It really is a bit much, especially for a sensitive, high-minded man like him, constantly to be exposed to those hostile, vulgar hints at nothing in particular.'

The following day was Whit Sunday. The weather was glorious, and according to custom the women of the village went into the woods to wreathe garlands for themselves; on their way there they came up to the big house and began to sing and perform dances. Marya Pavlovna and Varvara Alekseyevna came out on to the porch dressed in fine clothes and carrying parasols, and went down to stand near the circle of dancers. This year the two women were accompanied by one of Yevgeny's uncles, a corpulent lecher with a weakness for alcohol, who was spending the summer at the house; he was wearing a little Chinese tunic.

As always, a gaily coloured circle of young married women and unmarried girls, vivid with flowers, formed the central axis, around which in succession and from every side, like planets and satellites that had torn themselves free of it and were now in orbit around it, went girls holding hands, rustling the new silk of their peasant gowns, young boys sniggering at something and chasing one another to and fro, older lads in red shirts, black long-waisted coats and black caps, keeping up an incessant spatter of sunflower-seed husks, and the manor serfs and bystanders looking on from a distance. The two ladies went right up to the circle. They were followed by Liza, who was wearing a light-blue dress and had ribbons of the same colour and material in her hair; the dress had wide sleeves that exposed her long, white arms and her angular elbows.

Yevgeny did not really want to go out, but it would have looked odd for him to hide himself away. He too came out on to the porch, smoking a cigarette; he exchanged greetings with the lads and muzhiks and had a brief conversation with one man. All the while the peasant women continued to yell out a dance tune at the tops of their voices, snapping their fingers, clapping their hands and dancing.

'The lady of the house is calling you, sir,' said a young boy, coming over to Yevgeny, who had not been able to hear his wife's voice above the din. Liza wanted him to come and watch the dancing of one of the peasant women she thought looked particularly charming. It was Stepanida. She was dressed in a yellow skirt, a sleeveless cotton-velvet jacket and a silk kerchief; she was wide-hipped, energetic, flushed and elated. No doubt she was dancing wonderfully. He saw nothing of it.

'Well, well,' he said, taking off his pince-nez and putting it back on his nose again. 'Well, well,' he thought. 'So I'm not going to get away from her, after all.'

He could not bring himself to look at her, as he was afraid of her attractiveness. For that very same reason, in the brief glimpse he had of her she seemed to him particularly attractive. What was more, he could tell from the way her eyes had flashed that she had seen him and seen that he was enthralled by her. He remained there just as long as good manners dictated and then, having seen Varvara Alekseyevna summon Stepanida to her side and address her rather awkwardly and artificially, calling her 'my dear', turned away and went back to the house. He had left so as to avoid seeing her, yet as he reached the house's top storey, not knowing why he did it, not even aware of doing it, he found himself going to a window. For as long as the peasant women remained below the porch, he stood at that window and looked and looked at her, feeding his eyes on her.

Before anyone could catch sight of him, he ran downstairs and quietly went out on to the balcony. There he lit a cigarette and, as if he merely had the intention of taking a walk, set off into the garden following the direction she had taken. He had hardly gone a couple of yards along the path when behind some trees he caught a glimpse of a cotton velvet jacket against a pink skirt and a red kerchief. She was going off somewhere with another woman. Where could they be going?

Suddenly he was burned by a terrible lust that gripped hold of him like a hand. As if in obedience to some alien will, he looked round and went towards her.

'Yevgeny Ivanych, Yevgeny Ivanych! May I have a word with your honour?' came a voice from behind him. Yevgeny saw that it was the old man Samokhin, who was digging a well on his land. Turning quickly, he went back towards Samokhin. As he talked to him, he looked to one side and saw

Stepanida and the other woman going down the hill, evidently to the well or at least with the well as a pretext. They stayed by the well for a short time, and then went back to the dancing.

XIII

When he had finished talking to Samokhin, Yevgeny returned to the house. He felt completely crushed, like someone who has committed a crime. It was perfectly obvious that she had read his mind, knew that he wanted to see her, and wanted it herself. What made it even worse was that the other woman – this Anna Prokhorova – clearly knew what was going on.

What he felt more than anything else was that he had been beaten, that he no longer had any will of his own, that he was being propelled along by some force that was extraneous to him. He felt that today he had only been saved by a lucky chance, and that if not today, then tomorrow, or the day after, he would be ruined.

'Yes, ruined.' There was no other way of putting it. 'To be unfaithful to one's young and loving wife with a peasant woman from the village, for everyone to see, is that not ruin, the most terrible ruin, after which life must cease to be possible? No, I must act, I must do something.

'Oh God! God! What can I do? Am I really to go to my ruin like this?' he said to himself. 'Is there really nothing I can do? There must be something. You mustn't think about her,' he ordered himself. 'You mustn't!' And immediately he began to think about her, saw her in front of him, in the shade of the maples.

He recalled once having read about a *starets*, a holy man, who when faced with the holy duty of laying his hand on a woman in order to cure her had, in order to ward off temptation, placed his other hand in a brazier and burned his fingers to ash. He reflected on this. 'Yes, I'd sooner burn my fingers to ash than be ruined.' And, taking a quick look round to make sure there was no one else in the room, he lit a match and put his finger in the flame. 'Right, now think about her,'

he said to himself, ironically. He started to feel pain, withdrew
his soot-blackened finger, threw the match away, and laughed
at himself. 'What rot. This isn't what I ought to be doing. What
I ought to be doing is making sure I never see her again – I
ought either to go away myself or make arrangements for her
to go away. Offer her husband money to move to town or to
another village. People would find out, the word would get
around. So what, anything would be better than this constant
risk. Yes, that's what I must do,' he told himself, continuing to
watch her from the window. 'Where's she going now?' he
wondered, suddenly. He had a feeling she had seen him at the
window. She was going off in the direction of the garden, arm
in arm with some other woman, letting her free arm swing
briskly as she went. Without knowing why or for what
purpose, allowing his thoughts to take over, he went along to
the estate office.

Vasily Nikolayevich, wearing his Sunday best, his hair
sleeked with pomade, was sitting in the office having tea with
his wife and a female visitor in a carpet shawl.

'I wonder if I might have a word with you for a moment,
Vasily Nikolayevich?'

'Why, certainly, sir. Go right ahead. We've finished our tea.'

'No, I think it would be better if you came outside with me.'

'Just as you wish, sir. Wait till I get my cap. You can let the
samovar go out now, Tanya,' said Vasily Nikolayevich gaily as
he went outside.

Yevgeny thought Vasily Nikolayevich looked as though he
had been drinking, but there wasn't anything to be done about
that; anyway, it might even help matters – make Vasily
Nikolayevich more sympathetic.

'It's the same thing I was telling you about last time,' said
Yevgeny. 'It's that woman.'

'What? I told them on no account should they hire her.'

'No, it isn't that. You see, what I've been thinking, and what
I wanted to ask your advice about, was whether it wouldn't be
possible to have them move, have the whole family move?'

'Where would you have them move to?' asked Vasily, in a
displeased, mocking tone of voice, Yevgeny thought.

'Well, I thought I might give them some money, or even a bit of land at Koltovskoye – anything, so long as she isn't here.'

'But how would you ever get them to move? It would mean him having to tear up his roots. And what's it to you? What harm has she ever done to you?'

'Oh, Vasily Nikolayevich, surely you must understand what a dreadful thing it would be for my wife if she were ever to find out about this.'

'But who's going to tell her?'

'And how can I go on living in this constant fear? Anyway, the whole business is just too awful for words.'

'I don't know what you're getting so worked up about, sir, truly I don't. You must allow bygones to be bygones. Let him that is without sin . . .'

'All the same, it would be better if they could be made to go away. Couldn't you have a word with her husband?'

'There'd be no point, sir. Dear me, Yevgeny Ivanovich, what's got into you? That's all over and done with now. It was just one of those things. Anyway, who is there that's going to say anything bad about you now? After all, you are in the public eye, you know.'

'Yes, but I want you to have a word with him, all the same.'

'Very well, sir, I'll talk to him.'

Even though he knew already that nothing was going to come of it, this conversation did have the effect of calming Yevgeny down a little. Above all, what it made him feel was that in his disturbed state of mind he had exaggerated the danger.

Had he really come out in order to meet her? No, of course he hadn't. He had simply taken a walk in the garden and she had happened to be there, too.

XIV

On the afternoon of that very same Whit Sunday, Liza went for a walk in the garden with Yevgeny. As she was crossing a little ditch on her way out of the garden into the meadow, where her husband wanted to take her in order to see the clover, she missed her step and fell down. Her fall was a gentle one, and she landed on her side; but she gave a moan, and in her features her husband could read an expression not only of fear, but of pain. He made as if to help her to her feet, but she pushed his hand away.

'No, wait a moment, Yevgeny,' she said, smiling weakly, and looking up at him rather guiltily, he thought. 'I went over on my foot, that's all.'

'It's what I'm forever telling her,' said Varvara Alekseyevna. 'How can she possibly expect to go jumping over ditches in her condition?'

'Oh mother, it's nothing. I'll be on my feet in a second.'

With her husband's help she managed to get up, but the moment she did so she turned pale, and looked frightened.

'No, there's something wrong,' she said, and whispered in her mother's ear.

'Oh, merciful heavens, what have you done to yourself?' exclaimed Varvara Alekseyevna. 'I told you not to go out walking. Wait here, all of you – I'll call the servants. She mustn't try to walk. She'll have to be carried.'

'Liza, you won't be afraid if I carry you, will you?' said Yevgeny, putting his left arm around her. 'Put your arms round my neck. Like this.'

And, bending down, he took hold of her legs with his right arm and lifted her up. The expression of beatific martyrdom on her face remained in his memory for ever after.

'I'm quite heavy, you know, darling,' she said with a smile. 'Mother's running, do tell her!'

And she tilted her head towards him and gave him a kiss. She obviously wanted her mother to see him carrying her.

Yevgeny shouted to Varvara Alekseyevna not to hurry, he would carry Liza back to the house. Varvara Alekseyevna stopped running and began to shout in a voice even louder than his: 'You'll drop her, you're bound to drop her. Do you want to kill her? You've absolutely no conscience.'

'I'll manage perfectly.'

'I don't want to watch you murdering my daughter, I don't

want to look and I can't look.' And off she ran, until she disappeared round the corner of the pathway.

'Don't worry, it'll pass,' said Liza with a smile.

'Just as long as there aren't any consequences like there were the other time.'

'No, I'm not talking about that. There's nothing wrong with me, it's mother I'm talking about. You're tired, you ought to take a rest for a minute.'

But even though she was rather heavy, Yevgeny carried his burden all the way to the house with proud delight. He did not even give her up to the housemaid and the cook whom Varvara Alekseyevna had found and sent out to meet them, but carried her up to their bedroom and put her down on the bed.

'All right, you can go now,' she said and, pulling his hand towards her, kissed it. 'Annushka and I will manage.'

Marya Pavlovna also came running in from her annexe. Together the women undressed Liza and put her to bed. Yevgeny sat in the drawing-room with a book in his hand, waiting. Varvara Alekseyevna swept past him with an expression of such gloom and reproach on her face that he was gripped by a sudden fear.

'How is she?' he asked.

'How is she? I'm surprised you bother to ask. She's just the way I expect you wanted her to be when you made her leap over those dikes.'

'Varvara Alekseyevna!' he burst out. 'This is intolerable. If you want to torment people and make their lives a misery . . .' he was going to add, 'go somewhere else and do it,' but managed to restrain himself in time. Instead he said: 'Don't you feel sorry for us?'

'It's too late for feeling sorry now.'

And with a triumphant toss of her cap she went out through the doorway.

Liza's fall had really been quite a bad one. She had gone over on her foot in an awkward way, and there was a real danger that she might have a miscarriage. Everyone knew there was nothing to be done, that she would just have to lie quietly, yet all the same they decided to send for the doctor.

'Dear Nikolay Semyonovich,' Yevgeny wrote to the doctor. 'You have always been so kind to us in the past that I hope you will not refuse to come to the aid of my wife on this occasion. A few days ago she . . .' and so it went on. When he had finished the letter, he went to the stables to see about the horses and the carriage. It was necessary to get ready one set of horses to bring the doctor, and another to take him home again. When a household is not run on a grand scale, such things cannot be arranged at once, but require careful thought. By the time he had sorted the matter out and dispatched the coachman on his way, it was nearly ten o'clock. When he got back to the house, he found his wife lying down as usual. She told him she felt fine and was not in any pain; but Varvara Alekseyevna was seated by a lamp that was shielded from Liza by a book of music, and was knitting a large red coverlet with a look on her face which plainly said that after what had happened there could be no reconciliation. 'Whatever anyone else may have done, I at least have performed my duty,' was what that look declared.

Yevgeny was aware of this, but in order to pretend he hadn't noticed anything, he tried to simulate a cheerful, light-hearted air, telling them how he had fitted out the horses, and how the mare Kavushka had made an excellent left-side trace-horse.

'Yes, of course, you couldn't have thought of a better time for breaking in wild horses, just at the very moment when you have to send for help. I dare say the doctor will end up in a ditch, too,' said Varvara Alekseyevna, casting a swift glance through her lorgnette at her knitting, bringing it right up under the lamp as she did so.

'But we had to send someone to get him. I did the best I could.'

'Yes, Yevgeny, I well remember how your horses went charging under that train with me.'

This was an old exaggeration of hers, and now Yevgeny was careless enough to protest that it had really not been like that at all.

'It just goes to prove what I'm always saying. I'm forever telling the prince the same thing, that there's nothing more terrible than living with people who are untruthful and lacking in sincerity. Anything I can endure, but not that.'

'Well, if anyone's sorry about what's happened, it's me,' said Yevgeny.

'Yes, that's obvious.'

'What do you mean by that?'

'Oh, nothing, I'm counting my stitches.'

At that moment Yevgeny was standing beside the bed; Liza was looking at him. With one of her moist hands, which were resting on top of the coverlet, she caught his and pressed it. 'Put up with her for my sake. After all, she can't stop us loving each other,' her gaze said.

'I won't do it again. Really I won't,' he whispered, kissing first her long, moist hand, and then her lovely eyes, which closed as his lips brushed against them.

'It's not the same thing again, is it?' he asked.

'I'm frightened to say in case I'm wrong, but it feels as though it's alive and it's going to be all right,' she said, looking down at her abdomen.

'Oh, it's terrible, too terrible even to think of.'

Even though Liza insisted that he should go away, Yevgeny spent the night by her bedside, only occasionally allowing himself to nod off to sleep, and ready to attend to her at any moment. But she passed the night without incident, and might have got up next morning, had it not been for the fact that the doctor had been sent for.

The doctor arrived towards noon, and announced, predictably, that although a recurrence of the symptoms might give cause for concern, there were no positive indications that anything was wrong, but that as there were no counterindications it was possible to suppose one thing, while from another point of view it was possible to suppose something else entirely. And so she must go on lying down, and although he did not like prescribing drugs, she must take this medicine none the less, and not get out of bed. The doctor also delivered a lecture to Varvara Alekseyevna on the subject of the female anatomy, in the course of which Varvara Alekseyevna nodded her head meaningfully. When he had taken his fee, slipping the money, as doctors do, into the rearmost part of his palm and securing it there with his thumb, the doctor left, and the patient was consigned to a week of lying on her back.

XV

Yevgeny spent the greater part of his time by his wife's bedside, attending to her needs, talking to her, reading to her and, most difficult of all, putting up with Varvara Alekseyevna's shows of hostility without a murmur, and even contriving to make light of them.

But he could not spend all his time at home. For one thing, his wife kept sending him away, declaring that he would fall ill if he stayed with her all the time, and, for another, the practical affairs of the estate were developing in such a way that his presence was required at every step. He could not stay at home; he had to be out in the fields, in the wood, in the garden, at the threshing barn – and wherever he went he was haunted not only by the thought of Stepanida, but also by her living image, to such an extent that only rarely was she absent from his mind. Not that that in itself was so significant; he might have been able to overcome that feeling. What made it so much worse was that while previously he had gone for months without seeing her, now he was constantly running into her, she was constantly before his eyes. She evidently understood that he wanted to renew his intimacy with her, and she contrived to cross his path whenever she was able to. Neither of them ever spoke to the other, and they made no arrangements to meet, but simply tried to be in the same place as often as possible.

This was most likely to happen in the woods where the women from the village went with sacks to cut grass for their cows. Yevgeny knew about this, and took a walk along the edge of the wood every day. Each day he would tell himself he was not going to go there, and each day he would end by going off to the wood; hearing the sound of voices, he would stand still behind a bush and peep out, his heart beating violently, to see if it was her.

Why he wanted to know if it was her, he was not sure. If it was her – so he imagined, at any rate – he would run away; but he did want to see her. On one occasion he did encounter her: as he was going into the wood, she emerged from it with two other women; she was carrying a heavy sack full of grass on her shoulders. A little earlier, and he might perhaps have come across her in the wood itself. Now, however, with the other two women looking on, it was out of the question for her to turn back and join him. But even though he knew it was out of the question, he stood behind a hazel bush for a long time, running the risk of attracting the other women's attention. Needless to say, she did not come back. But he continued to stand there for a long time. And, merciful heaven, how lovely did she appear to him in the picture his imagination painted for him! Not only once did she appear, but five, six times, and each time she seemed lovelier than the last. Never had she seemed so attractive to him. Not only that: never had she had such a complete hold over him.

He felt he was losing control of himself, was going insane, even. His severe attitude towards himself had not slackened by one iota. On the contrary, he was perfectly aware of the utter loathsomeness of his desires, and of his actions – for his going to the wood was an action. He knew that it would be enough for him to meet her unexpectedly in the dark, close to, and for him to touch her, and he would give himself up to his passions. He knew it was only shame – before others, before her and before himself – that was holding him back. And he knew that he was looking for circumstances in which that shame would not be noticeable – darkness, or the kind of physical contact in which shame is anaesthetized by animal passion. It was for that reason that he knew he was a loathsome criminal, and he despised and hated himself with all the strength of which his soul was capable. He hated himself because he still had not succumbed. Each day he prayed to God to give him strength, to save him from ruin, each day he resolved that from now on he would not take so much as one step in her direction, would never look at her again, would erase her from his memory. Each day he thought up new methods of delivering himself from his infatuation, and he put these methods into practice. But it was all to no avail.

One of the methods he used was to keep himself constantly occupied; another was fasting, combined with strenuous physical labour; yet another was imagining to himself in vivid detail the shame that would descend upon him when everyone – his wife, his mother-in-law, the servants and farm-hands – got to know about his affair. He would do all these things, and think he was gaining the upper hand; but then a certain time of day – noon, the time of their former rendezvous and the time he had met her carrying the grass – would arrive, and he would go into the wood.

Five agonizing days went by like this. He only glimpsed her from a distance, and never once met her face to face.

XVI

Liza gradually recovered. Now she was up and about, but she was perturbed by the change that seemed to have taken place in her husband, which she did not understand.

Varvara Alekseyevna had gone away for a while, and now the uncle was the only guest in the house. Marya Pavlovna was there, as ever.

Yevgeny was still in the same state of semi-insanity when, as often happens after thunderstorms in June, there were two successive days of pouring rain. The rain made it impossible for anyone to work. They even had to give up carting the manure because of the mud and damp. Everyone stayed at home. The herdsmen had a terrible time rounding up the cattle, but finally managed to drive them back to the houses. Cows and sheep strayed on to the common pasture and went scampering about all over the grounds. The peasant women, barefoot and in shawls, ran splashing through the mud in search of cows that had got loose. The roads became rivers, the leaves and grass were saturated in water, and steady rivulets flowed from the roof-gutters into bubbling pools. Yevgeny stayed at home with his wife, who was being particularly trying that day. Several times now she had asked him why he was so unhappy, and on each occasion he had irritably replied that nothing was the matter. Now she had stopped asking, though she was obviously annoyed.

After lunch they sat in the drawing-room. For the hundredth time, Yevgeny's uncle was telling invented stories about his acquaintances in high society. Liza was knitting a bed-jacket and sighing, complaining about the weather and the pains in the small of her back. Yevgeny's uncle advised her to lie down, and told the servant to bring him some vodka. Yevgeny was horribly bored. Everything was so insipid, so tedious. He smoked cigarettes and tried to read a book, but took in nothing of what he read.

'Well, I'll have to be getting along now. I must take a look at the new beet grater; it was only delivered yesterday,' he said. He got up and went out.

'See you take an umbrella with you.'

'Oh no, I've got my leather coat. Anyway, I'm only going as far as the refinery.'

He put on his boots and leather coat and set off in the direction of the sugar factory; but he had hardly gone twenty paces when he suddenly caught sight of her coming towards him, her skirt tucked up high above her white calves. As she walked along she held down with both hands the shawl in which her head and shoulders were swathed.

'What are you doing?' he asked, not recognizing her at first sight. By the time he had recognized her, it was too late. She stopped and looked at him slowly, smiling.

'I'm looking for a calf. Where are you off to in this weather?' she said, as if she were used to seeing him every day.

'Come to the hut,' he said suddenly, hardly aware of doing so. It was as if someone had uttered the words from inside him.

She bit her shawl, flashed him a look of assent, and ran off in the direction she had been following when he had met her

– into the garden, towards the hut. Meanwhile he continued on his way, intending to turn back under cover of the lilacs and go to the hut as well.

'Master,' he heard a voice behind him say. 'The mistress is asking for you, sir, she wants you to go in and see her for a moment.' It was Misha, their servant.

'My God, that's the second time I've been saved like this,' thought Yevgeny, and he went back to the house immediately. His wife wanted to remind him that he had promised to deliver later that day some medicine to a woman who was ill, and to ask him to take it with him now.

It was some five minutes before the medicine was ready. When he emerged from the house with it, he decided not to go to the hut, in case someone saw him from a window. As soon as he was out of sight, however, he turned back and went to the hut after all. He could already see her in his imagination, halfway inside the hut, smiling and laughing; but she wasn't there, and there was nothing in the hut to say that she had been there. He was already beginning to suspect she was not going to turn up, had not heard or had misunderstood the words he had spoken to her. He had muttered them under his breath, as if he had been afraid she might hear them. Perhaps she had not wanted to come? And anyway, where had he got the idea that she would just fling herself at him? She had a husband. It was only he, Yevgeny, who was such a low individual. He had a wife, and a good one, too, yet here he was running after the wife of someone else. Such were his thoughts as he sat down in the hut, the thatched roof of which leaked in one place, letting in a steady drip of water. 'How good it would be if she did come, though. Alone here in the rain, just the two of us. If only I could have her again, just once, and then let things turn out as they may. Yes, of course,' he reflected, 'if she's been here I'll be able to tell by her footprints.' He examined the area of trodden ground that led up to the hut and the path where it was overgrown with grass, and found the fresh imprints of a bare foot that had slithered on the mud. 'Yes, she's been here all right. But I'm fed up with this. Wherever I see her now, I'll go to her. It's as simple as

that. I'll even go to her at night.' For a long time he remained
sitting in the hut. When he emerged from it, he felt exhausted
and depressed. He delivered the medicine, and then went
home and lay down in his room to wait for dinner.

XVII

Before dinner was served, Liza came to see him in his room.
Still trying to fathom why he seemed so unhappy, she began
to tell him that she had been afraid he would disapprove of
her being taken to Moscow to have her baby, and that she had
decided to remain at Semyonovskoye. There was nothing that
would induce her to go to Moscow. He knew that it was really
the birth she was afraid of, and the risk that she might have a
deformed or sickly child, and he could not help being touched
when he saw how ready she was to make this sacrifice because
of her love for him. Everything in the house was so pleasant,
so cheerful, so clean; everything in his soul was so dirty,
loathsome and foul. All evening Yevgeny was tormented by
the knowledge that, in spite of the outright disgust he felt at
his weakness, in spite of his firm intention of breaking off all
relations with Stepanida, everything would be the same again
tomorrow.

'No, this is impossible,' he told himself, as he paced up and
down his room. 'Surely there must be something I can do? Oh
God, what can I do?'

Someone knocked at the door, in the foreign manner. He
knew this would be his uncle.

'Come in,' he said.

His uncle had come to see him of his own accord, as a kind
of emissary from Liza. 'You know, I really have noticed a
change in you recently, old chap,' he said, 'and I can understand how worrying Liza must find it. I'd advise the two of
you to go and take a vacation somewhere. I can see it will be
hard for you to leave all the fine work you've started here, but
what can you do, *que veux-tu*? It'll be better for both of you. My
advice to you both would be to go to the Crimea. The climate

there's better than any obstetrician, and you'll arrive right in the middle of the grape season.'

'Uncle,' said Yevgeny, suddenly, 'can you keep a secret – a terrible, shameful secret?'

'My dear boy, surely you trust me?'

'Uncle, you've got to help me. Not only help me, but save me,' said Yevgeny. And the thought that now he was going to reveal his secret to his uncle, whom he did not respect, that he was going to show himself to his uncle in a most disadvantageous light and degrade himself before him, this thought was pleasing to him. He felt loathsome and guilty, and he wanted to punish himself.

'Go right ahead and tell me all about it, dear boy. You know how fond of you I am,' said his uncle, obviously tickled that there was a secret, that it was a shameful secret, that he was about to be told it and that his services were required.

'First of all I must tell you that I'm a loathsome individual, a good-for-nothing, a real cad.'

'I say, what's got into you?' said his uncle, puffing himself up angrily.

'How can I possibly be anything but a cad when what I want, I, Liza's husband – you know how pure she is, how much she loves me – when what I, her husband, want is to be unfaithful to her with a peasant woman?'

'What do you mean, want? Are you saying you haven't been unfaithful to her?'

'Yes, but it's the same as if I had, because the matter wasn't under my control. I was ready to do it. Something happened to stop me, but if it hadn't, by now I'd have . . . I'd have . . . I don't know what I'd have done.'

'I'm afraid you'll have to explain it to me.'

'Look, it's like this: I was once stupid enough to get physically involved with a woman here, one of the women in the village. What I'm saying is that I used to meet her out in the woods, in the fields . . .'

'And was she pretty?' asked his uncle.

This question made Yevgeny frown, but so desperate was he for some outside support that he pretended not to have heard, and continued: 'Well, I didn't think anything of it at the time, I thought I'd break it off eventually, and then it would all be over. And I did break it off before I got married, and I didn't see her or think about her for nearly a year.' Yevgeny had a strange feeling as he heard himself giving this description of his situation. 'And then suddenly, I don't know how it happened – you know, sometimes I really do believe in witchcraft – I saw her, and a worm crept into my heart – and it's gnawing me away. I curse myself, and I'm conscious of the utter hideousness of that act, that act I may commit at any moment, and yet I go looking for an opportunity to commit it, and if I haven't committed it yet it's only because God has saved me. I was on my way to see her yesterday when Liza called me to the house.'

'What, out in the rain?'

'Yes. Uncle, I've had all I can take, and I've decided to confide in you and ask you to help me.'

'Well, of course, you know, it's not a good idea on your own estate. People will get to hear of it. I realize Liza isn't strong, of course, and that you have to go easy on her. But why on your own estate?'

Once again Yevgeny tried to ignore what his uncle was saying, and proceeded instead to the heart of the matter.

'Please save me from myself. That's what I'm asking you to do. Today it was chance that prevented me; but tomorrow, or another time, it may not prevent me. And she knows about it now. Please don't leave me all on my own.'

'Yes, very well, then,' said his uncle. 'But are you sure you're really so in love with her?'

'Oh, it's nothing like that. It's a kind of force that's taken hold of me and won't let me go. I don't know what to do. Perhaps I'll recover my strength, and then . . .'

'Well, what about my suggestion?' asked his uncle. 'Why don't we go to the Crimea?'

'Yes, yes, let's go – and in the meantime I'll stay with you, talk with you.'

XVIII

Confiding his secret to his uncle, in particular the agonies of guilt and shame he had experienced after that rainy day, had a sobering effect on Yevgeny. A trip to Yalta was arranged, and the date of their departure fixed for a week hence. During that week Yevgeny visited town in order to draw the money for the trip, and made the necessary practical arrangements for the running of the house and the estate office while they were away; he became noticeably more cheerful, was on friendly terms with his wife again, and his mental state began to improve.

So it was that, without once having seen Stepanida since that rainy day, he set off with his wife for the Crimea. There they spent two wonderful months. There were so many new impressions that it seemed to Yevgeny as though all that had gone before had been completely wiped from his memory. In the Crimea they met some old friends with whom they got along extremely well; they made some new friends, too. For Yevgeny, this time in the Crimea was a perpetual holiday; what was more, it was instructive and useful for him. While they were there they became friendly with the ex-marshal of their province, an intelligent man of liberal views who conceived a liking for Yevgeny, took him in hand and won him over to his side. At the end of August, Liza gave birth to a fine, healthy baby girl; the birth passed off with surprising ease.

In September the Irtenevs went home with two additions to their ménage – the baby and a nurse, since Liza could not breast-feed the baby herself. Completely free now of his former black mood, Yevgeny returned home a new and happy man. Having gone through everything a man usually goes through when his wife is having a baby, he loved her even more. The feeling he had for his new daughter, when he took her into his arms, was an amusing, novel, pleasant one, the sort of sensation one has on being tickled. Another novel aspect of his life was that now his mind was occupied not only with the running of the estate, but also, thanks to his recent contact with Dumchin (the ex-marshal), with a new-found interest in the affairs of the local zemstvo, an interest that stemmed partly from personal vanity and partly from a sense of duty. In October there was to be an extraordinary session of the zemstvo at which he was to be a candidate for election as a member. When he got home he made one visit to town, and another to see Dumchin.

The tortures of his former allurement and his struggle with it had slipped from his mind; now he could only recall them with difficulty. They seemed to him like some fit of temporary insanity he had undergone.

So free of all that did he feel now that, on the first occasion he was alone with the estate manager, he was not afraid to ask about her.

'How's Sidor Pchelnikov getting along these days – still living away from home?' he asked.

'Yes, sir, still living in town.'

'And what about his wife?'

'Some wife, if you ask me, sir. Gallivanting around with Zinovy now, she is. Gone right off the rails.'

'Well that's fine,' thought Yevgeny. 'I really feel extraordinarily indifferent. How I've changed!'

XIX

Everything had worked out as Yevgeny had wanted it to. He had managed to retain the estate, the sugar factory was in operation, the beet crop had given an excellent yield and they could expect to make a large profit from it; his wife had had her baby without mishap, his mother-in-law had gone, and he had been elected to the zemstvo by a unanimous vote of all the members.

Yevgeny was returning home from the town after his election. People had congratulated him, and he had thanked them. Afterwards there had been a dinner at which he had drunk about five glasses of champagne. Entirely new plans as to the way his future life would develop had risen before him. During the drive home, he thought about these. They were having an Indian summer that year. The road surface was excellent, the sun was shining brightly. As his carriage approached the house, Yevgeny reflected that as a consequence of his election he would now be able to serve the people of the village in the way he had always dreamed of doing, not merely by providing work for them but by exercising a direct influence on them. He wondered what his peasants, and the others, would be saying about him three years from now. 'That man, for example,' he thought, as he drove through the village and in front of the carriage saw a muzhik carrying a full tub of water across the road, helped by a peasant woman. They halted to let the carriage go past. The muzhik was the old man Pchelnikov, and the woman was Stepanida. Yevgeny glanced at her, recognized her, and found to his satisfaction that he was able to remain quite calm. She was as pretty as ever, but that had no effect on him now. As he arrived at the house, his wife came out to meet him on the porch. It was a beautiful evening.

'Well, can I congratulate you?'

'Yes, I was elected.'

'Why, that's marvellous. We'll drink to it!'

Next morning Yevgeny went for a ride around the estate, which he had been neglecting. A new threshing-machine was being tried out at one of the farms. As he watched it at work, Yevgeny strolled among the peasant women. He tried not to pay any attention to them, yet no matter how hard he tried, he could not help once or twice catching sight of Stepanida's black eyes and red kerchief. She was carrying the chaff away. Once or twice he took a surreptitious glance at her, and felt that something was taking place inside him again, though he wasn't sure what it was. It was only the day after, when he took another ride over to the farm to watch the threshing, and spent two hours there, quite unnecessarily, unable to take his eyes off the young woman's familiar, appealing figure, that he suddenly knew he was lost, utterly and irrevocably lost. Once

again he experienced those torments, that fear and horror.
And there was no way out.

It happened to him, the very thing he had been dreading.
The following evening he somehow found himself outside her
back yard, opposite the hay barn where they had once made
love the previous autumn. As if he were merely out taking a
stroll, he stopped there and lit a cigarette. A woman who lived
in one of the neighbouring cottages saw him, and as he started
to turn back he heard her say to someone: 'Go on, he's waiting
for you. Cross my heart, it's him. Go on, you silly idiot!'

He saw a woman – it was her – run towards the barn, but it
was too late for him to retrace his steps now, as a muzhik was
coming, and he went home.

XX

When he entered the drawing-room, everything somehow
seemed wrong and not as it should be. That morning, when
he had got out of bed, he had still been in a cheerful frame of
mind; he had formed a resolve to cast the whole matter aside,
to forget about it and forbid himself to think about it. But
somehow, without even really being aware of it, all that
morning he found that not only could he not arouse any
interest in his work, he was even trying to avoid it. Everything
that had previously been important to him and had brought
him such satisfaction now seemed utterly insignificant.
Unconsciously he found himself trying to get out of attending
to the business of the estate. He felt he must get away from it
in order to be able to review the situation and think things
over. And get away from it he did, and kept himself to himself.
As soon as he was alone, however, he began to make forays
into the garden or the wood. Each place he visited bore the
taint of memories, memories that obsessed him. He told
himself he was just taking a walk in the garden and thinking
things over, whereas in actual fact he wasn't thinking anything
over at all, but simply waiting for her, waiting quite irrationally

in the hope that by some miracle she would realize that he
desired her and would come either here to the garden or over
there to the wood where no one would see anything or better
still to either place, but under cover of night, when there was
no moon, and no one, not even she herself, would be able to
see anything – that was the time she would come to him, the
time when he would touch her body . . .

'Yes, I thought I could break it off when I wanted to,' he said
to himself. 'I thought I could make love with a clean, healthy
woman for the sake of my health! No, it's obvious I can't play
around with her like that. I thought I'd taken her, but it's she
who has taken me, she's taken me and she won't let me go. I
thought I was free, but I wasn't free at all. I was deceiving
myself when I got married. All that was mere nonsense and
deception. From the first time I made love with her, I
experienced a new feeling, the true feeling of a husband. Yes,
it was her I should have lived with.

'There are two lives open to me: one is the life I've begun
with Liza, involving my work at the zemstvo, the running of
the estate, our child, the respect of other people. If that's the
life I'm to lead, there's no room for Stepanida. She'll have to
be induced to move, as I was talking of doing, or else done
away with, so she doesn't exist any more. The other life is
right here: I'd have to take her away from her husband, give
him money, close my eyes to the shame and disgrace, and live
with her. But then there would be no place for Liza and Mimi,
our child. No, that's not right, Mimi wouldn't be any problem,
but there'd be no room for Liza, she'd have to go away. She'd
have to find out about it, curse me and go away. She'd have to
find out that I'd exchanged her for a peasant woman, that I'm
a trickster and a cheat. No, it's too dreadful to contemplate! It's
out of the question. But what if,' he continued to reflect, 'what
if Liza were to fall ill and die? If she were to die, everything
would be perfect!

'Perfect? You miserable worm! No, if anyone's got to die, it
had better be the other one. If only Stepanida were to die, how
wonderful everything would be.

'Yes, that's how it's done, that's how a man poisons or

shoots his wife or his mistress. He just takes a revolver, tells her to come to him and then, instead of embracing her, he fires a bullet into her breast. And that's that.

'After all, she's a devil. Just that – a devil. She's taken possession of me against my will. Shall I kill her? Yes. There are only two ways out: either I kill Liza or I kill her. Because I can't go on living like this.* I can't. I must think things over and look to the future. If I leave everything as it is, who knows what may happen?

'What will happen will be that I'll start telling myself I'm going to give her up, but it'll just be words, and by the time it's evening I'll be standing in her back yard again, and she'll see me and come out. And either the servants will find out and tell my wife, or I'll tell her myself, because I can't go on lying, I can't go on living like that. I can't. I'll be found out. They'll all get to know about it – Parasha, the blacksmith, all of them. Well, honestly, how can I live like that?

'I can't. There are only two ways out: either I kill Liza or I kill her. Or . . .

'Ah, yes, there's a third way: I can kill myself,' he said aloud, softly, and a sudden shiver ran over his flesh. 'Yes, if I kill myself, I won't have to kill either of them.' He grew afraid, because he knew that this was in fact the only possible way out. 'I've got a revolver. Am I really going to kill myself? I'd never have thought of that before. How strange it will be.'

He returned to his study and without further ado opened the cupboard where he kept his revolver. No sooner had he opened it, however, than his wife came in.

XXI

He threw a newspaper over the revolver.

'Again,' she said, giving him a frightened look.

'What do you mean, "again"?' he asked.

'You've got the same look on your face again, the one you had before, that time when you wouldn't tell me what was

* The alternative ending begins here (see Appendix 2).

wrong. Zhenya darling, tell me what's wrong. I can see you're dreadfully worried about something. Tell me what it is, then you'll feel better. Whatever it is, tell me – anything's better than seeing you suffer like this. Anyway, I know it's nothing so very terrible.'

'You know? I'll tell you what it is presently.'

'Tell me, tell me. You're not going to get away without telling me.'

He smiled at her pathetically.

'Tell you? No, I can't do that. Anyway, there isn't really anything to tell.'

He might very well have gone ahead and told her, had not the nurse come in just then to ask if it was all right for her to take the baby out in the pram now. Liza went off to get the baby dressed.

'All right, so you'll tell me, then? I'll be back in a moment.'

'Yes, perhaps . . .'

She never forgot the look of suffering he gave her as he said this. She went out.

Quickly, furtively, like a burglar, he whipped the revolver out of its case. 'It's loaded, but that was ages ago, and one of the cartridges is missing. Well, so be it.'

He put the muzzle to his temple, and then hesitated. Almost immediately, however, he remembered Stepanida, his decision not to see her any more, his struggle, temptation, fall and resumed struggle. He shuddered with horror. 'No it's better this way.' And he pulled the trigger.

When Liza came running into the room – she had only just left the balcony – she found him lying on the floor, face down. Warm, dark blood was spurting from the wound, and his body was still twitching.

There was an inquest. No one was able to understand or explain the causes of Yevgeny's suicide. It never even entered his uncle's mind that it might be in some way linked with the confession his nephew had made to him two months previously.

Varvara Alekseyevna claimed to have seen this coming all along. She said she had observed it in his eyes on all those occasions when he had argued with her. Neither Liza nor Marya Pavlovna had the slightest notion as to why it should have happened; on the other hand, neither of them believed what the doctors said, that he had been mentally ill. On no account could they agree with this diagnosis, as they knew he had been more sensible and level-headed than hundreds of people of their acquaintance.

And indeed, if Yevgeny was mentally ill, then everyone is mentally ill, and most of all those who claim to perceive in others symptoms of the madness they fail to perceive in themselves.

THE
FORGED COUPON

PART ONE

Fyodor Mikhailovich Smokovnikov, the head of a government tax department, a man of incorruptible integrity and proud of it, a gloomy liberal who was not only a free-thinker but also a hater of every manifestation of religious tendencies, which he considered a throwback to the superstitions of earlier times, had come home from his office in a very sour frame of mind. He had just received a most stupid memo from the governor, and from it the inference could be drawn that Fyodor Mikhailovich had acted in a dishonest fashion. Bitterly angry, Fyodor Mikhailovich had immediately dashed off to the governor a stinging and caustic reply.

When he got home it seemed to him as if everything were going against him.

It was five to five. He had expected dinner to be served as soon as he made his appearance, but it wasn't ready yet. Fyodor Mikhailovich banged the door and stalked off to his study. There was a knock. 'Who the devil is it now?' he wondered, and he shouted: 'Who is it now?'

Into his study came a fifth-form grammar-school boy, his fifteen-year-old son.

'What do you want?'

'It's the first of the month today.'

'Money, is it?'

They had an arrangement whereby on the first day of each month the father gave his son an allowance of three rubles to cover the cost of entertainments. Fyodor Mikhailovich made a sour face, took out his wallet, searched inside it and extricated from it a two-and-a-half-ruble bond coupon;[15] then he fished out his small change and counted out another fifty copecks. His son said nothing and did not take the money.

'Papa, please let me have some more in advance.'

'What?'

'I don't like to ask you, but I borrowed some money and promised on my word of honour to pay it back. As a man of integrity, I can't . . . I have to have another three rubles, really I do, I wouldn't ask you, or at least, well . . . Please, papa.'

'You were told . . .'

'I know, papa. Look, it's just this once . . .'

'You get an allowance of three rubles, and still it's not enough. When I was your age I didn't even get fifty copecks.'

'All my friends get more than I do now. Petrov and Ivanitsky get fifty rubles a month.'

'And I'm telling you that if you go on like this you'll end up as a swindler. That's it, now, I've told you.'

'So what if you have? You'll never be able to put yourself in my shoes; now I've got no alternative but to be a swindler. It's all right for you.'

'Get out of here this instant, you idle good-for-nothing! Get out!'

Fyodor Mikhailovich leapt to his feet and rushed towards his son.

'Out! You ought to be given a good whipping!'

His son was overtaken by fear and a sense of bitter resentment; his resentment, however, was greater than his fear. Bowing his head, he walked quickly to the door. Fyodor Mikhailovich had no intention of laying a finger on him, but he was enjoying his fit of anger, and he continued to hurl abuse at his son for some considerable time, until the latter had disappeared.

When the maid came in to say that dinner was served Fyodor Mikhailovich rose to his feet.

'At last,' he said. 'I don't even feel hungry now.' And with a black scowl on his face he went to have dinner.

At the dinner-table his wife started to talk to him, but so angrily did he bark out his replies that she fell silent. His son, too, said nothing, keeping his eyes steadily fixed on his plate.

In silence they continued to eat, and silently they rose from the table and went about their separate tasks.

After dinner the grammar-school boy went back to his room, where he took the coupon and change out of his pocket and threw them on to his writing-desk; then he removed his school tunic and put on a jacket. After he had spent some time poring over a tattered Latin grammar, he got up, closed the door, and fastened its hook, then swept the money off the desk top and into a drawer. From the same drawer he took some Russian cigarette papers with their cardboard holders, stuffed a quantity of tobacco into one of them using a piece of cotton wool, and started to smoke.

He continued to pore over his grammar and his exercise books for a couple of hours without taking anything in. Then he stood up and began to pace to and fro in his room, stamping his heels as he recalled the scene he had had with his father. All his father's abusive talk and, in particular, the malevolent expression there had been on his face, came back to him as clearly as if it had all just been a moment ago. 'You idle good-for-nothing! You ought to be given a good whipping!' And the more of the scene he remembered, the more his anger at his father grew. He remembered his father saying to him: 'It's easy to see what you'll end up as – a swindler. Just you wait.' 'He said I'd end up as a swindler if I went on like this. It's all right for him. He's forgotten what it's like to be young. Anyway, what crime have I committed? All I did was go to the theatre, and because I didn't have any money I borrowed some off Petya Grushetsky. What's wrong with that? Anyone else would have shown some sympathy and given the matter some consideration, but all he could do was bellow at me and think of himself. When he hasn't got something he wants he shouts the whole house down, but I'm a swindler. No, even though he is my father, I don't like him. Maybe all fathers are like he is, but I still don't like him.'

The maid knocked at his door. She had brought a note for him. 'You're to reply to it at once,' she said.

The note read: 'This makes three times now that I've asked you to return the six rubles you borrowed from me, but you always try to get out of it. Men who are honest don't behave like that. Please send the money at once via bearer. I'm really broke myself. Surely you can get it for me? Your – depending on whether or not you give me my money back – respectful or contemptuous friend, Grushetsky.'

'I don't believe it. The greedy pig, he can't wait. I'll have another go.'

Mitya went to see his mother. This was his last hope. She had a kind heart and was never able to refuse him anything, and she would probably have helped him on this occasion too, except that she was in an anxious state about the illness of two-year-old Petya, her youngest boy. She was angry at Mitya for coming in and making a noise, and she turned down his request point-blank.

He muttered something to himself under his breath, and went out of the room. His mother immediately felt sorry for him, and called him back.

'Wait, Mitya,' she said. 'I haven't got it right now, but I'll get it for you tomorrow.'

But Mitya was still burning with resentment against his father.

'What's the good of waiting till tomorrow, when I need it today? I may as well tell you that I'm going to ask one of my friends to lend me it.'

He went out, finally this time, banging the door behind him.

'There's nothing else for it. At least he'll be able to tell me where I can pawn my watch,' he thought, fingering the watch in his pocket.

Mitya took the coupon and the change out of the desk drawer, put on his coat and set off to visit his friend Makhin.

II

Makhin was a fifth-former with a moustache. He played cards, knew women and always had money. He lived with his aunt. Mitya knew that Makhin was a ne'er-do-well, but when he was with him he unconsciously let him take the upper hand.

Makhin was at home, getting ready to go to the theatre: his grimy little room smelt of scented soap and eau-de-Cologne.

'That's too bad,' said Makhin, after Mitya had related his woes to him, shown him the coupon and the fifty copecks, and told him he needed nine rubles more. 'You can pawn your watch, of course, but you can do better than that,' said Makhin, giving him a wink.

'How do you mean, better?'

'It's very simple.' Makhin took the coupon. 'If you insert a 1 before the 2 r. 50 it'll read 12 r. 50.'

'But do coupons for that amount exist?'

'Of course they do, on thousand-ruble bonds. I put one of them into circulation myself, once.'

'I don't believe it!'

'All right then, shall we do it?' said Makhin, taking a pen and smoothing out the coupon with the index finger of his left hand.

'But it's not right.'

'Rubbish.'

'He was right,' thought Mitya, remembering the things his father had shouted at him. 'A swindler. I'll be a swindler now.' He looked Makhin in the face. Makhin was watching him with a quiet smile.

'Well then, shall we?'

'All right.'

Makhin painstakingly wrote in a figure 1.

'Right, now we'll go to a shop. There's one on the corner here that sells photographic supplies. It just so happens that I need a frame for this lady.'

He produced a photograph of a round-eyed girl with vast tresses of hair and magnificent breasts.

'How do you fancy her, eh? Eh?'

'Yes, yes. But how . . . ?'

'It's very simple. Come on.'

Makhin put on his coat, and they left the house together.

III

The bell in the entrance to the photographic supply shop gave a tinkle. The two grammar-school boys went inside and looked around the deserted shop with its shelves of photographic equipment and its counters on which stood showcases. From a doorway at the back of the shop a plain woman with a kindly face emerged. Taking up her position behind the counter, she asked them what they wanted.

'A nice frame, miss.'

'How much do you want to spend?' asked the lady, running the swollen-jointed fingers of her mittened hands swiftly and deftly over various types of frames. 'Those are fifty copecks each, but these are a little more expensive. This one here is very nice, it's a new line, priced at a ruble twenty.'

'All right, I'll take that one. But wouldn't you let me have it for a ruble?'

'All our prices are fixed,' said the lady, with dignity.

'Oh, all right then,' said Makhin, putting the coupon down on one of the glass showcases. 'But please hurry up and let me have my change. I don't want to be late for the theatre.'

'Oh, you're in plenty of time,' said the lady, and she began to examine the coupon with eyes that were obviously short-sighted.

'She'll look stunning in that frame, won't she?' said Makhin, turning to Mitya.

'Haven't you any other money with you?' asked the shop-lady.

'That's just it, I'm afraid I haven't. My father gave me this, and told me to get it changed.'

'Are you sure you haven't got a ruble twenty on you?'

'I've got fifty copecks. Anyway, what's the matter, are you afraid we're trying to pass a forgery off on you?'

'No, nothing like that.'

'Then give me the coupon back, please. We'll have it changed somewhere else.'

'How much change do I have to give you?'

'Well, let's see, it works out at eleven something.'

The shop-lady flicked the beads on her abacus, unlocked the till, took out a ten-ruble note and, running her hands through the change, raked together six twenty-copeck pieces and two five-copeck bits.

I'd like it wrapped up, please,' said Makhin, taking the money in a leisurely fashion.

'It won't take a moment.'

The shop-lady wrapped the frame and tied the parcel up with string.

Mitya only dared to breathe again after the entrance bell had tinkled and they were out on the street once more.

'All right, here's ten rubles for you; let me keep the rest. I'll give you it back.'

And Makhin went off to the theatre, while Mitya visited Grushetsky and settled his debt.

IV

An hour after the two grammar-school boys had left the shop, the proprietor returned and started to count his day's takings.

'Oh, you idiot of a woman! You idiot!' he shouted at his wife when he saw the coupon and immediately spotted the forgery. 'And what are you doing accepting coupons, anyway?'

'But I've seen you accept them, Zhenya, twelve-ruble coupons exactly like this one,' said his wife, who was by now confused, upset and on the point of tears. 'I don't know how they managed to fool me,' she said. 'Grammar-school boys, they were, too. One of them was such a handsome young man, he seemed so *comme il faut*.'

'I'll *comme il faut* you, you idiot!' shouted her husband, keeping up a steady stream of abuse at her as he continued to count the takings. 'When I accept a coupon I make sure I know what's printed on it, but you, all you can see is those boys from the grammar-school with their ugly mugs.'

This was too much for his wife, and she too flew into a rage.

'There's a man for you! All you can do is put the blame on other people; I suppose losing fifty-four rubles at cards is neither here nor there?'

'That's something else entirely.'

'I'm not going to waste any more breath on you,' said his wife, and she went off to her room. There she started to remember how reluctant her family had been to consent to her marriage, as they had considered that her husband belonged to a lower social class than theirs, and how she had had to insist; she remembered the child she had had who had died, and her husband's indifference to this loss, and she felt such hatred for him that she wished it had been him that had died. This thought frightened her, however, and she quickly put on her coat and went out. When her husband got back to their apartment, she was gone. Without waiting for him she had taken her coat and set off alone for the house of a teacher of French who had invited them to a soirée that evening.

V

At the home of the teacher of French — a Russian Pole — there was a gala tea with sweet pastries. After it was over, everyone sat down at several tables to play bridge.

The photographic supplier's wife shared a table with the host, an officer, and a deaf old lady in a wig who was the widow of a music-shop owner and had a passion for cards, which she was very good at. This particular game seemed to be going in favour of the photographic supplier's wife; twice now she had made a grand slam. Beside her was a plate that contained a bunch of grapes and a pear, and she was in the best of spirits.

'What's keeping Yevgeny Mikhailovich?' asked the hostess from another table. 'He's supposed to be our fifth hand.'

'Oh he's probably still doing his accounts,' said Yevgeny Mikhailovich's wife. 'Today's the day he always pays the grocery and firewood bills.'

And, remembering the scene she had had with her husband,

she frowned, and her mittened hands trembled with resentment towards him.

'Talk of the devil,' said the host, turning to greet Yevgeny Mikhailovich, who had just walked in. 'What held you up?'

'Oh, various bits of business,' replied Yevgeny Mikhailovich cheerfully, rubbing his hands. Then, much to his wife's astonishment, he went over to her and said: 'You remember that coupon? Well, I've managed to pass it on.'

'You have?'

'Yes, I gave it to a muzhik for some firewood.'

And with great indignation Yevgeny Mikhailovich proceeded to tell everyone the story of how some dishonest grammar-school boys had tricked his wife, while his wife supplied the details.

'Right, now let's get on with it,' he said at last, sitting down at the table when his turn came, and shuffling the cards.

VI

Yevgeny Mikhailovich had indeed managed to pass the coupon on: he had persuaded a peasant named Ivan Mironov to accept it in exchange for some firewood.

Ivan Mironov made his living by buying up single loads of firewood in the wood-yards and then carting them for sale around the town; he split the loads into five, and sold each part for what a quarter-load cost at the wood-yards. Early on the morning of this day that was to prove so unlucky for him, Ivan Mironov had carted out an eighth-load and, having quickly sold it, had brought out another eighth in the hope of selling it, too. This time, however, he could not find a customer, and spent all day until evening carting the load around in search of someone who might possibly buy it. He kept running across canny townsfolk who were wise to all the sharp practices of muzhik firewood salesmen, and were not so credulous as to believe that he had brought the wood in from the country, as he said he had. He was thoroughly famished, and felt chilled to the bone in his worn sheepskin jacket and his ragged undercoat; by evening the temperature had dropped to minus twenty; his horse, which he had been driving without mercy, since he was about to sell it to the knacker, refused to go any further. Ivan Mironov was even thinking of selling the firewood at a loss when he encountered Yevgeny Mikhailovich, who had gone out to buy some tobacco and was now on his way home.

'Would you like to buy some firewood, sir? I'll sell it to you cheap. My horse won't go any further.'

'Tell me where you're from first.'

'From the country, sir. The wood's all my own. It's good, dry stuff.'

'I know your sort. Well, what do you want for it?'

Ivan Mironov named an exorbitant price, then started to reduce it, and finally parted with the firewood at his normal price.

'Just for you, sir, seeing it's not far to deliver,' he said.

Yevgeny Mikhailovich did not make too much fuss about the price. He was pleased at the thought that now he would be able to pass on the coupon. Pulling the cart along by his own efforts, Ivan Mironov somehow managed to manoeuvre the firewood into the yard; he unloaded it and stacked it in the shed himself. The yard-keeper was not on duty. At first Ivan Mironov was unwilling to accept the coupon, but Yevgeny Mikhailovich was so persuasive and seemed to be such an important gentleman that in the end he agreed to take it.

As he entered the servants' room through the tradesman's entrance, Ivan Mironov crossed himself, wrung the icicles from his beard and, turning back the lapel of his sheepskin jacket, produced a leather purse from which he counted out eight rubles and fifty copecks change. He handed the money over, took the coupon, rolled it up in a piece of paper and put it in his purse.

Having proffered his thanks, in a manner befitting the conclusion of a transaction with a gentleman, Ivan Mironov proceeded to set the legs of his doomed, frost-encrusted horse in motion, not with the lash of his whip now, but with its handle, forcing it to drag the empty cart as far as the local inn.

At the inn Ivan Mironov ordered eight copecks' worth of tea and vodka. Once he had thawed out and even begun to perspire a bit, his mood became thoroughly amiable, and he got into conversation with the yard-keeper, who was sitting at his table. He really warmed to the conversation and told the yard-keeper that he came from the village of Vasilevskoye, some twelve versts outside town, that he had been given his share of the family fortune and now lived independently of his father and brothers with his wife and two sons, the elder of whom was undergoing professional training and so was not yet able to help him out. He told the yard-keeper that while he was in town he was staying in lodgings, and that tomorrow he was going to the knacker to sell his old jade, and might possibly buy a new horse. He said he had now managed to save up the sum of twenty-five rubles and that half of the money was in the form of a coupon. He took out the coupon and showed it to the yard-keeper. The yard-keeper could neither read nor write, but he said he had changed money like that for the tenants, that it was all right, but that there were forgeries around, and for that reason he advised him to play safe and have it changed at the bar. Ivan Mironov gave the coupon to the waiter and asked him to bring him the same amount in ready cash. The waiter went off, but did not return. Instead, the inn's bald-headed, shiny-faced manager appeared, clutching the coupon in his pudgy hand.

'Your money is no good,' he said, indicating the coupon, but not returning it.

'It's perfectly good, I was given it by a gentleman.'

'No, my fine fellow, this coupon's been tampered with.'

'Give it back to me, then.'

'No, my fine fellow. You'll have to be taught a lesson. You forged this coupon yourself, you and your swindler friends.'

'Give me my money back; you've got no right to do this.'

'Sidor! Call the police!' said the barman to the waiter.

Ivan Mironov was slightly the worse for the drink he had had. And being slightly the worse for drink, he was also getting rather agitated. He seized the manager by the collar and shouted: 'Give me it back, I'll go and see the gentleman. I know where he lives.'

The manager tore himself free of Ivan Mironov's grip, but as he did so his shirt began to split.

'Oh, so that's how you want to play it! Take him!'

The waiter seized hold of Ivan Mironov, and at that very instant the local policeman appeared. As master of the situation, he listened to both sides of the story, and then brought the whole episode to a speedy conclusion.

'You've got to come down to the station!'

The policeman put the coupon into his own wallet, and then escorted Ivan Mironov and his horse to the police station.

VII

Ivan Mironov spent the night in the cells at the police station, together with the drunks and the pickpockets. Not until around noon the following day was he summoned to appear before the station chief. The station chief asked him a lot of questions and then told the policeman to take him along for an interview with the proprietor of the photographic supply shop. Ivan Mironov could remember the name of the street and the number of the house.

When the policeman knocked on Yevgeny Mikhailovich's front door and confronted him with the coupon and with Ivan Mironov, who confirmed that this was the gentleman who had given him the coupon, Yevgeny Mikhailovich's expression of astonishment was quickly replaced by one of grim severity.

'What? Have you taken leave of your senses? I've never seen this man before in my life.'

'Master, be sure your sins will find you out. One day we all must die,' said Ivan Mironov.

'What's the matter with him? You must be dreaming. It was someone else you sold your firewood to,' said Yevgeny Mikhailovich. 'In any case, wait a moment, I'll go and ask my wife if she bought any firewood yesterday.'

Yevgeny Mikhailovich went off and immediately summoned

the yard-keeper. The yard-keeper was a very strong, handsome, agile fellow who seemed to be perpetually in a good mood, gave himself airs, and went by the name of Vasily. Yevgeny Mikhailovich instructed him that if anyone should ask him where the last load of firewood had come from he was to say they had got it from the wood-yards, and that they never bought firewood from the muzhiks.

'There's a muzhik here claiming I gave him a forged coupon. He's a stupid nitwit, talking a lot of nonsense, but you're an intelligent chap. You tell him we only ever buy our firewood at the wood-yards. Oh, by the way, I'd been meaning to give you this towards a new jacket,' Yevgeny Mikhailovich added, giving the yard-keeper a five-ruble note.

Vasily took the money, and his eyes flashed from the note to Yevgeny Mikhailovich's face; he tossed back his hair and gave a little smile.

'It's common knowledge they're a stupid lot. Uneducated. Don't you worry, sir, I know what to say to the likes of him.'

No matter how tearfully Ivan Mironov beseeched Yevgeny Mikhailovich to admit that the coupon was his, and the yard-keeper to confirm that this was so, both men stuck to their story: they never bought firewood off carts. And the policeman took Ivan Mironov back to the police station, where he was charged with forging a coupon.

It was only by following the advice of his cell-mate, a drunken office clerk, and slipping the station chief a five-ruble note, that Ivan Mironov was able to procure his release from detention. Now he was minus the coupon and had only seven rubles left out of the twenty-five he had had the day before. Ivan Mironov spent three of these seven rubles on drink. Dead drunk, looking utterly crushed, he crept back to his wife.

His wife was in the last stages of a pregnancy, and she was feeling ill. She started to shout at her husband, he pushed her away, and she began to pummel him with her fists. Making no attempt at retaliation, he lay face down on the plank bed of the lodging-house and wept loudly.

Not until the following morning did his wife discover what had happened; believing her husband's story, she spent a long

time cursing the fraudulent gentleman who had tricked her
Ivan. And Ivan, who was now sober, remembered what the
factory hand with whom he had been drinking the night
before had advised him, and decided to find a lawyer and
lodge a complaint.

VIII

The lawyer agreed to take on the case, not so much for any
money he could hope to receive, as because he believed Ivan's
story and was angry that anyone should so shamelessly
defraud a poor muzhik.

Both parties attended the hearing, at which the yard-keeper
Vasily was the sole witness. The hearing was a repetition of all
that had gone before. Ivan Mironov made allusions to God,
and to the fact that one day we all must die. Yevgeny
Mikhailovich, though troubled by an awareness of what he
was doing as both shabby and dangerous, was unable now to
go back on the testimony he had already given, and he
continued to disclaim all responsibility with an appearance of
outward calm.

Vasily the yard-keeper pocketed another ten rubles and
calmly asserted that he had never set eyes on Ivan Mironov in
his life before. And when he was summoned to be sworn in,
even though he quailed inwardly, he none the less repeated
the words of the oath after the old priest who had been
specially brought in for the occasion, and swore on the crucifix
and the Holy Gospel that he would tell the whole truth and
nothing but the truth.

The court proceedings ended with the judge rejecting the
action brought by Ivan Mironov and making him forfeit court
costs to the tune of five rubles, which Yevgeny Mikhailovich
magnanimously paid for him. Discharging Ivan Mironov, the
judge cautioned him to be more careful in future about
bringing accusations against decent, law-abiding citizens, and
told him he should be grateful to the defendant for paying his
court costs for him, instead of prosecuting him for slander, an

offence for which he could have been sent to prison for at least three months.

'I thank your honour kindly, sir,' said Ivan Mironov, and he left the chamber, shaking his head and sighing.

The whole episode seemed to have ended well for Yevgeny Mikhailovich and Vasily the yard-keeper. But that was only the way it looked on the surface. No one perceived what had really happened – something far more grave than what could be discerned by human eyes.

It was getting on for three years now since Vasily had left his village and gone to live in the town. With every year that passed he gave less and less of what he earned to his father, and he had not sent for his wife, since he did not need her. Here in the town he could have as many women as he wanted, and they were no useless old hags like her. With every year that passed Vasily forgot more and more of the country laws and customs, and adapted himself more and more to the ways of the town. Back there, life had been crude, cheerless, impoverished and messy; here it was tasteful, comfortable, clean and luxurious – everything had been taken care of. Increasingly he had grown convinced that those countryfolk lived blindly, like beasts in the forest, while all the real people were here. He read books by good authors, novels and went to stage performances at the People's House.[16] One could never see anything like that in the country, not even in one's dreams. In the village he had come from the old men had used to say: 'Live with your wife according to the law, work hard, don't eat too much, don't give yourself airs.' But here people were clever, educated – that meant they knew what the real laws were – and they enjoyed life. Everything was just perfect. Until the hearing concerning the coupon, Vasily had refused to believe that the upper classes had no laws to govern the conduct of their lives. He had thought they did have laws, but that he, Vasily, did not know what they were. But after the hearing, and in particular his perjury, which in spite of all his fears had had no negative consequences for him and had indeed resulted in his being ten rubles better off, he became fully persuaded that there were no laws and that all one was supposed to do was to enjoy life. This he did and this he continued to do. At first he merely fiddled a bit of money on the purchases he made for the tenants, but this was not enough for all his expenses, and he started, whenever he got the chance, to pilfer money and valuables from the tenants' apartments; once he even tried to steal Yevgeny Mikhailovich's wallet. Yevgeny Mikhailovich caught him in the act, but did not bring proceedings against him in court: instead, he saw to it that Vasily got the sack.

Vasily did not find the idea of going back to his village particularly appealing, and he stayed on in Moscow with his mistress, looking for work. He found a low-paid job as yard-keeper to the proprietor of a small shop. Vasily started in the job, but in the very second month of his employment he was caught stealing sacks. His employer did not make an official complaint against him, but gave him a beating and drove him off the premises. After that it was impossible for Vasily to find work, his money was all spent, soon he had pawned most of his clothes and in the end all he had left was a tattered coat, a pair of trousers and some ragged footwear. His mistress left him. But Vasily did not lose his cheerful, high-spirited disposition, and when spring came round he set off home for his village on foot.

IX

Pyotr Nikolayevich Sventitsky, a thickset little man who wore smoked glasses (he had trouble with his eyes and was threatened by total blindness), got up before dawn, as was his custom, and, after he had had a glass of tea, put on his knee-length fleece coat, trimmed with lambskin, and set off to make the rounds of his estate.

Pyotr Nikolayevich had been a customs officer and had managed to save some eighteen thousand rubles of what he had earned. Almost twelve years previously he had gone into retirement, not quite voluntarily, and had bought the poky little estate of a young landowner who had squandered his fortune. Pyotr Nikolayevich had married while he had still been on government service. His wife was the poor orphan of an old aristocratic family, a plump, attractive woman who had borne him no children. Pyotr Nikolayevich was, in all his dealings, a man of persistence and thoroughness. The son of a Polish gentleman, he had known nothing about agriculture, yet so skilful at it had he proved to be that the ramshackle, three-hundred-desyatina estate had, within the space of ten years, become a very model of perfection. All the structures he put up, from the house itself to the granary and the shelter over the fire-hose, were solid and reliable, covered by sheet iron, and given a coat of fresh paint whenever they needed it. In the implement-shed there was an orderly collection of carts, harrows and wooden and iron ploughs. The horses' harness was kept properly greased. The horses themselves were medium-sized animals, nearly all from the same stud – well-fed, sturdy greys, matched in pairs. The threshing-machine was operated in its own covered barn, the feed was kept in a special shed, and the liquid manure flowed into a pit with a paved base. The cows were likewise all of the same stock, medium-sized, but giving a high milk-yield. The pigs were the 'English' variety. There was a poultry-yard with several breeds of hen notable for their laying properties. The fruit trees in the orchard were sprayed and coated, and new ones had been planted. Wherever one looked there were signs of thrift, reliability, cleanliness and good order. Pyotr Nikolay-evich drew a great deal of satisfaction from his estate, and was proud of the fact that he had achieved all this not by making his peasants' lives a misery but, on the contrary, by exercising the most scrupulous fairness in their regard. Even when mixing with the local nobility he tended to hold to a middle-of-the-road point of view, one that was closer to a liberal rather than a conservative position, and he always defended the common people to the advocates of serf-ownership. 'Be good to them, and they'll be good to you,' was his motto. It was true that he would not tolerate slips and blunders on the part of those who worked for him, and sometimes he would urge them along himself; he demanded that they work hard for him, but on the other hand the accommodation and the food he offered them were of the very highest quality, their wages were always paid on time, and on holidays he treated them to vodka.

Stepping carefully over the melting snow – this was in February – Pyotr Nikolayevich made his way past the farm-hands' stable to the *izba*[17] where the farm-hands lived. It was still dark; the fog made it even darker than it might have been, but light was visible in the windows of the *izba*. The farm-hands were getting out of bed. His intention was to hurry them up: this morning six of them were supposed to be taking the cart over to the thicket to gather in the rest of the firewood.

'What's this?' he thought, suddenly noticing that the door of the stable was open.

'I say, who's in there?'

There was no answer. Pyotr Nikolayevich went into the stable.

'Who's in here, I say?'

Still there was no answer. It was dark, the ground under his feet felt soft, and there was a smell of manure. A pair of young greys occupied a stall to the right of the door. Pyotr Nikolayevich stretched out his hand – but there was nothing there. He moved his foot forward. Perhaps they had lain down. His foot met empty air. 'Where have they taken them?' he wondered. They couldn't have been taken for harness, the sleigh was still out there. Pyotr Nikolayevich went back outside and shouted, loudly: 'Hey, Stepan!'

Stepan was the head farm-hand. He was just coming out of the *izba*.

'I hear you!' Stepan shouted back in a jovial voice. 'Is that you, Pyotr Nikolayevich, master? The lads are just coming.'

'Why is the stable door open?'

'The stable door? I don't know, sir. Hey, Proshka, give us a lantern.'

Proshka came running with a lantern. They went into the stable. Stepan knew at once what had happened.

'It's thieves, Pyotr Nikolayevich. The lock's been smashed.'

'Never!'

'They've taken them, the villains! Mashka's not here. Neither's Yastreb. No, here's Yastreb. It's Pyostry that's missing. And Krasavchik.'

Three of the horses were missing. Pyotr Nikolayevich said nothing. He was frowning, and breathing heavily.

'Just wait till I get my hands on them. Who was supposed to be keeping watch?'

'It was Petka, sir. Petka fell asleep.'

Pyotr Nikolayevich reported the theft to the police. He told the chief constable about it, informed the leader of the zemstvo and sent his men to comb the entire neighbourhood. The horses were not found.

'Filthy peasants!' said Pyotr Nikolayevich. 'Look what they've done to me. As if I hadn't been good to them. Just you wait. Thugs and villains, the lot of you. From now on I'm going to deal with you rather differently.'

X

But meanwhile the horses – three greys – had been taken away to the outlying districts. The raiders sold Mashka to the gypsies for eighteen rubles, bartered Pyostry for the horse of a muzhik in a village forty miles away, and rode Krasavchik until he dropped from exhaustion and then slaughtered him, selling his hide for three rubles. The man who organized the raid was Ivan Mironov. He had worked for Pyotr Nikolayevich in the past, and knew his way around the estate, and he had decided to recoup his losses by doing a little horse-stealing.

After his misfortune with the forged coupon, Ivan Mironov had spent a long time drowning his sorrows, and indeed he would have drunk away everything he possessed, had his wife not hidden his horse-collars, his clothes and everything else he could have sold to buy vodka. During his drunken binge, Ivan Mironov never for a moment ceased to think not only about the gentleman who had wronged him, but also about all the gentlemen and not-so-gentle men who lived by milking his fellow peasants. On one occasion Ivan Mironov happened to be drinking with some muzhiks from the area around Podolsk. As they journeyed along, the muzhiks told him the story of how they had made off with the horses that had belonged to one of their number. Ivan Mironov began to chide these horse-thieves for wronging a muzhik in this manner. 'It's a sin,' he said. 'A horse is like a brother to a muzhik, yet you took all his horses from him. If you're going to steal horses, then steal them from the higher-ups. Those sons of bitches deserve it.'

As the conversation developed, the muzhiks from Podolsk said that you had to be pretty crafty to be able to steal horses from the gentry. You had to know your way around, and you needed the help of someone on the inside. Then Ivan Mironov remembered about Sventitsky, on whose estate he had once lived and worked as a farm-hand; he remembered that Sventitsky had once deducted one and a half rubles from his wages as compensation for a broken coupling bolt, and he remembered the greys he had used in his farm-work.

Ivan Mironov went to call on Sventitsky, making it appear as though he wanted Sventitsky to hire him, but really in order to spy out the terrain and to familiarize himself with Sventitsky's arrangements. Once he had seen that there was no night-watchman, and that in the stable the horses were kept in separate stalls, he summoned the thieves and the deed was done.

After he had split the proceeds with the muzhiks from Podolsk, Ivan Mironov went home to his village with five rubles in his pocket. At home there was no work he could do: he had no horse. And from that time onwards, Ivan Mironov began to associate with horse-thieves and gypsies.

XI

Pyotr Nikolayevich Sventitsky spared no effort in attempting to track down the thieves. He knew that the raid would not have been possible without the connivance of one of his own employees. So he regarded them all with suspicion, and tried to find out if any of them had been away from the farm on the night in question. He discovered that there was one such peasant. This was Proshka Nikolayev, a young lad who had just come back from his military service. He was a handsome, agile fellow, and Pyotr Nikolayevich employed him in place of a coachman, to look after the horses and carriages, and drive them on occasion. The chief constable was a friend of Pyotr Nikolayevich's, as were the district police inspector, the leader of the local zemstvo and the investigating magistrate. Each year all four were invited to Pyotr Nikolayevich's name-day festivities, and they were well acquainted with his delicious liqueurs and pickled mushrooms – white, honey-agaric and milk-agaric. Now they were sympathetic to him and tried to help him.

'You see, that's what you get for taking the side of the muzhiks,' said the chief constable. 'I wasn't making it up when I told you they were worse than wild animals. You won't get anywhere with them if you don't use the whip and the rod. So you think it was Proshka, do you, the chap who works as coachman for you?'

'Yes, it's him.'

'Let's have him in here, then.'

Proshka was summoned, and they began to question him.

'Where were you that night?'

Proshka shook his hair back, and his eyes flashed. 'At home, sir.'

'What do you mean, at home? All the farm-hands say you weren't.'

'As you please, sir.'

'What I please has nothing to do with it. Where were you?'

'At home, sir.'

'All right, then. Constable, take this man into custody.'

'As you please, sir.'

The reason why Proshka would not say where he had been on the night of the theft was that he had spent it at the house of his girl-friend Parasha, and had promised not to get her into trouble. There was no evidence, and Proshka was released from custody. But Pyotr Nikolayevich was convinced he had been responsible for the raid, and he conceived a hatred for him. Once, when he had taken his carriage out with Proshka as driver, he sent him off to buy some fodder. Proshka did what he usually did, and bought two measures of oats at a wayside inn, giving one and a half measures to the horses, and exchanging the remaining half for vodka. Pyotr Nikolayevich found out about it, and made a complaint to the local JP. The JP sentenced Proshka to three months' imprisonment.

Proshka was a man of self-esteem. He considered himself a cut above the rest, and had a degree of personal pride. His spell in prison was a humiliating experience for him. No longer could he strut with pride before his fellows, and his spirits sank at once.

Proshka went home from prison embittered not so much against Pyotr Nikolayevich as against the whole world.

Everyone said the same thing: after he came out of prison, Proshka went to pieces. He grew too lazy to work, took to drink and was soon caught stealing clothes from the trades-man's wife. Once again, he ended up in prison.

As for the horses, all Pyotr Nikolayevich could find out about them was that someone had discovered the hide of a grey-coated gelding which he was subsequently able to iden-tify as once having belonged to Krasavchik. To an ever-increasing degree, he was infuriated by the thieves' impunity. Now he could not set eyes on a muzhik without a sense of anger. The very mention of them was enough to make his blood boil, and he tried whenever he could to make their lives a misery for them.

XII

In spite of the fact that, once he had passed it on, Yevgeny Mikhailovich had stopped thinking about the coupon, his wife, Marya Vasilevna, could neither forgive herself for having been taken in, nor her husband for all the unkind things he had said to her, nor – and this was what rankled most – the two young louts for having so skilfully deceived her.

. From the day she had been tricked onwards, she kept a watchful eye on every grammar-school boy who came along. On one occasion she encountered Makhin, but failed to recognize him because when he saw her he distorted his features in a way that completely altered his appearance. When, however, some two weeks after the event, she ran smack into Mitya Smokovnikov on the street, she recognized him immediately. She allowed him to go by and then, turning round, she set off in pursuit. When she reached the entrance of the apartment where he lived, she took a note of his parents' name. Next day she went to the grammar school. In the vestibule she encountered Mikhail Vvedensky, the school's religious instructor. He asked her if he could help. She said she wanted to see the headmaster.

'I'm afraid the headmaster isn't here today: he's unwell. Perhaps I can deal with your inquiry, or at least take a message for him?'

Marya Vasilevna decided to tell the religious instructor everything.

Father Vvedensky was a widower, a traditionalist and a man of considerable personal vanity. The year before, he had met Smokovnikov's father at a soirée and had had a difference with him during a conversation on the subject of religion, in the course of which Smokovnikov had outmanoeuvred him on all counts and had made a laughing-stock of him. Father Vvedensky had resolved to single out the son of this man for special attention. When he discovered that the son showed the same indifference to religion as that displayed by his infidel father, he began to persecute him and even failed him in an exam.

Father Vvedensky could not help feeling a certain satisfaction when he heard from Marya Vasilevna what the young Smokovnikov had done, as he saw in the incident a confirmation of his hypotheses concerning the immorality of those who did not follow the guidance of the Church. He decided that he would make use of the incident in order, as he tried to persuade himself, to highlight the risk run by all who stray from the Church and its teachings. His real reason for doing so was, however, to take revenge on a man whom he considered to be a proud and self-opinionated atheist.

'Yes, very sad, very sad,' said Father Mikhail Vvedensky, smoothing with one hand the smooth edges of the confessional crucifix he wore at his chest. 'I'm so glad you've told me about this. As a servant of the Church I shall of course endeavour not to leave the young man without guidance; but I'll also try to make his edification as painless as possible.'

'Yes, I shall act in accordance with my vocation,' said Father Mikhail to himself, in the belief that he had completely forgotten the hostility of Smokovnikov senior and desired nothing but the welfare and salvation of the son.

During the scripture lesson the following day Father Mikhail told his pupils the whole episode of the forged coupon, and said this had been done by one of the boys at the grammar school.

'It was a vile, wicked thing to do,' he said. 'But not to own up is even worse. I don't believe it was one of you; but if it was, that boy had better own up now, and not try to hide behind others.'

As he said this, Father Mikhail gave Mitya Smokovnikov a fixed look. The other pupils, following his gaze, turned round to look at Mitya, too. Mitya turned red and began to sweat; at last he burst into tears and ran from the classroom.

When Mitya's mother learned of this, she made her son tell her the whole story, and then hurried off to the photographic supply shop. She paid the supplier's wife back the twelve rubles fifty, and made her promise to keep quiet about the grammar-school boy's identity. She instructed her son to deny everything, and on no account to make a confession to his father.

And indeed, when Fyodor Mikhailovich found out what had happened at the grammar school, and his son, on being interviewed, denied all knowledge of the matter, he went to see the headmaster and laid the facts of the case before him, saying that the religious instructor had behaved in a most reprehensible manner and that he, Fyodor Mikhailovich, was not going to let the affair rest there. The headmaster sent for the religious instructor, and a heated exchange of opinions ensued.

'First a stupid woman makes insulting and damaging accusations against my son, and then withdraws them, yet all you can do is blacken the name of an honest, truthful boy.'

'I have blackened no one's name, and I will not permit you to talk to me like that. You forget my vocation.'

'I spit on your vocation.'

'Your mistaken ideas,' said the religious instructor, his chin quivering so that his beard trembled, 'are familiar to the whole town.'

'Gentlemen, gentlemen,' remonstrated the headmaster, trying to pacify the two adversaries. This, however, proved to be impossible.

'My holy calling imposes upon me the duty of concerning myself with the moral and religious upbringing of the young.'

'That's enough of your hypocrisy. Do you think I don't know you've got no more religion than a common heathen?'

'I consider it beneath my dignity to continue holding a conversation with an individual such as yourself,' said Father Mikhail, who had taken particular offence at Smokovnikov's last remark, as he knew it was perfectly correct. He had gone through the complete course at the Theological Academy, and so had long ago ceased to believe what he practised and preached. All he believed now was that it was everyone's duty to compel themselves to believe the things he had compelled himself to believe.

Smokovnikov was less incensed by the religious instructor's behaviour than he was by this illustration of the way the influence of the clergy was beginning to manifest itself in Russian society, and he told all his friends and acquaintances about this incident.

Father Vvedensky, on the other hand, saw in it yet one more manifestation of the nihilism and atheism which were becoming established not only among the younger generation, but among older people as well, and which he believed it necessary to combat. The more he censured the unbelief of Smokovnikov and of those like him, the more convinced he was of the unshakeable solidity of his own faith, and the less he felt the need to put that faith to the test or to make himself live in accordance with it. His faith, recognized as it was by the world at large, was his principal weapon in his struggle against its repudiators.

These thoughts, engendered in him by his confrontation with Smokovnikov, and by the unpleasant events at the grammar school that had followed in the wake of that confrontation – namely the reprimand and black-marking he had received from the school authorities – finally induced him to do something that had been enticing him for a long time, ever since the death of his wife, in fact: to become a monk, and thus embark upon a career already chosen by several of his fellow students at the Academy, one of whom was already an archbishop, and another of whom was the Father Superior of a monastery, in line for appointment as a diocesan.

At the end of the academic year, Vvedensky relinquished his post at the grammar school, took monastic vows and the name 'Misail', and was very soon given the rectorship of a theological seminary in a town on the Volga.

XIII

Meanwhile Vasily the yard-keeper had set out on foot down the high road to the south.

By day he tramped, and at night a local gendarme would show him to the lodgings that were always reserved for travellers. Wherever he put in he was given bread, and sometimes people would invite him to sit down at table and have supper with them. In one village in the province of Oryol where he spent the night he was told that a merchant who had leased an orchard from the local landowner was looking for able-bodied night-watchmen. Vasily had by this time had enough of the beggar's existence he had been leading. He did not, however, want to return to his village, so he went to see the merchant who had leased the orchard and got himself taken on as a night-watchman for a wage of five rubles a month.

Vasily found life in his watchman's hut very pleasant, particularly when the sweet apples had been picked, and the other watchmen brought enormous bundles of straw that had been gathered from under the threshing-machine in the master's shed. He could lie all day long on the fresh, fragrant straw beside the even more fragrant heaps of spring and winter windfall apples, and all he had to do was keep a lookout to see that none of the young lads tried to steal the apples that were on the trees, whistle, and sing songs, which he was very good at, since he had a fine singing voice. The peasant women and girls would come up from the village in quest of apples. Vasily would tease them a bit, giving apples to the ones that caught his fancy, or exchanging lesser or greater quantities of apples for eggs, say, or a few copecks – and then he would lie back again, only getting up in order to have his breakfast, dinner and supper.

Vasily only possessed the one shirt: it was made of pink cotton and was full of holes. On his feet he wore nothing at all, but his body was strong and healthy, and when the pot of kasha was removed from the fire, Vasily would eat enough for three men, to the perpetual astonishment of the old head watchman. Vasily never slept at night, and either whistled or called out from time to time in order to keep himself awake; he could see a long way in the dark, like a cat. One night some big lads from the village started climbing the trees and shaking the apples to the ground. Vasily crept up and pounced on them; they tried to escape, but he knocked them all to the ground, and then took one of them back to his hut and handed him over to the master.

Vasily's first hut was at the far end of the orchard, but his second, into which he moved when the sweet apples were picked, was situated only forty yards or so from the master's house. Vasily found life in this hut even more pleasant. All day long he could see the gentlemen and young ladies playing games, going out for drives or taking walks together; and later on, when it got dark, he would observe them playing the

violin or the piano, singing or dancing. He would see the
students and the young ladies sitting in the windows fondling
one another, and later, some of them walking together in the
dark avenues of the lime trees, where the moonlight only
filtered through in stripes and patches. He would see the
servants running to and fro with refreshments, and would
note how the cooks, the laundresses, the managers, gardeners
and coachmen were all working for the sole purpose of
supplying their masters and mistresses with food, drink and
entertainment. Sometimes the young gentlefolk would drop
by to see him in his hut, and he would pick out the best,
juiciest and reddest apples and give them to them; the young
ladies would munch them on the spot, praising them and
saying a few words in French – Vasily would understand that
they were about him – and they would insist that he sing for
them.

Vasily viewed this way of life with admiration and, as he
thought back to the life he himself had led in Moscow, more
and more did he grow convinced that what mattered most of
all in life was to have money.

Vasily began to spend more and more time trying to think
how he could quickly get his hands on a large sum of money.
He remembered how he had fiddled bits of money for himself
on the side, and he decided that that was not the way to go
about it; it was not enough simply to attempt to grab whatever
lay in temptation's way – one had to plan things in advance,
observe the lie of the land, and do the deed neatly, leaving no
loose ends.

When it was nearly Christmas, the last of the winter apples
were picked. The fruit-grower had made a handsome profit,
and he paid off and thanked all the watchmen, including
Vasily. Vasily put on the coat and hat the fruit-grower had
given him, but he did not go home – the mere thought of that
brutish, peasant existence was enough to make him feel
positively ill. Instead, he went back to the town in the company
of the drunken ex-conscripts who had worked as watchmen
with him. Once there, he decided he would break into and
burgle the shop where he had once worked as yard-keeper,

and whose proprietor had given him a beating and driven him off the premises without giving him his wages. He knew the place inside out, including where the money was kept. He stationed one of the ex-conscripts outside the shop as a guard, smashed a window at the rear, climbed inside and took all the money. It was all so skilfully managed that no one was ever able to find out who had done it. Vasily got away with three hundred and seventy rubles. He gave a hundred to the man who had helped him, and took the rest to another town, where he spent it on a wild binge with his mates and girl-friends.

XIV

Meanwhile, Ivan Mironov had become a skilled, fearless and successful horse-thief. Afinya, his wife, who previously had been critical of him for his 'bungling', as she called it, was pleased with her husband and proud of him because he now owned a sheepskin coat with a hood, and she had a shawl and a new fur coat.

Everyone in the village and the surrounding district knew that there was not one local instance of horse-stealing in which he was not somehow involved, but they were all afraid to give evidence against him, and so whenever the finger of suspicion pointed at him he came out as clean as a whistle. His most recent raid had been on the night-grazing over at Kolotovka. So far as he was able, Ivan Mironov tried to choose the people he stole from, and his favourite victims were landowners and merchants. It was also, however, more difficult to steal from them. So when their horses seemed out of reach, he stole the muzhiks' horses instead. Thus, from the night-grazing at Kolotovka he stole as many as he could get his hands on. He didn't do the thieving himself, but employed a smart young lad by the name of Gerasim to do it for him. Not until daybreak did the muzhiks realize that their horses were missing; then they took to the roads in a mad rush to look for them. By that time, however, the horses were standing in a deep ravine in the middle of the State forest. Ivan Mironov intended to keep them hidden there until the following night, and then take them to a yard-keeper he knew in a village forty versts away. Ivan Mironov visited Gerasim in the forest, brought him pie and vodka, and then went home again by a forest path on which he hoped he would not meet anyone. He was unlucky enough to encounter one of the forest watchmen, an ex-conscript.

'Been looking for mushrooms, have you?' asked the ex-conscript.

'I can't find any today,' replied Ivan Mironov, pointing to the basket he had taken along with him just in case he did happen to find any mushrooms.

'Aye, it's not the mushroom season yet,' said the ex-conscript. 'They only start coming up after Lent.' And he walked past.

The ex-conscript was aware that something here was not as it should be. Ivan Mironov had no business to be walking through a State forest that early in the morning. The ex-conscript went back the way he had come and began to probe around in the forest. Near the ravine he heard the snorting of horses. Silently he crept up to the place it had come from. The floor of the ravine had been trampled by hooves, and there were horse-droppings everywhere. A little further off sat Gerasim, eating something, and two horses stood tethered to a tree trunk.

The ex-conscript ran off to the village and fetched the elder, the constable and two men to act as witnesses. From three sides they approached the place where Gerasim was sitting, and then seized him. Gerasim made no attempt to protest his innocence; being drunk, he immediately confessed to everything. He told them that Ivan Mironov had plied him with drink and put him up to the whole thing, and that he had said he would come to the forest to fetch the horses that day. The muzhiks left Gerasim and the horses in the forest, and set an ambush for Ivan Mironov. When night fell, a whistle was heard. Gerasim whistled back. As soon as Ivan Mironov started to come down the slope, the muzhiks rushed at him and took him to their village.

The next morning a crowd assembled in front of the elder's *izba*. Ivan Mironov was led out and questioned. Stepan Pelageyushkin, a tall, stooping, long-armed muzhik with an aquiline nose and a dour expression was the first to question him. Stepan had done his military service and now lived independently with his wife and children. It was only very recently that he had moved out of his father's house; just when he had been starting to find his own feet, his horse had been stolen. By working for two years in the mines he had managed to buy two new horses. Both had now been stolen.

'Tell me where my horses are,' said Stepan, pale with anger, staring from the ground to Ivan's face and back at the ground again.

Ivan Mironov said he knew nothing about it. Then Stepan struck him in the face, breaking his nose, from which blood began to trickle.

'Tell me, or I'll kill you.'

Ivan Mironov said nothing, and inclined his head. Stepan struck him once with his long arm. Then he struck him again. Ivan still would not say anything, but merely swung his head from side to side.

'Everyone stone him!' said the elder.

And they all began to stone him. Ivan fell silently to the ground, and then shouted: 'Barbarians, devils, stone me to death! I'm not afraid of you!'

Then Stepan took a stone from the pile he had ready, and smashed Ivan Mironov's skull with it.

XV

Ivan Mironov's murderers were brought to justice. Stepan Pelageyushkin was among those put on trial. The charge brought against him was more serious than those that were brought against the other men, because they all testified that he had been the one who had smashed Ivan Mironov's skull with a stone. Stepan made no attempt to conceal anything at his trial. His explanation was that when his pair of horses had been stolen he had gone to the police station to report the matter – it would probably have been possible to track the horses down with the help of the gypsies – but the constable had refused to see him, and had made no effort to look for the animals.

'What were we supposed to do with a man like him? He'd ruined us.'

'Why were you the only one to stone him?' asked the prosecutor.

'I wasn't. We all stoned him; the *mir*[18] had sentenced him to death. I just finished him off. What was the point of making him suffer unnecessarily?'

The judges were shocked by Stepan's expression of utter calm as he told of what he had done, of how they had stoned Ivan Mironov, and how he had finished him off.

Stepan really did not consider that the murder he had committed was such a terrible act. During his military service he had taken part in a firing squad, and then as now he had seen nothing wrong in this type of killing. If you killed a man, you killed him. Today it was his turn; tomorrow it might be yours.

Stepan was let off lightly. He was given one year in prison. His muzhik's clothes were taken away from him and locked away in the prison stores under a numbered tag, and he was given a convict's overall and boots to wear.

Stepan had never had a great deal of respect for authority, but now he was fully convinced that all the powers that be and all the nobility except the Tsar, who alone took pity on the common people and was just in his dealings with them, were nothing but robbers and bandits, sucking the life-blood of the poor. The stories of the deportees and hard-labour convicts with whom he associated in the prison confirmed him in this view. One man had been sentenced to hard labour for exposing the pilfering of some local officials, another for striking an official because he had unlawfully confiscated the property of peasants, yet a third for forging banknotes. The gentry and the merchants could get away with anything, it seemed, while the poor muzhiks were sent to feed the lice in prison for the slightest misdemeanour.

During the time that Stepan spent in prison he received visits from his wife. Things had been bad enough for her with him gone from home, but now she had become completely destitute and had had to go begging with her children. His wife's misfortunes made Stepan even more embittered. He was viciously aggressive towards everyone in the prison, and on one occasion he nearly killed one of the prison cooks with an axe, for which he was given another year. During the course of that second year he learned that his wife had died, and that his household had ceased to exist . . .

When Stepan's term was up, he was summoned to the stores and his muzhik's clothes were taken down from the shelf and handed back to him.

'Where am I to go now?' he asked the quartermaster-sergeant as he put his own clothes on again.

'Home, of course,'

'I haven't got a home any more. I suppose I'll just have to take to the road and rob folk.'

'If you rob folk you'll be back to see us again.'

'Well, that's as may be.'

And Stepan went away. In spite of what he had said, he set off in the direction of his home. There was nowhere else for him to go.

On his way there he stopped to spend the night at a roadside inn and drinking-house he knew.

The innkeeper was a fat tradesman from Vladimir. He knew Stepan, knew that he had gone to prison as a result of misfortune, and agreed to let him stay the night.

This rich tradesman had run off with the wife of a muzhik in the neighbourhood, and she now lived with the tradesman both as spouse and employee.

Stepan knew all about the episode – how the tradesman had injured the muzhik's honour, how this vile woman had left her husband and then grown fat from overeating. Just at that moment she was treating her sweaty personage to tea;

charitably, she asked Stepan if he would like some. There were no other guests at the inn. Stepan was allowed to sleep the night in the kitchen. Matryona cleared away the dishes and went off to her room. Stepan lay down on top of the stove, but he couldn't sleep, and kept snapping beneath his weight the lengths of kindling that had been placed on the stove to dry. He could not for the life of him get the tradesman's fat belly out of his head; in his mind he saw it bulging from the waist of his cotton shirt, which had been washed and rewashed so many times that it had grown faded. Again and again the thought recurred to him of slashing that belly with a knife and letting out the fatty intestines. And of doing the same to the woman, as well. One moment he would say to himself: 'Oh, to hell with them, I'll be gone tomorrow,' and the next he would remember Ivan Mironov and start thinking once again about the tradesman's belly and Matryona's white, sweaty throat. If he was going to kill, he'd better kill them both. The second cock-crow sounded. If he was going to do it, he had better do it now, or it would be daylight. The night before he had spotted a knife and an axe that had been left lying out. He climbed down from the stove, took the axe and the knife, and went out of the kitchen. Out in the hall he heard the latch click on the other side of the door. The tradesman opened the door and came out. This was not the way Stepan had been planning it. The knife would be no good now, so he swung the axe and split the tradesman's head in two. The tradesman fell against the lintel and slumped to the floor.

Stepan went into Matryona's room. Matryona leapt up and stood on her bed, dressed in nothing but her nightshirt. With the same axe Stepan killed her, too.

Then he lit a candle, took the money from the till and fled.

XVI

In the chief town of a country district lived an old man who had once been a civil servant, but had now taken to drink. He owned the house in which he lived with his two daughters and son-in-law, and which stood some way from the other buildings in the town. The married daughter also drank and led a disreputable life, and it was the elder, widowed daughter, Maria Semyonovna, a wrinkled, emaciated woman of fifty, who kept them all on her pension of two hundred and fifty rubles a year. The entire family lived on this money. Maria Semyonovna also did all the housework. She looked after her drunken, enfeebled old father and her sister's baby, she cooked the meals and did the laundry. And, as always happens in such cases, they each of them unloaded all their wants and requirements on to her, yet never ceased to shout abuse at her; the son-in-law would even beat her when he was drunk. She endured it all in silence and humility and, as is also usual in such cases, found that the more she was compelled to do, the more she was able to do. She even offered assistance to the poor, leaving herself short; she gave away her clothing and helped to look after the sick people in the neighbour-hood.

On one occasion Maria Semyonovna hired the services of a crippled, one-legged country tailor. He altered her father's long overcoat and re-covered her fur-lined jacket with new cloth so that she could wear it when she went to market in winter.

The crippled tailor was an intelligent, observant man who had come across a lot of people in the course of his work and whose disability had compelled him to spend much of his life sitting down, and thus predisposed to reflection. He had stayed for a week in Maria Semyonovna's household, and had been lost in wonderment at the life she led. Once she came into the kitchen, where he did his sewing, in order to wash some towels, and as she did them she talked to him about his life – how badly his brother had treated him and how he had taken his patrimony and left to live on his own.

'I thought it would be better, but I'm poor just the same as I was before.'

'It's better not to change, but to live in the way you've always lived,' said Maria Semyonovna.

'That's what I find so wonderful about you, Maria Semyonovna: you're always putting yourself out for others, yet you seem to get precious little good back from them in return.'

Maria Semyonovna did not say anything.

'You must have decided that it's true what the good book says, and you'll get your reward in the world to come.'

'We know nothing of that,' said Maria Semyonovna. 'All I know is that it's better to live that way.'

'And is that what the book says?'

'Yes, it is,' she said, and out of the Gospels she read him the Sermon on the Mount. The tailor began to reflect. Even after he had been paid and had set off home, he still continued to reflect on what he had observed in the house where Maria Semyonovna lived, and on what she had told him and read to him.

XVII

Pyotr Nikolayevich had changed his attitude towards the common people, and the common people had changed their attitude towards him. Within the space of barely a year the local muzhiks had felled twenty-seven of his oak trees and burned down a threshing-barn that had not been insured. Pyotr Nikolayevich decided he could not go on living among people such as these.

At about this time, a family called the Liventsovs were looking for a manager to run their estate, and the marshal of nobility had recommended Pyotr Nikolayevich as being the best farmer in the district. The Liventsov estate was enormous, but it was failing to yield any profit and the peasants were helping themselves to the land. Pyotr Nikolayevich undertook to put everything to rights. He leased out his own estate and went with his wife to live in the remote Volga province where the Liventsov holdings were situated.

Pyotr Nikolayevich had always been a stickler for law and order, and this made him all the more determined that these wild, uncivilized muzhiks were not to be allowed to take illegal possession of land and property that did not belong to them. He was glad of this opportunity to teach them a lesson, and he set about his task with severity. He had one peasant sent to prison for stealing timber, and another he flogged personally and without mercy for not getting out of the way and doffing his cap when he was supposed to. As for the meadows which were in dispute, and which the peasants regarded as theirs, Pyotr Nikolayevich let it be known that if they allowed their cattle on to them he would have the beasts impounded.

Spring came, and the peasants, as they had done in previous years, let their cattle out on to the manorial meadows. Pyotr Nikolayevich called all the farm-hands together and instructed them to drive the cattle into the manorial stockyard. The muzhiks were out ploughing, and so in spite of the warning cries of the peasant women, the farm-hands were able to round up the cattle. When the muzhiks came back from work, they gathered together and came over to the manorial stockyard to demand the return of their animals. Pyotr Nikolayevich came out to meet them with a rifle slung across his shoulder (he had just come back from making a round of inspection) and told them he would only give them back their cattle upon payment of a fine of fifty copecks per cow or steer and ten copecks per sheep. The muzhiks began shouting that the meadows were theirs, that they had belonged to their fathers and their grandfathers before them, and that he had no right to impound other people's cattle.

'Give us our cattle or it'll be the worse for you,' said one old man, advancing towards Pyotr Nikolayevich.

'What did you say?' exclaimed Pyotr Nikolayevich, his face drained of colour. He went up to the old man.

'Give us them back if you don't want trouble, shark.'

'What?' howled Pyotr Nikolayevich, and he struck the old man in the face.

'You wouldn't dare fight us. Lads, take the cattle by force.'

The crowd advanced. Pyotr Nikolayevich attempted to make his escape, but they would not let him. He tried to force his way through, and his rifle went off by accident, killing one of the peasants. A riot ensued, in the process of which Pyotr

Nikolayevich was crushed to death. Five minutes after it was all over, his disfigured corpse was dragged down into the ravine.

The murderers were tried by a military tribunal, and two of them were sentenced to death by hanging.

XVIII

In the village the crippled tailor hailed from, five of the well-to-do peasants leased from the local landowner a hundred and five desyatinas of rich, arable land as black as tar and distributed it among the other muzhiks in exchange for payments of eighteen and fifteen rubles per allotment. None of the allotments changed hands for less than twelve rubles. So the well-to-do peasants made a good profit. They each took five desyatinas for themselves, and these allotments cost them nothing. One of these muzhiks died, and the others asked the crippled tailor if he would like to come in on the deal with them.

When they began to divide the land up among themselves, the tailor refused to drink vodka with them, and when they got round to discussing who should get how much land, the tailor said he thought that everyone should receive the same amount, and that no charge should be made, but that everyone should receive according to his need.

'Whoever heard of such an arrangement?'

'Otherwise we won't be acting as Christians. That's all very well for the higher-ups, but we're peasants. We have to do things God's way. Follow the law of Christ.'

'Where's it written down, this law?'

'In the good book, in the Gospels. Here, I tell you what, you come over to my place on Sunday; I'll read you a bit of it, and then we can discuss it.'

Most of the peasants did not bother to go to the tailor's house on Sunday. Three, however, did, and the tailor began to read to them.

He read them five chapters of the Gospel according to St

Matthew. When he had finished, they proceeded to discuss what they had heard, but only one man, a peasant called Ivan Chuyev, thought it made any sense. So bowled over by it was he that he began to do everything according to God's law, and all his family followed suit. He refused to accept the extra land and would only take what was his proper share.

Other people began visiting Ivan and the tailor, and gradually they too were won over. They gave up smoking, drinking and swearing and started trying to help one another. They also stopped going to church, and they took down their icons and gave them back to the village priest. Eventually seventeen households – comprising sixty-five people in all – were involved in this movement. The village priest was frightened, and reported the matter to his bishop. The bishop wondered what he should do, and finally decided to send for Father Misail, the former grammar-school religious instructor.

XIX

The bishop asked Father Misail to sit down, and began to tell him about the strange new goings-on in his diocese.

'It's all caused by ignorance and spiritual weakness. You're a man of learning. I'm relying on you. I want you to go down there, call them all together and get the matter sorted out.'

'With Your Grace's blessing, I shall try,' said Father Misail. He was glad of this assignment, as he always was whenever he was given an opportunity of demonstrating his faith. Converting others was the best means he knew of persuading himself that he did in fact believe.

'Please do the best you can. I'm really awfully worried about my little flock,' said the bishop, accepting in leisurely fashion a glass of tea from the lay brother, with his white, pudgy hands.

'Why have you only brought one sort of jam? Bring some others,' he told the lay brother. 'I'm really most, most upset,' he went on, addressing Father Misail.

Father Misail was glad of this chance to show the stuff he

was made of. Being a man of modest means, however, he asked that his expenses be paid and, anticipating the opposition he would encounter on the part of the uncultured peasants, he also requested that the governor of the province should instruct the local police to give him assistance in case of need.

The bishop made all the necessary arrangements for him, and when Father Misail had, with the help of the lay brother and the cook, got together the hamper and provisions that were so essential when travelling to the back of beyond, he set off for his destination. As he set off on this mission, Father Misail had a pleasant sense of the importance of his vocation; at the same time he ceased to have any doubts concerning his own faith, and was on the contrary quite swept away by a conviction of its authenticity.

His thoughts centred not on the substance of his faith – that he considered an axiom – but on the refutation of these objections that were being made to its outer forms.

XX

The village priest and his wife gave Father Misail a most respectful welcome, and the day after his arrival they called all the peasants together in the village church. Father Misail, attired in a new silken surplice, wearing a confessional crucifix at his chest, his hair neatly combed, walked up into the ambo Standing by his side was the priest; a little further away stood the deacons and the choirboys; a number of policemen were stationed by the side-doors. Some of the sectarians had also arrived; they were dressed in dirty, ragged sheepskin coats.

After the public prayer, Father Misail delivered a sermon in which he exhorted the apostates to return to the bosom of the Mother Church, threatening them with the torments of hell and promising absolution to those who repented.

The sectarians fell silent. When they were actually questioned, however, they did make some reply.

To the question why they had broken away from the Church,

they replied that it had been because what people worshipped in the churches were wooden, man-made gods; not only was this not indicated by the Holy Scriptures, the prophecies actually forbade it. When Father Misail asked Chuyev whether it was true that they called the holy icons 'boards', Chuyev replied: 'Well, you just turn any old icon round and see for yourself.' When it was inquired of them why they didn't recognize the priesthood, they replied that in the Scriptures it was written: 'Freely ye have received, freely give,' whereas the priests would only offer their holy grace in exchange for money. All Father Misail's attempts to support his arguments by Holy Scripture were met with the calm but firm rejection of Ivan and the tailor, who referred to that same Scripture, which they knew inside out. Father Misail grew angry and threatened them with the secular authorities. To this the sectarians replied that the Scriptures said: 'They will persecute you, even as they persecuted me.'

Thus it all came to nothing, and all would have passed off peacefully, had not Father Misail delivered, at Mass the following day, a sermon about the harmful influence of false witnesses, in which he said that they deserved every form of punishment. As the peasants were shuffling out of the church afterwards, they started talking about what they could do to teach the atheists a lesson and prevent them from stirring up any more trouble among the village folk. And that very day, at the same time as Father Misail was nibbling smoked salmon in the company of His Holy Reverence and an inspector who had arrived from a nearby town, a riot broke out in the village. The orthodox believers had gathered together in a crowd outside Chuyev's *izba* and were waiting for the sectarians to come out so they could beat them up. There were about twenty sectarians, men and women. Father Misail's sermon and now this assemblage of orthodox believers with their threatening taunts had aroused a malevolent spirit in the sectarians, one that had not been there before. Evening approached, and it was time for the peasant women to go and milk the cows, but the orthodox believers continued to stand outside and wait. When a young lad ventured out of the *izba*, the crowd started to lay about him and drove him back inside. The sectarians discussed what they should do, but were unable to reach any agreement among themselves.

The tailor said they ought just to put up with it and not fight back. Chuyev, on the other hand, said that if they didn't do anything they would all be beaten up, and he grabbed a poker and went out into the street. The orthodox believers hurled themselves upon him.

'All right then, let's do things according to the law of Moses!' he shouted, and started to lay about the orthodox believers with the poker, putting one man's eye out in the process. The rest of the sectarians meanwhile slipped out of the *izba* and went back to their homes.

Chuyev was brought before the court for false witness and blasphemy, and was sentenced to deportation.

Father Misail, on the other hand, received a reward and was made an archimandrite.

XXI

Two years before all this happened, an attractive girl of healthy, oriental appearance called Katya Turchaninova arrived in St Petersburg from the territory of the Don Cossacks in order to take up her studies at the university. There she met the son of the leader of the zemstvo in Simbirsk province, a student by the name of Tyurin. Her love for him was not the ordinary kind of female love that expresses itself in the desire to become a man's wife and the mother of his children, but was rather a comradely affection which drew most of its strength from the couple's shared sense of outrage and hatred where the established social order was concerned, from a similar animus towards the representatives of that order, and from a consciousness of their own intellectual, educational and moral superiority to them.

Turchaninova was a capable student. She had no difficulty in memorizing her lecture notes and thus passed her examinations, managing at the same time to devour enormous quantities of the most recently published books. She was quite certain that her calling lay not in the bearing and nurturing of children – she looked upon such a vocation with disgust and contempt – but in destroying the existing social order, which put shackles on the finest aspirations of the common people, and in showing men and women the new way of life that had been revealed to her by the most modern European writers. Full of figure, fair-skinned, red-cheeked and attractive, with flashing black eyes and a thick tress of black hair, she aroused in men feelings she did not intend to arouse and indeed had no time for, so immersed was she in her labour of agitation and propaganda. Nevertheless, she liked the fact that she aroused these feelings, and although she never dressed to kill, she did not neglect her appearance, either. She liked the fact that she appealed to men, as it meant she was able to show that she despised that which was held in such esteem by other women. In her views on the methods to be used in the struggle with the established order she went further than Tyurin and the majority of her friends, maintaining that the end justified any means whatsoever, including murder. Yet this same revolutionary, Katya Turchaninova, was also a truly kind-hearted and self-effacing woman who was forever putting herself out for the sake of other people's advantage, enjoyment and well-being, and who was always genuinely glad of an opportunity to do favours, whether for children, old people or animals.

Turchaninova spent the summer months in the principal town of one of the Volga districts, where she stayed with a friend of hers who was a country schoolmistress. Tyurin also spent the summer in this district where his father owned a house. Turchaninova, her friend, Tyurin and the local doctor often met, exchanged books, argued with one another and got generally worked up about social issues. The Tyurins' estate bordered on the Liventsov holding where Pyotr Nikolayevich was now manager. As soon as Pyotr Nikolayevich arrived and started to set the place in order, young Tyurin, noticing that the Liventsovs' peasants seemed to have acquired a spirit of independence and a firm resolve to uphold their rights, began tc take an interest in them and often walked down to the village to talk to them, trying to promote the theory of socialism among them, with particular regard to the nationalization of the land.

When Pyotr Nikolayevich was murdered and the district sessions arrived, the circle of revolutionaries in the district town had a marvellous pretext for agitation in court, and they spoke out their opinions in no uncertain terms. Unfortunately, however, Tyurin's walks to the village and his conversations with the peasants were alluded to during the court proceedings. His house was searched, some revolutionary pamphlets were discovered, and he was arrested and taken away to St Petersburg.

Turchaninova followed him to St Petersburg and went to the prison to try to see him, but was not permitted to have a private interview with him; instead, she had to come on the public visitors' day, and could only catch a glimpse of him through two iron gratings. This meeting increased her sense of outrage still further. Her indignation finally reached its limit when, remonstrating with a handsome young officer of the gendarmes, she discovered that he was willing to offer her some concessions if she would agree to certain proposals he wished to make to her. This sent her into a violent rage against representatives of authority. She went to the chief of police in order to file a complaint. The chief of police repeated what the gendarme had said, that there was nothing they could do and that it was all in the hands of the Minister of the Interior. She sent a petition to the minister, requesting an interview with Tyurin; it was refused. Then she decided she would commit an act of desperation, and bought a revolver.

XXII

The minister received his visitors at the hour he usually set aside for this purpose. Three of his petitioners he avoided; he had a few words with the governor of a province and then went up to a pretty, dark-eyed young woman who was standing with a document in her left hand. A lecherous glint appeared in the minister's eyes at the sight of such an attractive petitioner, but remembering his status he assumed a serious countenance.

'What can I do for you?' he asked, drawing closer to her.

Without replying, she quickly produced her revolver from under her cape and, pointing it at the minister, fired, but missed.

The minister tried to grab her arm, but she stumbled backwards and fired a second shot. The minister took to his heels. The woman was trembling all over, unable to say a word; then, suddenly, she burst into hysterical laughter. The minister escaped without even a scratch.

It was Turchaninova. She was thrown into a cell to await trial. Meanwhile the minister, who had received the compliments and commiserations of those in the very highest places and even from the Tsar himself, appointed a commission to investigate the plot that had led to this attempt on his life.

There was, of course, no plot; but officials of both the civil and the secret police forces zealously applied themselves to the search for all the threads of the non-existent conspiracy, conscientiously earning their salaries and their keep. Getting up early in the morning, before it was light, they conducted search after search, copied documents and books, read diaries and personal letters and made extracts from these in beautiful handwriting on beautiful paper; they cross-examined Turchaninova any number of times, confronting her with witnesses and endeavouring to make her tell them the names of her accomplices.

The minister was a kindly man at heart and was really sorry for this healthy, attractive Cossack girl, but he told himself that he had grave responsibilities to the state which he must discharge, however painful they might be. And when an old friend of his, who knew the Tyurin family, met him at a court ball and started to ask him about Tyurin and Turchaninova, the minister shrugged his shoulders, crinkling the red ribbon that traversed his white waistcoat, and said: '*Je ne demanderais pas mieux que de lâcher cette pauvre fillette, mais vous savez — le devoir.'*

And all the while Turchaninova was sitting in her cell awaiting trial, exchanging tapped signals with her fellow prisoners from time to time and reading the books she had been given. On occasion, however, she would suddenly give way to rage and despair, hammering on the walls, screaming and laughing.

XXIII

One day, when Maria Semyonovna was on her way home from collecting her pension at the paymaster's office, she met a teacher she knew.

'Hullo, Maria Semyonovna, did you get your pension all right?' he shouted to her from the opposite side of the street.

'Yes, thank you,' replied Maria Semyonovna. 'It'll be enough to fill a few cracks, anyway.'

'Well, you've got enough there, you can fill the cracks and still have some over,' said the teacher, and with a goodbye he walked on.

'Goodbye,' said Maria Semyonovna. As she watched him depart, she ran straight into a tall man with very long arms, whose face wore a stern expression. Approaching her house, she was surprised to see this same long-armed man again. He watched her as she went into her house, stood around for a while outside and then turned on his heels and left.

At first Maria Semyonovna felt a sensation of fear, but this soon gave way to one of melancholy. None the less, once she was inside and had given sweets to the old man and her scrofulous little nephew Fedya and made a fuss over the dog Treasure, who yelped with joy to see her return, she felt all right again and, giving the pension money to her father, resumed the household chores with which she was never done.

The man she had bumped into had been Stepan.

After he had murdered the yard-keeper at the wayside inn,

Stepan had not gone home to Moscow. It was a strange thing: the recollection of the murder was in no way disagreeable to him; indeed, he thought about it several times a day. He liked the idea that he could do something of this nature so cleverly and skilfully that no one would ever find him out or prevent him from doing the same again to other people. As he sat in an eating-house in a provincial town sipping tea and vodka, he looked at all the customers with one thought in his head: how to murder them. He went to the house of a man who came from his village and worked as a drayman in order to ask him for a bed for the night. The drayman was out. Stepan said he would wait, and sat talking to the drayman's wife. Then, when she turned her back to him, leaning over the stove, he had the idea of killing her. Surprised at himself, he gave his head a shake, then took his knife from his boot-flap, threw the woman to the ground and cut her throat. The children started to cry, so he killed them too and left the town that same night. Once he was out of town he found a village and slept the night at its inn.

The following day he came back to the market town, and while he was walking along the street he overheard Maria Semyonovna's conversation with the teacher. Her gaze frightened him, but all the same he decided he would break into her house and steal the money she had drawn. That night he broke the lock and entered an upstairs room. The younger, married daughter was the first to hear him. She cried out. Stepan immediately cut her throat. The son-in-law woke up and grappled with him. He seized Stepan by the throat and struggled with him for a long time, but Stepan was too strong for him. When he had dealt with the son-in-law, Stepan, agitated now and aroused by the fighting, went behind the partition. In bed behind the partition lay Maria Semyonovna. She sat up and looked at Stepan with meek, frightened eyes and made the sign of the cross over herself. Once again Stepan found her gaze intimidating. He lowered his eyes.

'Where's the money?' he asked, without looking up.

She did not say anything.

'Where's the money?' Stepan repeated, showing her the knife.

'What are you doing? You can't do this.'

'Oh, can't I?'

Stepan moved closer to her, getting ready to seize her arms so that she could not stop him, but she offered no resistance and did not raise her arms, merely pressed them to her bosom, gave a deep sigh and said repeatedly: 'Oh, what a terrible sin. What are you doing? Have mercy on yourself. You think you're harming others, but it's your own soul you're ruining . . . O-oh!' she screamed.

Stepan could stand her voice and her gaze no longer, and with a cry of 'I'm not going to waste my breath on you!' he slashed her throat with his knife. She sank back on to the pillows and began to wheeze, soaking one of the pillows in blood. He turned away and walked through the upstairs rooms, gathering the valuable items together. When he had taken what he wanted, he lit a cigarette, sat down for a while in order to brush down his clothes, and then left the house. He had thought that this murder would pass off with ease, as the previous ones had done, but before he had reached the place where he intended to lodge for the night he suddenly felt so exhausted that he could hardly move a limb. He lay down in a ditch and stayed there for the rest of that night, all the following day and all the next night.

PART TWO

I

As he lay in the ditch, Stepan kept seeing Maria Semyonovna's meek, emaciated and frightened face, and hearing her voice. 'You can't do this,' it kept saying in that peculiar, lisping, plaintive way. And each time it spoke he relived what he had done to her all over again. He began to grow really afraid, and he closed his eyes and flailed his head from side to side in an effort to shake these thoughts and memories out of it. For a moment he would succeed in freeing himself from the memories, but they would be replaced first by one black devil, then by another, followed in turn by yet more black devils, with glowing red eyes, making dreadful faces, and all saying the same thing: 'You killed her – now kill yourself, or we won't give you any peace until you do.' And he would open his eyes and see her again and hear her voice, and he would start feeling sorry for her and experiencing fear and revulsion at himself. Once more he would close his eyes – and once more the devils would appear.

Towards the evening of the second day he got up and walked to a nearby inn. With much effort he got there, and began drinking. But no matter how much he drank, he could not get drunk. He sat at a table in silence, knocking back glass after glass of vodka. The village policeman entered the inn.

'Who might you be, then?' asked the policeman.

'Oh, I'm the one who slit everybody's throats up at Domotvorov's place the night before last.'

They bound him hand and foot. After he had been held for a day in the local police station, he was sent to the chief town of the province. The warden of the prison there, recognizing him as the unruly inmate he had once had to deal with in the past, gave him a sour reception.

'You'd better not play any tricks on me now, mind,' the warden said hoarsely, knitting his eyebrows and making his lower jaw protrude. 'At the first sign of it I'll have you flogged to death. You won't escape from my prison.'

'What would I be doing trying to escape?' retorted Stepan, looking at the ground. 'I gave myself up of my own free will.'

'Don't answer back when I'm around. And look up at a superior when he's addressing you,' shouted the warden, and gave him a sock on the jaw.

Just then Stepan was thinking once more about Maria Semyonovna and hearing her voice inside his brain. He had not heard a word the warden had been saying.

'What?' he asked, brought back to his senses with a start by the sudden blow on his chin.

'Come on, come on. Forward march. None of your nonsense, now.'

The warden had been expecting disorderly behaviour, machinations with other convicts, escape attempts. But of all this there was none. Whenever the orderly or the warden himself looked in through the peephole in the door of Stepan's cell, they would see him sitting on a sack that had been stuffed with straw, his head propped in his hands, constantly whispering something to himself. When he was questioned by the court investigator he again behaved differently from other prisoners. He seemed absent-minded, seemed not to hear the questions he was asked or, if he did take them in, was so truthful in his replies that the examining magistrate who was used to battling with ingenuity and subterfuge on the part of the defendants who appeared before him, now experienced a feeling akin to that of someone climbing a flight of stairs in the dark and suddenly putting his foot into empty space. Knitting his eyebrows and fixing his eyes straight in front of him, Stepan confessed to all the murders he had committed in the most unaffected, business-like tone of voice, doing his utmost to remember all the details: 'He came out,' said Stepan, describing the first murder, 'without any shoes or socks on, and stood in the doorway, so I gashed him once, and he croaked, and then I went straight to work on his missus . . .' – and so it went on. When the public procurator made his rounds of the prison cells and asked Stepan if he had any complaints to make or if there was anything he lacked, Stepan answered that he had everything he wanted and that no one had mistreated him. The procurator, having gone a few steps down the stinking corridor, stopped for a moment and asked the warden who was accompanying him what the behaviour of this convict was like in general.

'He baffles me,' replied the warden, gratified that Stepan had praised the treatment he had received. 'He's been with us nearly two months now, and he's been a model of good behaviour. All I'm scared of is that he's got something up his sleeve. He's a plucky chap, and incredibly strong.'

II

For the first month he spent in prison Stepan was incessantly tormented by the same thing: he saw the grey wall of his cell, heard the sounds of the prison – the buzz of voices in the communal cell below him, the footsteps of the sentry in the corridor, and the ticking of the clock – and in addition he saw *her*, with her meek gaze, the gaze that had vanquished him the first time he had encountered her in the street, with her scraggy, wrinkled throat which he had cut with his knife, and her sweet, plaintive, lisping voice saying: '*You think you're harming others, but it's your own soul you're ruining. You can't do this!*' Then the voice would die away and the three black devils would reappear. They would reappear irrespective of whether his eyes were open or closed. When they were closed, the devils appeared more distinctly. When they were open, the devils would fuse with the doors and the walls and gradually disappear, only to re-emerge from three different directions, making leering faces and saying over and over again: 'Kill yourself, kill yourself. You can make a noose, you can start a fire.' At this point Stepan would begin to shiver, and he would start reciting what prayers he knew – 'Ave Maria' and 'Our Father' – and initially this seemed to help. As he said these prayers, he would begin to remember his past life: he would remember his father and mother, his village, Wolf the family dog, his grandfather lying on top of the stove, the upturned benches on which he had tobogganed in the snow with the other boys; then he would remember the girls and their songs, and then the horses, and how they had been stolen, how they had caught the horse-thief and how he, Stepan, had finished him off with a stone. And then his first prison term would come back to him, and he would remember the fat yard-keeper, the drayman's wife and her children, and then again he would remember *her*. And he would feel hot all over, he would throw off his prison dressing-gown, leap up from his bunk and begin to pace up and down his cramped cell with rapid strides, like a wild beast in a cage, turning abruptly whenever he reached the damp, sweating walls. And again he would recite his prayers, only now they were to no avail.

On one of those long, autumn evenings, when the wind was howling and whistling in the chimneys, he sat down on his bunk, having had enough of pacing his cell, and knew that it was no use struggling any longer, that the devils had won, and he submitted to them. For a long time now he had had an eye on the stovepipe. If he were to wind some thin twine or thin strips of cloth round it, it would hold. But it would have to be done cleverly. He set to work and spent two days cutting long strips of cloth from the sack he slept on (when the orderly came in he covered the bed with his dressing-gown). He tied the strips together in double knots so that they would support the weight of his body. While he was engaged in this task, his mental anguish ceased. When everything was ready he made a noose, put it round his neck, climbed on to the bed and hanged himself. But his tongue had only just started to protrude when the strips of cloth broke and he fell to the ground. The noise brought the orderly running in. The medical orderly was sent for, and Stepan was taken away to the hospital. By the next day he had fully recovered, and he was discharged from hospital and taken, not to his solitary cell, but to the communal one.

In the communal cell he lived with twenty other prisoners as if he were alone: he saw no one, spoke to no one and suffered again from his former mental anguish. He suffered particularly when all the men were asleep except for him, and he would see her again as of old, hear her voice, and then witness once again the appearance of the black devils with their terrible eyes, mocking and tormenting him.

Once again, as formerly, he said his prayers and once again they were to no avail.

On one occasion when, after he had prayed, she appeared to him again, he began to pray to her instead; he prayed to her soul, begging it to let him go, to forgive him. And when, towards morning, he collapsed on to his tattered sack, he fell fast asleep, and as he slept she appeared to him again in his dreams with her scraggy, wrinkled, cut throat.

'Please forgive me.'

She looked at him with her meek gaze and said nothing.

'Won't you forgive me?'

Three times he begged her to forgive him. But she said nothing, and finally he woke up. From that time on he started to feel better, and it was as if his eyes had been opened: he looked around him and for the first time he began to make friends with his cell-mates and to talk to them.

III

One of the men in Stepan's cell was Vasily, who had been caught stealing again and been sentenced to deportation; another was Chuyev, who had also been sentenced to forcible settlement. Vasily spent his time either singing songs in his magnificent voice or telling his cell-mates the story of his exploits. Chuyev, on the other hand, either worked, mended some article of outer clothing or underwear, or read the Gospels and the Psalms.

To Stepan's query as to why he was being deported, Chuyev replied that it was because he was a true believer in Christ, because the deceiving priests could not tolerate the strength of spirit of those who lived according to the Gospels and thus laid bare their own sinfulness. When Stepan asked him what the law of the Gospels was, Chuyev explained to him that it consisted in not praying to man-made gods, but rather in worshipping in spirit and in truth. And he described how they had learned this true faith from a one-legged tailor when they had been dividing up the land.

'All right, so what's the punishment for evil-doing, then?' asked Stepan.

'It's all written in the Gospels.' And Chuyev read to him:

' "When the Son of man shall come in his glory, and all the

holy angels with him, then shall he sit upon the throne of his glory:

' "And before him shall be gathered all nations: and he shall separate them one from another, as a shepherd divideth his sheep from the goats:

' "And he shall set the sheep on his right hand, but the goats on the left.

' "Then shall the King say unto them on his right hand, Come, ye blessed of my Father, inherit the kingdom prepared for you from the foundation of the world:

' "For I was an hungred, and ye gave me meat: I was thirsty, and ye gave me drink: I was a stranger, and ye took me in:

' "Naked, and ye clothed me: I was sick, and ye visited me: I was in prison, and ye came unto me.

' "Then shall the righteous answer him, saying, Lord, when saw we thee an hungred, and fed thee? or thirsty, and gave thee drink?

' "When saw we thee a stranger, and took thee in? or naked, and clothed thee?

' "Or when saw we thee sick, or in prison, and came unto thee?

' "And the King shall answer and say unto them, Verily I say unto you, Inasmuch as ye have done it unto one of the least of these my brethren, ye have done it unto me.

' "Then shall he say also unto them on the left hand, Depart from me, ye cursed, into everlasting fire, prepared for the devil and his angels:

' "For I was an hungred, and ye gave me no meat: I was thirsty, and ye gave me no drink:

' "I was a stranger, and ye took me not in: naked, and ye clothed me not: sick, and in prison, and ye visited me not.

' "Then shall they also answer him, saying, Lord, when saw we thee an hungred, or athirst, or a stranger, or naked, or sick, or in prison, and did not minister unto thee?

' "Then shall he answer them, saying, Verily I say unto you, Inasmuch as ye did it not to one of the least of these, ye did it not to me.

' "And these shall go away into everlasting punishment: but the righteous into life eternal." ' (Matthew xxv, 31–46)

Vasily, who had squatted down on the floor opposite Chuyev in order to listen to the Scripture reading, nodded his stately head in approval.

'That's right,' he said, emphatically. ' "Go ye accursed into eternal torment, you never fed a poor man, but filled your own bellies instead." That's what they deserve. Here, give me the book, I want to read a bit, too,' he added, anxious to show off his reading ability.

'But won't there be any forgiveness?' asked Stepan, silently lowering his shaggy head to listen.

'Hang on a minute, and shut up,' Chuyev said to Vasily, who was still going on about how the rich had neither fed the poor wanderer nor visited him in prison. 'Hang on, will you?' said Chuyev again, leafing through the copy of the New Testament. When he found the place he wanted, Chuyev smoothed out the pages with a large, strong hand that had gone white from his long term in prison.

' "And there were also two other malefactors, led with him" – with Christ, that is,' Chuyev began, '– "to be put to death.

' "And when they were come to the place, which is called Calvary, there they crucified him, and the malefactors, one on the right hand, and the other on the left.

' "Then said Jesus, Father, forgive them; for they know not what they do. And they parted his raiment, and cast lots.

' "And the people stood beholding. And the rulers also with them derided him, saying, He saved others; let him save himself, if he be Christ, the chosen of God.

' "And the soldiers also mocked him, coming to him, and offering him vinegar.

' "And saying, If thou be the king of the Jews, save thyself.

' "And a superscription also was written over him in letters of Greek, and Latin, and Hebrew, THIS IS THE KING OF THE JEWS.

' "And one of the malefactors which were hanged railed on him, saying, If thou be Christ, save thyself and us.

' "But the other answering rebuked him, saying, Dost not thou fear God, seeing thou art in the same condemnation?

' "And we indeed justly; for we receive the due reward of our deeds: but this man hath done nothing amiss.

' "And he said unto Jesus, Lord, remember me when thou comest into thy kingdom.

' "And Jesus said unto him, Verily I say unto thee, Today shalt thou be with me in paradise." ' (Luke xxiii, 32–43)

Stepan said nothing, but sat reflecting, and although he appeared to be listening, he heard no more of what Chuyev was reading.

'So that's what the true faith is,' he thought. 'It's only the people that feed the poor and visit the prisoners who'll be saved, all the rest'll go to hell. All the same, the thief didn't repent until he was on the cross, and he went to heaven.' He saw no contradiction here. The one circumstance seemed rather to confirm the other: the merciful would go to heaven and the unmerciful would go to hell, and that meant that everyone had better be merciful; the fact that Christ had pardoned the thief meant that Christ too was merciful. All this was completely new to Stepan; he only wondered why it had all been previously concealed from him. And he spent all his free time with Chuyev, asking him questions and listening to Chuyev's replies. As he listened, the truth came home to him. The overall meaning of the doctrine – that all men were brothers and that they ought to love and have compassion for one another, and that then everyone would be all right – was revealed to him. As he listened, he perceived as something forgotten and familiar everything that confirmed the overall meaning of this doctrine, and simply let slip past his ears everything that did not confirm it, ascribing it to his lack of understanding.

And from that time onwards, Stepan became a different man.

IV

Even before this, Stepan Pelageyushkin had been a docile prisoner; but of late, with the change that had taken place in him, he had become a source of amazement to the warden, the orderlies and the other prisoners. Without being told to, even when it was not his turn, he performed all the most difficult and unpleasant tasks, including the emptying and cleaning of the night-pail. But in spite of this obedience, his cell-mates feared and respected him, knowing his will-power and his great physical strength; this was particularly so after an incident involving two vagrants who attacked him, but whom he repulsed, breaking the arm of one of them. These vagrants had set out to beat a well-to-do young prisoner at cards, and had fleeced him of every penny he owned. Stepan had interceded for him and had managed to get back from them the money they had won. The vagrants had started to curse him and had then tried to beat him up, but he had overpowered them both. When the warden made an inquiry as to the cause of the quarrel, however, the vagrants claimed it had been Stepan who had tried to beat them up. Stepan had made no attempt to protest that he had been in the right, and had meekly accepted his punishment, which had consisted of three days in the punishment block and transfer to a solitary cell.

He found solitary confinement irksome because it separated him from Chuyev and the Gospels, and also because he feared a return of his hallucinations involving Maria Semyonovna and the devils. But the hallucinations did not come back. His soul was entirely filled with a new, joyful radiance. He would have been glad of his solitude if only he had been able to read and had possessed a New Testament. The prison authorities would have given him the latter, but he was unable to read.

As a boy he had begun to learn the alphabet in the old-fashioned way – *az, buki, vedi*[19] – but because of his slow-wittedness he had got no further than learning the individual letters, had never been able to understand the way words were put together, and had remained illiterate. Now, however, he resolved to try again, and he asked the orderly for a New Testament. The orderly brought him one, and he set to work. He could recognize the individual letters, but he could not for the life of him work out how they were put together. No matter how hard he struggled to understand the composition of the words, he could make no sense of it at all. He was unable to sleep at nights, spent all his time thinking about this problem, even went off his food. In the end he grew so depressed that he had an attack of lice, and could not get rid of them.

'How's it going then? Still can't make it out, eh?' the orderly asked him one day.

'No.'

'I tell you what, do you know "Our Father"?'

'Yes.'

'Well, look, here it is; now you say it. There you are.' And the orderly showed him the text of the Lord's Prayer in the New Testament.

Stepan began to recite the Lord's Prayer, fitting the familiar letters together with the familiar words. And suddenly the mystery of words was revealed to him, and he began to read. He was overjoyed. And from that day forth he continued to read, and the meaning that little by little emerged from the words which he composed with difficulty acquired even greater import.

Stepan's solitude was no longer a burden to him – it was a joy. His whole life was filled with his task, and he was dismayed when he was transferred back to the communal cell so that his solitary cell could be made available to house one of the newly arrived political prisoners.

V

Now it was often Stepan, not Chuyev, who read aloud from the Gospels in the communal cell, and while some of the prisoners sang bawdy songs, others would listen to what he read and what he had to say about it. There were two men in particular who paid attention in this way: Makhorkin the executioner, who was doing hard labour for murder, and Vasily, who had been caught stealing and was being held in this prison while he awaited trial. On two occasions during his stay in the prison, Makhorkin had carried out his duties as an executioner, both times in other towns where no one could be found to carry out the sentences imposed by the judges. The peasants who had murdered Pyotr Nikolayevich had been tried by a military tribunal, and two of them had been sentenced to death by hanging.

Makhorkin was ordered to go to Penza to act as executioner in the prison there. On previous occasions such as this, possessing a degree of literacy that was above the average, he had immediately written a letter to the governor, explaining that he had been called away to Penza to carry out his duties and requesting the chief of the province to grant him a regulation daily maintenance allowance; this time, however, he declared, much to the astonishment of the warden, that he would not go and said he would never carry out his official duties ever again.

'Have you forgotten the whip?' shouted the warden.

'The whip's as may be, but killing's against the law.'

'Been talking to our prison prophet Pelageyushkin, have you? Just you wait.'

VI

While all this was going on, Makhin, the grammar-school boy who had shown his friend how to forge a coupon, had left school, gone to university and taken a degree at the Faculty of Law. Thanks to his success with women, and in particular with an ex-mistress of an aged cabinet minister with whom he was friendly, he had, at a remarkably early age, become an examining magistrate. He was a dishonest man who cheated on his debts, a seducer of women and a gambler, but he was also clever and keen-witted, and had a retentive memory and a shrewd eye for a case.

He was the examining magistrate in the district where
Stepan Pelageyushkin was being tried. Even at the first
examination he was taken aback by the simplicity, truthfulness
and calm of Stepan's replies to his questions. Makhin sensed
unconsciously that this man who stood before him in fetters
and shaven-headed, and who had been escorted to the prison
and placed under lock and key by two soldiers, was endowed
with a perfect freedom, and existed at a superior moral level
that was inaccessible to him, Makhin. So as he examined him,
he had constantly to keep rallying his spirits and egging
himself on, so as not to lose face and be put off his mark. He
was astonished by the way Stepan talked about what he had
done as though it were something that had happened long
ago, and as though it had not been him but someone else who
had been involved.

'And didn't you feel sorry for them?' asked Makhin.

'No. I didn't understand in those days.'

'Well, how do you feel about them now?'

Stepan smiled sadly.

'I wouldn't do it now even if you were to roast me on the
fire.'

'Why not?'

'Because now I know all men are brothers.'

'What, do you mean to say you think I'm your brother?'

'Of course I do.'

'What, I'm your brother, and yet I'm having you put away?'

'You're only doing that because you don't understand.'

'What don't I understand?'

'You don't understand, otherwise you wouldn't be having
me put away.'

'Oh all right, let's get on with it. So where did you go after
that?'

Makhin was astonished most of all by what the prison
warder told him about Pelageyuskin's influence on the executioner Makhorkin who, at the risk of receiving a flogging,
had refused to carry out his official duties.

VII

At a soirée in the house of the Yeropkin family, where there were two rich marriageable daughters, both of whom Makhin was courting, the singing of romances had just come to an end. Makhin was musically gifted, and he particularly excelled in the performance of romances, being both a fine singer and a fine accompanist. After the singing was over, Makhin gave a very objective, faithful and detailed account – he had an excellent memory – of the story of the strange criminal who had converted an executioner to Christ. Makhin was able to remember and describe everything so exactly because he was always totally uninvolved with the people he had to deal with. He neither entered into nor knew how to enter into the emotional condition of others, and this was why he had such a good memory for all the things that happened to people, all the things they said and did. Pelageyushkin, however, had awoken his interest. He did not attempt to put himself in Stepan's shoes, but he found himself asking himself the question: 'What's going on inside his head?' Although he was unable to come up with any answer, he none the less had a feeling that it must be something interesting, so at the soirée he related the entire case: the executioner's conversion, the warden's stories about Pelageyushkin's strange behaviour, his reading of the Gospels and the powerful influence he exerted on his fellow convicts.

Everyone took an interest in Makhin's story; most interested of all, however, was the Yeropkins' younger daughter, Liza, who was eighteen years old and had just completed her studies at a ladies' institute. It was only recently that she had woken up from the darkness and narrowness of the false surroundings in which she had been reared, and had burst like a swimmer to the surface, gulping in the fresh air of life. She began to question Makhin about the details of the story, about how and why it was that such a change had taken place in Pelageyushkin. Makhin informed her of what Stepan had

told him about his most recent murder, and about how the
meekness and docility of this extraordinarily kind-hearted
woman, who had known no fear of death but who had been
his victim none the less, had vanquished him and opened his
eyes, and how the reading of the Gospels had done the rest.

It took Liza Yeropkina a long time to get to sleep that night.
For several months now a struggle had been going on inside
her between the fashionable social life her sister had been
trying to get her interested in, and her love for Makhin, which
in her was connected with a desire to reform him. And now
it was this latter pull that took over. She had already heard
something of the woman before she had been murdered. Now,
however, in view of the terrible manner of her death and what
Makhin had told her about the things Pelageyushkin had said,
she inquired after all the details of Maria Semyonovna's
history and was quite shaken at what she learned.

Liza passionately longed to be another Maria Semyonovna.
She was rich, and she was afraid that Makhin was only
interested in her for her money. And so she decided she
would give all her land away, and told Makhin of her intention.

Makhin was glad of this opportunity of showing how
disinterested he was, and he told Liza that her money had
nothing to do with his love for her and that her decision,
which he thought a very magnanimous one, had touched him
deeply. Meanwhile a struggle had developed between Liza
and her mother – the estate had been given to her by her father
– who would not allow her to give the land away. Makhin
went to Liza's aid. And the more he acted in this way, the
more he came to understand this new world of spiritual
aspiration, which he perceived in Liza and which until now
had been a complete mystery to him.

VIII

In the communal cell, all had grown quiet. Stepan was lying
in his berth on the plank bed, not yet asleep. Vasily went
across to him and tugged his foot, winking to him as a signal

to get up and come over to where he was standing. Stepan clambered down from the plank bed and approached Vasily.

'Now, my friend,' said Vasily. 'You see if you can't help me.'

'How can I help you?'

'Escaping is what I have in mind.'

And Vasily told Stepan that he had made all the arrangements for an escape.

'Tomorrow I'll start a bit of trouble with them' – he pointed to the prisoners lying asleep – 'and they'll complain to the orderlies. They'll take me to the cells upstairs, and from then on it'll be plain sailing. Only you'll have to help to get me out of the mortuary.'

'All right, then. But where'll you go?'

'I'll go where fortune leads me. Do you think there's any shortage of villains out there?'

'That's true, Vasily, but it's not for us to judge them.'

'Well, I mean, it's not as if I was a murderer, is it? I've never killed a person in my life, and what's stealing? What's wrong about it? Don't they rob us poor blighters?'

'That's their business. They'll have to answer for it.'

'Well, and are we supposed to just stand still and watch? Look, I burgled a church once. What harm did that do anyone? What I want to do now is make one really big haul – not just break into some little shop or other – and give the money away to them that need it.'

Just then one of the convicts sat up on the plank bed and began to eavesdrop. Stepan and Vasily went their separate ways.

On the following day Vasily carried out his plan. He began complaining about the bread, saying it was mouldy, and egged on the convicts to send for the warden and make an official complaint. The warden arrived, showered them with abuse and, discovering that Vasily was the ringleader, ordered him to be locked up separately in one of the solitary cells upstairs.

This was exactly what Vasily had wanted.

IX

Vasily was well acquainted with the upstairs cell into which
he had been put. He knew how its floor was constructed, and
as soon as he arrived there he started to take the floorboards
up. When he was able to wriggle under the floor, he prised
open the planks on the ceiling of the room that lay directly
below, and jumped down. This room was the prison mortuary;
that day there was only one corpse on the mortuary table. It
was in this mortuary that the sacks used for making the
convicts' straw mattresses were kept. Vasily knew this and
was counting on it. The padlock on the door of the room had
been unlocked and pushed inside. Vasily opened the door and
went out along the corridor to its far end, where a new latrine
was under construction. In this latrine there was a hole leading
from the third floor down to the basement. Feeling for the
door, Vasily went back into the mortuary, removed the shroud
from the ice-cold corpse (his hand touched it as he pulled the
shroud away), then took some sacks, tied them together with
the shroud so as to make a long rope, and lowered the rope
into the latrine hole; then he tied the rope to a cross-beam and
climbed down it. The rope was not long enough to reach all
the way down. How much of a gap was left, he did not know,
but there was nothing to be done about it now, so he hung
down as far as he could, and then jumped. He hurt his legs,
but was able to continue walking. There were two windows in
the basement. They were wide enough for him to crawl
through, but were fitted with iron gratings. One of the iron
gratings would have to be dislodged. What could he use to do
that? Vasily began to rummage about. Lying in the basement
were some sections of boards. He found one section that had
a pointed end and began using it to force the bricks that held
the grating in place. This work took a long time. Second cock-
crow came, but still the grating held. At last one side of it came
loose. Vasily shoved his pointed section of board into the gap
and heaved; the grating came away, but a brick fell to the

floor, making a noise. The sentries might hear. Vasily froze.
All was quiet. He climbed out of the window. He would have
to scale the prison wall in order to make his escape. In a corner
of the yard stood an outhouse. He would have to climb on to
the roof of this outhouse and get over the wall that way. He
would have to take a section of board with him, for otherwise
he would not be able to get on to the roof. He climbed back
through the window, came out again with a section of board
and froze, listening for the sentry. As he had been counting
on, the sentry was marching on the other side of the courtyard
square. Vasily went over to the outhouse, placed his piece of
board against it, and started to climb. The board slipped and
fell. Vasily was wearing socks, but no shoes. He took off his
socks, so as to get a better grip with his feet, positioned the
board again, leapt on to it and seized the roof-gutter with his
hand. 'Oh God, don't let me fall, keep me up,' he prayed. He
hung on to the roof-gutter, and then managed to get up on to
the roof by one knee. The sentry was coming. Vasily lay down
and froze. The sentry did not notice anything and continued
on his rounds. Vasily leapt to his feet. The iron roofing
clattered under his feet. He took one step, two. Then he was
at the wall. He could reach it easily with his hand. One hand
first, and then the other, he stretched up, and there he was, on
the wall. All he had to do now was to be careful and not hurt
himself as he jumped down. He turned round, hung by both
hands, stretched to his full length, lowered one arm, then the
other and – praise the Lord! – he was on the ground. It was
soft ground, too. His legs were unharmed, and off he ran.

When he reached his house in the suburbs, Malanya opened
the door for him, and he crawled under the warm, patchwork
quilt that was steeped in the smell of sweat.

X

Pyotr Nikolayevich's large and attractive wife, childless, forever placid, and plump as a dry cow, stood at the window and
watched her husband being killed by the peasants and his

body being dragged away somewhere into the fields. The feeling of terror Natalya Ivanovna (such was the name of Pyotr Nikolayevich's widow) experienced at the sight of this bloody deed was – as is generally the case – so powerful that it blotted out all other feelings in her. When, however, the crowd of peasants had disappeared from sight behind the garden fence and the hubbub of voices had died away, and Malanya, the barefoot girl who worked as a servant for them, came rushing in with her eyes sticking out of her head as though she were about to relate some joyous event, to say that Pyotr Nikolay-evich had been murdered and his body thrown in the ravine, Natalya Ivanovna's feeling of horror was gradually supplanted by another emotion: a sense of joy at her liberation from the despot in the smoked eyeglasses who had kept her in slavery these past twelve years. She was deeply shocked by this feeling, and tried not to acknowledge it to herself, and even more not to tell anyone else about it. When his yellow, hairy, disfigured corpse was washed and dressed and laid in its coffin, she was filled with horror, and she wept and sobbed. When the examining magistrate with special responsibility for serious cases interrogated her as a witness, he confronted her, right there and then in his office, with two peasants in fetters who had been charged with being the principal culprits. One of them was quite old, with a long, white curling beard and a face that was calm, stern and handsome; the other was of gypsy appearance and was somewhat younger, with shining black eyes and curly, dishevelled hair. Natalya Ivanovna thereupon testified that to the best of her knowledge these were the same two men who had been the first to seize Pyotr Nikolayevich by the arms, and even though the peasant who looked like a gypsy flashed and darted his eyes under his flickering eyebrows, and said reproachfully: 'It's a sin, ma'am! We'll all die some day, you know' – even in spite of this, she did not feel in the slightest sorry for them. On the contrary, during the investigation a hostile feeling rose up in her, coupled with a desire to take revenge on the murderers of her husband.

But when a month later the case, which had been transferred

to a military tribunal, ended in eight men being sentenced to penal servitude and the two ringleaders – the white-bearded old man and the swarthy 'gypsy' as he was called – being sentenced to be hanged, she experienced an unpleasant sensation. This soon disappeared, however, under the influence of the solemn ritual of the court. If this was what the higher authorities considered to be necessary, then it must be all right.

The executions were to be carried out in the village. And, returning from Mass one Sunday, Malanya, wearing a new dress and new shoes, told her mistress that a gallows was being put up, that an executioner was expected to arrive from Moscow on Wednesday, that the two men's relatives were wailing without cease, and that the noise could be heard all over the neighbourhood.

Natalya Ivanovna stayed indoors, so as not to see the gallows or the people, and wished only for one thing: for it all to be over as soon as possible. She took thought only for herself, and not for the condemned men or their families.

XI

On the Tuesday, the chief constable, who was a friend of Natalya Ivanovna's, dropped in to see her. Natalya Ivanovna treated him to vodka and her own pickled mushrooms. When the chief constable had sampled both, he told her that there was to be no execution the following day.

'What? Why is that?'

'It's an odd story, really. We can't find a hangman. There was one in Moscow, but my son was telling me that he started reading the Gospels and now says killing's against his conscience. He got hard labour for the murders he committed, but now all of a sudden he says he can't kill even if he's got the law behind him. He was told he'd be whipped. Whip me, he says, but I still won't do it.'

Natalya Ivanovna suddenly blushed, and her thoughts even started to make her perspire.

'But can't they be pardoned now?'

'How can they be pardoned when they've been found guilty by a court of law? Only the Tsar can pardon them.'

'But how will the Tsar ever find out about them?'

'They have the right to appeal for mercy.'

'Anyway, it's for my sake that they're being executed,' said Natalya Ivanovna, who was not very intelligent. 'And I forgive them.'

The chief constable laughed. 'Why don't you put in a petition for them?'

'Can I?'

'Of course you can.'

'But won't it be too late now?'

'You can send a telegram.'

'To the Tsar?'

'Of course, you can send a telegram even to the Tsar.'

The discovery that the executioner had refused to do his job and was prepared to suffer rather than kill anyone caused a sudden upheaval within Natalya Ivanovna; the sense of horror and compassion which had already surfaced a few times in her now broke through and took possession of her.

'Dear Filipp Vasilyevich, please write the telegram for me. I want to ask the Tsar to show mercy to them.'

The chief constable shook his head. 'What if we were to be punished for it?'

'I'll take the responsibility. I won't mention you at all.'

'There's a kind woman,' thought the chief constable. 'A really kind woman. If my wife was like her I'd be in clover now.'

And the chief constable wrote a telegram to the Tsar: 'To his Imperial Majesty the Sovereign Emperor. Your Imperial Majesty's loyal subject, the widow of the collegiate assessor Pyotr Nikolayevich Sventitsky, murdered by peasants, prostrating herself at the sacred feet of Your Imperial Majesty' (the chief constable was especially proud of this passage in the telegram), 'begs You to have mercy on the condemned men, the peasants so-and-so, of such-and-such a village, *volost*,[20] district and province.'

The chief constable dispatched the telegram himself, and Natalya Ivanovna began to feel much happier. She felt that if she, the widow of the murdered man, forgave his murderers and asked for mercy for them, the Tsar could not refuse to grant her request.

XII

Liza Yeropkina was living in a state of continuous exaltation. The further she progressed along the Christian way of life that had been revealed to her, the more convinced she became that this was the only true way, and her heart grew lighter and lighter.

Now she had two immediate objectives: the first was to convert Makhin, or rather, as she put it privately, to return him to himself, to his good and beautiful nature. She loved him, and by the radiance of her love she saw into the divine nature of his soul, which is common to all human beings, seeing in this universal principle of life, however, a goodness, tenderness and exaltedness that were peculiar to him alone. Her other objective was to cease being rich. She wanted to get rid of all her land, in the first place in order to put Makhin to the test, and secondly for her own good, for the good of her soul – and she wanted to do this according to the letter of the Gospels. She began by dividing up the land and announcing her intention of giving it away, but she was prevented from carrying out this plan in the first instance by her father, but even more effectively by the deluge of personal and written applications that flooded in on her. Then she decided to turn to an elder who was noted for the holy life he had led, and asked him to take her money and do with it whatever he thought fitting. When her father found out about this, he was furious, and in the course of a heated conversation with her called her a madwoman and a psychopath, and said he was going to take steps to protect her from herself.

Her father's angry, irritable tone of voice had its effect on her, and before she was aware of it she burst into resentful tears and said insulting things to him, calling him a despot and even a shark.

She begged her father to forgive her; he said he was not angry, but she could see that he was hurt and had not really forgiven her. She was reluctant to tell Makhin about what had happened. Her sister, who was jealous of her because of Makhin, shunned her completely. She had no one to talk to about her feelings, no one to whom she could confide.

'It's God I must confide in,' she told herself, and since it was Lent she decided she would fast and take holy communion, and that during confession she would tell the Father Confessor everything and ask his advice as to what her future actions should be.

Not far from the city was the monastery where the elder lived, the one who was renowned for his way of life and for the teachings, prophecies and cures that were ascribed to him.

The elder had had a letter from Yeropkin senior, warning him of his daughter's arrival and of the abnormal, hysterical state of mind she was in; the letter expressed his confidence that the elder would be able to put her on the right track, the way of moderation and of the good, Christian life, in harmony with existing circumstances.

Tired after a long succession of visitors, the elder received Liza and quietly began to impress upon her the importance of moderation and obedience to the existing circumstances of her life and to her parents. Liza blushed, perspired and said nothing, but when he had finished she began to remind him, timidly at first, with tears in her eyes, that Christ had said: 'Leave thy father and thy mother, and follow me,' and then, with an increasing degree of animation, went on to explain her entire conception of Christianity. At first the elder just smiled and made some routine points of dogma, but then he grew silent and began to sigh, muttering 'Oh God!' to himself now and again.

'Well, all right, then, come to me for confession tomorrow,' he said, and blessed her with his wrinkled hand.

The following day he heard her confession, and without continuing their conversation of the day before, he sent her away, curtly refusing to take upon himself the disposition of her property.

The purity of this girl, her fervour and complete subservience to the will of God had made a deep impression on the elder. He had long wanted to turn his back on the world, but the monastery needed his services, as they brought in money. And so he had agreed to stay on, although he had a vague awareness of the falsity of the position he was in. He had been turned into a saint and worker of miracles, while really he was just a weak man who had been carried away by his own success. And the soul of this girl, which she had just revealed to him, had opened to him a revelation of his own soul. He had seen how far he was from what he wanted to be and from what his heart was drawing him towards.

Soon after Liza's visit, he went into a retreat and it was not until three weeks later that he came out into the church, conducted the service and after it delivered a sermon in which he reproached himself and castigated the world for its sinfulness and called it to repentance.

Every two weeks he delivered a new sermon. Each time they were attended by more and more people. His fame as a preacher spread further and further afield. There was something unique, bold and sincere about his sermons, and this was the reason for the powerful effect he had on other people.

XIII

Meanwhile Vasily had been doing exactly as he pleased. One night with some companions he broke into the house of Krasnopuzov, a rich man. He knew that Krasnopuzov was miserly and debauched, and he broke open the writing-desk and took thirty thousand rubles from it. And he did what he pleased. He even stopped drinking and gave the money away to poor girls who wanted to get married. He provided dowries, paid off debts and kept a low profile. All he worried about was how to distribute the money fairly. He even gave some of it to the police, who as a result did not spend much time looking for him.

His heart rejoiced. And when in the end he was arrested none the less and brought to trial, he laughed and boasted, saying that the pot-bellied Krasnopuzov's money had been lying idle, that its owner had not known its true value, while he, Vasily, had put it into circulation and had used it to help good folk.

And indeed, so good-humoured and kind-hearted was his defence that the jury almost acquitted him. He was sentenced to deportation.

He thanked the judge and told him in advance that he was going to escape.

XIV

Sventitsky's widow's telegram to the Tsar produced no result whatsoever. It was decided by the petitions office not even to report the matter to His Majesty. One day, however, when the Tsar was having lunch, the Sventitsky affair came up in the course of the table talk, and the director of the petitions office, who was present, told him about the telegram that had been received from the murdered man's wife.

'C'est très gentil de sa part,' said one of the ladies of the Imperial family.

The Tsar merely sighed, shrugged his epauletted shoulders, and said: 'The laws's the law.' Then he set up his glass, into which the valet poured some sparkling Moselle. Everyone pretended to be overwhelmed by the wisdom of the Tsar's words. And after that there was no more mention of the telegram. The two muzhiks – the older man and the younger fellow – were hanged with the help of a cruel and bestial murderer, a Tartar executioner who had been summoned especially from Kazan.

The old man's widow had wanted to dress her husband's corpse in a white shirt, white foot-cloths and new shoes, but they would not let her, and both men were buried in a common grave outside the wall of the cemetery.

'Princess Sofya Vladimirovna was telling me he's the most marvellous preacher,' said the Tsar's mother, the Dowager Empress, to her son one day: '*Faites le venir. Il peut prêcher à la cathédrale.*'

'No, it'd be better to have him preach at home,' said the Tsar, and gave orders that elder Isidor was to be summoned to court.

All the generals assembled in the court chapel. A new and out-of-the-ordinary preacher was, after all, something of an event.

A little, grey-haired, emaciated old man came out and looked everyone over: 'In the name of the Father, and of the Son, and of the Holy Ghost,' he said, and began his sermon.

It started off all right, but the longer it went on, the worse it became. '*Il devenait de plus en plus aggressif*,' was how the Empress described it afterwards. He fulminated against everything and everyone, spoke of the death sentence and ascribed its necessity to bad government. Can it really be permissible, he asked, to kill people in a country that is supposed to be Christian?

Everyone looked at one another, and everyone thought only of the impropriety, and of how displeased the Tsar must be, but no one said anything. When Isidor said 'Amen', the Metropolitan approached him and asked him to come and have a word with him.

After a talk with the Metropolitan and the Chief Procurator of the Synod, the old man was immediately sent off to a monastery – not his own, this time, however, but the one at Suzdal, where the Father Superior and prison commandant was Father Misail.

XV

Everyone pretended that there had been nothing untoward about Isidor's sermon, and no one made any mention of it. Even the Tsar felt that the elder's words had left no impression on him, although a couple of times during the day he did find

himself thinking about the execution of the peasants, and
Sventitsky's widow's telegram of intercession for them. There
was a parade that afternoon, followed by a drive through the
streets, then there was a reception of ministers, dinner, and in
the evening he went out to the theatre. As usual, the Tsar fell
asleep as soon as his head touched the pillow. That night he
was awoken by a terrible dream: in a field stood a gallows
with corpses dangling from it; the corpses' tongues were
protruding, sticking out further and further. And someone
was shouting: 'It's all your doing, it's all your doing!' The Tsar
woke up in a sweat and started to think. For the first time in
his life he began to think about the responsibility that rested
with him, and he remembered everything the old man had
said . .

But he could see the human being in himself only from afar,
and he could not give himself up to the demands of the human
being because of all the demands that are made on a Tsar from
every side; as for admitting that the demands of the human
being might be more binding than the demands made on him
as a Tsar – he did not have the strength to do that.

XVI

Proshka, that high-spirited, dandified, proud young lad came
out from his second term in prison completely broken. When
he was sober he merely sat around and did nothing, and, no
matter how much his father shouted at him, he lived as a
parasite and did no work – not only that, he was in the habit
of stealing things and taking them down to the public house
to sell for drink. He slouched around, coughed, hawked and
spat. The doctor he visited auscultated his chest and shook his
head.

'What you need, my friend, is something you haven't got.'
'I know, it's what I've always needed.'
'Drink plenty of milk and don't smoke.'
'But it's Lent, and anyway we haven't got a cow.'
One night that spring he was unable to sleep; he felt

depressed and wanted to drink. There was no drink in the house. He put on his fur hat and went out, making his way along the street until he came to the houses where the clergy lived. There was a harrow leaning against the fence outside the deacon's house. Proshka went over, slung the harrow over his shoulder and carried it off to Petrovna at the drinking-house. 'Maybe she'll give me a bottle of vodka for it.' He had not gone far when the deacon came out on to his porch. It was already broad daylight, and he could see that Proshka had taken his harrow.

'Hey, what do you think you're doing?'

The deacon's servants came out, seized Proshka, and threw him in the lock-up. The justice of the peace sentenced him to eleven months in prison.

Autumn came. Proshka was transferred to the prison hospital. He could not stop coughing, his chest was nearly bursting, and he could not keep warm. Some of the patients must have been fairly healthy, for they at least were not shivering. But Proshka shivered by day and by night. The warden liked to economize on firewood, and did not start heating the hospital until November of each year. Proshka suffered physical agonies, but spiritually he suffered even worse. Everything disgusted him, he hated everyone: the deacon, the warden who refused to heat the hospital, the orderly and even one of the patients near him who had a red, swollen lip. He also conceived an intense dislike of the new convict who had just been brought in. This was Stepan. He had caught an inflammation of the head, had been transferred to the hospital and had been put in a bed next to Proshka. Although Proshka hated him at first, he subsequently grew so fond of him that all he cared for was the chance of talking to him. It was only after his conversations with him that Proshka's intense depression ever lifted.

Stepan was forever telling the other patients about his most recent murder and about the effect it had had on him.

'She didn't yell or scream or anything,' he would say. 'She just said: Go on, then, cut my throat. It's not me but yourself you ought to feel sorry for, she said.'

'Yes, I know, it's a terrible business killing anything. I once killed a sheep, but I wasn't proud of myself for doing it. And here I am, I haven't killed a soul, but they've gone and ruined me anyway, the rats. I've never harmed a living soul in all my life . . .'

'Never mind, it'll all be counted in your favour.'

'Where, might I ask?'

'What do you mean, where? Where's your faith in God?'

'You don't see much of Him, somehow; you know, I don't believe in Him. I think you just die and the grass grows over you. That's all.'

'How can you say that? I've killed that many folk, but she was kind, all she did was help people. Do you think we'll get the same treatment, she and I? No, you wait and see . . .'

'So you think that when you die your soul stays alive?'

'What else? It stands to reason.'

Death was not coming easily to Proshka, and he was gasping for breath. But at the very last moment he suddenly felt at ease. He called to Stepan.

'Well, brother, farewell. I see it's time for me to die now. I was that scared, but now I can see there's nothing to it. I just want it to be over as soon as possible.'

And Proshka died in the hospital.

XVII

Meanwhile the affairs of Yevgeny Mikhailovich were going from bad to worse. He had had to mortgage his shop. Business was bad. Another photographic supply shop had opened in the town. The interest on his mortgage was due. He had to borrow more money in order to pay off the interest. And the upshot of it all was that the shop was earmarked for sale, and all the goods in it as well. Yevgeny Mikhailovich and his wife ran all over town, but nowhere could they raise the four hundred rubles they needed in order to save their business.

They had had a faint hope that the merchant Krasnopuzov, whose mistress was friendly with Yevgeny Mikhailovich's wife, might help them. But by now the whole town knew that an enormous amount of money had been stolen from Krasnopuzov. It was said that the sum amounted to half a million.

'And who do you think stole it?' said Yevgeny Mikhailovich's wife. 'It was Vasily, our old yard-keeper. They say he's throwing the money around like anyone's business, and he's even bribed the police with it.'

'He never was any good,' said Yevgeny Mikhailovich. 'Perjured himself as easy as blinking that time, he did. I'd never have believed it of him.'

'They say he called by at our place one day. The cook said it was him. She says he paid the dowries for fourteen poor girls who wanted to get married.'

'Yes, well people do make things up, you know.'

Just then a strange-looking elderly man in a woollen jacket came into the shop.

'What can I do for you?'

'There's a letter for you.'

'Who's it from?'

'It says on it.'

'Well, they'll want a reply, won't they? Wait a moment.'

'I can't.'

And having handed over the envelope, the strange-looking man left in a hurry.

'Funny.'

Yevgeny Mikhailovich tore open the fat envelope and could hardly believe his eyes: it contained hundred-ruble notes. There were four of them. What on earth was this? And there was a badly spelled letter addressed to Yevgeny Mikhailovich, which read: 'The Gosspels tell us to render good for evil. You cauzed me a lot of truble with that cupon and a lot of truble to that muzhik as well, but I feel sory for you. Here's four undred for you, and remember your old yard-keeper Vasily.'

'Well, isn't that extraordinary!' said Yevgeny Mikhailovich; he said it both to his wife and to himself. And whenever he remembered this subsequently or mentioned it to his wife, the tears would come to his eyes and her heart would be filled with joy.

XVIII

In the prison at Suzdal there were fourteen clergymen who had all been sent there in the first instance for apostasy; this was where Isidor too had been sent. Father Misail received Isidor according to the instructions he had been given and, without interviewing him, ordered him to be put in a solitary cell, as befitting a serious criminal. In the third week of Isidor's stay in the prison, Father Misail made the rounds of the inmates. Going into Isidor's cell he asked if there was anything he required.

'There are a lot of things I require, only I can't tell you what they are in front of the other men. Let me have a private talk with you.'

They looked at each other, and Father Misail saw that he had nothing to fear. He ordered Isidor to be brought to his retreat and, when the two of them were alone, he said: 'All right, go ahead, then.'

Isidor fell on his knees.

'Brother!' said Isidor. 'What are you doing? Have mercy on your own soul. You're the worst villain alive, you've spat on everything that's holy . . .'

A month later Father Misail filed documents for the release, on the grounds of penitence, not only of Isidor but also of seven other men, with a request that he himself be allowed to retire to a monastery.

XIX

Ten years went by.

Mitya Smokovnikov had graduated from the technical institute and was now an engineer on a large salary; he was engaged in gold prospecting in Siberia. It was necessary for him to make an exploratory tour of the area. The director of the project suggested that he take the convict Stepan Pelagey-ushkin along with him.

'One of the hard-labour men? Won't that be rather dangerous?'

'He'll not be any trouble. He's a holy man. Ask anyone you like.'

'What's he in for?'

The director smiled. 'He murdered six people, but he's a holy man. I promise you.'

And so Mitya Smokovnikov agreed to take Stepan, who was now a balding, emaciated, weather-beaten old man, along with him, and they set off together.

On the journey Stepan looked after Smokovnikov as if he were his own child, and told him his whole story, and all the whys and wherefores of his present existence.

And it was a strange thing. Mitya Smokovnikov, who until that time had lived only in order to eat, drink, play cards and chase women, now thought about life for the very first time. And these thoughts gave him no peace; indeed, they gradually turned his soul upside down. He was offered a very advantageous position. He turned it down and decided to use the money he had in order to buy some property, get married and serve the common people as best he could.

XX

And that was what he did. But first he went to see his father, with whom he had been having difficulties on account of his father's new family. Now, however, he decided to make it up with his father. And so he did. And his father, surprised, laughed at him at first, but later recalled the many times he had been guilty with regard to him.

AFTER THE
BALL

A Tale

'What you're all saying, you see, is that on his own a person can't distinguish the good from the bad, that it all depends on his environment, that a person's a prey to his environment. But the way I see it is that it's all up to chance. Listen, I'll tell you something that happened to me personally . . .'

This was how our universally respected Ivan Vasilyevich began to address us after a discussion we had been having on the subject of whether all that was necessary in order to achieve individual perfection was to alter the conditions under which people lead their lives. It should be pointed out that none of us had actually said that on his own a person cannot tell the good from the bad, but Ivan Vasilyevich had a peculiar way of answering questions of his own that had occurred to him in the course of the discussion, and of making these the pretext for tales concerning episodes in his own life. Quite often he would completely forget the point from which he had started, and would get carried away by his stories, all the more so since he told them with a high degree of sincerity and truthfulness.

It was no different on this occasion.

'I'll tell you what happened to me. The whole of my life's been like this; it hasn't been influenced by my environment, but by something else entirely.'

'What?' we all wanted to know.

'Oh, it's a long story. It'll take quite a bit of telling if you're really to understand.'

'That's all right, go ahead and tell us.'

Ivan Vasilyevich thought for a moment, and then nodded his head.

'Yes,' he said. 'The whole of my life changed as a result of one night, or rather one morning.'

'But what happened?'

'What happened was that I'd fallen deeply in love. I've fallen in love many times, but this was my deepest love. It's all an age ago now: she's got married daughters nowadays. The girl's name was B——, yes, Varenka B——. (Ivan Vasilyevich mentioned the family's name.) Even at fifty she was a remarkably attractive woman. But when she was young, eighteen years old, she was stunning: tall and graceful, with a lovely figure — majestic, truly majestic. She always maintained an unusually erect posture, as though she could not do otherwise, with her head thrown slightly back, and this, together with her beauty and her tall stature, and in spite of her thin, almost bony physique, gave her a queenly appearance which would have been intimidating had it not been for her lovely, joyous smile, her beautiful, shining eyes and her overall charm and youthfulness.'

'I say, hark at Ivan Vasilyevich's description!'

'No description could possibly tell you what she was really like . . . but that's not important. The events I'm going to tell you about took place in the eighteen forties. In those days I was a student at a provincial university. I don't know whether it was a good thing or a bad one, but at the time I was there our university contained no circles or theories of any kind. We were simply young and we lived as the young do: pursued our studies and enjoyed ourselves. I was a very jolly, lively fellow, and I had money, too. I owned a magnificent pacer, went tobogganing with the young ladies (skating had not yet come into fashion), and lived it up with my companions (in those days we never drank anything but champagne; if we were out of money we didn't drink at all, and never turned to vodka, as students do nowadays). But what I enjoyed most were the soirées and balls. I was a good dancer, and was tolerably good-looking.'

'Come, come, you needn't be so modest,' said one of the ladies in our company. 'We know what you look like in your daguerreotype, don't we? You weren't just tolerably good-looking, you were handsome!'

'That's as may be, but it's not important, either. The important thing was that during this time, when my love for her was reaching its highest point – the last day of Shrovetide, it was – I went to a ball at the house of the local marshal of nobility, a good-natured old man who was well off, liked throwing parties and was a gentleman-in-waiting at the court. The guests were received by his wife, who was also very good-natured, wearing a velvet dress, a diamond ferronière on her forehead, her white, puffy, aged shoulders and breast exposed, as in the portraits of the Empress Elizabeth Petrovna. It was a wonderful ball: a fine big reception room, with choirs, an orchestra, famous in those days, composed of the serfs of a landowner who was also an amateur musician, a magnificent buffet and a veritable ocean of champagne. Although I was fond of champagne, I didn't drink any, as I was already drunk, without need of wine, drunk on love; on the other hand, I danced until I dropped: quadrilles, waltzes, polkas, all as far as possible with Varenka, of course. She wore a white dress with a pink sash, white kid gloves that reached almost to her thin, pointed elbows, and white satin shoes. I had the mazurka poached from me by a really terrible fellow called Anisimov, an engineer · I still haven't forgiven him to this day. He had asked her for this dance at the very moment she had arrived, while I had been delayed by having had to go back to the barber's to fetch the gloves I had left there by mistake. So instead of getting to dance the mazurka with Varenka, I had as my partner a young German girl I'd once run after. I'm afraid I wasn't very considerate to her that evening, hardly spoke to her or looked at her and only had eyes for that tall, shapely figure in the white dress with the pink sash, for her flushed, radiant face with its dimples, and for her tender, affectionate eyes. I wasn't the only one: everyone was looking at her and admiring her, men and women alike, even though she put them all in the shade. It was impossible not to admire her.

'Officially, so to speak, I had another partner for the mazurka, but in reality I danced most of the figures with her. Without the slightest embarrassment she would walk the whole length of the room and come straight up to me, I would jump to my feet, not waiting to be asked, and she would thank me with a smile for my quick-wittedness. When we were led before her to choose one of us, she would give her arm to another gallant, unable to guess my quality,[21] shrug her thin shoulders and smile to me as a sign of regret and consolation. When the figures of the mazurka were being danced as a waltz, I waltzed with her for a long time, and smiling and breathing fast she said: *'Encore!'* And I waltzed and waltzed, until I was no longer conscious of my body at all.'

'What do you mean you weren't conscious of it? I bet you were very conscious of it when you had your arm around her waist, not only of your body but of hers as well,' said one of the guests.

Ivan Vasilyevich suddenly turned a deep red and in his anger almost shouted: 'Yes, there you are, there's the youth of today for you! You don't see anything apart from the body. It wasn't like that in our day. The more deeply I fell in love, the more disembodied she became for me. Nowadays you study their legs, their ankles and a bit more besides; you undress the women you're in love with. But for me, as Alphonse Karr used to say (he was a good writer, by the way), the object of my love was always dressed in vestments of bronze. It wasn't just that we didn't undress our women mentally; like the good sons of Noah, we tried to conceal their nakedness. Well, you wouldn't understand . . .'

'Don't pay any attention to him. Carry on with the story,' said one of us.

'Yes, all right. Well, there I was dancing with her, and I completely lost track of the time. The musicians were strumming away at the same old mazurka tune with a sort of desperate weariness – you know how it is at the end of a ball – the mamas and papas had already risen from the card tables and were waiting for supper to be served, the manservants were running to and fro, carrying things. It was already after

two a.m. I would have to make the most of the last few
minutes. Yet again I asked her to dance with me and for the
hundredth time we sailed through the ballroom together.

' "May I have the quadrille after supper?" I asked her, as I
took her back to her seat.

' "Of course, if they haven't taken me home by then," she
said with a smile.

' "I won't let them," I said.

' "Give me back my fan," she said.

' "It breaks my heart to do even that," I said, as I returned
her inexpensive white fan to her.

' "Well, here you are, so your heart doesn't break," she said,
plucking a feather from her fan and giving it to me.

'I took the feather, and was only able to express my joy and
gratitude by the way I looked at her. I was not merely light of
heart, contented; I was blissfully happy, I overflowed with
goodness, I was no longer myself but some unearthly being
that had no knowledge of evil and was capable only of doing
good. I hid the feather in my glove and remained standing
there, unable to summon up the strength to leave her.

' "Look, they're trying to get papa to dance," she said,
pointing out the tall, stately figure of her father, a colonel in
silver epaulettes who was standing in the doorway with the
hostess and some other ladies.

' "Varenka, come over here," we heard the hostess, with her
diamond ferronière and Empress shoulders, call in a loud voice.

'Varenka went over to the doorway. I followed her.

' "Ma chère, do try to talk your father into taking a round of
the floor with you. Come along now, please, Pyotr Vladislav-
ych," said the hostess to the colonel.

'Varenka's father was a very tall, stately, handsome, well-
preserved old man. His face had a rubicund complexion, he
had a white, curly moustache à la Nicolas which joined a pair
of side-whiskers, also white, and his hair was combed forwards over his temples. A happy, affectionate smile like that
of his daughter played in his brilliant eyes and around his
lips. He was magnificently built, with his broad chest thrown
forwards, military style, and adorned with a tasteful clutch of

medals, his powerful shoulders and his long, elegant legs. He
was a military commander with the bearing of an old cam-
paigner from the days of Nicholas I.

'As we approached the doorway, the colonel was on the
point of refusing, saying that he had forgotten how to dance;
none the less, smiling and reaching with his right arm for his
left side, he drew his sword from its scabbard, gave it to an
obliging young man and, putting a suede glove on his right
hand – "Everything according to regulations," he said, smiling
– led his daughter out on to the dance floor, made a quarter-
turn and waited for the mazurka tempo to begin.

'When it did, he stamped one foot smartly on the floor, put
the other one forward, and his tall, stout figure began, now
quietly and smoothly, now noisily and impetuously, to move
around the ballroom with a thudding of boot soles and of foot
against foot. Beside him floated Varenka's graceful figure,
imperceptibly lengthening or shortening the steps her small
feet took in their white satin shoes. All who were present in
the room followed each and every movement of the couple.
Not only was I lost in admiration as I watched them, I was
filled with a moved, ecstatic feeling. I was particularly moved
by the colonel's boots, which were fastened by foot-straps –
they were good, calf-leather boots, though not of the pointed,
fashionable kind, but with the old-style square toecaps and
without heels, obviously the work of a regimental cobbler. "In
order to bring out his favourite daughter and set her off he
hasn't bought fashionable boots but is just wearing his
ordinary, home-made ones," I thought, and those square
toecaps continued to move me. It was evident that he had
once been an excellent dancer; now he had grown stout,
however, and his legs were no longer supple enough for the
swift, elegant dance steps he was trying to perform. All the
same, he managed to make two rounds of the floor with
considerable dexterity. And when he swiftly planted his feet
apart and then rejoined them and fell to one knee, albeit
somewhat heavily, and when she, smiling and patting her
skirt where he had caught it, circled him gracefully, everyone
burst into loud applause. Getting to his feet again with a

certain amount of effort, he embraced his daughter tenderly and affectionately by the ears and, kissing her forehead, led her over to where I stood, thinking that I was dancing with her. I told him that I was not her escort.

' "Well, never mind, you take her for this dance," he said, smiling kindly and putting his sword away in its scabbard.

'Just as a single drop poured from a bottle is followed by the gushing forth of the entire contents, so my love for Varenka released the entire amorous capacity of my soul. At that moment I embraced the whole world with my love. I loved the hostess with her ferronière and Empress Elizabeth bust, I loved her husband, her guests, her manservants and even Anisimov, the engineer who was now giving me a rather cool look. As for her father, with his regimental boots and his affectionate smile that was like hers, for him I felt an emotion that was composed of enthusiasm and tenderness.

'The mazurka came to an end, the host and hostess asked the guests to come in to supper, but Colonel B— refused, saying that he had to get up early next morning, and he took his leave of them both. I was beginning to worry that Varenka too would have to go, but she remained with her mother.

'After supper I danced the quadrille with Varenka, as she had promised, and although my happiness already seemed infinite, it continued to grow and grow. We said nothing on the subject of love. I did not ask her, any more than I asked myself, whether she loved me. And the only thing I was afraid of was that something might spoil my happiness.

When I got home I undressed and thought about sleep, and then realized that sleep was quite out of the question. I was still holding the feather from her fan and one of her gloves which she had given me as she had been leaving (I had helped both her and her mother to get into their carriage). I looked at these objects and, without closing my eyes, saw her before me, now as she had been at the moment when, choosing between two escorts, she had tried to guess which quality I represented, and I had heard her charming voice say "Pride? Yes?" – and had joyfully given me her hand; and now as she had been at supper, taking little sips from her goblet of

champagne and looking at me with affectionate mistrust. But
most clearly of all I saw her together with her father, circling
around him and surveying the admiring spectators with pride
and joy both at him and at herself. And I found myself linking
them both in a single emotion of tender rapture.

'At that time I was living with my brother, who is dead
now. In general, my brother wasn't much disposed towards
society life and didn't go to balls; just then he was studying
for his final-year university exams and was leading a very
regular life. He was asleep. As I looked at his head, buried in
the pillow and half covered by a flannel blanket, I felt sorry for
him in a brotherly sort of way, sorry that he neither knew nor
shared the happiness I was experiencing. Our household serf
Petrusha came to meet me with a candle and wanted to help
me undress for bed, but I sent him away. I found the sight of
his sleepy face and tousled hair charmingly touching. Trying
not to make any noise, I went into my room on tiptoe and sat
down on the bed. It was no good, I was too happy, I would
never be able to sleep. What was more, I found the heated
rooms far too warm, and without taking off my uniform jacket
I went quietly into the hallway, put on my overcoat, opened
the front door and went out on to the street.

'It had been after four a.m. when I had left the ball; since my
arrival home two hours had passed, which I had spent sitting
about; thus it was already light when I emerged on to the
street. It was real Shrovetide weather – there was a fog, patches
of snow saturated with water were melting on the roads, and
there was a steady dripping from the roofs. In those days the
B—s lived on the outskirts of town near a large field, at one
end of which there was a Shrovetide fair, and at the other an
institute for young ladies. I walked down the deserted lane
outside our house and came out on to the main road; here
even at this hour I began to meet pedestrians and draymen
with firewood on their sledge-carts that grazed the road-
surface with their runners. Everything – the horses rhythmic-
ally swaying their sopping heads under the glossy shaft-
bows, the cab-drivers, their shoulders covered in bast matting,
trudging along beside their cabs in enormous boots and, on

either side of the streets, the houses, which in the fog seemed extraordinarily tall – for me it was all charged with a peculiar fascination and significance. When I came to the field where their house was situated, I saw at its opposite end, near the fairground, something large and black; I could hear the sound of a fife and drum coming from over that way. My head was still full of music, and every now and then I had been silently hearing the tune of the mazurka. What filled my ears now, however, was another kind of music, harsh and unpleasant.

'"I wonder what that is?" I thought, and made my way along the slippery path that had been trampled across the middle of the field in the direction the sounds were coming from. When I had gone about a hundred yards or so, I began to be able to make out through the fog a large number of people dressed in black. They were obviously soldiers. "They must be on manoeuvres," I thought, and together with a blacksmith in a dirty apron and dirty sheepskin coat who was walking in front of me, carrying something, I went closer. Black-uniformed soldiers were standing perfectly still in two rows, their rifles at rest. Behind them stood a drummer and a fifer who kept playing the same shrill, unpleasant melody over and over again.

'"What are they doing?" I asked the blacksmith, who had stopped beside me. "Giving a Tartar a hiding for desertion," said the blacksmith gruffly, his eyes trained on the far end of the rows of men.

'I followed his gaze, and between the rows saw something terrifying coming towards me. It was a man stripped to the waist and tied to the rifles of the two soldiers who were escorting him. Beside him, in an overcoat and peaked cap, walked a tall colonel who looked familiar to me. His whole body twitching, his feet slapping on the melting snow, the man who was being punished was moving towards me under a hail of blows that descended on him from all sides, now throwing himself backwards – whereupon the NCOs who were dragging him along on their rifles would push him forwards – now falling forwards, whereupon the NCOs would pull him backwards in order to keep him upright. And by his side, with a firm, slightly quivering step, walked the tall colonel. It was her father, with his rubicund face and his white moustache and side-whiskers.

'Each time he was struck, the man who was being punished turned his face, which was contorted with suffering, in the direction from which the blow had come, as if in surprise, and, baring his teeth, kept repeating the same words. It was only when he was quite close to me that I was able to make out what they were. In a voice that was more of a sob, he was mouthing: "Have mercy on me, lads. Have mercy on me, lads." But the lads were not having any mercy on him, and when the procession drew level with me, I saw the soldier standing opposite me take a determined step forwards and bring his stick whistling down on the Tartar's back with a violent slash. The Tartar convulsed forwards, but the NCOs restrained him, and another similar blow landed on him from the other side; this was followed by another from the side I was on, then by a further one from the other side, and so it went on. The colonel maintained his accompanying presence, and looking now at his feet and now at the man who was being punished, he took deep gulps of air, blowing out his cheeks and letting the air escape through his protruding lips. When the procession had gone past me, I caught a glimpse of the Tartar's back through the ranks of men. It looked so lurid, wet and unnaturally red that I could hardly believe it was a man's back.

' "Oh, Christ," said the blacksmith, who was standing beside me.

'The procession began to move off into the distance, the blows continued to rain down from both sides on the stumbling, writhing man, the drum went on beating and the fife went on shrilling, and the tall, stately figure of the colonel continued to move alongside the Tartar with its firm step. Suddenly the colonel stood still. Then he went up to one of the soldiers.

' "I'll teach you to miss the mark," I heard him say in an angry voice. "Going to miss the mark, were you? Going to miss it, eh?"

'And I saw his powerful, suede-gloved hand strike a puny, frightened little soldier in the face for not bringing his stick down on the Tartar's back hard enough.

' "Give them fresh sticks!" he shouted, and as he looked round he caught sight of me. Pretending not to know me, he wasted no time in turning away, frowning angrily and menacingly as he did so. I was so embarrassed that, not knowing where to look, as though I had been caught red-handed in the most shameful misdeed, I lowered my eyes and hurried off home. All the way back I could hear either the beating of the drum and the shrilling of the fife and the man sobbing, "Have mercy on me, lads," or the self-assured, angry voice of the colonel shouting, "Going to miss the mark, were you? Going to miss it, eh?" And all the while I was filled with an almost physical anguish that rose in me to the point of nausea, and so powerfully that several times I had to stand still and thought I was going to vomit up all the horror that this spectacle had aroused in me. I don't even remember how I managed to reach home and get into bed. But no sooner had I fallen asleep than I heard and saw it all over again, and I leapt out of bed.

' "He obviously knows something that I don't," I said to myself, thinking of the colonel. "If I'd known what he knows, I'd have understood what I was seeing and it wouldn't have upset me." But no matter how hard I tried, I couldn't imagine what it was the colonel knew, and it was not until that evening that I was able to fall asleep, and even then only after I had gone to the house of a friend and got completely drunk with him.

'Well, do you suppose I made up my mind then that what I had seen was something sickening? Not a bit of it. "If it was done with such assurance and everyone thought it was necessary, then they must have known something I didn't," was what I thought, and I tried to find out what it was. But I couldn't, no matter how hard I exerted myself. And since I couldn't, I couldn't join the army as I'd planned to, and not only did I not join the army, I couldn't find a place for myself anywhere in society, and ended up being no good for anything, as you can see.'

'Oh yes, we know all about how you're no good for anything,' said one of us. 'But tell us: how many men would be no good for anything if it weren't for the likes of you?'

'Oh, come, that's just plain stupid,' said Ivan Vasilyevich with unfeigned irritation.

'Well, and what about that love of yours?' we asked.

'My love? Oh, from that day on it started to fade. Whenever she grew pensive, with that smile on her face, as she often did, I'd immediately find myself thinking about the colonel on the field, and I'd feel awkward and unwell; so I started to see her less often. And my love for her just disappeared. That's the way it is with some affairs, and those are the sort of events that change the course of a man's entire life. But you say . . .' he concluded.

APPENDIX 1:

POSTFACE TO *THE KREUTZER SONATA*

I have received, and continue to receive, a large number of letters from people I do not know, asking me to explain in clear, simple terms what I think of the subject of the story I wrote entitled *The Kreutzer Sonata*. This I shall endeavour to do; that is, I shall attempt briefly to express, within the limits of the possible, the substance of what I was trying to say in that story, and the conclusions which in my view may be drawn from it.

The *first point* I was trying to make was that in our society there has been formed the solid conviction, common to every class and receiving the support of a mendacious science, that sexual intercourse is an activity indispensable to health, and that since marriage is not always a practical possibility, extramarital sexual intercourse, committing a man to nothing except the payment of money, is something perfectly natural and therefore to be encouraged. So firm and widespread has this conviction become that parents, following the advice given by their doctors, make arrangements for the depravation of their children; governments whose sole purpose is to care for the moral welfare of their citizens bring in institutionalized debauchery by regularizing the existence of an entire class of women who are obliged to suffer both physically and emotionally in order to satisfy the imaginary needs of men, so that the unmarried give themselves up to debauchery with a perfectly clear conscience.

And what I was trying to say was that this is not a good state of affairs, for it cannot be right that for the sake of the health of some the bodies and souls of others should be caused to perish, just as it cannot be right that for the sake of the health of some it should be necessary to drink the blood of others.

The conclusion it seems to me natural to draw from this is that one ought not to yield to this delusion, this fraud. And in order not to yield to it, it is necessary, in the first place, not to lend credence to immoral doctrines, whatever the pseudo-sciences that give them their support and, in the second place, to understand that sexual intercourse in which men either extricate themselves from its possible consequences – children – or else shift the entire burden of those consequences on to the woman, or practise contraception – that such intercourse is an offence against the most elementary requirements of morality, is an infamy, and that therefore unmarried men who do not wish to live a life of infamy must not indulge in it.

In order to be able to abstain from it they must, in addition to leading a natural way of life – not drinking, not eating to excess, not eating meat and not shirking physical toil (not gymnastic exercises, but fatiguing, genuine toil) – exclude from their thoughts the possibility of having intercourse with chance women, just as every man excludes such a possibility between himself and his mother, his sisters, his relations and the wives of his friends.

Abstinence is possible, and is less dangerous and injurious to the health than non-abstinence: every man will find around him a hundred proofs of this.

That is the first point.

The *second point* is that as a result of this view of sexual intercourse as being not only a necessary precondition of health but also a sublime and poetic blessing that life bestows, marital infidelity has become in all the classes of society (especially, thanks to conscription, among the peasantry) a most common occurrence.

The conclusion that follows from this is that men should not act in this way.

In order for men not to act in this way, it is necessary that carnal love be envisaged differently, that men and women be educated by their families and by public opinion in such a way that both before and after marriage they view desire and the carnal love that is associated with it not as a sublime, poetic condition, as they are viewed at present, but as a condition of animality that is degrading to human beings, and that the violation of the promise of fidelity given at the time of marriage be censured by public opinion in at least the same degree as it censures commercial fraud and the non-payment of debts, and that it not be sung to the skies, as is done at present in novels, poems, songs, operas, etc.

That is the second point.

The *third point* is that in our society, as a consequence of the same false significance accorded to carnal love, procreation has lost its meaning: instead of being the goal and the *raison d'être* of marital relations, it has become no more than an obstacle to the agreeable protraction of love relations. Because of this, and as a result of the advice given by the servants of medical science, there has begun either the spread of an employment of means which prevent the woman from conceiving, or else a certain practice has started to become common, one which did not exist formerly and is still unknown in the patriarchal families of peasants: the extension of marital relations into pregnancy and nursing.

And I think this is a bad thing. It is a bad thing for people to use contraceptive devices, in the first place because it frees them from the care and hard work which children bring and which serve as an expiation of carnal love, and in the second place because this is something very close to the act which is more repugnant to the human conscience than any other: the act of murder. Non-abstinence during pregnancy and nursing is likewise undesirable, because it damages the physical, and more importantly, the emotional strength of the woman.

The conclusion that may be drawn from this is that men should not act in this way. And in order not to act in this way, they must understand that abstinence, which forms the essential condition of human dignity outside marriage, is even more necessary in marriage itself.

That is the third point.

The *fourth point* is that in our society, where children are considered either as a hindrance to pleasure, as an unfortunate accident, or as a particular form of pleasure (when born in predetermined quantities), they are brought up not with any

view to those tasks of human life that may await them as
thinking, loving beings, but solely with a view to the enjoyment they may be able to afford their parents. In consequence
of this, the children of men are raised like the young of
animals, and the principal concern of their parents is not to
prepare them for an active life worthy of human beings but
(and here the parents receive the support of that mendacious
science that is called medicine) to feed them as well as
possible, to make them as tall as possible, to make them clean,
white, replete and attractive (if this is not done among the
lower classes, it is only because necessity will not permit it —
their view on the matter is the same). And in these pampered
children, just as in all animals that are overfed, there is an
unnaturally early appearance of an unmasterable sensuality
which is the cause of horrible torments during their adoles-
cence. Their clothes, their books, their entertainments, the
music they play and listen to, their dancing, the sweet food
they are given, the whole environment of their lives, from the
pretty pictures on their tins of candy to the novels, stories and
poems they read, inflame their sensuality even more; in
consequence, the most fearful sexual vices and illnesses
become a normal condition of growing up for children of both
sexes, and often retain their grip even in adulthood.

And I think this is a bad thing. The conclusion that may be
drawn from it is that we must stop raising the children of men
as if they were the young of animals, and set other goals for
the education of the children of men than merely an attractive,
well-groomed body.

That is the fourth point.

The *fifth point* is that in our society, where the love between
a young man and a young woman, the foundation of which is
none the less carnality, is elevated into the loftiest poetic goal
of all human aspirations (all the art and poetry of our society
are the witness), young people devote the best years of their
lives, if they are men, to spying out, hunting down and taking
possession of the objects most worthy of their love by means
of an affair or of marriage, and if they are women and girls, to
enticing and drawing men into an affair or marriage.

Because of this the finest energies of human beings are wasted on work that is not only unproductive but also harmful. This is the source of most of the mindless luxury of our day-to-day lives, and it is also the cause of the idleness of our men and the shamelessness of our women who think nothing of parading, in fashions borrowed from prostitutes, those parts of their bodies that excite men's lust.

And I think this is a bad thing. It is a bad thing, because the achievement of union either in marriage or outside it, with the object of one's love, no matter how poeticized, is not a goal that is worthy of human beings, any more than is the goal, considered by many as the highest good imaginable, of procuring large quantities of delectable food for oneself.

The conclusion that may be drawn from this is that we must give up thinking of carnal love as something particularly exalted, and must understand that a goal worthy of man, whether it be the service of mankind, of one's country, of science or of art (not to mention the service of God) is, as soon as we consider it as such, not attained by means of union with the object of our love either inside marriage or outside it; on the contrary, love and union with the object of that love (no matter how hard people may try to prove the opposite in verse and prose) never make the achievement of a goal worthy of man any easier, but always render it more difficult.

That is the fifth point.

This is the substance of what I was trying to say, and of what I thought I had indeed said, in my story. It seemed to me that while one might argue about the best way of remedying the evil designated in the above propositions, it was impossible for anyone not to agree with them.

It seemed to me impossible that anyone would not agree with these propositions in the first place because they are fully in accord with the progress of humanity, which has always proceeded from libertinage towards an ever greater degree of chastity, and with the moral awareness of society, with our conscience, which always condemns licentiousness and esteems chastity; and in the second place because these propositions are merely the inevitable conclusions to be drawn from the Gospels, which we profess, or at least admit to be the basis of our conception of morality.

Things have turned out differently, however.

No one, it is true, contests outright the propositions that one must not indulge in lust either before marriage or after it, that one must not prevent conception by artificial means, make of one's children an entertainment, and place the love-bond higher than all else – in short, no one will deny that chastity is better than libertinage. But people say: 'If celibacy is better than marriage, then it follows that people must do what is better. But if they do it, the human race will come to an end, and surely the ideal of the human race cannot be its own extinction?'

But quite apart from the fact that the extinction of the human race is not a new idea for mankind, that for the religious it is an article of faith and for the scientifically inclined an inevitable deduction to be drawn from observations concerning the cooling of the sun, there is concealed in this objection a grave, widespread and ancient misunderstanding.

People say: 'If human beings attain the ideal of complete chastity, they will cease to exist, and so this ideal must be a false one.' But those who talk like this are, wittingly or unwittingly, confusing two things that are different in nature: the law – or precept – and the ideal.

Chastity is neither a law nor a precept but an ideal, or rather one of the preconditions of an ideal. An ideal is only genuine, however, when its realization is only possible in idea, in thought, when it is only attainable in the infinite and when, consequently, the possibility of approaching it is an infinite one. If there were an ideal that was not only attainable but could be imagined by us as being attainable it would cease to be an ideal. Such is the ideal of Christ – the establishment of the Kingdom of God upon earth, the ideal, already announced by the prophets, concerning the advent of a time when all men, instructed by God, will beat their swords into ploughshares and their spears into pruning-hooks, the lion will lie down with the lamb and all beings will be united by love. The entire meaning of human existence is contained in the movement towards this ideal, and thus not only does the striving towards the Christian ideal in its totality and towards chastity as one of the preconditions of that ideal not exclude the possibility of life; on the contrary, it is the absence of this Christian ideal that would put an end to that forward movement and consequently to the possibility of life.

The opinion that the human race would cease to exist if people were to devote all their energies to the attainment of chastity is similar to the opinion (still held today) that the human race would perish if people, instead of continuing the struggle for existence, were to devote all their energies to loving their friends, their enemies and the whole of living creation. Such opinions stem from a lack of understanding of the difference between two types of moral guidance.

Just as there are two ways of indicating to the traveller the path he should follow, so there are two methods of moral guidance for the person who is seeking the truth. One of these consists in pointing out to the person the landmarks he must encounter, and in him setting his course by these landmarks. The other method consists simply in giving the person a reading on the compass he carries with him; he keeps this reading steady as he travels, and by means of it he is able to perceive his slightest deviation from the correct path.

The first type of moral guidance makes use of external precepts, or rules: the person is given the clearly defined characteristics of actions he must and must not perform.

'Keep the sabbath, practise circumcision, do not steal, do not drink alcohol, do not kill, give a tenth of what you own to the poor, do not commit adultery, make your ablutions and say your prayers five times a day, be baptized, take communion,' and so on. Such are the precepts of the external religious doctrines: the Brahminic, the Buddhist, the Muslim, the Hebraic and the Ecclesiastic, mistakenly referred to as the Christian.

The second type of guidance consists in showing the person a state of perfection impossible for him to attain, the striving for which he acknowledges in himself: he is shown the ideal, and he is forever able to measure the degree of distance that separates him from it.

'Love thy God with all thy heart, and all thy soul, and all thy mind, and love thy neighbour as thyself. Be perfect like your Heavenly Father.'

Such is the doctrine of Christ.

One can only verify the fulfilment of the external religious doctrines by the concordance of men's actions with the requirements of those doctrines; such a concordance is possible.

One may verify the fulfilment of the doctrine of Christ by one's awareness of the degree of distance that separates one from the ideal of perfection. (The degree of approximation is not visible: all that can be seen is the distance that separates a human being from perfection.)

A person who follows the external law is like someone standing in the light of a lantern that is suspended from a post. He stands in the light shed by this lantern, its light is sufficient for him, and he has no need to go any further. A person who follows the teaching of Christ is like someone carrying a lantern before him on the end of a pole of indeterminate length: its light is always in front of him, it constantly prompts him to follow it and at each moment reveals to him a new expanse of terrain that draws him towards it.

The Pharisee thanks God for the fact that he is able to fulfil all his duties.

A rich young man may have fulfilled all his duties ever since his childhood, and yet be unable to see that he is lacking in anything. Such young men cannot think otherwise: there is no goal before them towards which they might continue to strive. They have given away a tenth of what they own, they have kept the sabbath, they have honoured their father and mother, they have not committed adultery, theft or murder. What more is left to them? For the person who follows the teaching of Christ, however, the attainment of any degree of perfection makes it necessary for him to climb to a higher degree, from whence a yet higher degree is revealed to him, and so it continues.

The person who follows the doctrine of Christ is perpetually in the situation of the publican. He always feels imperfect; he cannot see behind him the path he has already travelled; instead, he constantly sees in front of him the path along which he has still to go.

Herein lies the difference between the doctrine of Christ and all the other religious doctrines. It is not a difference in moral demands, but in the way human beings are guided. Christ laid down no rules as to how one should live one's life; he never established any institutions, not even the institution of marriage. But people who do not understand the special nature of the doctrine of Christ, people who are accustomed to external doctrines and who want to feel righteous in the way that the Pharisee feels righteous have, contrary to the entire spirit of the doctrine of Christ, interpreted his teachings according to the letter, and constructed a body of external precepts called ecclesiastical Christian doctrine, and have substituted this for Christ's authentic doctrine of the ideal.

In the place of Christ's doctrine of the ideal the ecclesiastical teaching calling itself Christian has, with regard to every manifestation of life, instituted external rules and precepts which are alien to the spirit of that doctrine. It has done this with regard to the authority of the State, justice, the armed forces, the Church and the holy ritual, and also with regard to marriage: in spite of the fact that not only did Christ never advocate marriage, but, if one looks to the matter of external precepts, took a negative attitude towards it ('leave thy wife and follow me'), the ecclesiastical doctrine which calls itself Christian has established marriage as a Christian institution; in other words, it has determined certain external conditions in which carnal love is supposed not to contain any sin for the Christian, and to be completely lawful.

But since there is no basis in the true Christian doctrine for the institution of marriage, the result has been that the people of our world have fallen between two stools: they do not really believe in the ecclesiastical dispositions concerning marriage, for they sense that this institution has no basis in Christian doctrine, and at the same time they lose sight of Christ's ideal, which is now obscured by the teaching of the Church, they lose sight of the ideal of chastity, and are left without any guidance where marriage is concerned. Hence there arises a phenomenon that seems at first sight strange: among the Jews, the Muslims, the Lamaists and others who profess religious doctrines of a far lower order than the Christian one, but who have precise external rules governing marriage, the family principle and conjugal fidelity are incomparably more deeprooted than they are among us so-called Christians.

They practise a form of concubinage, a polygamy that is regulated within certain limits. Among us, on the other hand, there exist outright licence and concubinage, polygamy and polyandry, subject to no rules and disguised as monogamy.

Solely because, in exchange for money, the clergy performs a special ceremony, called Christian marriage, over the heads of a certain number of couples, the people of our world imagine, either naively or hypocritically, that they are living in a state of monogamy.

There never has been and there never will be a Christian marriage, just as there never has been nor can there be a Christian ritual (Matthew vi,5–12; John iv,21), Christian teachers and fathers (Matthew xxiii,8–10), Christian property, or a Christian army, justice of State. This was always understood by the true Christians of the earliest times, and by those who lived thereafter.

The Christian's ideal is the love of God and of one's neighbour; it is the renunciation of self for the service of God and of one's neighbour. Marriage and carnal love are, on the other hand, the service of oneself and are therefore in all cases an obstacle to the service of God and men – from the Christian point of view they represent a fall, a sin.

The contraction of marriage cannot promote the service of God and men even when the partners have as their aim the propagation of the human species. It would make much more sense if such people, instead of entering into marriage in order to produce children, were to sustain and rescue those millions of children who are perishing all round us because of a lack not of spiritual, but of material food.

A Christian could only enter into a marriage without any consciousness of having fallen or sinned if he could be absolutely certain that the lives of all existing children were assured.

It is possible not to accept the doctrine of Christ, that doctrine which impregnates the whole of our lives and on which our entire morality is based; if, however, one does accept it, one cannot but recognize that it points towards the ideal of total chastity.

The Gospels, after all, tell us quite plainly and without any possibility of misinterpretation that a married man must not divorce his wife in order that he may take another, but must live with the one he originally married (Matthew v,31–2; xix,8); second, that it is a sin in general, and thus just as much for the man who is married as for the man who is not, to look upon a woman as an object of pleasure (Matthew v,28–9), and third, that it is better for a man who is single not to marry at all, to remain, that is, completely chaste (Matthew xix,10–12).

To very many people these ideas appear strange and even contradictory. And indeed they are contradictory, but not of one another; they contradict our entire way of life, so that involuntarily a doubt arises: Who is right? These ideas, or the lives of millions of people, our own included? I experienced this very same feeling most acutely when I was in the process of arriving at the convictions I am now setting forth: I never expected that the train of my thoughts would lead me where it did. I was horrified at my conclusions. I tried not to lend them any credence, but that was impossible. However much they might contradict the entire fabric of our lives, however much they might contradict all that I had previously thought and even said aloud, I had no alternative but to accept them.

'But these are all merely general reflections, and they may very well be correct; however, they relate to the doctrine of Christ and are obligatory only for those who profess it; after all, life is life, and one cannot, having pointed to the unattainable ideal of Christ, abandon people at the heart of a problem that is one of the most urgent, universal and productive of catastrophes with nothing but his ideal, yet at the same time fail to provide them with any sort of guidance.'

'A young man, full of enthusiasm, will be carried away by this ideal at first, but he will not persevere, he will break loose and, no longer taking account of any kind of rules, will sink into utter depravity.'

That is how people usually reason.

'The ideal of Christ is unattainable, and so it cannot serve us as a guide in our lives; it can be talked and dreamed about, but it cannot be applied to life, and so it should be left alone. What we need is not an ideal, but rules and guidance that are within our power to follow, that are within the power of the average moral level of society to follow: honest marriage in church, or even marriage that is not completely honest, where one of the partners – in our case, the man – has already had relations with a large number of women, even civil marriage, or even (following the same logic) the Japanese type of marriage, which only lasts for a definite period of time – why not go the whole way, and allow licensed brothels?'

People say that this is better than allowing debauchery in the streets. That is precisely the trouble: once one has permitted oneself to lower an ideal to the level of one's own weakness, one can no longer discern the limits beyond which one should not go.

This line of argument is mistaken right from the outset; above all, it is mistaken to assert that an ideal of absolute perfection cannot be a guiding force in our lives, and that in its presence we must either wave it aside, saying it is of no use to us because we will never be able to attain it, or lower it to the level our weakness desires.

To argue in this way is to be like a navigator who tells himself that since he cannot follow the course indicated by his compass he will throw his compass away or stop paying any attention to it (abandon his ideal, in other words), or else that he will fix the needle of his compass on the point that corresponds to the course of his vessel at any given moment (lower his ideal to the level of his weakness, that is). The ideal of perfection set by Christ is not a dream or a subject for rhetorical sermonizing – it is a most necessary and universally accessible form of guidance for the moral conduct of men's lives, just as the compass is a necessary and accessible instrument for the guidance of the navigator; all that is required in either case is for one to believe that this is so. In whatever situation a person may find himself, the doctrine of the ideal set by Christ will always be sufficient for him to be able to receive the most reliable indication of those actions he must or must not perform. But he must believe in this doctrine completely, and in this doctrine alone, he must give up believing in all the others, just as the navigator must believe his compass, and cease to look at and be guided by what he sees to either side of him. A person must know how to be guided by Christian doctrine as by a compass, and for this he must above all be sure of his own situation, and not be afraid to determine precisely how far he has diverged from the ideal course. At whatever level a person finds himself, it will always be possible for him to approach this ideal, and he can never attain a situation where he can say that he has reached it and is unable to come any closer to it. Such is the nature of man's striving for the Christian ideal in general, and for chastity in particular. If, where the problem of sexuality is concerned, one envisages to oneself all the different situations – from the innocence of childhood up to marriage – in which abstinence is not practised, at each stage of the way between these two situations the doctrine of Christ and the ideal it represents will always serve as a clear and definite guide as to what a person should or should not do.

What should pure, young, adolescent lads or girls do? They should remain free of temptation and, in order to be able to devote all their energies to the service of God and men, strive for an ever greater chastity of thought and intention.

What should pure, young, adolescent lads or girls do, who have fallen prey to temptation, are swallowed up by thoughts of an objectless love or by a love for a specific person, and have thus lost a certain part of their ability to serve God and man?

The same thing: not connive at a further fall, in the knowledge that such connivance will not deliver them from temptation but merely reinforce it, and continue to strive towards an ever greater degree of chastity in order to be able to serve God and men more fully.

What are those people to do who have been vanquished in this struggle and have fallen? They should consider their fall not as a legitimate source of enjoyment, as is done at the present time when it is absolved by the rite of marriage, nor as a carnal pleasure in which they can indulge repeatedly with others, nor as a misfortune, when the fall occurs with someone not their equal or without the consecration of marriage, but regard this initial fall as the only one, as the contraction of an indissoluble marriage.

For those who are able to enter upon it, this contraction of marriage, together with its consequences – the birth of children – specifies a new and more limited form of the service of God and men directly, in the most various forms; the contraction of marriage reduces the scope of man's action and obliges him to rear and educate his offspring, which is composed of future servants of God and men.

What are a man and woman to do who are living together in marriage and performing this limited service of God and men through the rearing and education of their children, consequent upon their situation?

The same thing: they should strive together to free themselves from temptation, to make themselves pure, abstain from sin, and replace conjugal relations, which are opposed to the general and the particular service of God and men, replace carnal love with the pure relations that exist between a brother and a sister.

Thus it is not true to say that we cannot be guided by the ideal of Christ, because it is too exalted, too perfect and unattainable. The only reason we can fail to be guided by it is because we lie to ourselves and deceive ourselves.

Indeed, when we tell ourselves that we need rules that are more practicable than the ideal of Christ, that if we fail to attain this ideal we sink into debauchery, what we are saying is not that the ideal of Christ is too exalted for us, but only that we do not believe in it and do not want to make our actions conform to it.

When we say that having once fallen we will sink into debauchery, all we are really saying is that we have already decided beforehand that a fall with someone who is not our equal is not a sin but an amusement, a diversion which we are not obliged to atone for by what we call marriage. On the other hand, if we could only understand that such a fall is a sin which must and can be redeemed only by the indissolubility of marriage and by the whole of the activity involved in the rearing of the children born of that marriage, our fall can never be the cause of our sinking into debauchery.

This is, after all, just the same as if a farmer were not to consider those seeds which failed to germinate as seeds at all, but only the ones that, sown elsewhere, gave a yield. It seems obvious that such a person would waste a great deal of land and seed, and would never learn how to sow. As soon as one makes of chastity an ideal and realizes that every fall, no matter who the partners in it are, is a unique marriage that shall remain indissoluble for the whole of one's life, it becomes clear that the guidance given by Christ is not only sufficient, but is the only guidance that is possible.

'Man is weak, he must be set a task that is within his power,' people say. This is just the same as saying: 'My hands are weak, I cannot draw a line that is straight, the shortest one between two points, that is, and so, in order to make it easier for myself, instead of drawing the straight line I should like to draw, I shall take as my model a crooked or a broken line.'

The weaker my hand is, the greater is my need of a model that is perfect.

It is impossible, once one has understood the Christian doctrine of the ideal, to behave as if one were ignorant of it and to replace it by external precepts. The Christian doctrine of the ideal has been revealed to mankind precisely because it is capable of guiding mankind at the stage it has presently reached. Mankind has outgrown the era of external religious precepts, and no one believes in them any more.

The Christian doctrine of the ideal is the only doctrine that is capable of guiding mankind. One cannot, one must not, replace the ideal of Christ by external rules; on the contrary, one must keep this ideal firmly before one in all its purity and, most important of all, one must believe in it.

One may say, to a man who is navigating close to the shore: 'Steer by that rise, that cape, that tower,' and so on. But there comes a moment when the navigators sail away from the shore and only the unattainable stars and the compass may indicate the direction they should follow, and serve as their guides. We have been given both.

APPENDIX 2:

ALTERNATIVE CONCLUSION TO *THE DEVIL*

[*From p. 172*] . . . he said to himself and, going over to the desk, took out his revolver. Examining it, he found that one of the cartridges was missing. He stuck the gun in his trouser pocket.

'My God! What am I doing?' he exclaimed suddenly, and putting his hands together began to pray: 'Oh Lord, help me, deliver me. You know that I don't desire any evil, but I can't manage on my own. Help me,' he said, crossing himself before the icon.

'I *can* control myself. I'll go for a walk and think it all over.'

He went out to the hallway, put on a sheepskin coat and galoshes and emerged on to the porch. Without him really being aware of it, his footsteps took him past the garden along the country road towards the farm. The threshing-machine was still droning away there, and the cries of the drover lads could be heard. He went into the threshing-barn. She was there. He caught sight of her at once. She was raking up the ears of grain, and when she saw him she made her eyes laugh and started to trot pertly and skittishly here and there among the scattered grain, skilfully gathering it together. Yevgeny did not want to look at her, but could not prevent himself from doing so. He only recovered his senses again when she had disappeared from view. The estate manager came over to him and told him that they were threshing the flattened corn and that this was taking longer and giving a lower yield. Yevgeny went up to the threshing-drum, which rattled every now and then as the inadequately separated sheaves were fed into it, and asked the manager if there were many of these flattened sheaves still to come.

'There's another five cartloads, sir.'

'Then listen, I tell you what . . .' Yevgeny began, but did not get to the end of his sentence. She had gone right up next to the drum of the threshing-machine to rake the grain from under it, and as she did so she turned on him her incandescent, laughing gaze.

That gaze spoke of the happy, carefree love between them, of her knowledge that he desired her, that he had come to her barn, that she was, as ever, willing to make love with him and have a good time with him, without regard to the consequences. Yevgeny felt that he was in her power, but he did not want to give in.

He remembered his prayer, and tried to say it over again. He started to say it to himself, but felt at once that it was no use.

He was now wholly absorbed by a single thought: how could he make a rendezvous with her without anyone noticing?

'If we get through this stack today, do you want us to start on a new one, or can it wait till tomorrow?' asked the manager.

'Yes, it can wait,' replied Yevgeny, following her mechanically over to the pile of grain she had raked together with another woman.

'Is it really true that I can't control myself?' he wondered. 'Am I really ruined? Oh God! But there is no God, there's only the Devil. And it's her. It's taken possession of me. But I won't let it, I won't! She's the Devil, yes, the Devil.'

He went right up to her, took the revolver out of his pocket and shot her in the back once, twice, a third time. She teetered forwards and fell on to the pile of grain.

'Almighty Lord! Sisters and brothers! What's happened?' cried the women.

'No, it's not an accident. I meant to kill her,' shouted Yevgeny. 'Send for the police.'

He returned home, and without saying a word to his wife went into his study and locked himself in.

'Don't try to get in,' he shouted to his wife through the door. 'You'll find out soon enough.'

An hour later he rang for the manservant, and told him: 'Go and find out if Stepanida's still alive.'

The manservant already knew what had happened, and told him that Stepanida had died an hour ago.

'Very well. Now leave me alone. Tell me when the police arrive.'

The police arrived the following morning. When Yevgeny had said goodbye to his wife and child, he was taken away to prison.

He was put on trial. These were the early days of trial by jury. He was found to have been temporarily insane, and was sentenced only to do ecclesiastical penance.

He spent nine months in prison and a month in a monastery. While he was in prison he began to drink. He continued to drink in the monastery and went home an enfeebled, irresponsible alcoholic.

Varvara Alekseyevna claimed to have seen this coming all along. She said she had observed it in his eyes on all those occasions when he had argued with her. Neither Liza nor Marya Pavlovna had the slightest notion as to why it should have happened; on the other hand, neither of them believed what the doctors said, that he had been mentally ill. On no account could they agree with this diagnosis, as they knew he had been more sensible and level-headed than hundreds of people of their acquaintance.

And indeed, if Yevgeny was mentally ill, then everyone is mentally ill, and most of all those who claim to perceive in others symptoms of the madness they fail to perceive in themselves.

NOTES

1 (page 27). The Nizhny Novgorod summer fair: Nizhny Novgorod (now known as Gorky) was a major Volga port, and one of the centres of trade and navigation on the river. Each summer an important trade fair was held there.

2 (page 27). Kunavino: suburb of Nizhny Novgorod, place of amusement for visitors to the fair.

3 (page 32). *Domostroy*: a medieval Russian treatise on domestic life.

4 (page 42). Rigolboche: the *nom de théatre* of the French dancer and cabaret singer Marguerite Bodel, who had a great success in Paris during the 1850s and 1860s.

5 (page 44). I let her read my diary: a recurrent trauma in Tolstoy's own life which haunted him until he died. He refers to it in *Anna Karenina* (IV,16), and it is a theme that is obsessively present throughout the *Intimate Journal* of 1910.

6 (page 54). Hartmanns: the reference is to Eduard von Hartmann (1842–1906), pessimistic philosopher, author of *The Philosophy of the Unconscious*. He wrote a refutation of Schopenhauer's *The World As Will and Idea*.

7 (page 56). Shakers: the members of the religious sect which emerged in England during the mid eighteenth century. The Shakers preached celibacy, communal ownership of property, obligatory physical labour, conscientious objection to military service, etc. During his work on *The Kreutzer Sonata* Tolstoy received letters and books from Shakers in the United States, and grew interested in their teachings (see p. 14).

8 (page 63). Trubnaya Street, the Grachevka: Trubnaya Street, also called the Truba, was the centre of a low-class district of Moscow where the brothels were situated. Tolstoy was in the habit of referring to the Imperial Court as 'the Truba'. The Grachevka was another street in the same district.

9 (page 91). Zemstvo: elective district council in pre-revolutionary Russia.

10 (page 102). Verst: one verst is approximately two miles.

11 (page 106). Vanka-Klyuchnik: the hero of a Russian folk-song that

exists in a number of variants. He is the lover of either the wife or the daughter of his master, and he boasts about the relationship. Denounced by a serving-maid, he pays for his bragging with his life, but not before he has taken a last mocking dig at his master, who in most versions is the Prince Volkonsky.

12 (page 106). Yard-keeper: the entrances to apartment houses in Russian towns were generally patrolled by a yard-keeper or concierge whose task it was to keep the yard and the street in front of the house clean, and to keep an eye on visitors.

13 (page 118). *Prostite . . . proshchayte*: *proshchayte* is the customary Russian form of farewell. *Proshchat'* (perfective aspect *prostit'*) also means 'to forgive'.

14 (page 120). Desyatina: one desyatina is 2.7 acres.

15 (page 175). Coupon: a detachable voucher of Tsarist government bonds, used for obtaining interest on them.

16 (page 189). The People's House: the People's Houses (*narodnyye doma*) were the working men's club of pre-revolutionary Russia, places of popular entertainment, vaudeville, etc. Towards the end of the nineteenth century the People's Houses in the main urban centres also acquired an educational function, and began to contain libraries and reading-rooms.

17 (page 197). *Izba*: hut, small wooden dwelling.

18 (page 206). *Mir*: village community.

19 (page 231). *Az, buki, vedi*: mnemonic names for the first three letters of the Russian alphabet. One of Tolstoy's educational projects was a new presentation of the alphabet and a system for learning to read.

20 (page 242). *Volost*: small rural district.

21 (page 258). *Quality*: c.f. Tolstoy *Childhood* Chapter 22.